CLAIMING

HER

KRIS KENNEDY

Acknowledgments

To my family, because they totally 'got' that this story was wrecking me, and driving me, and devouring me, and gave me all the time I needed to do what I needed to do with it.

To my Pixie Chick buddies, for plotting and brains that are different from mine.

To my Irish friend Richie and his Irish buddy Pól, for the Irish translations. Richie, buy that man another drink for me. I'll come over myself and buy you both one, one day soon.

Here's to castle towers and hard, hot, good men who know who they are, and know just what they want.

I once told myself I was going to write a story comprised of two people in a room, alone, together, for the whole story. This isn't *quite* the whole story, but it sure tried.

Notes On Pronouncing The Hero's Name

The hero's name is 'Aodh.' It can be pronounced: Ae, Aí, Eh, Ee, or Ay.

In my mind, I hear it as 'ay' with the faintest emphasis of a 'd' on the end, as you would say the beginning of 'Aidan.'

It means 'fire.' It is a royal name.

ROGUE WARRIORS

PROLOGUE

1589
Whitehall, England

"THERE ARE QUESTIONS OF TREASON out on the Rardove estate. I intend to see them settled, once and for all."

The men of Queen Elizabeth's Privy Council lifted their heads in unison at the queen's startling announcement.

Treason at Rardove?

More to the point: *Again?*

Questions of loyalty had swirled around the Irish barony ever since the thirteenth century, when the then-lord of Rardove quite lost his mind and tried to blow up half of Ireland by means of a legendary explosive dye—a ridiculous legend, that. But in the event of this madness, he died without issue, in a state of treason, and quite violently too, at the hands of a vengeful Irishman and, the legend went on to say, a vengeful English merchant widow.

Life beyond the Pale certainly was a vicious thing, even in legend.

In the ensuing centuries, the Crown had tried to bring the land back under submission by creating new lords of Rardove. The Englishmen granted the honor invariably sailed over, enraged the countryside, then promptly died in alarmingly violent ways.

Simply put, Rardove could not be kept in Englishmen.

Which honed the point to an even sharper tip...*how* did the queen intend to settle the matter of Rardove, once and for all?

The men of her Council exchanged uneasy glances.

"What an...unforeseen development," ventured one of the men, treading cautiously into the adjective.

"Is it?" the queen replied drily, scribbling her signature on a parchment. "I should say rather that Rardove breeds rebellion."

The men exchanged another look. "And how does Your Grace intend to 'settle the matter'?"

"I'm restoring the title."

Again.

A collective, if silent, groan swept the table.

This was not the first time Elizabeth had taken her stab at restoring the Rardove lordship. Over twenty years ago, she'd granted the barony to one of her favorites.

At first, it had appeared to be a success, for Henri de Macie had not angered the Irish at all; indeed, he'd gone quite the opposite direction and fallen in *love* with one of them. Then married her. Then engaged in treason by defending her.

The man had been overcome by passion and entirely lost his head.

It was placed on a pike outside London Bridge.

The Irish wife fled, too frightened to face the queen's wrath, leaving behind an eight-year-old dispossessed heiress.

The title and lands had gone back to the Crown, of course, but the queen had seen something in the young girl. She'd civilized Katarina as best she could, then sent her back to Ireland under the protection of her stepbrother, the baron's son from a previous marriage, a man intent on restoring his father's titles and wresting the land back to England, once and for all.

He was dead within five years. Slipped off a cliff one bright spring morning. While engaged in mortal combat. With an Irishman.

The Council hardly batted an eye that time; such was the way with the lords of Rardove.

Which is why a lady ruled there now. Katarina of Rardove, the only issue of the treasonous union between the Baron

Rardove and the Irish woman he never ought to have fallen in love with. Bearing no title, she'd ruled there for the past seven years, holding the desolate castle in the name of the queen.

She had done quite well, too, to the Council's surprise. Not the queen's, though; Elizabeth always said she'd seen a bit of herself in the young woman she allowed to rule her Irish marchlands. By all accounts, it had been a wild success.

Until the recent rumors of treason.

Again.

Which quite honed the point of *why* the queen was restoring the title.

But the potentially deepest puncture of this development was…to *whom* would she grant it?

Rardove encompassed vast tracts of land. Wild land, rich land, lands of legend and rumor, beset by rain and wind and Irish warriors.

Surely she would not cede it to…an Irishman?

Surely not the one who intermittently showed up to *serve* on the Council? That is, when he was not out fighting the Armada or capturing Spanish treasure fleets, or engaged in any of the other deeds of derring-do he did so well, that so captured the queen's fancy?

Their sovereign had an unnatural affinity for male Celts.

Tall, with long hair and unfashionable clothing—Aodh Mac Con dressed more like a pirate than a gentleman—he was rumored to be pricked by paint all over his body like the Native men Raleigh had brought back from the New World.

But although this Irishman was just as much a savage as they—any world outside England was—he was potentially more dangerous, for he claimed *he* was the rightful heir of Rardove.

No. The queen would never do such a dangerous thing as give Ireland to an Irishman.

Would she?

The Council members exchanged uneasy glances.

Cecil took the van. He cleared his throat. "And to whom is Your Majesty considering granting the barony?"

She glanced up from a sheaf of papers she'd been examining. "I am not considering it, I am doing it. Bertrand of Bridge."

The men exchanged another surprised glance. "Bertrand, your interrogator?"

She nodded. "I want these rumors of rebellion settled. Bertrand is the man to do it." The queen paused over the papers. "It is passing sad, really. I believed in Katarina, when you all spoke against her. But she reminded me of myself." There was the faintest tremble to her pen. "Ah well. What must be, will be. Bertrand will question her. If she proves loyal, she may stay and wed him. If not…"

Silence fell.

"And what of…Aodh Mac Con?" someone ventured.

The queen set down her pen with a decisive click. "I will explain it to him. I will give him…I don't know, a license for the wines. A monopoly on the nails. Some such. He will be wealthy. He will be made whole. He will *understand*."

It sounded as if she was asking if this could be so.

They had their doubts.

Aodh Mac Con invariably walked the edge of the pot, always ready to tip things over. He had a careless disregard and almost hostile impatience for any and all proprieties that did not serve him, which made him dangerous in any number of ways.

This should have infuriated the queen, but instead, had found a sympathetic haven in the heart of a woman who'd done things no one expected — or wanted — her to do, right up to ruling a kingdom, unwed, for decades.

The queen swept her gaze down the line of the most powerful men in England, then threw up her hands. "Well, after all, I cannot simply *give* Ireland to the Irish, can I?"

A sigh of relief flowed over the table.

As one, they sat back and smiled and began talking of other things, now that the matter of Ireland was settled.

Because in the end, really, what could the Irishman *do* about it?

CHAPTER 1

Early Spring, 1589
Northern Ireland, Beyond the Pale

TREASON WAS a dirty word. Especially when it ran in the family.

Which was why Katarina of Rardove found herself awaiting the queen's man, bound to wed him to save her lands, her title, and herself.

"My lady, he is come!"

The cries went up from her soldiers all along the walls. A sharp gust of cold spring air rushed through the bailey while up on the battlement walls, soldiers pointed into the valley below. Wicker, her youngest man-at-arms, peered down at her, waving his arm and shouting.

"There must be sixty of them, my lady! Well armed enough to scare away the wind!"

All her guardsmen were young and hardly gentle born — not a single knight among the lot — but they were brave and possessed the pragmatic, unvarnished warrior skills known to those who bobbed at the edge of a sea of war. This made them enthusiastic about anything that could be used as a weapon in an unabashed, *enveloping* sort of way: swords; pistols; the redheaded lass from the town below. Wicker in particular rather burst with fervor for all three.

"You can see them now, lady, cresting the rise of the valley."

He crouched at the top of the stairway and stuck out a hand for her. "You'll see when you come up."

"Excellent," she replied brightly. She did not come up.

"Right up here, on the walls, my lady." He patted the stone parapet. "That's where you'll see them."

There was nothing for it, then. Up she went, to witness the wondrous sight of her betrothed riding in with a small army to assess the degree of Rardove's loyalty, and then to ensure it, by becoming the new Lord of Rardove.

Not as reassuring as one would think.

The English Crown had long ago given up on conquest, and settled on maintaining what it had in Ireland, erecting a veritable wall of forts and castles around the perimeter of the Pale, a small arc of English settlements that huddled around Dublin like kittens around a bowl of milk. Rardove was one of the few English fortresses outside this protected ring, the Crown's longest claw, flung out far beyond the Pale. A lone royal watchtower over the edge of the wild.

It could be worse, she told herself as she lifted her skirts and started up the stairs. Bertrand of Bridge, the man the queen had sent to question her and, assuming he was satisfied with her answers, the one given the right to wed her and assume the title Lord of Rardove, was a most excellent queen's man. Powerfully built, fierce, ready to the fight.

He would fit perfectly out here.

Which, most assuredly, was not reassuring.

Queen Elizabeth had become increasingly brutal to those suspected of treason, and as it was ever a more simple matter to be labeled suchly, Katarina was grateful the queen had allowed her to be questioned here in her home, indeed to be questioned at all, rather than simply accused and dispatched.

But to be wed into the bargain...well, it was difficult not to see *that* as punishment from the queen she'd always served so loyally.

But then, such things were always in question, were they not, when one's father had lost his head on account of treason.

Katarina would acquiesce. Again.

It was the only way.

As she neared the top of the stairs, her men gave a shout and all but hauled her the rest of the way up, attending her with the sort of energetic devotion that at times left her exhausted and slightly bruised. They gently manhandled her to the nearest crenel opening and pointed over the wall.

"There, my lady."

The wind sliced through her cloak and burned her cheeks, but the shiver that moved though her was entirely unrelated to the weather. Wicker had not misspoken.

Her soon-to-be-betrothed traveled at the head of a fearsome-looking contingent, large and bristling with armaments. They rode at a leisurely pace over the sere grass, for even the maddest of the mad Irishry would not dare attack such a group. All bore long swords and a legion of other steely weapons. Armor peeked through long woolen cloaks and hoods, glinting in the dim, cloudy morning light.

One of the men riding in the van lifted his helmed head and swiveled it slowly. It stopped when it was aimed directly at the walls where Katarina stood.

She pressed her palm to her temple, pressing her hair down. Her skirts blew out to the side. After a moment, she lifted her hand in case he was watching.

His rose in reply.

A smile tugged at her lips. Silly, to smile over such an exchange.

The small army started down the hill, and she turned toward the stairs. Her guards sprang to assist, but Wicker won and grinned back up at his companions as he preceded her down the stairs.

He looked back at her, still smiling but his gaze full of silent questions.

Katarina, fingertips touching the wall as she descended, lifted her brows in equally silent permission.

"He's brought a proper force, hasn't he, my lady?" he burst out. "We didn't expect so many, did we?"

"No, we did not," she agreed.

"'Tis a bold force."

"Very bold."

"And their armor, did you see their armor?"

"I most certainly did."

"Toledo, do you think?"

"At a distance of several hundred yards, I found it difficult to assess. It was exceptionally...steely." It had reflected the pale sun in sharp daggers of light.

Wicker's grin never faltered. "Toledo," he assured her. "And their horses." His voice crossed over into the territory of reverence. "Warhorses."

"Yes, their horses," she echoed. It seemed Bertrand of Bridge had brought everything but a cannon.

At the bottom of the stairs, Wicker, so nicknamed because he was so tightly wound, his energy braided but ready to burst, turned and put out a hand for her, tilting his helmed head up, his exuberance suddenly extinguished. "We are fortunate, are we not, my lady? Now that he is come?"

Things will go easier now? Things will be better? You will be safer? Aye?

He would never say such things aloud, but he was thinking them. They were *all* thinking them. Beyond the Pale, one was either a wife, a warrior, or dead.

Thus far, Katarina was none of those things.

Everyone knew it was only a matter of time.

God knew life was harder than stone out here, and this last year had been boulder hard. Everyone was past ready for life to become a simpler matter, by any means necessary. Even if it meant Bertrand of Bridge.

Everyone except Katarina.

She patted Wicker's mailed arm. "Fortunate, indeed. Now go tell Sir Roger you need to be relieved of your post. I want you to roll up the wine barrels from the cellars."

His exuberance rushed back. "Very good, my lady! Wine and mayhap...butter?"

She gave him a level look, intended to censure such bold forays into their larders, then said, "Of course."

He emitted an improper whoop, all but swung her off the

bottom step to the ground, gave an irreverent salute, and bolted off to do as he'd been told.

She was still catching her breath and righting her skirts when a voice came in from the side.

"You ought make them show more respect, my lady," the voice said.

Katarina closed her eyes briefly. "Walter." Her clerk and steward. "What have they done now?"

"*They* do nothing, my lady. *You* allow much. Wicker ought not treat you as if you were his sister. And your maidservant ought not tug on your sleeve when she is excited, and chatter inexhaustibly at all other times."

"Susanna is...ebullient," Katarina admitted about her sole lady's maid.

"She is a bubble," he said dourly. "A great, noisy, impudent bubble."

"She is vibrant, Walter. In these dark times, we need all of that we can get. I am surprised to hear you disapprove of such things." She started toward the gate. Walter stepped with her, taking her arm to assist her over the rutted cobbles.

How she hated being assisted over rutted cobbles.

"I disapprove of maids acting like ladies, soldiers acting like councilors, and men and women of all ages forgetting their place."

"Just so, Walter. I will counsel Susanna to flatten herself forthwith."

Gray-browed and disapproving, he regarded her levelly. "You should rein them in, my lady."

A fissure of irritation opened up inside her. "They are not horses, Walter."

"They most certainly are. Stallions too loose on their lead. They need restraint."

She looked away. He was right. The boundaries of propriety had broken down rather tragically at Rardove. It simply seemed so...unnecessary. So unhelpful. So ungrateful.

And there was the truth of it. Her men, most of whom were barely men at all, were steadfast and loyal when they need not be. There were far richer, less remote, and less dangerous gates to guard south and east. She had no notion why they stayed with her, but in consequence, in *gratitude*, she gave them a great deal of meat, a great deal of ale, and a great deal of leeway when it came to matters of propriety.

She relied upon them. She cared for them. And they knew it.

No doubt she was in error with this approach. But it was the only one she could think of short of shouting, and Katarina knew very well her voice would not carry far in the wilds of Ireland.

Even so, irritation at her steward rose up more sharply than usual. She wanted to shout *No, no, no!* at him, like a petulant child. But the familiar inner voice called up, *Simply agree with the man.*

Her inner voice was extremely sensible.

"You are right, of course," she said quietly.

They stared at each other. Or rather, he stared, while she looked intently at his eyebrows, since they were so pronounced, and looking directly into his eyes might cause her to do something highly *in*sensible, like grab his ears and yank.

"Now, Walter," she went on brightly, "we seem to have been caught unawares by Bertrand of Bridge, and I without my good hood."

He shifted his frown to her blowing hair.

"Might you see to it for me? The green, if you will. And inform the servants of Sir Bertrand's arrival? So that we might make the proper impression?"

That, of course, was Walter's weak point, and she aimed for it ruthlessly.

"It would be more proper yet for you to wait indoors and have Sir Bertrand brought to you," he grumbled but, realizing the futility of arguing, turned and strode off to the keep. Walter had, after all, been her father's steward before hers, and had seen her at her most improper yet.

He went, clearly resigned to minimizing the damages of Katarina's improprieties.

She gestured to the door warden standing at the inner bailey gate, and he ducked inside the gatehouse. A moment later, the winches began to turn, and the squeal of iron streaked through the bailey like a cold star. The gate began to lurch upward.

She stood, waiting, letting the wind blow back her cloak. It was no use trying to stop such things. Doors opening, winds blowing, the warrior about to ride through her gates; these sorts of things were unstoppable.

A moment later, hooves clattered over the cobblestones and the riders swept into her home.

CHAPTER 2

SIXTY-FOUR MEN rode through her gates.

Katarina saw only one.

Hooded and helmed, riding a pale gray horse, their leader resembled mist taking shape. A simple dark gray woolen cape was draped over his horse's dappled rump, and silver-gray armor covered his legs and forearms.

Under helm and hood, it was impossible to see where he was looking. But Katarina did not need to see. She *felt* his gaze on her, as if a cord had been strummed inside her.

Swinging off his horse, he spoke a quiet word to his men, then started over with long, confident strides, somewhat like a mountain in motion. It wasn't that he was so very large, although he was tall. It was more a sense of the space he took up, the *certainty* of him being in that space, moving aside the air to inhabit it.

But then, "presence" was to be expected when an armed knight strode through one's bailey, cape tugged back in the steely winds, a heavily armed detachment spreading out behind him like an unsheathed blade.

She did not recall such presence in Bertrand of Bridge.

He bent a knee, bowing his head. "My lady."

It was a simple male rumble, but it sent something entirely unsimple tingling through her limbs. She returned a curtsey and extended her hand.

"You are well met, sir. I am pleased to see you."

Liar.

He closed his fingers around hers and straightened. They were warm in the winter cold. She could barely make his face out amid the shadows of hood and helm. Indeed, the steel accentuated all the hard, capable things about his face.

The nose, broken no doubt sometime in the past, the hard slash of a mouth, lined with small crescent curves along each side, the rough growth of hair that brushed his cheeks and jaw, but above all, the eyes peering out at her. They were blue-gray, reflecting the steely sky. Hard, perceptive, uncompromising eyes. Just what was needed for the Irish marches.

Mayhap the distant Crown had chosen well this time.

Although she did not recall Bertrand having blue-gray eyes.

"My lady, we must speak at once, on a matter of some urgency." His voice was pitched low.

A chill pierced down her spine. "Is it the Irish?"

Slate-blue eyes dropped to hers. "When is it not?"

She nodded, but felt honor-bound to add, "When it is the English, my lord."

He ought to be told such things, and who else but Katarina was going to inform him of the shifting realities and immutable truths of life on the marches?

"If we might speak?" he said quietly. "Alone?"

"Of course." She gestured to the castle. "Come inside."

He released her fingers. Behind them, the outer gate lowered with a creaking thud. She slid a sideways glance at his hooded profile as they hurried across the bailey: grim, serious, silent. Intent on the castle doorway.

"Tell me of the defenses, lady."

"The west wall is weakest, but it will hold."

"The garrison? Your outer gate was unmanned."

"We have been understaffed of late," she admitted. Miserably so. For years.

"That is unfortunate," he said. In truth, it sounded as if he'd said *that is fortunate,* but his voice was pitched so low, the wind must have whipped away his prefix.

As if in answer, a rogue blast of wind roared through the bailey, rattling the castle windows and ripping a section of thatch off one of the outbuildings. It almost tore Katarina's cape off her shoulders. She spun to the side to ward it off, catching her hood against the side of her face.

He was there at once, hand on her back, one of his hard legs behind hers, righting her. She lifted her head and stared into the broad expanse of an armored chest, then up further to his eyes.

"My thanks, my lord," she said, rather breathlessly, from inside her billowing hood. The winds did that every so often, took one's breath away.

Ice-blue eyes looked down at her. "The garrison?"

"Ten in total," she told him, ignoring the armored leg pressed up against hers. "Armed to the teeth and most bold."

The hand at her back tightened, and he spun her around to face him. She came to a stop opposite him, their capes snapping in the air between them.

"*Ten?*" he repeated. "You hold the barony of Rardove with ten men?"

Winds whipped her hair across her face. "I had to, my lord. I had no more."

He stared. A knot tightened in Katarina's stomach. Clearly the queen had not relayed the sad news about the state of Rardove's garrison. Perhaps because Katarina had neglected to inform the queen of it in any *meaningful* way. But then, no one had ever asked. Being in Ireland meant being forgotten.

It was one of the things she loved best about it.

So. They were about to witness how Bertrand of Bridge dealt with disappointment.

"That is impossible," he said slowly. He sounded quite certain of this, although she had been doing it for years.

"I have found, sir, that one does not know the limits of possibility until one reaches them." She pressed a palm to her temple to catch her flying hair. "I have not yet reached mine."

Something shifted in the shadowed eyes holding hers. "I see. And am impressed."

A cascade of unfamiliar heat flushed through her belly. She waved her hand dismissively. "For no need. 'Twas more stubbornness than anything."

"And yet..." His gaze swept the bailey, then came back.

She smiled faintly. "And yet."

His smile in reply, though small, was rather devastating.

"But be assured, sir, my men are most brave, and have had occasion upon which to prove it."

"And so they shall have to again," he said, and quite grimly too, as only a wise soldier would. That was hopeful. One did not want a braggart with a sword out beyond the Pale.

No, Katarina most certainly did not recall Bertrand of Bridge having such restraint of manner, nor such piercingly pale blue eyes. But then, she'd only seen him twice, once from a distant of several hundred yards, the other from a much closer distance—far too close—but then, it had been dark.

Far too dark.

Perhaps Bertrand had changed, she thought hopefully. People did. It was known to happen. On occasion...very rarely.

They started toward the castle. He kept a hand at her back in case any more gusts of wind bore down on them, but he did not take hold of her elbow to assist with the ruts. He thought her capable of ruts. More hopeful yet.

Being a wise woman, she would take help with the wind wherever it appeared.

Hay blew past, and hard bits of snow began swirling around them as they hurried toward the keep. She realized he'd put his arm behind her back.

The grim intensity of him grew, expanding like a breath being taken. He was closer to her now, moving her across the bailey, propelling her faster and faster. She felt pressed upon. They took the stairs two at a time. The door squealed as he pushed it open and ushered her inside.

The brittle winds ceased abruptly. Cavernous and stone-walled, the great hall opened below them, a vast expanse fifty feet long and arching overhead to a cathedral ceiling. It was filled with half-erected trestle tables and low fires, but empty of souls. The servants would be in the kitchens and storerooms, frantically trying to prepare for the extra mouths to feed.

His body was an inch behind hers. Behind him, the door, heavy and rusted, stood open. She could see the sharp blue sky and the way his men were spreading out along the walls.

Uneasiness crept down her spine. "Perhaps I should call for my men, apprise them…"

"Your men are being apprised of the circumstances as we speak."

Circumstances?

He peered over her shoulder, down into the great hall. "'Tis larger," he murmured.

Confusion swirled in her belly, then fear crept up behind on cold, pricking spider legs. "Larger than what, my lord?" she said sharply and began to push past him, back outside. "Good, my lord, I shall call for my men—"

His gaze snapped down. "Stay."

Something in it chilled her from her breasts to the back of her spine. Dim, sharp shouts pierced in through the open doorway. The shouts of soldiers.

She took a step backward. "What news, my lord? You said the Irish…?"

"Oh, aye," he said, very low. "It is the Irish."

"What have they done this time?"

"Taken Rardove Keep."

Seconds ticked away as her heart beat harder, as she stared into his fire-ice eyes, his *Irish* eyes, as she finally discerned the faint Irish lilt to his softly spoken words.

"What did you say?" she whispered dumbly.

He slid off his helm, revealing a handsome face and partially shaved head. Shocking, barbaric, illegal. The pricks of fear became a cold wash of it, a river through her skull, so she could not even hear herself think.

He brought those steel-blue eyes very close to hers and bent the granite of his jaw into a smile.

"The Irish have taken Rardove Keep, my lady. My thanks for opening the gates."

Rogue Warriors

Chapter 3

AODH LOOKED DOWN at Katarina, the woman known as the Beauty of Rardove. She was, indeed, beautiful.

She was also, quite literally, standing in his way.

He was prepared for anything—screaming, running, fainting, begging—which rendered him entirely unprepared for nothing. The dark feminine eyes locked on his burned with an entire mountain range of emotions, but everything about her remained calm, motionless, almost serene.

Her cheeks, though, did grow slightly more pale.

At least that was something.

"You'll not be harmed if you do as I say, my lady," he sought to reassure her. Although she did not appear to be particularly in need of reassurance.

In fact, she did not appear to be listening.

Her gaze flicked over his shoulder, to the open door. Cold air rushed through it, along with the sounds of his men taking over the castle. She moved nothing else. Nothing at all, except her nostrils, which flared slightly as she inhaled. She was all but motionless. Perhaps stunned.

"Where is Bertrand of Bridge?" she asked finally.

He reflected a moment. "Wandering on a hill somewhere in Northumbria, one hopes."

Her gaze slid back. "Who are you?"

"Aodh Mac Con."

No need to mention the 'Rardove' part just yet. Or ever. It

would only complicate things. Ship her out, get on with the rebellion.

More motionless regard. She seemed to be working that out. The early spring winds had dislodged a great number of strands of hair from the threadbare hood enclosing her head. They hung beside her mouth like dark russet ink strokes.

"Aodh, son of the Hound." She anglicized his name in a low, throaty voice.

He gave a small bow.

"That is unfortunate."

"I will endeavor to make it less so, lady." He extended an arm toward the stairs behind her. "If you would but — "

"I meant unfortunate for you, Aodh Mac Con."

He stopped, arm in the air.

Her face was extremely pale but fixed and determined. "You have defied the Queen of England, sir. You will be cut down like a sapling."

He smiled. "Ah, but we are beyond the Pale, are we not, where wild things hold sway more than queens?"

Something flashed in her eyes. "You do not know your history, sir."

"I know some," he said grimly. The bloody, betrayal-thick, grave-laden parts.

"Then you know Rardove had always held for England." Her brown eyes held his steadily as she mouthed such idiocies.

He smiled faintly. "Not always."

Her face paled slightly more, but her chin also lifted to the same degree. Fear and defiance, then, in equal measure.

"*I* am Rardove, sir," she said boldly, quietly, and foolishly. "And I hold for England."

"That has just become a matter for negotiation. From here on, let us say England shall have to *earn* Rardove's loyalty."

She stepped back, her lips parting. He'd shocked her.

The realization caused a small, strange tinge of disappointment in him, that a woman who'd held an English castle beyond the Pale with only ten men would be shocked by such a thing. It seemed somehow…diminishing. But then, Aodh had a taste for rebellion today, and nothing but more of the same would serve.

Still.

A movement at the far end of the hall caught his attention. One of his captains, Cormac, poked his head through a door, caught his eye and nodded, then ducked back out. Good. They'd made it to the north side, which meant they'd secured the entire castle. Rardove was his.

And so where was the hot satisfaction of conquest? The rush of triumph? Where was…everything?

Lying at the bottom of the same cold pit that had marked his life for too many years to count, no doubt. Intrigues, battle, courtly maneuvers, it was all the same: naught.

Apparently even coups of castles did not rise to the level of interest anymore.

He turned his attention back to Katarina. "My lady, if you will—"

All he saw was a blur of green silk, then her small, bunched fist smashed into his face.

The impact, hard and square, landed directly on his jaw.

Caught utterly unaware—as he'd never been before, *never*, not even when his father had his head cut off—Aodh reeled sideways.

The retreat gave enough room for her to launch forward and slam her shoulder directly into his ribs so hard and fast, he grunted and stumbled backward and hit the ground, her on top, twisting like a hellcat.

She jammed a knee into his bollocks, and he doubled over protectively, at which point she grabbed one of his fingers and twisted it back almost to breaking, while her other hand—so sinuous and slender it was all but ungrippable—snaked between their writhing bodies and tugged his accursed dagger out of its sheath.

Disappointed, indeed.

With a roar, he lunged up off the ground, lifting her with him, and backed her to the wall. Predictably—dimly, he noted he was already predicting things about her—she wrestled like a firebrand. Whirling hair, arms, legs. Kicking, biting, punching, swiping with the knife.

First things first.

He caught hold of the feminine fist snaked around the hilt of his blade and slammed it to the wall above her head, gripping her wrist so hard she cried out, but she did not, of note, stop fighting.

He finally had to pin her to the wall with his entire body, her toes dangling half a foot in the air, their faces pressed together, cheek to cheek, until he stilled everything that was writhing and flailing and kicking on her curving, rampant, berserker body.

Fire burned in his veins, urging him to smash and destroy. He reached over with his other hand and wrenched the blade out of her grip and tossed it onto the ground behind him.

He inhaled slowly, forcing himself to calm. They stood like this for a moment, her body pinned between him and the wall. He supposed she could still kick his shins, but she'd impact against his greaves, and it would hurt her far more than him.

She seemed to agree. At least, she didn't move.

He pulled back a few inches, let her feet drop to the ground, and peered down at her. Breathing fast, she tossed her head, spraying hair across her face. It was pale and beautiful, with slim, dark brows arcing over what appeared to be intelligent brown eyes. A shocking discovery.

"If you were a man, I would kill you right now," he said in a low voice.

He waited for her response—everything now was a test, every moment a potential tipping point. Would she recoil? Be wise and retreat, apologize, surrender, run scared?

Would she be like everyone else?

She shifted the only thing he didn't have restrained, her left hand, and laid what turned out to be the cold edge of a blade against the side of his throat.

"If I were a man, sir," she whispered back, "you would already be dead."

God*dammit*.

It was his dagger, one of many strapped to his body. In the

mêlée, she'd succeeded in getting it free. In the distraction of staring into her eyes, trying to ascertain if she was mad, she'd succeeded in lifting it to his throat.

A rush went through him, hot and intense. "You are left-handed," he observed grimly.

"When necessary."

A humming filled his stomach, deep and low. He'd come for battle, and that this slim audacious woman had given it to him, undefended, in a hopeless situation, outmatched and overpowered, bespoke great boldness. Of a kind he'd not seen in a long time.

Either that, or idiocy.

She did not appear idiotic. Of course, she'd not appeared reckless either, out in the bailey. She'd seemed calm, clever, pale, and beautiful. Then she'd launched her body into his and turned into a bold, roaring-mad hellcat.

Perhaps *everything* in her was latent. Who knew, idiocy might rear its head at any moment. Or more boldness.

Although it was difficult to see how she could become *more* bold than she was at the moment.

Small wisps of hair brushed beside her mouth. Aodh knew battle and fights; her lips ought to be dry with fear, parched and tight. But they were wet. Parted and wet, her chin up, her cheeks a sort of hot red. Her slim body was pressed hard against his, female curves barely detectable through his armor. But the vivid flush of *her* was clear. Her mad, energizing, fearless self was the clearest thing on his mind.

That and the blade pressed against his neck.

He laughed low in his throat. It had been a long time since he'd felt this hum inside him, this energized, this vital.

He leaned closer until his mouth was an inch from hers, until he felt the honed edge of his own blade indent the flesh of his throat.

"Do it, lass," he whispered. "Or drop it. *Now.*"

CHAPTER 4

MAD IRISHRY.

The thought pounded through her brain with each beat of her heart. Her insides rattled like a winter leaf. This moment was constructed of madness. A pit of madness.

The sensible voice inside her, the one she *relied* upon to restrain her from acts of recklessness just such as this, had utterly failed her. She was alone with the bright fire of passion. It had taken over like an ember tossed back onto a dry forest bed.

"Do not push me," she warned in a shaky voice.

"Oh, but I will." He shifted on his booted feet, pushed his hips harder against hers, until she felt a part of the wall. A part of him. "You lifted a blade to me, Katarina. I'm going to push you hard."

Fear spiked through her.

"Tell me, how do you foresee this ending? Shall I help you think it through?"

She jerked her head in an abbreviated shake. "Stop."

"You will either kill me or be very sorry you tried. Neither ends well for you."

"One ends poorly for you," she pointed out.

"Then do it."

"Y-you are not in a position to issue commands, sirrah."

But he was. Even with a blade held against his throat, he was a mighty presence, and her hand was growing sweaty around the hilt.

Her breath was coming too fast, her heart hammering too hard, her hand — the one she'd punched him with — throbbed as if she'd punched a wall, not a man. Steel before and stone behind, she was, most literally, between a rock and a very hard place.

He was all wild thing, untethered and unafraid. His hair had been shaved close on the sides, growing long down the middle, banded at the base of his neck, so he looked familiar and yet utterly foreign. His face was all cut planes of male fury, hard cheekbones, dark brows above the ice-blue eyes pinned on her. She felt like she was staring at a flame burning inside a shard of ice.

"The blade is exceptionally sharp," he assured her, his voice a rumble of cold, calm advice. "If you press the slightest bit, you shall see results."

"Then stop pushing me," she almost begged.

"No."

She began to tremble outwardly. The rush of fury was fading; fear would soon settle in. Terror would come on its heels. And then, sanity, sense, reason, restraint.

The column of his neck, strongly muscled, pressed against the blade. Sheer hard will was the only thing that kept her from lowering it, for the moment she did, she was a dead woman.

His icy gaze roamed her face. "I see 'I shall do it' in your eyes."

Her hand tightened on the slippery hilt. "Indeed I shall."

"Ah, but I see a thousand 'I shall do its' in your eyes, and yet, you do not."

Swoosh. The blood coursing through her body washed cold, then hot. How had he done that, seen straight through to the heart of her?

"Are you going to drop it?"

"Are you going to kill me?"

Another mad smile. "Drop it and see."

She squeezed the blade tighter, because that was terrifying.

Then, God save her, he leaned in closer yet, until she felt his breath on her cheek and he put his mouth by her ear and said,

"I dare you."

Dare? "To what?" she whispered back, as if they were in secret council and this was his whispered advice.

For a beat of her heart, he remained still. Then, like some animal, like some untamed, unbroken, undaunted sensual being, he ran his tongue across her ear, his breath hot and male.

She felt struck by lightning. Burnt, charged, dangerous. Whatever had been coursing through her before became a flood. Hot and raging.

She flung her head and leapt backward, but there was nowhere to go, and as she rebounded between his rock-hard body and the stone wall, she dropped the blade.

In a single move, he kicked it away and clamped a fist around her wrist, pinning it to the wall high above her head. He caught her other wrist and held it low beside their hips, their bodies still pressed together. Then he went suddenly, absolutely, terrifyingly motionless.

She felt the beat of his heart against her chest—it was not racing as fast as hers, but it was a strong, hard beat. She saw the vein on his neck thudding.

She had no idea what a warrior might feel inclined to do at such a moment—hanging; a simple, swift beheading—but none of them occurred. Nothing happened, nothing but the tension slowly rising through her body the way a flood tide rises on a riverbed. She was awash in awareness of him, pinning hers from chest to knee, in the way he was watching her with inscrutable eyes, in the hard, absolute motionlessness of his body.

She was doomed. Walter had been saying it for years, and now all the predictions were coming true.

Boots sounded on the stairs, then stopped short. A loud male gasp sliced through the stony entry chamber. "Dear God in *heaven*."

Walter.

"My lady, what have you *done*?" It was barely short of a wail. "Did I not *tell* you this habit of the blades would turn out poorly?"

Aodh Mac Con moved his gaze to the steward. "They are not

her blades."

"My lord," was Walter's next attempt to reinsert sanity into the moment, and she had to admire him for it. "I beg you, sir, go gentle with her."

She felt the Irishman's hard body shift against hers. "Gentle with *her*?"

She almost laughed.

She was losing her mind.

Walter cleared his throat. "Sir, I will make her stand down —"

The Irishman cocked a brow. "Will you? How?"

Walter fell silent, struck dumb. A feat only a barbarian could achieve. A perverse bolt of satisfaction surged through Katarina.

"My lord, take heed," Walter spoke in a confidential tone. "There are reasons for my lady's mania. There was a murrain in the sheep last spring that almost wiped out the flock, then the fire less than a twelvemonth past, and all those Spaniards washing up on our shores, and…well, in truth, sir, it has been a most trying year for us all, Lady Katarina more than most, of course, as she is a woman and as such, not as well equipped as you or I…"

Walter's voice drifted off in momentary pity for her less equipped nature. "But she has never done *this* sort of thing before," he concluded carefully. Implying she'd done other sorts of things.

She felt an urge to stab him. With the Irishman's blade.

Aodh Mac Con's face turned down to hers. "He thinks you ill-equipped to handle murrains."

"I am not fond of them," she admitted in a whisper.

And there it was again, the faintest hint of a smile.

By the stairs, Walter tutted in an impotent, clerical way. "Sir Bertrand, I beg you, if you and I could but speak —"

"He is not Bertrand of Bridge," Katarina said loudly, but her voice sounded as if it was coming from a long way off. "His name is Aodh Mac Con, and his men have taken over the castle."

Finally, finally, Walter stopped talking. He might have

stopped breathing, the silence was so complete. Then he gasped, and boots scraped against the stony ground, and then...

"He is running," the Irishman said, sounding surprised.

A strange bubble rose up inside Katarina, an iridescent sort of lightness. Buoyant. Dreamlike. Perhaps she was going into shock. "He is frightened."

"So were you."

She shook her head the slightest bit. "No. But it shall come."

He never looked away from her. His eyes were so blue, so intensely, palely blue, so utterly focused on her, it was like being immersed in a sea. An ocean of consideration.

It was the oddest moment, so quiet, so...connected, his body pressed to hers as they conversed quietly about her cowardly steward. The Irishman had taken away all her choices. She was shorn of responsibility as she'd not been since she was eight, and in consequence, she felt...like a soap bubble.

She became aware they were breathing in unison.

Shock, certainly.

Then she heard Walter cry out, "Oh sweet and merciful Lord," and a contingent of Irishman thundered into the entryway, foaming up the stairs like a steel river.

One of the warriors bounded up from behind and stopped short, perhaps taken aback by the sight of his master pinning the lady of the castle against a wall, an assortment of blades scattered on the ground around them.

"Aodh?" the warrior said carefully.

Aodh Mac Con tossed his reply over his shoulder. "What news?"

His captain took a cautious step forward. "We've taken the keep."

"The walls?"

"Our men are stationed the entire length. The gatehouse and all the outbuildings are secured."

"The garrison?"

His captain shook his head. "Must be in hiding. We found only nine, and a handful of youths."

Aodh Mac Con's gaze honed back in on her. "Where is he?"

She swallowed. "He?"

"The tenth of your garrison."

Self-disgust burned in her throat. *She'd* told him that. Still, she hesitated, debating whether to withhold any more specific information regarding Wicker's whereabouts. Might it give him a chance to escape? Rally a counterattack?

Get himself killed.

"He is in the cellars," she said in a flat voice. "Bringing up barrels of wine. For the celebration."

The irony seemed to elude him. He cast orders over his shoulder.

"Retrieve him, *Réalta Farraige*," he said, saying the Irish words, sea star, as if they were a name, elongating the vowels into a sensual rumble, so the latter sounded a bit like *barrage*, which was entirely fitting and quite unnerving. "Have the men search the outbuildings and upper floors. Round up all the servants."

The captain nodded. "The others are being held in the yard, at blade point."

Aodh didn't move. From the corner of her eye, Katarina saw the captain's gaze drift in her direction.

"We await your instructions, Aodh."

So, this barrage of a captain was more than a captain. He was a friend.

A ripple moved through Aodh Mac Con's body, like a statue awakening. He stepped back, releasing her from the wall, leaving her strangely cold without his armored body pressed up to hers.

"Take her ladyship to the solar." He waved a young man of his guard forward and turned away, and was immediately ensconced in a phalanx of armed men. They moved toward the door like a flock of birds, boot heels clattering.

Katarina stared after them, stunned and reeling without the support of the wall or his armored body. The young guardsman put his hand on her elbow and turned her toward the stairs.

Behind them, Walter's voice rang out with vague encouragements. "My lady, do not lose courage! If ever it has been needful for English blood to come to your aid, now is that time," he called, then huffed, "Leave off me," to someone who was evidently restraining him.

"Heed me, Katarina," he called again. "Many's the Englishman who's found himself in straits even more dire than these, and though you are but a woman, even you can attend the need for restraint and—"

"Oh, Walter, please do shut up," she said, not looking around. One could only take so much, after all, and the inner voice of reason had fallen blessedly silent.

So did Walter.

It was all oddly…satisfying.

ROGUE WARRIORS

CHAPTER 5

AS HE CROSSED the bailey, a strange quietness rode under the more savage thrill Aodh now felt, finally, at accomplishing the task no one thought he'd attempt: take the castle the Queen of England refused to give him.

Aodh was an opportunist. From the moment of his birth to this one, every move had been aimed at gaining the next foothold, and a bloody climb it had been. Rardove was the prize.

Sent out in the world almost twenty years ago with a single mission—to regain his ancestral homeland—he'd meant to do great things, and by those deeds win favor and honor, and return, Rardove in his fist.

Over the years, Aodh had seen much and done much, most of it hard and brutal, the sort that did not make for suppertime conversation.

First as one of Elizabeth's sea dogs, then as courtier and councilor, Aodh had grown adept at both war and court life, at politics and power and the furtive maneuverings of mind and man. These were the skills requisite to and consequence of being favored by Queen Bess.

Rardove had been his father's dream. And his grandfather's. And his grandfather's grandfather. And so on, marching back down the family line for centuries. Everyone had dreamed of returning as lord of Rardove.

And now here he stood, within its walls, feeling...cold.

29

He glanced up at the castle. *His* castle.

The battlements loomed over the surrounding countryside, forty feet of stone to the top of the walls, the towers rising higher yet, all painted a vibrant cobalt blue and white. Pennants snapped wetly at intervals along the battlements.

Still, nothing like the mythic images his father had drawn in his mind. It was just a wall.

Not the castle of Finn MacCumhail, or the fortress of Conchobor Mac Nessa. Nothing great, nothing out of the mists of legend. Just rubble and stone, with frightened people inside.

Except Katarina.

No doubt she *had* been frightened, but she'd come at him like a warrior. Like a berserker in a coif. A beautiful, nay, carnally made woman who, in a moment of great fear, had attacked instead of fled and made his heart beat more fiercely than it had in years.

At his side, his captain Ré walked in companionable silence. His proper name was as simple and unfitting as his origins—John—so Aodh had promptly renamed him after he dragged Aodh out of the sea and pumped the water from his lungs.

Ré's father had been a poor peasant farmer, but even at thirteen, Ré held ambitions higher than furrows of dirt. He'd latched his ambitions to Aodh's and followed him up.

Aodh's name for him was as succinct as his English one, but it meant a great deal more.

Now, after sixteen years of a friendship that had included bloody flashes of battle and the low-burning flame of courtly intrigue, there was little that needed saying aloud. Each would watch the other's back, be there when needed, and say a thing only if it needed saying.

"By any chance, did the lady of the castle have a blade at your throat?" Ré asked, breaking the companionable silence.

Aodh stifled a sigh. Apparently this was a thing that needed saying. "Aye."

"By any chance, was it *your* blade?"

"Aye."

"Ah. Because that's what it looked to be. Your blades. Saw

them both."

"Your eyesight is remarkable."

Ré grinned. He was not one to resist many things, neither danger nor dare.

It had been that way since the moment they'd met, and was partly why they were so close—both of them saw the edge of the cliff as a thing to skirt *very* close. Occasionally to dive over.

And so, Ré stepped closer to this particular cliff.

"What I can see, friend, is that we're in for trouble if you cannot keep your blade out of a woman's hands."

Oh, the innuendoes. They looked at each other as they walked.

"So, how did she get your blades in the first—"

"I was distracted."

Ré looked delighted by this. "Were you? That is fascinating."

"By Cormac," Aodh explained, dispersing blame.

"Is that so? For I did not see him anywhere—"

"He was there, a moment earlier. Stuck his head through the north door."

"I see. So you were chatting with Cormac, and the lady of the castle put a blade to your throat. Entirely understandable. Could have happened to anyone."

Aodh looked over. "Must we?"

Ré gave him a happy grin. "We must."

He exhaled noisily. "She surprised me."

"Did she? How?"

"The usual way. Punched me in the jaw then kneed me in the bollocks."

This granted him almost full minute of relief, since that was how long Ré spent doubled-over laughing.

Aodh took the respite to debate whether he actually required Ré's services any longer.

Ré finally composed himself, but after a long examination of Aodh's profile, all he said was, "Clever. Surprising."

Clever, surprising…beautiful, reckless, roiling. "Very."

"Well, I venture she's done with surprises now that we have her castle."

The corner of the barracks came into view as they circled the huge keep. Gray and dark except where its dullness was sprinkled with cold darts of white snow, it was as monochromatic and cheerless and cold as everything else in Ireland. Except Katarina.

Red cloak, thick reddish-brown hair that seemed to glow as strands floating beside the fire in her eyes, she was like a lick of flame in a bleak, barren landscape.

"She held Rardove with ten men, Ré," Aodh said quietly.

Ré glanced over. "Your meaning?"

"She is not yet done with surprises."

Ré pushed back his sweaty hair, then wiped his palm across his forehead. "Aodh?"

"Aye?"

"You are not...thinking anything, are you?"

"Thinking?"

"Planning."

"Planning?"

"Anything reckless," Ré said, gaze still on the soldiers ahead.

Aodh smiled faintly. Reckless as in marching up to Queen Elizabeth at fourteen years of age and offering your already-bloodied sword in exchange for your family's ancestral lands?

Reckless as in rising to the top of her councilors and captains, despite all odds being against a dirty Irishman?

Reckless as in feeling fire for the first time in your life whilst pinning a mad, beautiful woman against a wall, with *your* blade in *her* hand?

Reckless as in planning to warm your hands over that fire?

"When am I ever reckless?" he asked quietly.

"Ever and anon?"

Aodh snorted.

"But never foolhardy. One hopes this is not a first. Because if it were, I'd feel an overwhelming urge to caution you—"

"I'd tell you to resist it."

"—that this is not the time to dally with ladies who steal blades."

They finished circling the rounded tower of the keep. "'Dally?' When have I ever 'dallied?'"

"When you are being reckless," came his friend's blunt reply.

"Ré, I have countermanded orders, broken faith with the queen, sent false messages to misguide the nobleman she *meant* to send here on a wild goose chase through northern England. I have sailed the Irish Sea and marched halfway across Ireland to take a castle explicitly forbidden to me. One would say recklessness has already been done on a rather grand scale."

"Which is why a wise man might refrain from indulging in any additional bouts of the stuff just now."

"Aye. A wise man might."

Ré's jaw tightened. "We are here to force the queen's hand, Aodh. We are here because—"

"We are here because I am not the queen's plaything." Curt and hard, his words cut Ré off. "We are here because my cloth was cut to fit Rardove, and I will have it. It is mine."

Snow began to settle on the shoulders of Ré's cloak, a faint winter landscape across the dark green wool. It slid off in a whispery avalanche as he gave a last exasperated shake of his head.

"I hope you know what you're doing," Ré muttered, then pointed. "There they are."

Ahead in the tilting yards, abutting the battlement wall, stood a group of sullen, defeated Rardove soldiers.

Christ, they were young. Were any above twenty?

They'd been disarmed and placed in the center of a ring of Aodh's soldiers, who had their swords out. But despite the overwhelming odds and the fact that they'd been entirely disarmed, they looked belligerent and unruly, not particularly willing to bend. But bend they would, if they cared for their lady.

"They are all yours," said Ré.

"And I shall take them," he said, striding forward. Soldiers required attention, but not a great deal. There were the swords and pikes and the occasional firearm, but all in all, soldiers were not a complicated lot.

Katarina, though...complicated.

In twenty-nine years of hard living, Aodh had seen much and done even more. Little of it was pretty, much of it was brutal. As a child, his life had been a hedgerow of spears. His adult life had been much the same, except he was the one brandishing the weapons, and not all were wrought of steel; intrigue oft had the sharper bite. Queen Elizabeth expected nothing less from her most loyal men.

Little surprised or upended Aodh, and nothing, absolutely nothing, enchanted.

But Katarina had.

Granted, few men would find a woman laying a blade to their throat enchanting. But Aodh had always been the cross-grain, the thing that didn't fit, and it had taken approximately two seconds in Katarina's presence to know, without a doubt, she was just like him.

Katarina of the lonely castle.

Katarina of the bright eyes and curving body.

Katarina the flame, who knew very well she ought to have submitted but in a moment of great passion, had not.

Lovely, reckless, hotheaded Katarina.

Aodh was hardly above a challenge.

Sooth, he *craved* a challenge. But the way to Katarina was not by breaking. It was by bending. Of her own free will.

Aodh's specialty. Making people bend.

Chapter 6

SHE'D BENT. Dropped the only protection she had when the Irishman *ran his tongue over her ear.*

Katarina shivered again, even now, hours later.

Idiot. Unbridled, hotheaded, reckless *fool.*

She stood in the exact center of the solar chamber, where she'd been escorted hours earlier, her spine erect, chin up, gaze unmoving on the door, running through the list of self-recriminations. It was a sort of paternoster.

Unfortunately, it did not calm. Nor did it penetrate the true depths of her madness.

If one was going to be so *precipitate* and *idiotic* and *reckless* as to steal a man's blade, one must then *use* it. Not be upended by his shiver-blue eyes and his…his tongue.

She stood motionless, gaze on the door. Motionless was the way to approach this thing. Akin to stone or steel. Untouched and untouchable.

It shouldn't be difficult. She'd had a great deal of practice.

A single candle burned in the leaded glass window. Cold air moved in intermittent drafts, running through the castle like children, particularly here in the solar, which had been damaged in the fire. She hardly felt it. All her attention was focused on detecting sounds from below.

Unfortunately, there were no sounds from below. At least nothing clear. Or human. Animals occasionally bleated or barked or whinnied, but the Irishman's soldiers had clearly conquered, then gone indoors. The castle grounds were eerily quiet. The only sounds were faint ones, creeping through the castle like winding vines, a steady low hum punctuated by occasional whoops and crashes.

Aodh's men might be playing music, conducting races, or beheading people. There was no way to know. Until someone chose to tell her.

How...infuriating.

She shifted her gaze to the young soldier standing guard duty. He leaned against the wall, furs draped over his shoulders, arms crossed, hands shoved up into his armpits, watching her watch the door.

"You are an admirable guard," she told him. "You have not once looked away from me."

"Aye, well, my lord would have my head if anything happened to you, my lady."

That sounded forbidding.

He watched her warily. He was only just coming into his youthful strength, and a rough spray of facial hair dusted his jawline. His gaze swept down her briefly, taking in her somewhat threadbare cloak and exceedingly hard, good boots.

"Are you warm enough?" he asked, sounding doubtful.

"Yes, very," she assured him.

The tip of his nose was red-tinged. She supposed hers was as well. They examined each other's noses.

"You should take my furs, my lady," he urged with a sort of quiet desperation.

"So you have suggested." Repeatedly. But Katarina's old wrap was sufficient, and the thought of being indebted to Aodh Mac Con for anything, anything at all—even a wrap—was, well...infuriating.

"I think not," was all she said.

"A fire, then."

"There is no need." Fuel must be kept for even greater need, which was always coming; he'd learn that soon enough.

He regarded her morosely. "My lord will not be happy."

36

"That I will not take your wrap?"

"That you've been made cold."

"Why ever should he care about such a thing?"

He shrugged. "You're under his protection now."

A terrifying thought, that. "And how would he know of our failed treaty over the furs?"

He looked at her red-tipped nose.

She touched it lightly. "Of course. And for this, he will have your head?"

"He might," he replied grimly.

The terrifying thoughts continued to pile up, did they not? "He does this often, this collecting of heads?"

Surprise crossed his face, then was swept away, shuttered beneath a soldier's mask. He rolled his shoulder slightly, turning away, perhaps to distance himself from any more of her heresy.

After a moment, he said quietly, "I'm sure he'll call for you soon, my lady."

"Yes, but how will that help?"

To that, he had no reply.

Steps sounded outside the room, and a muffled voice came through the door. "Bran, my lad, open up. He wants her."

Pure, cold fear shot through Katarina. *He wants me.*

Her young guard swung the door open. One of Aodh's older captains stood on the landing, clad in his disguising English armor, but the shaggy hair spilling down over his shoulders was entirely Irish. He looked foreign and terrifying, standing on her landing.

His gaze flicked to her briefly. "Bring her down, Bran."

A disconcerting buzz started in Katarina's head, the sort that accompanied faints and watery knees, or so she'd been told. It was ridiculous. Katarina's knees were made of steel.

One did what one did, then dealt with the consequences. She'd taken her captor's blade and used it against him, in front of his men, and in the end, he'd prevailed.

It was like tossing a rock into the air. Eventually, it was going to land.

R℞W

THEY CIRCLED the curving staircase, down through the flickering glow of torches. Her young guard had the lead, the stern-eyed captain strode behind, creaking with leather and clinking with steel.

She kept her fingertips on the curving wall. Composure and control were all in the moment to come, and Katarina was a master of such arts.

She'd spent years honing them against the whetstone of the Irish wilderness, restraining anything reckless inside her, anything that might make her misstep and lose everything.

One did not maintain an English castle beyond the Pale by being reckless. Impolitic. Emotional. Tempestuous.

All things of Katarina.

Oh, she knew very well she was not fitted to rule. How many times had she been reminded of this fact?

No, she'd learned the way through, and it was not her way. So, she'd hammered herself anew. She was akin to steel now. Tempered, capable of great harm.

To this dismal end.

It made one wonder why one hammered oneself at all.

Even now, anger pushed at her. Anger was dangerous. It made her do intemperate things, like steal blades from warriors.

She pressed the anger down where it belonged, deep inside, with all the other dangerous things, like passion and hope.

And that madness downstairs? Naught but a misstep, a regrettable error in judgment, harkening back to the old ways. It must not be repeated.

It would not be. She was calmer now, prepared, reasoned. Leashed.

It was for the best.

All she had to do was see what punishment the Irishman thought fitting. The Irishman who had possession of her castle. The Irishman with eyes of blue ice, who had pressed his neck into a blade with terrifying intensity. Who had run his tongue across her ear and dared her to…to…

To what?

She stumbled on the stone steps.

They stepped out on the landing before the lord's chambers. A crowd of soldiers milled there, as if they'd just left and were about to disperse to the various tasks attendant on conquerors.

Bran walked into their midst. Loud conversations and a general sort of self-approving masculine din died down as she followed after. There was absolute silence as she waded into the thicket of sword-bearing, hard-eyed, long-haired warriors.

Her fingertips were so cold, it felt as though they would break off if she were bumped too hard.

Every man tilted his head down to peer at her as she passed by. She felt as though she was in a forest of men.

Her young guard stopped at the outer chamber door and rapped hard.

The men stared at her back, and Katarina knew, quite suddenly, what creatures on display must feel like. The giraffes and lions in the queen's menagerie, the bears muzzled until their fight. They were fodder for food or fight. Entertainment. Not even prey anymore. Simply…doomed.

To the good, doomed things did not need to wrestle with options or consider consequences. The future was laid out rather neatly, if uncomfortably. So she returned a regard as disdainful as the ones fixed on her, sliding her gaze across them, man by man.

A few raised their eyebrows, one laughed, and then a low, male murmur rippled through their steely midst.

"You're wasting your fight on the wrong mark, my lady," one observed drily, nodding toward the chamber behind her. A few rumbles of appreciative laughter followed.

She returned a cold smile. "I waste nothing. You are all my mark."

A surprised hush swept the landing. Then, almost as one, they threw back their shaggy heads and burst into laughter.

It shook the room. Or mayhap that was inside her.

Bran, the young guard at her side, spoke quietly. "He's ready for you, my lady."

She turned, skirts gripped in her fingertips. The door to the outer bedchamber had been pushed open. A pair of boots could be heard moving in the inner chamber.

"My lady?" Bran's voice was quiet at her side. "You may go in."

She peered at the antechamber. This was not an insurmountable distance. One simply took the next, natural step.

"My lady?"

She looked down at her feet. They were not moving.

Unable to determine a way free from this paralysis except to be dragged, she put her fingertips on Bran's forearm and said quietly, "Please, escort me in."

He stared.

"Physically," she explained.

Understanding flooded his face in the form of a blush. He laid his hand over hers and took a swift, decisive step forward, pulling her into the room.

The boot steps in the inner chamber stopped.

Bran, who now seemed a great friend, gave her hand a faint squeeze.

"Just go easy, my lady," he murmured, a quiet warning tossed to the passenger of a sinking ship: *Do not fight it; in the end, you will sink.* He lowered his arm and stepped back into the throng of men.

She felt their gazes like the points of invisible swords, poking at her back.

She glanced over her shoulder. They were watching her, grinning. No one said a word, but the energy was voice enough: *menagerie girl.* She met their gazes, fierce and silent, hands fisted at her sides.

"That's enough, lads," said a low, familiar voice behind her.

Like a rumble of thunder, chills skipped across her skin, hot and cold and absolutely everywhere.

A muscular arm appeared at her side and reached past her to push the door shut. She stared down. Her heart skipped a beat.

Why, his wrist and hand were *painted*. Almost engraved.

Covered in thick, dark lines, curving and swirling as they roped up his forearm, some resembling the shapes of mystical animals, some simply bursting into curves and flourishes.

God save her, he'd adorned his body with paint, like a wild thing. Like a barbarian.

Like an illumination.

She swallowed and lifted her head.

He certainly looked the barbarian. Gloriously so. His dark hair was untethered now, hanging freely, so she could no longer see the shaved sides. Divested of most of his armor, he still wore his arming doublet, the fustian fabric of the vest dyed a smoky black, so the mail encasing his arms seemed to grow out of the darker bulk of him like tree limbs. The metal rings winked dully in the firelight.

Hose encased his powerful legs. A black and red tunic hung to mid-thigh, and his calves were clad in high, muddy leather boots. But his body was rock-hard and pulsed with masculine vitality in the cold, almost bare antechamber. A painted body that sculpted of stone, and eyes wrought of icy steel.

He was magnificent.

What a terrible, terrible thing.

Any moment now, he was going to do something wild and barbaric.

He stared at her face then his demon-eyes narrowed. He tipped closer, his gaze pinned on her.

"Why is your nose red?"

Rogue Warriors

Chapter 7

STARTLED, KATARINA'S HAND flew to her nose. She touched it, shielded it. It seemed suddenly important to protect her nose from observation.

Because I refused your wood. And your man's cloak.

She finally settled on, "Because I am stubborn," for if you could not tell the awful truth to your enemy, who else could bear the strain?

His gaze trailed across the rest of her face. "Stubborn people end up dead before their time."

She blinked. "Indeed?" she retorted, having no other reply to hand. "Whereas I'd been told it is the reckless ones who end up in early graves."

"You were misinformed. Recklessness gets you admirers."

"And enemies, who then get you dead," she said tartly.

He smiled. "Only if you are stubborn too." His gaze sailed down her body, as if examining it for signs of stubbornness.

A sizzling thrill arced through her. "Some call it loyalty."

"Others call it idiocy."

She sniffed. "I see. So you will deal with any devil."

A smile touched his mouth, a lopsided, sensual, self-approving thing. "Well, I've dealt with England."

"And yet live on," she observed darkly.

He bent closer, his face angled slightly away, and put his mouth directly beside her ear. "As do you, my lady, and recklessness marks you like a brand."

The breath caught in her throat. He turned on his heel and strode into the inner chamber, asking over his shoulder, "Wine?"

She stared at him. "Wine?"

"Wine. 'Tis a drink."

"Of course. Wine," she said stupidly. "I should very much like wine." A large, potent pot of it. Perhaps two.

Why was he not chaining her to the walls?

She followed him into the chamber and stopped short in amazement.

A monstrous fire roared in the gaping maw of the hearth, orange and red and blue flames dancing merrily, so different from the low range of flames that flickered across the single log Katarina allowed herself every day.

Tapestries hung on the walls, wool and silk weaves that seemed to undulate in the light of the conflagration. A far cry from her threadbare tapestries.

On the floor lay plush pelts and on the walls, every oil lamp was ablaze. The lord's huge oak table still dominated the chamber, host to thousands of meetings of Rardove lords over the centuries, secret councils to plot coups and rebellions and marriage alliances. Now, a river of candles streamed down its center, little islands of wine jugs and plates of bread and cheese scattered along its shores. The room practically pulsed with light and heat.

A shockingly profligate approach to warmth. Not at all how Katarina managed heat.

Aodh Mac Con stood by the table, pouring a stream of silky-looking wine into a silver goblet. His gaze flicked up and caught her standing by the door.

"You'll have to come in to get it."

He extended the wine, hand overturned to cup the bowl. The filigreed stem rested between his thick fingers, which were dark against the delicate silver. The illustrations adorning his wrist and hand wound up several of his fingers like beautiful snakes.

"Do not be frightened," he said quietly. "'Tis naught but wine. I've no intention of harming you. Yet."

A roguish smile accompanied this minimally reassuring

statement, but the mockery within was sufficient to help her regain her wits.

"Is that a jest?" she asked.

His look grew serious. "Do you wish me to harm you now and get it over with?"

Every fiber of her being screamed *"Run!"* and *"Flee!"* or at least *"Do not engage with madmen!"*

But the fibers of her being were almost numb from cold, so instead of doing any of these sensible things, she tipped her head to the side and studied her captor.

"Would you?" she asked quietly.

"Do I look as though I am about to harm you?"

"You look as though weather is not safe from you."

A smile touched one corner of his mouth. "That bad?"

"Worse," she assured him. "And yet, I ask myself, why would he waste the wine on me? But then, perhaps it is not very *good* wine."

He smile grew. "'Tis exceptionally good wine. If only you were not too frightened to try."

She made a little sound in her throat. "You underestimate me, sir."

"To think wine would frighten you?"

"To think an angry Irishman would."

His smile grew to encompass both sides of his mouth. He had an uncommonly handsome smile. How unfortunate.

The goblet remained in the air, a silent challenge.

She reached for it, careful not to touch the winding dark flames that licked across his hand and fingers. She took the stem and tugged.

He did not let go.

She looked up, surprised to find she wasn't surprised, but instead…prepared.

Surprise did not haunt his features either. So, neither of them were surprised. And neither were letting go.

No doubt there were several paths of wisdom through this moment. Unfortunately, Katarina knew none of them. Wisdom had fled. It was as if she'd been blindfolded and dropped in a foreign land, and told to reach the shoreline. Diplomacy and experience meant nothing; previous knowledge was of no use. There was only Aodh Mac Con and whatever he wanted.

Something small and fiery charged through her, a miniature lightning bolt.

Surely, clinging to the wine cup just now was not wise. But she did not let go. Neither did he. Her fingers were locked on the goblet's stem, her gaze on his. There developed the distinct possibility they would go to battle right here, over its gilded rim.

"If you ever take my blade again, lass, death will be the least of your worries," he said amiably.

"I shall recall that to mind," she murmured.

"Do." He uncurled his fingers, releasing the cup. "'Ware. 'Tis ever strong."

It was an ambiguous victory, but what could she do but claim the spoils? She lifted the cup, tipping her head back to taste his wine, his soft, exquisite—*St. Vincent, it was velvety*—wine.

A half smile played at his mouth as he watched her drink, a dark brow slightly raised. It was not so much a challenge as…something else.

Which unfortunately triggered a *something else* inside of her, not unlike the reverberations from a struck bell.

Papa would have called it anger, Mamma would have named it pride, but Katarina knew precisely what it was: danger.

She drank the entire cup of wine without stopping, holding his ice-blue gaze over its rim. She drank it down until there was nothing left but dregs. Exceptional dregs.

The half smile became a whole smile, and he nodded slowly. As if she'd said something. Or rather, told him something.

That could not be good.

She reached around him to set the cup on the table, careful not to come any closer than necessary to his body, while also demonstrating she did not *care* how close she came to his body.

He leaned his hip against the table and watched.

"That was speedily done," he said in an admiring tone. "More swiftly than I've ever seen a cup of wine downed." He reflected a moment. "Even by Cormac."

"I am sure your Cormac has other talents," she demurred modestly. "I am also quite skilled with a cup of ale."

He laughed, a low, entirely masculine sound.

"It is not a terribly useful talent."

He crossed his arms. "I would say that depends entirely upon the occasion."

"Would you? And upon what occasions do you deem it wise to render yourself witless, Aodh Mac Con?"

Certes not the wisest thing to say, but then, this moment was not made for wisdom. It was parry and thrust, stand and deliver or die. Life over the Pale in Ireland: the edge of a knife.

Especially when one had an Irish warrior standing in one's bedchamber.

One who was...smiling at her.

He stood, hip against the table, arms crossed, head tilted slightly to the side, not talking, just...watching her, as a hawk might do, if hawks smiled.

Why, this was just how young Bran had stood in the solar, absent the hawkish smile. It was unsurprising, and doubtless unconscious. Aodh Mac Con emanated a presence like air or light. Elemental. The sort men wished to emulate, the kind one absorbed without intent, as a sheet laid on the grass absorbs the morning dew, or a rag tossed on a spill absorbs the wine.

Water. Wine. Aodh.

A flush moved across her cheeks. She had to physically force herself not to cover them with her fingertips.

He slid his gaze down her body, forehead to boots, a swift, masculine appraisal.

"It depends," was all he said.

A hot ribbon unfurled down her belly.

He'd been correct; the wine was quite strong. She had the smallest, waviest feeling of being out of her senses.

"I am unsurprised you find such a thing relative, sir," she retorted, rallying. "And yet most folk take a certain comfort in knowing that coups of castles are almost *always* a poor occasion upon which to render oneself witless."

He nodded toward her empty wine cup. "Then why did you just do so?"

She looked at it too, then said with soft precision, "Aodh Mac Con, you do not think me witless, now, do you?"

A smile of something, perhaps delight?, crossed his face. "I do not know, you *did* take my blade."

"And you did take my castle."

"Ah." His gaze roamed her face. "Was that unwise of me?"

"Exceptionally."

"Alas, I have done many unwise things in my time."

"As have I."

"How unwise?"

"Enough to almost get me kicked out of Ireland."

"That would be bad indeed. Mine was enough to bring me back again. And since then, lass, how has your wisdom fared?"

Rough and low-pitched, his questions were like little tools, chipping away at her composure.

"At times, 'tis practically nonexistent," she whispered.

A dangerous smile crossed his face. "Good."

"My steward would not agree how fare my men?"

She threw out the question the way an anchor is thrown off a ship, so it became a single unstoppable sentence, for it seemed imperative to slow down this thing Aodh had set in motion, this river comprised of their locked gazes and their low murmured conversation about wisdom and the things they had done, and the things they might do, and how dangerous it all could be.

He pushed off the table and leaned over her so she had to tip her head back to hold his gaze.

His mouth was bare inches away, his tongue so close, so able to do the things it had done before. *He will take me now*, she thought wildly, her body charged, and she, standing here with her lips parted, not to receive him—not at all, that would be *madness*—but to draw air into her breathless body.

He smiled just above her mouth and said, "Stubborn," then turned and strode into the room.

CHAPTER 8

SHE TRIPPED backward, almost reeling at the…nothingness of it.

At the way her expectations had not been met.

"Stubborn?" she echoed. "My men are stubborn?"

He moved deeper into the room, touching small things as he went: the edge of her dressing table; the long oak table that dominated the side of the room; the corner post of the bed. He skimmed his hand over everything he passed, little more than brushes of his fingertips, as if testing its quality.

Or laying claim.

"They are reluctant to surrender." He touched a small beveled glass perfume bottle on her table. It rocked slightly but did not fall. "It seems they await a word from you on the matter."

"Fools," she said aloud, but inside she smiled. Loyal, wonderful fools.

"Aren't they?" His gaze slid her way, ice blue and piercing. "I do not need their allegiance, of course. But neither can they stay at Rardove in their condition."

Their defiant condition.

"No, of course not," she agreed softly.

His red and black tube tunic, belted at the waist, stretched taut across the flat plane of his stomach as he reached across the table for the jug of wine. She saw a thin tendril of paint curling up the back of his neck like a vine or a lick of dark flame. She felt breathless.

Good God, was he painted *everywhere*?

The corded muscles in his neck flexed as he looked over his shoulder at her. She ripped her gaze up. "And you are their fire. More wine?"

She stared stupidly at the jug in his hand. "I am...what?"

"Their fire. The thing they kindle themselves on."

This was a shocking observation. *"Me?"*

"Aye. You."

"You are mistaken," she said, intensely startled. "I assure you, Mac Con, I am as baffled as you why my men would be so reckless in such a lost cause."

"I did not say I was baffled."

Something about the low, slow way he said it sent another ribbony trail of heat fluttering through her body, up her breasts this time.

Ribbons of heat were entirely unwelcome. What was one to *do* with a ribbony trail of heat?

He set down the refilled cup of wine on the table next to her.

She regarded it grimly, then looked away, not without effort, because it truly was exceptional wine. He was toying with her. Dragging out whatever punishment or unpleasant consequences he had plann—

"Have you been treated well?" he asked as he circled the huge table.

"I have been locked in the solar, and have not yet had the opportunity to learn how your men take to their role as conquerors, nor how they treat their plunder."

His gaze swung to her. "You mean rape."

She hesitated, then nodded.

He watched her a moment more, then lowered himself into the huge lord's chair at the head of the table and sprawled back, his fire-ice eyes unreadable beneath dark brows, hard fingers interlaced on his lap, his body in the pose of ease, but Katarina could *feel* him from across the room.

His entire being was barely leashed power, like a bow drawn back, taut and ready.

From the first, he'd been nothing she could have expected, and it had been brutally effective. She had no notion how to proceed, but right now, she desperately wanted him to say something. Anything.

She also wanted more wine.

She wanted to throw something at his head.

Anything to break the tension.

"Where do we begin?" she asked abruptly.

"We have begun."

The simple, ominous reply occasioned a host of chills across her chest. She swallowed. "You'll want to see the ledgers."

"No."

She frowned, then tugged the castle keys from her girdle. Armory, storerooms, castle doors, and coffers: they held access to everything of value in Rardove.

She gave them a silvery-iron jingle and held them up.

He shook his head.

"They open all the doors and coffers," she told him, unnecessarily. Surely he knew what keys did. "You will find the account rolls. The ledgers. Coin."

He shook his head again.

What conqueror did not want coin?

"The only other way in is to smash them open," she said, then reversed step to examine the padlocks of the nearest chest, sitting under the edge of the table. Perhaps they'd already been broken open.

No, the locks were intact, as flat black and foreboding as ever. She turned back, oddly and unaccountably embarrassed.

Their eyes met. He shook his head again, very slowly.

A trail of fear slid down her belly like a drop of cold rain. Their eyes locked.

"I did not bring you here for coin or keys," he said in a low voice.

She rested her fingers on the worn but lovingly polished surface of her small dressing table. "I know why you brought me here."

"Do you?"

"To punish me."

"Why would I punish you?"

She waved in the direction of the door. "For what happened. Downstairs."

"Ah. What happened. Downstairs."

His echo was a long, drawn-out affair. Heat flared up her cheeks, hot streaks across her skin.

"'Twas an…aberration," she said quickly. "It is not like me."

"Aye, it is." He leaned his hard body back, slung an arm over the side of the chair and let it hang, deceptively relaxed, for she knew he was as relaxed as a wolf. "What 'happened downstairs' is very much a thing of you, Katarina."

Her jaw unhinged at his use of her Christian name. On his lips, it had not sounded Christian *at all*. He'd rendered it into something else entirely. The words were English, but the intonation, the inflection, the way it rolled over his tongue… No, this was not her language. This was his. Some melding of English and Irish. Something old, foreign. Ensorcelled. Enchanted.

She dragged her mind from the things he was doing to her name.

"Y-You are wrong about me, Aodh Mac Con."

He smiled faintly and bent to the floor beside him, lifted something, and tossed it onto the table. It was a lightweight sword belt, blades attached.

Her blades.

Other weapons followed soon after, hitting the table with muted thuds: the long clumsy dagger; the short, fierce knife; the sleek, keen-edged *misericorde*. Her wheel-lock pistol. The newer snaphances. All five of them.

He'd found everything. How…unsettling.

They stared at the deadly cache in silence a moment. She cleared her throat. "Ireland is a dangerous land."

He gave a low laugh. "Aye. With you in it."

Now she felt as if *she* were the bow being strung, inexorably drawn back, the tension torquing.

"I do not want my men to suffer on account of my deeds, sir. I offer my…apologies." She scraped the word out and wiped it through the air. "I am sorry."

"No you are not." He pushed the weapons to the side, inconsequential anymore. "'Tis time to clarify a few things, lass. I do not rape women."

His voice was hard steel, and it made her feel cold inside. "Oh."

"I do not smash open coffers to steal coin."

"I meant only—"

"I do not deal in feigned apologies—"

"I—"

"And I do not punish men for defending what is theirs."

It was an impressive litany of the restraints of a warrior. Katarina was not impressed.

"Do you not?" she said sharply. "How noble of you. And yet what of women, sir? For I have found there are so often different rules for them."

Something dark entered his regard, and he said softly, "I do not follow many rules, Katarina."

Whoosh, directly through the center of her belly. With her name strung on the end like a pearl, in his rough, dark lilt, it sounded like a promise.

"Ah," was all she could conjure up, a sad reply to this admission of his mutinous nature.

"What 'happened downstairs' is exactly what I'd expect from someone with wits enough to see when their opponent was distracted. And the bollocks to seize that moment."

Something that carried chills in its pockets swept over her. It was not so much coldness as a slapping sort of alertness, like drawing the furs off a slumbering body in winter. The splash of cold water in the heat of a fever.

Alert, aware, awake.

His eyes never left hers. "I do not disapprove."

Oh, *now* she saw the danger. Felt it as surely as she felt the heat from the fires he'd lit. Now, when it was far too close.

"Then you are different from any man I have ever known," she said quietly.

"That I am, Katarina. As for most men, they are fools. I rarely do the things they do. I proceed where they stop, I sail when they waver, and I take the castles they negotiate over."

A thread of chills scalded across her breasts, hardening her nipples. *Why?* Why when he spoke of such mercenary, acquisitive arrogance, why did she feel as if he'd touched her with a feather on fire?

"I think you are the same." He pushed out the chair opposite him with the tip of his boot and extended a palm toward it. "Sit with me."

"Why?"

"To negotiate."

She could not help it; she laughed. "Negotiate? Over what? I have nothing."

He just nodded toward the chair.

"Aodh Mac Con, you have my castle, my men, the coffers and the coin. You tell us what to do, and we shall do it. What more could you possibly want?"

"You."

Her heartbeat slowed. "Pardon?"

"I have a proposition."

"What sort?"

"The sort where you marry me."

ROGUE WARRIORS

CHAPTER 9

AODH WATCHED HER.

She went absolutely still, so still even the loosened hair laddering beside her cheeks didn't move. As motionless as she'd been when he told her he'd taken over her castle.

But this time she was truly rocked. He saw it in the way her lips parted, the way her fingers tightened in her skirts, the swift rush of blood into her pale cheeks.

Good. Kindle the fire inside her, then watch it burn.

He had no idea how she would respond specifically, though. She'd surprised him at every turn thus far. He greatly hoped she would do so again.

Perhaps she would lunge directly for his throat.

Maybe try to grab one of the pistols that had so shocked his squire Bran when they were searching the room and the boy pulled them out from under a pile of worn silk stockings.

He waited. And waited.

She lifted her chin a miniature inch, an infant inch, the smallest lift one could give a chin in a tight situation, then swept her skirts out to the side and sat down opposite him at the far end of the table.

"What do you offer in consideration of your suit, Sir Irish?"

Aodh burst out laughing.

Good girl.

"You've got bollocks, lass."

"I have been told that," she replied with the same liquid

grace she'd evidenced in everything thus far: greeting him in a cold bailey; handing over the keys to her castle; holding a blade at his throat.

He wanted to push her back on the bed and make her stop being graceful, become naught but heat. Roaring flames.

He shoved the heels of his boots into the ground and maintained his seat. Ravishing her would not encourage her to bend of her own free will.

Accursed free will.

To give his body something to do besides ravishing her, he grabbed the wine jug and tipped the spout her direction in silent query. The fire reflected in her dark eyes as she looked at him. Then she reached out and took it.

A small surrender, but Aodh was on a path. Small accessions, small agreements, accumulating like snow.

He waited until she finished pouring, then said, "I can think of half a dozen persuasive reasons to join me."

"By persuasive, do you mean 'mad'?"

He shrugged. "Some might call it that."

"*Sane* folk might call it that."

"On the other hand, folk who drink an entire bowl of wine in a single swallow might see merit in the notion."

She settled back in her seat. "I see. You *do* think me mad."

"I think you reckless and bold. To your arguments, Katarina: firstly, my men and I are already here."

"Yes, I had noticed that."

"For some, that alone would be sufficient motivation."

She smiled thinly. "So now you think me easily swayed."

"The dagger at my throat suggested otherwise," he said briskly. "Secondly, I have sixty-odd men who can commandeer a castle in less than ten minutes."

She settled back in her seat, wine cup balanced between the fingertips of both hands. "Oh, yes, we were all appropriately awed."

"*They* were. You were not."

"I was entirely awed, Mac Con. One might even say awestruck."

"Might one?"

A secret little smile touched her mouth. "It would depend upon the one."

He greatly liked when she smiled. "I think you will find sixty-odd men of use, Katarina."

"To what end would *I* use them? I have no troubles with the Queen of England."

He smiled. "Perhaps in your troubles with the Irish, then."

Her eyes snapped at him, no longer filled with cool consideration, but more like the fire-eyes of the woman he'd had to back up against a wall.

State of war notwithstanding, this was how he preferred her.

She jerked up in her seat, toward the table, toward him, as if she could no longer tolerate being reclined.

Good.

"Your boldness implies a certain ignorance of what is to come, Aodh Mac Con, so let me enlighten you. Sixty-odd warriors will never hold the line against the mighty forces the Queen of England will send marching for your head the moment she learns of your traitorous deeds here."

"I agree. That is where you come in."

Her cheeks flushed. "As your consort?"

"As the sword wielder. And wheel-lock-gun wielder. Or the snaphances," he said brightly. "You could wield those. All *five* of them."

Her jaw dropped. "You...jest."

"Neither of us are laughing."

At that, she *did* expel a short, sharp sound, half laugh, half incredulous gasp. "I, fight on *your* behalf? Are you mad?"

"Your array of weapons is inspiring. I presume you know how to use them. I am impressed."

The words brought her up short. Outrage and indignation faded. Something contemplative came into her eyes as she looked at the guns. "That is the second time you said that."

"'Tis the second time I felt it."

The third. Fourth. Everything she did.

"Would you say that if I were a man? Be impressed with my

weapons?"

He shook his head. "I would ask where your lance was."

She gave a strange little smile. Almost bitter. "There, you see: There *are* different rules for women."

"There is a difference between a rule and a regularity, Katarina. You are highly irregular."

She laughed then, a burst of unexpected amusement. It was a goodly thing, this laughter of hers. Musical and low, almost throaty. Pleasing. Very. As was the faint flush that washed across her pale cheeks.

"You've no idea how many men have told me that, Aodh Mac Con, if not quite in that way."

"And were they all as pleased by it as I?"

Her body became a study in frozen moments: stilled smile, furrowed brow, startled eyes pinned on his.

"I thought not," he concluded briskly. "They've no idea what to do with you."

"Who is 'they'?"

"Every man you've ever met, Katarina. Every one but me."

He could almost *feel* the chills race across her skin. Silence spread, except for the crackling fire.

She glanced into the depths of whatever wine was left in her goblet. Probably none. Then she rested an elbow on the table and considered him from across its length, somewhat like a battle commander in her war tent.

It was an uncommonly uncomfortable moment, having this woman's appraising, clever gaze inspect him.

"You do not like Ireland overly much, do you, Aodh Mac Con?" she said softly.

Surprise spiked through his body, and with it, all the changes that mark vigilance, as when you hear the snick of a lock in a darkened room, or feel the thud of a boot stepping where there should only be sleeping bodies.

Beyond the faintest jerk, though, he didn't move; too much experience with being scared half to hell and never showing it.

Clever, clever Katarina.

"Not overly," was all he said.

"And yet, here you are."

He spread his hands, palms up, to indicate he was, indeed, here.

The fire picked up the strands of reddish-gold amid her falling brown locks. "Ireland is a wild, fierce land, but I have discovered that for all its savagery, it is not a land of want. In fact, one discovers things here that are lacking in every other place in the world."

"Rain?" he suggested.

She smiled faintly.

"Cold? Darkness? The number of savages?" he went on absently, not interested in a discussion of the limited charms of Ireland. He was far more interested in the way her lips formed words. Full, wet, faintly red, and ever so slightly crooked.

"Indeed, sir, Ireland is all those things. Cold, dark, wet, although as you say, the worst menace are the warriors who paint their bodies like pages in a manuscript."

He slid his gaze from her mouth to her eyes. "You noticed."

Her face flushed. "Barely."

"Ha."

"But amid such trials," she went on, "Ireland bears unimaginable gifts."

"For instance?" he said doubtfully.

"No one cares what you do if you are in Ireland, so long as it does not inconvenience them. And as they are hundreds of miles and a sea away, it rarely does."

He sat back, slung his arm over the arm of the chair. "I see."

"Do you? Send the receipts, ship the wool, imprison any shipwrecked Spanish soldiers you may stumble across, and you become…chaff."

"I know," he agreed grimly. One benefit of being in a cold hell: no one bothered you. Until they came to crush you.

"You do not," she pressed, as if it mattered that he understand her strange affection for his homeland. "What I mean is, one may do as one wishes. One becomes…beneath notice. Blurred. A mote of dust. Taken"—she lifted a hand and let it fall—"for granted. This would not please one such as you—"

"Why do you say that?"

She arched an eyebrow, delicate and incredulous. "You stole a queen's castle and thereby issued an invitation for the entire royal army to come marching for you. One assumes you are not averse to...attention."

He grinned.

"But for one such as me, that has never served. I prefer to be a dust mote. Indeed, this invisibility, and the freedoms it brings, creates the strong, one might say *intense,* desire to never again become a thing to be 'done with.'"

The fire crackled through a moment of silence. Then, in case her meaning not been clear, she said in a low voice, "I am not a thing to be *done with*, Aodh Mac Con."

Although, of course, she was.

He knew it, she knew it, every member of her stubborn, currently locked-up garrison knew it. There was nothing clearer in all the world than that women were chattel and plunder.

But for all the talk of Fate and Heaven and Hell, the world let a man make of himself what he would. Required him to.

Men were as persuadable as sheep, and the world, be it civilized and courtier-laden or savage and howling with wolves, responded to whatever a man made of himself. If a man acted great, a great man he was. If he sold himself as a pastry, he would be consumed as one.

How could it not be true for women as well? The world did with one as one allowed it to do. No one knew its vicious appetites better than Aodh.

So, instead of laughing at Katarina and her ridiculous statements about being something other than chattel, he said simply, "Then you will suit just fine."

She closed her eyes for a moment and shook her head, releasing a small puff of air that might be a laugh. Or might not.

"You *are* mad," she said softly.

"Is that a yes?"

"And if *you* do not suit equally well?"

He grinned. "I shall."

"Saying yes would make me quite as reckless as you, sir."

"I am relying on it."

"And if I turn out to be stubborn instead?"

"Then I will have miscalculated." But he hadn't. He knew it. He was as sure of it as anything in his life: she was just like him.

And he *would* have her.

Deep inside, desire began to move thickly through his blood. It was her smile. This one was so small and enclosed, like a house with all the curtains drawn; anything might be happening inside.

He wanted in.

Her cheeks flushed, but her clever gaze never strayed from his. "You might be sorry, you know. I neither stitch nor sing, and most consider that a blessing, as I am without talent in either."

"I consider myself forewarned."

"Neither do I play an instrument."

"No mind. I do."

"The tennis court is entirely ornamental; I cannot play."

"But you have a wheel-lock," he said admiringly. "And a snaphance. *Five* of them."

She laughed and leaned back against the chair, momentarily relaxed. The bodice of her green gown tossed off darts of light from the silvery threads, and her long dark hair was still tousled, coif long forgotten, smiling at him. He wanted more of that from her. Wanted it badly. He had no idea why, and was not wont to examine it too closely. All he knew was he must keep Katarina upended. Keep her smiling. Keep her looking at him.

"That is the oddest measure of matrimony I have ever heard," she mused.

"Aye, we'll be quite a pair."

Head still back against the chair, she met his eye. "You do not fool me, Aodh Mac Con. This is not a pairing. You are a conqueror to the marrow of your bones. Your coup will be complete if you wed me. You will have the lady."

"I will have the fire."

One eyelid drifted down in suspicious regard. "I do not know where you have collected your notions of me, sir, but I am the furthest thing from a fire of rebellion that exists in all of Ireland."

But Aodh wasn't thinking about rebellion. He was thinking about the fire of Katarina. The heat, the passion, the *fuel* of her.

Aodh was comprised of ice, so hard and carven and unstoppable he'd achieved everything everyone had ever intended for him, and more. He felt like a glacier that had pushed aside even the intentions of a queen. Nothing could stop him. He was a block of ice, moving through the world. Not even fire could penetrate him. Nothing could warm him. Nothing touched him. He barely felt the flames roaring only a few feet away.

But he felt Katarina.

He sat forward, chest pressed to the hard edge of the table, surprised to find his heart beating fast.

"Lass," he said, very low. "Are you going to marry me?"

CHAPTER 10

KATARINA felt as if she was a candle he'd lit. Chills and heat warred across her skin.

How in God's name had it come to this?

She'd been facing a small query from one of the queen's interrogators about a faint rumor regarding a minor crack in the loyalty of Rardove — almost entirely unfounded — and she was being offered full-on rebellion in its stead.

Marry Aodh Mac Con, thief of castles, warlord who made her blood boil and who did not punish her, soldier unafraid of the Queen of England, who had trekked across hostile lands and — *I do not disapprove* — dispensed velvety wine and said her name like a hymn?

It was unfathomable, outrageous…unattainable.

She could not marry an Irish warlord. It was ludicrous. It would be treason at best. At worst…

Every man you've ever met.

Every one but me.

Simple, then. Say no. Get to her feet, decline this treasonous offer, close the strange, unforeseen door Aodh had thrust open with his coup and his eyes that heralded ice and sadness and his offers of marriage and *I do not disapprove.*

Just say no.

And then, through the long skein of the rest of her days, what then?

A jagged-edged chill cut down her belly.

"Katarina, regard," he said quietly. "Whether you wish it or no, I have uncovered the truth. You hold Rardove with ten men. I cannot fathom how you did it, but that time is over. People are going to come for this place."

"Yes, Bertrand of Bridge." A tragically, violently well-suited man for the task of subduing anyone.

"And you wish for that?"

The question disrupted her tenuous composure more than anything else that had happened this day, and a great many things had blown against that thin veil. This *detecting* of her inner thoughts was most unnerving.

"What does it matter what I wish for?"

"Right now, it matters to me."

A ribbon flicked inside her, hot and low in her belly, raising paradoxical little chills across her skin.

I do not disapprove.

He sat in the chair, his head resting against the high, carved wooden back, his gaze steady on hers.

The lord's chair was a deep, elaborately cushioned and ornately carved oaken affair, befitting a mystical forest prince more than a mortal man. But then, her father had been so very ambitious. And yet even so, he'd always seemed dwarfed by the grandness of the chair. Katarina avoided it entirely.

Aodh Mac Con looked like the King of the Wood.

She got to her feet, but could not look away.

He sat watching her, the power of him flickering in shadow and light. Dark hair, pewter eyes, warrior's body, weapons hanging across him, he was everything she knew to fear.

That *must* be fear, rushing through her in hot, shaky sweeps.

"Is that an aye?" he asked as her silence extended.

One beat, two. His eyes never left hers.

Then he pushed to his feet.

She felt dizzy, almost faint. She couldn't think straight. She half turned away. She was breathing too fast. Her head spun. Her lips parted around panted breaths, but not, of note, the simple word 'No.'

She heard him coming, the silvery jingle of spurs, the soft

tread of boots on plank floors. She curled her hand around a hairbrush on her dressing table, its gilt silver handle a cool thing of solid sanity, for this thing happening now, it could not be real.

But it was.

He came up behind her, stood at her back, not touching, *emanating*. He was like a fire burning in the room.

She tried to slow her racing breath, her spinning mind, her thundering heart.

"I cannot," she whispered. To her horror, she realized it sounded like a question: *Can I?*

He bent his head beside her hair. "Aye you can. Your people are frightened, Katarina. They need you to calm them, guide them. You and I have armies to integrate," his dark coaxing went on. "My men...they have been too long amid the fight. They need civilizing."

She gave a broken laugh. "They will hardly find that here."

"And you." His body was heat and hard power, a bare inch away. "You must ache for a husband."

She meant to shake her head, deny his words, deny everything. She moved nothing.

"On occasion, aye?"

She tilted her chin up.

"At night, when you are alone?"

He tread too close. In every way.

His fingertips touched down low on her back. "I would do my part to make it pleasing for you."

Her breath stopped as his fingertips skimmed up. He might as well have raked a hot poker up her spine, dragging streams of fire behind it. His hand slipped under the weight of hair at the base of her neck and brushed it aside.

He lowered his mouth to hover just above the exposed skin.

"Breathe," he said quietly.

The breath rushed out of her.

He did not touch her, but his breath skimmed across her skin as he spoke. "You would not suffer for the union."

He presented it as a choice, but all would bend to his will.

She knew it, he knew it; his presence was a decree. Still, he stood, restrained, head bent, a hand brushing the hair off the nape of her neck, coaxing her.

Seducing her.

Inside, she felt like dying coals awakened, as when a door is opened and the wind sweeps in.

"Contrary to what you might think, Katarina…" Oh, he *must* stop saying her name in that dark, lilting Irish voice. It would make her do something *mad*. "I do not take my pleasure in unwilling women."

"No?" she whispered.

"Nay." He rested a hand on the curve of her hip. "I prefer to make them willing."

Fire coursed through her body. "How?"

She meant, 'How *could you ever think to make me willing?'* It was a rhetorical device, a defiant query, a breathless taunt.

He took it as an invitation.

He pressed his knee to the back of hers and lowered his mouth to her neck, and if Katarina had thought him dangerous before, now she was educated on the true peril of Aodh Mac Con.

He was spark, and she was nothing but tinder.

Hot and confident, his mouth laid whisper-light kisses across the base of her neck, raining chills down her spine, then his wide palm came to rest flat against her stomach.

Shock reeled through her. She made the smallest push against his arm, and he dropped it at once. He did not move his mouth, though, and she did not move her body.

Wicked girl, she did not move anything at all.

He gathered her hand in his. Not hurrying in the least, he entwined their fingers and lifted them to his mouth and kissed each of her knuckles in turn. It was as if he'd laid tiny torches to the never-tended skin.

She was breathless and had to open her mouth to inhale. He touched each finger until he reached her orphaned thumb, then turned their hands over and pressed a kiss into the center of her palm, a slow, lingering kiss, his head to the side.

Her knees almost buckled.

The day's growth of hair on his jaw scraped against her palm, and she curled her fingers into it for a brief, mad second. Her head was a whirling thing, a dervish mind.

Which had to explain what happened next. How she allowed him so much. How she took so much.

He shifted behind her and his hand slid up her belly, over the mound of her breast. No, not his hand, *hers*, their fingers still entwined, sliding over her breast, brushing her knuckles over her nipple, coaxing it to a hard nub.

He was making her caress herself.

Their breaths were loud in the room. She felt as if she'd drunk a dozen cups of wine. She should have shouted no, stopped this thing. But she said nothing, for she knew if she so much as *whispered* no, Aodh would stop.

And if he stopped, she would die.

Passion had never served her.

But oh, how it pleased.

What Aodh was doing, how it pleased.

He curled a finger around the collar of her gown and slowly dragged it to the side, then bent his head and *exhaled* over the exposed territory. Then he skimmed the tip of his tongue over her skin.

Her head jerked back in shock and then she, wanton she, tipped her head to the side to allow him in.

He moved into the surrendered territory, went up the length of her neck with no hesitation, his mouth a weapon of sin and desire, marking her cool skin with hot, lingering, open-mouthed kisses, the barest grazing of his teeth, feasting on her neck and shoulders. Chills rampaged across her skin, armies of them.

He took the final step in, so his body was pressed up full against the back of hers, heat and hard power. The curve of his maleness pressed against the small of her back, and the thread binding her to sense quite snapped.

She arched her spine, pressing her breasts forward into the hard cupping heat of their entwined hands, pushing her hips back, her bottom rubbing against the hard length of his erection.

"Aye, like that," he said hoarsely against her neck. He bent them forward, guided their cupped hands down to the seam of her legs, until the silk was bunched high between her thighs, then he had them push in, hard and slow.

She gave a broken gasp.

"Do you see how we shall do it?" he asked in a dark murmur, and moved their hands again.

She was that close to lost, that close to taking everything Aodh was offering, when a shout from outside the room broke through the miasma of their passion like shattering glass.

Her body gave a single, sinful shudder, then she wrenched free.

For a half second, his arm tightened, then he released her.

She backed up a step, then another, and another, until she bumped into the table.

He watched go like some otherworldly being, cast in shadow and flickering light, his head bent, eyes half-lidded, dark painted lines inked across the hand fisted at his side. He was breathing as hard as she.

Another tentative call came from the antechamber. "Sir? You're wanted belowstairs."

"Leave," she whispered.

His gaze darkened. "Katarina." It almost sounded like...a question. A plea.

Oh, that would *never* do.

She pointed at the door. Her hand was shaking. "Get out."

Something shifted in the eyes holding hers, a hardening, like black ice forming, and he laughed, once, a harsh sound.

"If you wish to order me from my bedchamber, Katarina, you must first share it with me."

The breath strangled in her throat. He was right. This was not her room anymore. Nothing was hers anymore. He'd taken it all.

He turned for the door without another word.

Pressure whirled in Katarina's body like a tempest, a storm comprised of thwarted fury and thwarted desire and something so thwarted it frightened and could not be named.

But Aodh Mac Con suffered none of these things. If he wanted a thing, he took it; if he was angry, he smashed things: walls, houses, lives.

His confidence was his armor. His right to pass through the world was assured, mayhap not safely, but as he wished. Oh, men were mirrors of one another. They took what they wanted and left ashes in their wake.

"You think I have no choice," she said coldly to his back.

He stopped, his painted hand curled around the edge of the door as he turned and pinned her in his gaze.

"If I wanted what came from a woman who had no choice, Katarina, we would not be having this conversation."

Whoosh.

"Come to me willing, or do not come at all."

ROGUE WARRIORS

CHAPTER 11

AODH BARRELED out of the chamber, gripped in a vortex of lust.

It had turned him into a churning, roaring creature of want he'd never known before. His body, his mind, his intentions, everything had been consumed, wrested from his control, under the all-consuming power of wanting her.

If someone hadn't called, if he hadn't reached for self-control like a drowning man and let her go by an act of sheer will, he'd have had her up against the wall like some rutting beast, the very thing he'd spent his life proving he was not, all intentions of wooing and bending her will scorched away by the conflagration of his desire.

The conflagration of Katarina.

From the moment he'd touched her, he'd *known*.

He charged out the door and was halfway across the antechamber before he slammed to a halt to avoid tumbling over a youth, perhaps nine or ten years old, milling nervously about.

The boy froze like a hare at the sight of him. Aodh's seventeen-year-old squire, Bran, snapped to attention too, then, as he looked at Aodh, Bran's hand moved slowly to the hilt of his sword.

"What?" Aodh demanded.

"You...your..." Bran's hand made a circling motion to indicate Aodh's face.

Aodh was breathing as hard as if he'd run a footrace—and

lost. No doubt his face was flushed too, and was that sweat on his brow?

"Stay your sword, Bran, there is no danger," he said curtly, then glanced at the young boy. Bran shrugged.

"Says he's here to see you. And her."

The boy, small but seemingly determined, circled the landing like a wild creature about to bolt, then, face pale, he cleared his throat and stepped forward.

"I had a question, sir. My lord," he revised abruptly, then immediately retreated from it. "Sir. Milordsir," he settled on the mongrel word, and Aodh couldn't fault him for it.

"A question?" Aodh repeated in the same solemn tones.

"Is my lady...in need of anything?"

That was a loaded question.

The boy plunged on. "I'm to bring her things, you see, milordsir. 'Tis my duty, and I don't know if she"—he met Aodh's eye with a sudden spurt of reckless bravery—"if she needs anything."

A list of things Katarina needed entered his mind.

"'Tis my duty, sir," the boy repeated stoutly.

"If that is your duty, lad, then you should get to it."

The page's body slumped with relief.

"Never let someone stop you from doing what you know must be done, not even a big ugly Irishman."

The boy drew himself up straight, reinvigorated by this camaraderie and renewed sense of purpose. "Aye, sir! My lord! Sir! And you are not ugly, sir!"

Bran rolled his eyes and, at a gesture from Aodh, searched the boy then allowed him into the bedchamber. When the door was shut, Aodh gestured Bran over.

"Allow the boy out when he is done, but search him first. If the lady wishes to speak with any other members of her household, allow it, but search them fore and aft. Her ladyship is to remain inside, under lock and key, unless and until she wishes to see me. Then she is to be brought directly, and only, to me."

His squire drew up straight as an arrow. "Aye, sir. Do you

want her...bound?"

Yes, bind her, bring her to me like a feast. He forced in another deep breath. "She is a lady, Bran. We do not bind ladies. But we do escort them, everywhere." He paused. "Even the privy."

Bran gave a clipped nod, absorbing the new rule. "Do I search her as well?"

Aodh paused to imagine his squire trying to search Katarina. "No, but clear the room of weapons. And then, even so, should you hear anything that sounds like a wheel-lock being loaded," he added grimly, "investigate."

Bran's face paled. "As you say, sir. Should I locate her maidservant?"

He shook his head slowly. "Not yet you don't."

Bran looked unhappy about this. "What if she...needs anything?"

"Bring it to her. Or her to me. Those are her only options now."

Aodh clapped him on the shoulder, feeling oddly...buoyant. It was there, under everything else, deep inside him, a sense of being lifted. As if he were back at sea. Despite the fact that he had not succeeded.

Mayhap *because* of it.

"We wanted Ireland, Bran," he said. "This is it."

He took the stairs to the hall two at a time, hurtling down them.

"Good Christ, Aodh, where have you been?" called Cormac, crossing the hall, his broad, bearded face split by a huge grin.

"Busy."

"Are you mad? When the celebration is down here?"

People roamed everywhere. As Aodh had instructed, fires roared in every trough and hearth, tapestries were being hung, servants bustled to and fro, and the scent of duck and mutton wafted in from the stone kitchens.

There was an air of jubilation, even from the conquered. And why not? No one had been killed, food had been brought in plenty, and the isolation of early spring had been lessened by the influx of new people, new stories, new blood. And notwithstanding the fact that the Rardove garrison was at present being held at blade point, what could have been a night of bandages and mourning had turned into almost riotous celebration.

Rardove's legacy — legend — was the mollusks that populated the beaches at the base of its sea cliffs, rumored to have made the finest dyes far back into antiquity. But dyes were not necessary here. Rardove had a sheepfold that produced a wool that could be found nowhere else on earth. It also had thousands of acres of land, a seafront, and a stony castle fortress that could hold off an army for years.

Years.

Rardove was a gem in the Irish mists. Cold, diamond-hard opportunity. And it moved him not at all.

"Build the fires higher," he ordered a passing servant, and the man scurried off.

Cormac stood at his side and surveyed the bustle of the great hall. "Well, we did it." He flung out a beefy arm, indicating the hall, then turned and yanked Aodh into a heartfelt bear hug.

Aodh grunted as he was pulled into the Scot's chest. Eight years of service, eight years of battles and near escapes, and it still surprised the hell out of him when Cormac did these sorts of things.

"Christ's mercy," the gravelly, emotional, muffled voice came up. "We took accursed *Rardove Keep.*"

Aodh submitted to the embrace — it was easier than trying to wrestle free — and Cormac's burly arms sprang open and he stepped away, beaming.

"I'm no' ashamed to admit it, Aodh, I was skeptical about your god-awful plan at first, aye, but..." He swung his hand toward the hall, a silent, compelling conclusion.

"You're always skeptical of my plans," Aodh reminded him.

Cormac nodded happily. "That's because they're always so god-awful. Reckless and foolish with ne'er a chance of succeeding."

"Recall to me why you join me?" Aodh moved toward one of the tables.

Cormac grinned. "Because you're effective as hell."

"That would be why." He yanked out a bench and sat.

Cormac dropped down beside him, elbow sprawled across the table, then tipped forward and stopped a maidservant in her trembling tracks with a menacing, friendly roar. "We need ale, comely lass!"

She stared, wide-eyed, then hurried off.

Aodh sighed. "We're to *coax* the people of Rardove, not terrify them."

Cormac's bearded face compressed in indignation. "What did I do? I coaxed. Called her comely, I did. You heard me. An' she is."

"You frightened her."

Cormac swiveled to watch the girl, then shook his head. "No' a chance. She's been lurking around the edges for hours now."

"The edges of what?"

He grinned. "Me."

Aodh smiled faintly but said only, "Leave her be."

Cormac threw up his hands. "When do I ever do a thing I'm no' explicitly invited to?" he demanded. "E*xplicit*ly." He settled back with an indignant shuffle of his shoulders. "And frequently."

"I do not think she is a common serving wench. She looks finer than that."

"Aye, that she does," Cormac agreed, and folded his arms across the bulk of him, which was significant, and not an inch of it fat. He was hard, burly, Scottish muscle from chin to shins, and he was one of Aodh's most trusted councilors and captains.

He also had what some might call rustic manners. Others might call them loutish.

Aodh resigned himself to not receiving any ale until a less comely lass passed by.

Cormac yanked forward one of the low benches and threw his boots up on it. "Word came in not an hour past, while you were 'busy'."

Aodh's clerk came up, pen in hand, with questions about the

trunks in the office chamber. After he hurried off, Cormac went on.

"Lucius arrived."

Aodh felt a little quickening. "How did he get here so swiftly?"

"Chartered a boat, a cricky old thing, almost sunk him. We'll be hearing his complaints on that score until Michaelmas."

"And? Did he find Bertrand?"

Cormac's grin grew. "That he did. Found the fool sitting on the coast," he said, then added in a tone of gleeful derision, "waiting for the storm to pass."

They grinned at each other.

"Anyhow, Bertrand took the bait. Got your message and hightailed it out of there almost before he finished reading it, as if the hounds of hell were on his tail." He angled Aodh a sideways glance. "What did your message say, anyhow?"

Aodh shrugged. "That the queen was going to put the hounds of hell on his tail if he didn't find his way back to her right quick. In York."

Cormac roared in laughter at the idea of one of the queen's favorite interrogators being sent on a wild-goose chase to the north of England.

To Aodh, the resulting cold satisfaction he felt was a pale but welcome sensation. It didn't get much better than cold satisfaction these days.

Except it had with Katarina. Much more than 'satisfaction.' Much hotter.

Putting his elbows on the table, Cormac gazed across the bustling hall with cheerful good humor.

"Aye, well, good. Bertrand's taken care of for the time being then, seeing as the queen is in Windsor, not York. Elizabeth, o' course, now she's a different matter," Cormac went on with almost ghoulish glee. "She'll be deep in her royal passion by now. Send an army, she will."

"This pleases you."

Cormac shrugged. "'Twas inevitable. 'Twas the *point*, Aodh. She wouldn't give you what you rightfully earned, so you took it. And in fine fashion too. If she wants it now, she comes for it. With an army."

He shrugged again, pounding the subtle intricacies of political maneuvering on the anvil of his simple logic. He rubbed his chin with the side of his hand, reflecting. "A massive large one, if I'm any judge."

Shockingly, the comely maid reappeared, mugs of ale on a tray. She set the tray down with a curtsey, her pretty face tipped to the floor, but not far enough to hide the swift, appraising glance she took of Cormac before hurrying away.

Cormac grinned his thanks, handed a mug to Aodh, then sat back, his comfortable and dire predictions carrying on apace.

"The queen's going to want your pretty head, Aodh, and a few other body parts as well." Cormac eyed him appraisingly. "Your frightfully big bollocks, to start with. Dangle 'em right off the Tower if she gets a chance."

Aodh nodded. "Your insights are fascinating. Recall to me why I bring you with me?"

"Because I tell you what you need to hear, no' what you want to hear, like those English boys do." He sniffed. "In any event, you've naught to worry on. We shan't let her have your bollocks, nor your sorry arse, nor any other part of your sorry self, so don't get all worrisome now, Aodh." Cormac eyed him with a mixture of compassion and pity. "You worry too much."

Aodh drank. He had not worried for sixteen years, not since seeing his father hanged until he was half-dead, then taken down, bowels cut from his body and burned, his arms and legs torn from his body, his head cut off—it had taken four blows—and thrust on a spike outside Dublin Castle.

What was there to worry on? You grabbed what you could and then you died.

It was a motto that had served Aodh well, and, in turn, the men who followed him through all manner of exploits. It was also true, though, that his men had tried to make him see the mad recklessness and potentially suicidal nature of his plan to capture Rardove Keep.

Aodh had never disagreed.

He'd also never wavered.

And as 'reckless' was generally the sort of plan he devised anyhow, and always the sort they participated in, in the end, they followed him. As they always did. Honor, dauntlessness, a lack of other options, and a great deal of money ensured it.

He would make it worth their while.

He and Cormac drank in silence as the hall bobbed with life around them. Soldiers came and went on various tasks, and food was eaten as soon as it was brought, pulled off trays by celebratory soldiers.

"So, we send her off and settle in for a fight," Cormac concluded comfortably. "Keep your balls and pretty arse safe." He grinned and lifted his mug in toast.

Aodh returned the gesture but didn't drink. "Send who off?"

Cormac hooked a thumb at the ceiling. "The lady."

"Ah."

Cormac stilled, much as Ré had earlier, then turned his bearded face to Aodh and blew out an ale-gusted breath. "Christ on the Cross, you're planning something, aren't you?"

Aodh sighed. "When I have a plan, do I not tell you?"

"'Tis precisely what I'm sitting here wondering: *'What in God's holy name is he about to tell me he's planning?'*"

Aodh drank. "I asked her to marry me."

Cormac opened his mouth, shut it, opened it again, then flung out a hand in wordless astonishment and fell back in his chair. It rocked under the impact.

"Only the saints could persevere in the face of you, Aodh," he muttered. "How your mam did, I've no notion."

Aodh looked away, across the room, into the hearth. "She did not. She died when I was nine."

Cormac eyed him darkly. "You killed your mam," he muttered, then downed his entire mug in silence. It took three swallows. Aodh wondered idly how many it would have taken Katarina.

"Ré is not going to be happy," Cormac warned darkly.

"Nay, he is not," agreed Aodh, just as Ré himself appeared

at the top of the stairs.

"I'm not telling him," Cormac said peevishly.

"You won't have to."

The Scot snorted. "Aye, he'll see the madness in your eyes himself."

They looked across the bustling hall at Aodh's second-in-command, companion in intrigues that covered the map from Paris to Cadiz. Surely, if anyone would be prepared, it would be Ré.

Dirt-stained, sweaty, and smiling, Ré came to them, grabbed one of the mugs, and sat facing them, straddling a small bench. He drank deeply, then wiped his mouth with his forearm and grinned.

Neither of them returned it. Aodh kept looking at the fire.

Ré's grin faded. "What is it?"

Cormac gestured across the table with his elbow. "Aodh's lost his bleeding mind."

"How this time?"

A beat passed, then Cormac muttered, "Says he's going to wed her." This, despite his earlier vow of silence.

Ré continued to stare at Cormac, then turned his clear gray eyes to Aodh. "I understand the lady holds certain…charms…."

Aodh dragged his gaze off the fire.

"But can we not focus on the battle at hand?" Ré finished, his words hard.

Aodh smiled grimly. "You are not paying attention. She *is* the battle."

ROGUE WARRIORS

CHAPTER 12

KATARINA WATCHED Dickon, her young page, leave the bedchamber. He'd braved the Hound's wrath for her, and she was charmed, heart-warmed, and vaguely unsettled by how *pleased* he seemed after his encounter with Aodh Mac Con.

Outside the walls, the winds were picking up. A sudden gust moaned past the window and blew down the chimney, lifting the fire into hot roaring flames. Then it died away again to a lower burn. It would need to be fed to stay alive.

She crouched in front of it and laid another of Aodh's pieces of precious wood atop, then carefully arranged the grate in front. It was only then she realized her hands were shaking.

Voices sounded outside the door. She pushed to her feet as it swung open. Noise drifted in from the hall belowstairs, then Walter stepped into the room and closed the door, shutting out the sounds of revelry.

She exhaled a breath of…relief, of course. She was relieved. Who would not be relieved to see their advisor of many years at such a trying time?

"My lady," he said, sweeping into the room. "Are you well?" Tall and angular, he stopped and frowned as Bran poked his head in too, swept a wary eye over the room, then nodded to her and backed out again, shutting the door.

"Has the Hound hurt you?" Walter asked crisply as he came forward. He glanced at the bright, hot burning fire and lifted his bushy eyebrows in surprise.

"Of course not. I am unharmed." She felt for the arms of the carved lord's chair and sat down.

Walter's gaze swung away from the flames. "He has not threatened you in any way?"

"No." The cushion was still warm from Aodh.

"Taken anything?"

"Aside from the castle, Walter?"

Her curt replies seemed to recommend him to a different course. He paused, examining her with a frown, then sat down in the other chair and leaned toward her, folding his hands as if he were about to begin a prayer.

"This must be very trying for you, my lady."

She sighed. He was about to instruct her on herself.

"Such events tend to muddle the brain." He rolled his hand in the air to demonstrate muddling. "It can make one"—he pursed his lips—"less careful. Less discerning. Less capable of clear thought."

"More likely to run away?"

She hadn't meant to say it so sharply.

He stilled, then swallowed. His prodigious brow furrowed. "I swear to you, my lady, I was trying to help. I thought if I could get away, perhaps rally a few of the servants…"

She admitted this might be true. Walter, if pompous, had also proven stouthearted. Proof came in the fact of his continued presence out here on the Irish marches, when he could surely find employ somewhere else as an experienced, eagle-eyed clerk.

And that was Katarina's greatest gift: the ability to earn more loyalty than was her due. She ought to be appreciative. She *was* appreciative, deeply so. But Walter had a way of making even the deepest appreciation pale beside the depths of irritation he aroused.

"In this, my lady, my past is your good fortune. I know well how to manage an excess of passions of the sort Aodh Mac Con is exhibiting, the sort your mother exhibited—"

She could endure much, but not another recitation on the torments suffered by her father on account of her reckless mother. It was quite beyond her at the moment.

"Tell me, Walter," she interrupted sharply. "How does the castle fare?"

"The Irish Hound has prevailed unequivocally," he announced. "His men are ensconced in the hall right now with drink and meat" — he sent her a scathing look, as if she'd known they were to be conquered and had had the meat delivered specifically for their captors — "and showing untoward interest in the women. The women do not..." He sniffed. The sniff was a word. "...seem properly distressed by the men's attentions."

"Do they not?" she asked softly.

"Indeed, I warrant they return the interest, if smile and glance tell the tale."

I do not disapprove.

Every man but me.

Do you see how we shall do it?

"Walter," she said, watching the flames ripple across the top of the logs. "We float out on a sea here at Rardove, a sea of warfare and loneliness. We are surrounded by wolves and Irish tribes and mist, and little else. If they are not being injured or maligned, please leave the women be."

Leave me be.

His gaze sharpened to a veritable point. "My lady, the Hound has not done anything to *you*, has he? Anything...untoward?"

She leaned back against the chair and tilted her face up. "He has asked me to stay on. As his consort."

The words, once out, were not as shocking as she'd expected, but Walter flew up as if he'd sat on a pin. "He *what*?"

"Proposed a union." *Touched my neck. Entwined our fingers. Made me want.*

"An outrage!" he shouted, slamming the flat of his hand onto the table. His clerical face was as red as a holly berry. "That is madness!"

She assembled her expression into one of poised neutrality. "Is it not?"

He tugged on the row of buttons that ran the length of his velvet tunic. "To even *breathe* the idea that you should disparage yourself with a commoner, a...a barbarian, an Irishman" — he was sputtering with rage—"it is un*fathom*able. Out*rage*ous. *Lun*acy."

"Is it not?"

Something about how she said it made Walter's hands freeze on his gold-colored buttons. "Lady, you cannot— You cannot in earnest be considering…"

"How could one seriously consider such a thing?" she asked rhetorically. As rhetorical questions required no answer, she did not have to reply to its dangerous allure, of why she would turn herself over to Aodh Mac Con's untamed, perfect touch.

Walter breathed an audible sigh of relief. "Of course not."

She peered into the recklessly burning fire. "And yet, there is some merit, is there not? Some benefit to an alliance with the rebel?"

He gaped at her. "Benefit? Good God, my lady, to lie with a savage—"

"To distract him, waylay him, perhaps upend him, these things too. I do not mean a true union—"

I prefer to make you willing.

"—but a ruse. I shall feign agreement." She looked up. "Think you he brought his own clerk?"

Walter started. "His own…? No, of course not, he is a *savage*. Why would that matter?"

"Because if he had, he could prepare the betrothal papers. But if he has no clerk, and you were to suddenly take ill…or perhaps they were unable to locate you at all…"

Walter stopped talking. The proposal was worth it for that alone. She went on.

"In this way, we can hold what we may until the queen can send reinforcements. Recall, Walter, this 'savage' took Rardove Keep without so much as a shout. *No one knows he is here.* No one may know for weeks, months. Therefore, I think we would be wise to consider the advantages of feigning an alliance with the outlaw over adopting a more…combative stance."

Do you see how we shall do it?

Walter stared, dumbfounded. His jaw fell. She'd exceeded even his expectations for recklessness.

There was something madly gratifying about this. For a

second, she wished she could do more to shock him. Fling off her shoes and dance. Suggest *Walter* fling off his shoes and dance.

"Never." The word was a breath of clerical outrage. "I would see you burn on a funeral pyre first."

She lifted her eyebrows.

"Bertrand of Bridge is on his way here as we speak. When he arrives, he will sweep this outlaw and his rabble from our steps."

And bring in his own rabble, she thought. Vicious, wealthy rabble.

He frowned as if detecting her thoughts. "You cannot do this thing."

She slid her gaze to his slowly. "I am weary of being told what I cannot do."

A kind of tired sympathy entered Walter's eyes. He came a step closer and sat down opposite her. "Yet that is often the way of it, my lady," he instructed gently. "We do what is necessary, oft as others command. To bend one's will is no mean thing."

"I hardly require tutoring on how to bend my will." Hard as diamonds, the words spilled out of her as if tumbling from a pouch. "I know its taste far better than you."

"Katarina, child, I do but think of your welfare. Ever were you your mother's child, rash and tempestuous. It runs in the blood. No fault of your own, but still, it must be tempered."

"I have been tempered," she whispered.

Another gust of wind whipped past the windows, whistling, and a moment later whirled down the chimney. The fire was already burning down. It tried to rouse itself, but it was dying. Walter kept talking.

"I have seen the ravages of such states of passion. Your father was imprisoned on account of your mother's, and we saw how that ended." Her fingers tightened into a fist as he plowed on. "And when I stayed to watch over you, it was to guard against such passion ever rearing its head again." He frowned. "But it already had, had it not, child? Yes," he went on, pleased with his summary of the downfalls of the Rardove women. "Trust in me, then. Be as you are meant to be, quiet and circumspect. I shall guide us—"

For some inexplicable reason, she got to her feet.

Walter, mouth still open, stilled.

More inexplicably, she turned for the door.

"My lady, what— Wait! What are you..." He hurried after. "You cannot mean... You are not capable of executing something so vast as— Why, you cannot *imagine*—"

"I just did imagine it, Walter. I recommend you do as well. We serve two masters now: Elizabeth and the Irish warlord." She strode to the door, then paused and looked back. "And Walter? Please do bear in mind, there is nothing common about Aodh Mac Con. You have a habit of underestimating people. Please do not do so with him."

Walter's outrage froze.

She flung the oak door wide.

Young Bran, standing guard in the antechamber, whipped around.

Katarina gathered a thick handful of skirts in her fist and swept by him, announcing coldly, "I need to see your master."

Perhaps he was struck dumb. Or perhaps he saw the glint of determination in her eye. In any event, he did not stop her.

He did, however, turn and put a hand on Walter's chest as the clerk tried to hurry after.

"I'll need to search you, sir," he said.

"Good God in heaven, man!" Walter cried; he was becoming positively foul-mouthed in his desperation.

She would ensure the boy received extra rations the moment she made it back into the kitchens.

Katarina heard them arguing as she went down the stairs, Walter calling after. "My lady, heed me."

She did not heed him. Inexplicably.

"I forbid you to do this!"

She swept around a turn in the stairs.

"You are being *reckless*, girl."

It was the last arrow, a hissed word flung like a curse.

Still, she did not stop. She circled the lamplit stairs, down and down, then stepped out into the great hall and stopped short.

As Aodh Mac Con had done to the bedchamber, so too had he done to the hall. The huge, echoing space was, quite simply, alive.

Fires roared like dragons, gorgeously wasteful, in every hearth along the walls and down the huge center trough. Bright, leaping, reckless fires, red, orange, and blue flames licking the air like beating wings.

The vast stony hall, cool even in the dog days of summer, had been made, in the cold coil of early spring, warm. Bright. Bustling.

People were everywhere, more souls than Rardove had held in its belly for many a year, milling and talking, hurrying to and fro, laughing, intermingling—even her own people. No formal, seated meal, this; it was the butt end of a coup, and there was only sound and noise and movement.

A portly industrious clerk with a pen in his hand gestured to a man running by with a sheaf of papers, while a group of soldiers near the door plucked hunks of bread and cheese off trays being hurried past before turning for the door and striding out again. Calls came from all corners of the hall. Servants, both his and hers, frantically set up long trestle tables and benches down the length of the room, their voices swept up the vent holes in the roof. It was a hum of energy. Squires hurried everywhere, dodging dogs, helping soldiers remove their armor, and pounding iron spikes into the walls to dangle tapestries off them.

The bare stone walls were being made into a pageantry of color. Fluttering scenes of hunts and sea battles marched along all forty feet of the hall. Swords and armor were being hung, pennants and shields, testaments to the warrior prowess of the new, outlaw lord of Rardove.

The outlaw lord himself reclined on a bench at the near end of the hall. He sat at a common table, one boot kicked out, an elbow resting on the table, talking with two men sitting opposite him. Aodh regarded them with what appeared to be boredom.

The two men, his captain and another, red-bearded warrior, stared back with what appeared to be outrage.

His barrage of a captain, blond hair sweaty on his temples, leaned forward and said in an angry voice, "It serves naught." His words carried like light; they went everywhere.

Aodh swung his gaze across the room. It landed on her.

Something opened inside her, a ray of brightness.

Still looking at her, Aodh said, "It serves something," and pushed to his feet.

Behind him, his companions scrambled up too. At her back, she heard Walter, stumbling down the stairs.

"My lady, *you cannot do this.*"

But here she was, doing this.

"Aodh," warned Aodh's tall captain. "Do not be reckless now."

She almost smiled. The same accusations were being hurled at each of them. They were peas in a pod.

All around the hall, people turned as she stepped off the stairwell into the room. Silence rolled through the room like a wave rolling up the beach.

"Aodh, Christ's mercy, listen —"

"Katarina, you can*not* —"

Both their advisors frantically trying to stop a union neither of them could possibly want.

This time she did smile.

Everything faded to the buzzing of bees as Aodh, with his calm, devastating confidence, smiled back at her over all their heads.

I do not follow many rules.

"Yes," she said.

The word plunged the room into silence, the way a rock tied to a rope drags everything down into the river after it.

Then, in case it had not been clear, she said, "I will marry you."

There was a single, shocked gasp. Then Walter's vicious mutter broke the silence: "Christ on the goddamned *Cross.*"

"Leave us," Aodh ordered, and lifted his hand to her.

The stunned hall emptied in an exodus of silent, gaping people.

Katarina had no idea how long it took for them to leave, she knew only that Aodh held his hand out to her the whole time.

Then, as if it were the simplest thing in the world, she reached out and laid her hand in his.

ROGUE WARRIORS

CHAPTER 13

AODH TOOK HER HAND as if it were made of glass and led her to the dais, handed her down into a chair to the right of the lord's seat, then dragged out the heavy lord's chair and sat.

She'd repaired the damage that wind and coup had rent on her hair, even pinned a veil overtop. She looked as graceful and composed as ever save for...her breath. Light as gossamer and broken like glass, it was her tell, her secret revealed.

He felt as if he'd climbed a mountain. His blood came hot, the heat he had not known for years.

She'd bent. Bent to his hand, to his mouth, bent for his touch, and in the end, she would be his. The truth was clear: she wanted him the same way he wanted her. It emanated from her like scent from a flower. All he had to do was touch her, and she would be his.

Christ, he felt *that*.

He would have her undressed within the hour.

For a long while, she allowed his bold perusal, allowed the silence, not quite comfortable with it, for there was the shallow, staccato breath, but neither was she agitated.

Then, still facing forward, she murmured, "Well, it seems you were right after all."

"About what this time?"

This arrogance earned a faint smile. "My inclination for recklessness."

"Och, I'm sure you have a plan," he said companionably.

87

"Do you want to tell me what it is?"

"No," she said primly, then her cheeks flushed. "I mean to say, I have no plan."

"I highly doubt that."

Her clear eyes turned to him. "Then you are foolish to treat with me. I'm sure your councilors advised you on the matter."

"That they did. As did yours."

"Oh, did you hear?" she murmured, as if he might not have heard her steward shouting at her. Aodh smiled. "He made some valid points, you know."

"Such as me being a savage?"

"I believe he suggested the possibility."

Aodh shrugged. "And yet, here you are, with me."

Her dark eyes held his. "Perhaps I found your arguments more convincing upon reflection."

He smiled. *Within the half hour.* Where the hell was his clerk, Tancred? Doing something efficient and clerical, no doubt. Curse him. "I am glad to hear it."

One brow arched up, a little sweep of dark angles across her face. "Perhaps I expect it to be an extremely *short-lived* union," she said tartly. "In the event of you being beheaded for treason."

"I shall make your jointure a fine large one, to compensate you for your loss." He spread out a hand. "In the event."

"Yes," she echoed drily. "In the event."

He sat back and called for a servant.

"Bring me the leather chest in the lord's chambers," he ordered, and the man hurried off. Fires burned in the empty hall. She glanced at him, then quickly looked away, touching her fingertips to the smooth curve of her neck. A nervous gesture from the cool, graceful lady.

He smiled. Katarina was born to be enflamed, and he would see the deed done.

He slid a flask on the table her direction. It rumbled as it crossed the oak tabletop.

She looked at it. "Is that Irish whisky?"

"'Tis."

She sniffed. "I see Ireland still holds some charms for you."

"A few. Do you want a taste? 'Tis quite good."

"I do not drink your *uisce beatha*."

He sat back in surprise. "Whisky is one of the finest things about Ireland, and you've never tasted it?"

She tucked a strand of hair back under her veil. It seemed they were eternally springing free from her attempts at control.

"I did not say I never tasted it."

He shook his head sadly. "Lass, you don't know what you're missing."

"Yes, well, I have seen enough men facedown in the rushes to know what I *might* be missing."

He laughed. "Wine, then?" he asked, reaching for the jug.

"No! I mean…no." Her fingertips skipped down her neck, to the V of her collarbone, fluttering nervously.

"'Twasn't the wine, you know," he said gently.

Like glass, smooth and almost translucent, her gaze lifted to his. "What was not the wine?"

"What happened. Upstairs. What you did. With me."

A little shiver disrupted the otherwise calm façade of her gracefulness, then she shrugged dismissively. "You know naught of me, Aodh Mac Con. Perhaps I am eternally flinging myself at strange warriors whenever I drink wine from Gascony."

"Is that so? I shall inquire as to your habits at the first instance."

She sniffed. "Gird your loins, my lord. You will hear stories."

He grinned. Every move she made, every word she said, pleased him more. He sat back and pushed out his legs. The tips of his boots, black and mud-stained, came to rest just beside the green hem of her skirts. "Tell me, lady, why do you say the wine is from Gascony?"

"Is that not where most wine is from?"

"Some. 'Tis fine, if you like a claret."

She turned her face slightly toward him. "And if I do not?"

"Then you will like my wine. 'Tis a canary."

"Indeed? And what does that mean?"

"It is from the Canary Islands."

Her lips parted, into the smallest O. "And where, pray, are they?"

"I will show you," he said as the servant arrived back in the hall.

Puffing slightly from his labors on the spiraling staircase, he carried a leather chest in his arms. He placed it before Aodh, bowed deeply, then scurried out, leaving the hall once again empty but for burning fires and Aodh's marriage gift to Katarina.

His blood was starting to churn; desire fired through his veins, charging his blood, swelling his cock. Reveling in it and resisting it, he stood to unbuckle the leather straps lashing the chest, and creaked it open.

Beside him, Katarina straightened her spine as far as it could go, feigning disinterest while craning her neck to peer inside, practically vibrating with curiosity.

Claimed.

He removed the long, rolled parchments from within and began untying the laces that bound them. He set the first on the table and reached for candles, setting one at each top corner, to weight it down and hold it open, unrolling it as he went. Then he reached for another.

"Take an edge," he said, giving her an excuse to rise. She did, with alacrity, and helped him unscroll it.

Then they did the same to the other panels. There were six sections in total, and when they were all unrolled and set together, candles burning along the top and intersecting edges, Katarina stepped back and stared down at them.

He waited with a strange sort of anticipation. It made him think of his interminable wait in the queen's receiving corridor nearly two decades ago, a ragged Irish boy with nothing but a sword in his hand and cold determination in his heart: would his petition be enough?

Covered with gorgeous lines and shapes, the parchment was an explosion of color, in beautiful, vibrant sections, with scalloped and undulating edges, hues of red and green and yellow, with filigree-thin lines crisscrossing it, vertically and horizontally.

"What is it?" she whispered.

"It is a map. Of the world."

She gave softest intake of breath, not quite surprise. A little higher pitched, a little more silvery, a little more feminine, nigh onto a gasp of...pleasure.

His map had pleased her.

Savage satisfaction roared through him. Standing in a great hall, looking down at a map, he felt blown back by a wind.

"There are six panels," he told her quietly, as she bent over it. "Made by a friend of Mercator's. Abraham Ortelius."

They peered at it in silence a moment, then he tapped his index finger to a spot on the paper. "Jerusalem."

She ran a fingertip across the page, near but not touching his.

"And here," —he tapped again—"are the Canary Islands, where your wine came from."

"It is not my wine."

"It is now."

Their eyes met over the map of the world. "Not yet."

She was...testing him? Toying with him? Teasing him?

No matter; all stoked the flames of his lust.

She angled her face back down. "Where are we? Where is *Éire*?"

Ireland. She'd spoken the Irish word for the isle, and something moved inside him. Likely irritation; Irish was a convoluted language no one cared for anymore. Outdated, unnecessary. Anything of importance could be said in another language. Should be said in another language. Any other language. Surely you would be understood by more people.

He slid his finger closer to hers. A tiny oval of green and blue sat quite near the edge of the world, high up, as if it were hovering above all the rest, and hadn't quite descended yet.

"Oh yes," she exhaled, smiling faintly. "Yes, that is we." He looked at her sharply, but she was still staring at the map.

"And that..." —he pointed—"is the New World. America."

She leaned so close, her nose almost touched the parchment

and its bright colors. If he'd bent down too, Aodh knew he would see it all reflected in her eyes.

She spread a hand over it, hovering half an inch over it, as if she were casting spells. Her corset, laced up tight and proper, pressed against her ribs as she took swift breaths. She was excited.

And this, that this lass banished to the edge of the world, wished to go farther yet, this was wildly…exciting.

"What do you know of it?" she asked, so soft she was almost whispering. "The New World."

"'Tis abundant in wood and game and wild men."

He saw the curve of her cheek. She'd smiled. "Somewhat like Ireland, then?" she murmured, a teasing tone.

He looked at the back of her head. Under the sheer veil, her dark hair tumbled, silken thick lushness he would soon be dragging his fingers though. The curve of her shoulder, where it met her neck, held great promise as well. Earlier, he'd almost brought her to culmination simply by kissing that sensitive junction. He would do so again. This time open his mouth, rake her with his teeth, take her to the edge where pleasure met pain. And then there was her throat…

"Have you sailed, Mac Con?"

He dragged his attention back. "I have."

"Much?"

"Much."

She was still a moment, then turned her head to look at him. "Are you an Irish pirate?"

"I'd not call myself that."

"Would others?"

He laughed. "It would depend on how much money I earned them."

"Mm." It was a skeptical murmur, but it stood his cock at attention. "Have you ever been? To the New World?"

He shook his head, staring over her shoulder at the map. "Not yet."

"Yet?"

He met her gaze. "I am not yet done."

Her eyes lit with some spark, surely the reflection from the high, tapered candles burning on either side of the map, but it seemed to come from within her. And then she smiled. The small, secret smile. At him.

Something fierce awakened in his chest.

"And the queen's colony in the New World, Roanoke," she asked. "What do you know of it?"

"There has been no word," he said quietly.

"What do you suspect?"

He shrugged. "'Tis a hard world out there."

"Sad."

"Perils of the adventurer," was his careless assessment. "If one wishes to go adventuring, one must be prepared."

"In*deed*," she murmured with such dry meaning, he grinned.

She laid a hand on the table beside the map. The candlelight illuminated all its varied textures: small rounded knuckles; the pale blue line of veins; slim, curving fingers, nails unadorned, blunted from work. She leaned on her hand and craned her neck to look up at him.

"But that will not stop them, will it?"

"Would it stop you, Katy?"

Her eyes were bright as she shook her head. "I do not think it would." She turned back to the map. "I invested in an adventure company once."

He stared at the back of her head. "Pardon?"

"Yes, indeed. Does not every reckless fool with any spare coin? And even those without. The Gilbert Humphrey Trading Co. was my particular pitfall."

"Never heard of it."

She glanced up absently. "I am unsurprised. He was an Englishman, so how would you? He was desperately..." She pondered the correct word a moment. "Well, desperate. But bold. Oh, exceedingly bold." Her voice dropped to a conspiratorial tone, the sort used for secrets and bedrooms.

A long quiver unfurled inside Aodh, a misericorde-thin, daggerlike thrust through his chest, comprised of interest and...jealousy?

Good God. What was *that* doing inside him?

"Humphrey, was it, then?"

"Yes. Gilbert Humphrey. Tall and charming, full of tales of faraway places and derring-do. Oh, half were lies, no doubt, but I was fooled. He was a dreamer." She gave a helpless little shrug, her shoulders lifting under the force of her inability to fully express the charms of the most excellent Mr. Humphrey. "A dreamer, and a talker, and an…"

"Exceedingly bold man?"

She straightened away from the map. "Perhaps 'bold' overstates the matter. Better to say…" She touched her lips, and he felt it as if her finger had been laid upon his own mouth, the pad light, hot, pressing an oval onto his bottom lip. For a moment, everything, even her voice, faded away, while he imagined coaxing the tip of it into his mouth with his tongue.

"…be a more accurate description."

He dragged his gaze from her finger. "Pardon?"

"Mr. Humphrey was a cony catcher in the guise of a poet in the guise of a ship's captain."

He laughed, pleased with this tearing down of the bold and excellent Mr. Humphrey. "All ship captains are cony catchers, lass. Deceit and trickery are the wind under which they sail."

She laughed. "Yes, well, this one was that indeed. Foolhardy. Reckless."

Their eyes met.

"Stubborn?" he suggested.

Her eyes slid away. "He is dead now, if that is what you mean."

"And you miss him."

Her gaze arrested, stilled at some point in space between him and the map of the world. "Sir, I lost over a hundred pounds and my reputation because of him. 'Miss the man' hardly describes my feelings. His dream was not carefully dreamed. He was wild and careless and—"

"Exceedingly bold."

She looked at him sternly. "Reckless."

"And stubborn."

"And now he is dead."

Good. "So be it," was all he said.

She sighed. "So be it. 'Twas a waste of everything but the dream."

He smiled grimly. He knew the waste of dreams, far too well. Then, because he'd learned to listen deeply, he said softly, "Is money all you lost to Gilbert Humphrey, lass?"

Her jaw slowly fell, then color flowed across her cheeks and down her neck. Her chin dimpled. The response was gone in an instant. She shook her head sharply, just once, angrily, as if she was shaking something away.

"I was seventeen," she said quietly. "It was a mistake."

"I've made a few."

She gave a little laugh and shook her head while she traced the lines on the map, outlining Bohemia. "Such things are never the same for men." Her finger migrated west, into the Holy Roman Empire.

He reached out and swept up her hand, lifted it to his mouth. "I do not care for such things. They do not concern us."

Her gaze swept to his, her eyebrows slanted into a confused V. "How could such things not concern you?"

"Because they are the past. We are now." Still holding her gaze, he kissed the back of her hand.

She exhaled a long breath, her lips parted around it. Her eyes never left his. He nodded toward the map. "Do you like the world I've given you?"

She dragged her gaze off his and looked down at the map. "Why, yes, it's very nice." Then she laughed at herself and said softly, "It's breathtaking."

"I also have a gown for you."

She looked up sharply. "A gown?"

"Fabric, then. To be made into a gown. And seed."

The hand in his tightened.

"Wheat. And rye. For the spring plantings."

Her fingers curled around his. "You brought seed?"

"I brought seed. Tell me, Katy, will that suit?"

Rogue Warriors

Chapter 14

Katarina stared, stricken almost breathless. Who was this man, who conquered with gowns and wheat seed and maps of the world?

As if she'd forgotten *entirely* that this was a ruse, she smiled at him. "It suits quite well, sir."

He smiled back, the lazy, confident half-smile that couldn't be bothered to stretch all the way to the other side of his mouth.

From the far end of the hall came a bustle, and a figure appeared, hurrying toward them in the shifting amber light thrown by the leaping, roaring fires. Carrying another chest, the man tiptoed up to the dais table and leaned down to Aodh.

"The papers, my lord."

Still smiling faintly, she said, "Papers?"

Aodh pushed aside the map, while the tonsured clerk—Aodh had a *clerk?*—began setting down a sheaf of papers and pens and inkpots. Aodh glanced at her, his blue eyes level. "Betrothal papers."

She gave a start. *"Now?"*

"Aye. Now."

Her heart skipped a beat. Then another. Then it lurched forward in a cold staccato rhythm.

She stared helplessly at the preparations of Aodh and his clerk. Where had a *clerk* come from? "But—"

Aodh paused above the papers being spread in front of him. "But what?"

She swallowed thickly. She could not sign *betrothal papers*. Signing her name would be tantamount to treason. Her father had been *hanged* for less.

Oh, this was not going *at all* as she had planned.

Breathing fast, fingertips at her throat, she searched for a reason to delay this formalization of her subterfuge, some way to mitigate the damage. For as much as the Queen of England was not a woman to cross, neither was Aodh Mac Con a man to cross. And Aodh was much closer to hand.

And notwithstanding that they'd started as enemies, much as he could reasonably expect nothing approaching honesty from her, let alone loyalty, still, somehow…somehow, to say no now, felt like a betrayal.

To say yes felt like a binding.

If she wed Aodh Mac Con, he would never let her go.

Chills ran down her body. "What of the banns?"

He took a pen from his clerk. "There will be banns."

The clerk competently uncorked an ink bottle and laid it before Aodh. With a flourish, he set out a second pen. The bottle squatted above the papers, ready for dipping. The ink was red, like blood.

"But we must wait…three weeks…"

The clerk had taken his seat, a pouch of sand laid beside the parchment he was now scribbling on. Aodh stood looking over his shoulder, but at these words, he glanced her way.

"We shall not have the ceremony until three weeks." He leaned close and said in a low voice, "But to alleviate any concerns you may have, Katarina, know this: we shall consummate. Hard and well."

Her knees almost collapsed. She curled her fingers around the back of the lord's chair, holding on. In truth, the ceremony meant nothing. These papers were all. Her signature on them, their union afterward, this binding to Aodh.

It could not be.

"What of witnesses?" she whispered. It was a hopeless gesture, a shot in the dark, for she knew nothing would slow this down now. Aodh Mac Con meant to have her.

The rock she'd tossed into the air was coming down hard.

He snapped his fingers without looking over. "Call for Cormac and Ré," he ordered the soldier who appeared, then turned to her. "Who do you wish for, my lady?"

"Wish for?" A list of patron saints floated through her mind.

"As witnesses. I suppose you'll want the coward?"

"Walter?" *No.* "Yes. Of course."

"Bring her steward," Aodh ordered the soldier, and turned back to the clerk, murmuring something about jointure.

Her mind whirled as they talked through the time it took to round up several servants and Aodh's grim-faced soldiers, who looked no happier about this union than she. Then finally, Walter appeared, stern and disapproving.

A pen was placed in her hand.

His men stood arrayed around the front of the dais table. Walter stood like a monument of disapproval.

She stared down at the papers, covered in scrolling black scribbles. Words, surely these were words. But she could decipher none of them. Her heart was thudding too fast, the roar in her head too loud.

Aodh's clerk was speaking in Latin, saying something, saying their names...saying Aodh's name...*Aodh Mac Con Rardove.*

Aodh, son of the Hound of...Rardove?

Another cold blast struck her. She dragged her gaze up from the parchment. "You are the Hound of *Rardove*?"

"Aye."

Oh dear God.

She curled her hand tighter around the chair to steady herself, reeling. The Rardove clan was *dead*, or all but.

Living on the fringes of Irish society for centuries now, they were a pale shadow of their former selves, slowly dying out, notwithstanding a brief, if spectacular, resurgence a couple decades ago. But they posed no threat, they had no presence.

Legend said the Rardove chiefs were doomed to die young, half from heartbreak, half from drink, half from...oh dear God save her, *recklessness*.

"I thought...I thought you were all dead," she whispered.

His icy eyes flicked her way. "Not yet."

Her knees were bending now. Force of will was all that held them straight. She would *not* fall over, she would *not* sit down...or she might never get up again.

The clerk's voice droned on in Latin, and the Irish Hound was replying—*in Latin*—then the clerk read the terms aloud in French, and then in English, to ensure no confusion—oh, there was nothing *but* confusion—while Walter's grim, furious, yet vaguely triumphant face glared at her.

She had done precisely what she'd told him not to do: seriously underestimated Aodh Mac Con.

The pen in her hand shook slightly. She could not catch her breath. Everyone stared. Silence spread through the hall. A boot shuffled, leather creaked, a burning log shifted, then fell into hot ash in the hearth. All she had to do was sign her name.

If she signed, she was doomed.

Traitor. Treason.

Dead woman.

A drop of bright red ink hung, suspended, at the tip of the pen in her hand. Aodh's name was already on the page, scrawled in gorgeous, bold, *educated* letters, large enough to be read in Windsor.

He was afraid of nothing. This castle, this rebellion, Katarina—he claimed it all.

Trembling, she looked up into his eyes.

"Aodh," she whispered. It slipped out helplessly.

He went into motion. "Leave us," he ordered, taking the pen from her hand.

And once again, the people in the hall dispersed like pebbles running down a hill. His clerk and hers, the witnesses and soldiers, everyone turned and left, until she and Aodh were once again alone.

ROGUE WARRIORS

CHAPTER 15

SHAKING, she stood, head down, staring at the ground, braced for his fury. That is what men did, vent their fury. It would be over soon enough. He circled her once; she watched his boots make the circuit around her body.

"What is it?" he asked while behind her.

She inhaled, shook her head, looked at the papers, the signatures, then her gaze dropped to his sword. Everything about this was a conquest.

"I...cannot," she whispered.

He'd followed her glance at his sword, and with a swift sweep of his hands, he unbuckled it and let it fall to the ground. It clattered in a heap. He stepped over it and came nearer.

"Why are you saying no?"

"Because I would lose everything."

"Och, lass, you've already lost everything. All you can do now is gain."

She gave a broken laugh. "That is no good answer."

His gaze roved over her face, then he took the last, natural step and drew up before her. "Listen to me."

"No." She could not listen to his low resonate persuasions, spoken in that dark Irish lilt, the one that tempted as if it were touch.

He curled a finger beneath her chin and tipped her face up. "You cannot think it would have gone well for you when Bertrand of Bridge arrived? The queen's interrogator?"

She gasped. "Wh-what do you know of it?"

"In England, they are calling you a traitor. A priest-lover. An unwed dye-witch."

Shock made her hands fly to his chest. Fear curled them into fists, bunching his tunic. "No."

"Aye. So now, maybe, it is not so mad an idea to have something standing between you and England."

"Oh no," she whispered as he slid his fingers to the back of her neck and guided her closer, against the towering length of him, until they were touching from knees to stomach.

"I swear to you, Katy," he said in a low rasp. "I will protect you."

Confusion washed through her, an amalgam of shifting emotions. Protect her? When he was the danger, and England her salvation?

Protect her? No one protected Katarina. *She* was the protector, of Rardove, of the people within, of the queen's rights in Ireland.

But that this warlord had offered…

Their mouths were so close she could feel his breath on her. She wanted his breath.

"Now, Katy, let me show you the truth of us," he said, and bent his head.

She leaned back against the table before her knees buckled, her neck arched as he touched his lips to the base of her throat, raining a wash of chills down her body so potent she almost did not notice the wide palm skimming down her waist. She was far too focused on the other hand plunging into her hair, fingers splayed. He fisted his hand and tugged her head back.

The pressure was hard and exquisite, the pleasure undeniable.

The breath burst from her, a loud, stuttered gasp in the silent room.

His mouth worked his way up the line of her throat, a slow assault of carnal skill. He never hurried; she could have said 'no' at any moment. But as she didn't, he wasted no time on prelude, and when he reached the summit of her mouth, he simply claimed her. Slanted his mouth over hers and completed his conquest of Rardove by sliding his tongue between her already-parted lips, and deconstructed every notion she'd ever had of who she was, and what passion meant.

Showing her what he meant by their *'truth.'*

The moment their mouths touched, her body jerked. His tongue swiped against hers and the shock of it ripped another gasp from her. It would have been loud in the echoing hall, but Aodh captured it in his mouth and moved his hands around to cup the small of her back.

Stunned by the onslaught, whipped by fiery threads of desire, she could do nothing but follow the command of his hands to bend back more, the urging of his lips to open wider, to meet his tongue with her own in a hot swipe that made him groan deep into her mouth, which sent a shudder of excitement through her. And somehow, her hands were around his shoulders, and she was pushing her body up to his.

This emboldened a man who needed no more boldness, and he tore his mouth free far enough to suck her bottom lip into his mouth.

Her mind shut down, shocked by the carnal move, but her body, oh, her body reveled in it. She tipped her chin up, let him have her lip. With a low sound of approval, he swept a hand down to cup the underside of her knee and dragged it slowly up his thigh, as if he was caressing himself. With her.

She was all but lost. The hot center of her, high between her thighs, pulsed with heavy desire as their tongues tangled, hot and slippery. The table pressed against her bottom, supporting her as he pressed her knee against his hip and stepped between her legs.

She froze. He did too.

The room was silent but for the crackle and rush of roaring fires, her panted gasps, his slow, hard breath.

His eyes, darkened to indigo by firelight and passion, held hers as he rocked his hips forward, rubbing the length of his manhood against the juncture between her thighs, a slow, deliberate caress, so she could feel everything he wanted to do to her. *Would* do to her. If only she said yes.

Her head tipped back, her eyes barely open, ready to give him more.

More and more and more. It would never end. The fire-scorched clarity of her desire suddenly saw the truth: Aodh would ever demand more of her.

And she would give it.

"We are meant to be, Katy," he rasped, his voice passion-low. He brought his hands up to cup her face and hung his head beside hers, his mouth by her ear. "It will be so good, I will ensure it. Sign the papers, stand down your men, and we will be together."

Her heart leapt for a brutally long second, then crashed back down, yanked by cold reality.

But in that leaping, she saw the deeper danger of Aodh expanding like a storm on the horizon: he could make himself matter to her.

For a moment, at his words, her heart had been buoyed by...hope.

But this rebel was not hope. He was her downfall. She'd simply been seduced. By a warlord with an agenda.

And no matter how her body became a candle for him, this was no matter of seduction. This was politics and power and war.

This was treason.

Woe to her if she forgot it again.

Resist. Deny. But never, ever give him anything he wanted. For once she began, she might never stop.

As his head hung beside hers, his breath warm on her neck, she whispered, "No."

"No?" he repeated softly.

"No." With effort, she lifted her head. He was watching her, his ice-blue eyes searching.

"*Céard sa diabhal?*"

It was in Irish, but Katarina had spent her life in Ireland, and she knew very well what it meant: *what the hell?*

"No. No. No."

He straightened away from her. "What are you saying?"

"I cannot wed you."

"Why not?"

"Treason is why."

The dark brows descended. "If 'tis treason now, 'twas

treason before, when you were willing. What has changed?"

"I… The papers." She pointed at the table, inkpots and brightly colored sealing wax and long silk threads lying all about, a festive little documentary celebration of treason.

Still cupping her face, his fingers curled around the back of her head, he glanced at the table.

"You never meant it," he said in low accusation. "'Twas all a lie. You lied to me."

Anger rose up in her then, finally.

Lied to him?

"And who are you?" she whispered fiercely, feeling quite mad. For she was finally coming undone.

The restraint and rigid self-control of the past years were slipping away like ice in spring. She felt it sliding, slippery and wet, like a sheet of ice shearing off into a swift-moving river.

Further proof she'd slipped off the ledge of sanity entirely, she put her hands on his chest and *pushed* him.

"Who are you, Aodh Mac Con, that I may not lie to you?"

He dropped his hands, shock on his face.

"You, a usurper? A warlord? A thief?" And as madness abounded this night, she pushed him again, forcing him back a step. "And *I* may not lie to *you*?"

His jaw worked, but no words came out.

"I would not wed you if all the kings in the world begged me to. It would be treason, and I am not that woman."

For a moment, there was nothing but his hard body, motionless, and the long, slow breaths coming out of it, and the fierce, penetrating gaze, growing harder, harder, harder yet.

"Are you *mad*?" His words were low and barely controlled.

"Reckless."

"Veering perilously close to stubborn."

"So be it."

A beat of silence. Fury burned in his gaze. "You have already agreed."

"I signed nothing." Still, though, it had the whiff of a betrayal. Curse him. "I changed my mind. You cannot have my men, and you cannot have me."

A ripple moved through his jaw. Clearly, the Irish Hound was not used to being told no. His icy blue gaze burned into hers. "This will be done," he said, low and lethal.

"Over my dead body," she whispered back.

"So be it."

"You did not do so before."

"Do not use the past as a judge of what I am willing to make happen in the future, Katarina. Circumstances change."

She lifted her chin. "Do what you must, Aodh Mac Con. I refuse."

He spun on his heel and swept his sword belt up off the floor. "You *will* bend to me," he vowed.

"I will not."

The gaze he snapped to her was like a lance, slicing through her. "Then I will break you."

"I should like to see you try."

He reached her in two strides, roughly cupped the back of her neck, and plowed her mouth open with a violent, unforgiving kiss.

She stood cold beneath it.

Tearing his mouth away, he held her face just below his, and said in a rasping voice, "Katarina, do not make me do this."

"Do what you must. As have I." Their mouths were so close her hair was fluttering from their softly spoken words. "No," she whispered again. "I say no."

With a low sound of fury, he backed up, then leapt off the dais as if she were a rolling fire and he had to move fast to get out of the way. He strode halfway across the empty hall with its bright fires burning, calling as he went, "Ré!"

No reply. Apparently everyone had escaped farther away.

Abruptly, he spun on his heel and came back for her. Fear now joined the glorious rebellion, and she scrambled backward as he came toward her, his gaze fixed.

"Aodh," she exhaled in terror.

He took her by the wrist and propelled her in front of him, off the dais, across the hall, bellowing as they went, "*Ré!*"

There was a brief moment of silence, then came a distant

voice, very low: "Son of a bitch." From all corners of the castle came the sounds of men and boot steps, hurrying toward the hall.

A group of soldiers appeared at the top of the stairwell. Aodh flung himself away from Katarina and backed up, as if he could not trust himself to touch her any longer, leaving her standing alone in the hall, his men at the far end.

She stood straight and tall between them all.

The blond-haired captain looked between her and Aodh. He seemed to give her the faintest of nods then turned to Aodh. "My lord?"

Ah. He'd reverted to the respectful title in view of his master's fury. Something to learn from those who knew Aodh Mac Con better than she.

Too late now.

"Take her ladyship to the high tower," Aodh commanded, his voice like ice, like winter, so cold it was impossible to believe his mouth had been so hot on hers just a few moments ago. "Lock her inside."

Ré nodded. His face showed no emotion.

"Collect the rest of her household. Round them up, servants, hen maids, clerks. Lock them up. Lock them all up."

Katarina spun so fast, her hair, loosened by his attentions, whirled around her shoulders. "Aodh, you cannot—"

"What?" His question sliced her words off like a blade. "What can I not do? I can do anything, Katarina, and you cannot stop me. Rardove is mine. I need nothing from you."

He strode away, toward the stairs, buckling on his sword belt as he went. He leapt up the stairs and strode past his men without a word, out into the cold black night, without cloak or hood.

Katarina was led by yet another soldier to yet another tower, even higher than before.

ROGUE WARRIORS

CHAPTER 16

FURY FUELED her ascent up the circular staircase, flanked fore and aft by Aodh's soldiers. They stepped out onto the landing of the high tower and young Bran, heretofore the closest thing she'd had to a friend, glanced at her almost accusingly as he unlocked the door.

With an indignant squeal of iron hinges, it swung open. Darkness unfurled like a tongue.

Part of the original castle built in the twelfth century, the high tower had been designated a bedchamber for guests many years ago, then forgotten entirely when the guests disappeared. With walls five feet thick and an oak door four inches, the high tower was a testament of medieval power. No drafts here.

No luxuries either; the tower had escaped most of the renovations that swept the rest of the castle over the centuries. In fact, it had become a bit of a storage room.

A huge, pitted oak table was pushed up against one wall, benches atop it and chairs pushed carelessly beneath. Crates sat on and around it, stuffed with old bottles and bolts of fabric and the butt ends of candles that had yet to be remelted, all the various odds and ends that inhabited a marcher castle in constant flux on the edge of war.

A small hearth had been added at the turn of the last century, and a few old tapestries were pinned unevenly across the walls. A recessed cistern in the far wall held fresh water, and a large, canopied bed dominated the room, a twist of linen hanging from the ceiling above it to keep out drafts. Otherwise, there were few comforts.

That suited Katarina well; she wanted no comfort. She wanted to *bite* him. Gnash Aodh Mac Con in her teeth for having unleashed such dangerous passions. She'd spent years tempering herself, and in one day, he'd undone it all.

The barrage of a captain stayed by the door, watchful as Bran escorted her inside. He lit oil lamps that hung off wooden beams, casting wary glances her direction whenever her restless pacing took her near him, but when he crouched in front of the small hearth and made as if to light that too, she pointed at the door.

"Leave." She was the stern chatelaine now as she'd never been before, cold and regal.

Bran got to his feet, staring as if she was a wild thing. Which she was—wild and distressed and cornered and dangerous.

Bran joined his captain on the landing. Their gazes met, then slowly, the door swung shut with a thud. She heard a soft, heavy metal click, and the boots retreated.

She'd been locked inside.

The thing she loved so desperately about Ireland—her freedom—Aodh Mac Con had taken away.

She took a wild turn around the room, roiling with energy, furious, wanting to fling herself at Aodh, to hurt him, to ruin him as he was doing to her.

Her boots rang out loud on the floor as she circled endlessly through the night.

"SHE WILL NOT submit."

"I noticed," Ré said.

Down in the jousting yards, with moonlight to light their swordplay, he and Aodh circled each other, blades out. Ré was accustomed to such things; Aodh was an engine of movement in the best of times, and when he'd stormed out of the castle a few hours ago, venting a fury the likes of which Ré had never seen before, he'd assumed they were in for a night of…this.

Ré smashed Aodh's sword away and spun in a circle, coming around again, blade up.

The bailey was dark. Slivers of light from the castle windows broke the shadows cast by the surrounding buildings. Candle glow and soft sounds spilled from the hall. The barracks and gatehouse towers added some illumination. Tiny stars glittered here and there behind scuttling clouds.

"Are you asking my opinion?" Ré said.

"Have you one?"

"Perhaps you should send her away," he said as he slid his boot to the side, watching Aodh's sword in the moonlight. It moved in a wide sweep, and Ré leapt back. "As planned."

"No."

"Why not?"

"I am not yet convinced she cannot be of value."

"In what way?"

"Contacts, networks, alliances. She has lived here for years. She knows these people, these men."

They parried for a moment, then Ré said with deep suspicion, "So you want her for her…political connections?" Skepticism put a faint drag on the final words.

Aodh shrugged. "If I win her, we win those."

They both swept forward. Their swords met and held in the air, crossed like steely wings. "And if you do not win her?"

Aodh looked at Ré over the swords. "I will."

With a sharp squeal of metal, they separated and stepped back. "Perhaps you did not ask properly."

Aodh stared at his heretofore loyal captain and friend. "Am I to take some meaning from that?"

"Something happened in the hall, Aodh." Swipe right, swipe left. "Something that made her unwilling to sign, when she had been ready."

Aodh ground his teeth. Katarina had *not* been ready to sign. It had been clear as anything, which was why he'd sent them all away. To seduce her. And by it, convince her.

The former had worked. Not the latter.

He felt perilously close to being a fool, for it turned out she'd never intended to sign the betrothal papers at all. The whole thing had been a ruse.

Ré lunged forward, forcing Aodh to jump back. Ré pursued, sword cutting through the moonlight with swift strokes. "So what happened back there, to land her in the tower and us out here, fighting in the moonlight?"

Aodh let himself be backed up, engaging in swordplay by rote, reflecting on all the things that had happened in the firelit hall. Maps and long lingering gazes from dark eyes, throaty feminine laughter. The high curve of her breasts, the depth of her insights, the way she smiled at him, so that he felt as if fresh air had entered into his lungs, and when had he last felt that way?

Never.

"Aodh, do as you will," Ré said shortly, stepping back and lowering his sword. "But if you want her, and have somehow made her not want you, you shall have to…do something about it."

It was perhaps the most unhelpful advice he'd ever received. He lowered his sword as well. "Something?"

"Aye." Ré shrugged again. "Something."

Ré sounded as helpless as Aodh felt.

He suddenly realized his jaw ached from being clamped down so tight.

Do something?

What more did he have?

Thrice now, he'd touched her—in the entryway, in the bedchamber, and in the hall—and each time had been more intense. Gone deeper. Burned hotter. Why did she have this effect on him?

'Tis her eyes, he decided grimly. They saw too much.

Or mayhap her smile. The secret home of it.

Her mind. Quick, clever, insightful.

Her indomitable spirit.

The way she'd responded to his map.

Whatever the hell it was, Katarina had prised him open and tapped into some wellspring of passion and emotion he hadn't known existed in the world, let alone within himself.

And that was not enough?

He had nothing more.

A yawning chasm seemed to open beneath him as it had not done for years, sucking at him with cold winds of fury and…emptiness.

It *infuriated* him.

He had no time for cold sucking winds. He had a rebellion to conduct.

"Call the men," he said curtly, sheathing his sword with a vicious thrust and turning to the castle.

R⁄W

THEY ASSEMBLED in the great hall, before the huge hearth, sitting at tables with flagons of ale and wine and trays of bread and cheese, talking until late in the night.

They discussed the strategy of engaging the nearby town, and at the far end of the table, an argument broke out over whether it was worthwhile to send an emissary to entreat the town, or simpler to merely overrun it.

"We're not overrunning the town," Aodh said, moving his gaze down the long table to some of the younger soldiers who'd been involved in the discussions. "I told you before we sailed there would be no plunder. We are to live here. It will be our home. It is not our prey."

Cormac leveled a warning glance down the table after Aodh's words, and the men subsided.

"The town is rich, and its goodwill important," Ré explained calmly. "We will not squander it by a show of impatience."

"I'm off to visit it, in a day or so, when things are settled here," Aodh informed them. When Katarina was settled here.

Cormac shifted the bulk of his shoulders and reached for one of the earthenware jugs. "Anyway, there's no possible way we can garrison both a town and the castle when armies come marching. Nay, it must be won."

"And if it cannot be?" someone asked.

"Aye, if the lady won't submit?" someone else joined in. "If we cannot rely upon her allies, then we must need find other means. If the town sides with her, sacking it becomes ever more necessary."

Cormac smashed a fist on the table. All the mugs hopped and shuddered. "The lady. Will. Submit."

That settled it. The conversation moved onto less contentious matters, such as whether to roll up another barrel of ale, and which serving maids they were most interested in getting to know better, once the imprisoned women were released from their chambers.

Cormac said nothing, but he did shoot Aodh a dark look that could only be described as hurt. The comely maid with the bouncing breasts been locked up as well.

But Aodh's attention had moved away from impatient soldiers and defiant chatelaines to Tancred, his everyman—clerk, secretary, advisor in all things monetary—who sat at the next table over, assaying ledgers and poring over chests, while beside him sat the cowardly Rardove clerk, his face a monument of disapproval as he observed all the triumphant goings-on.

Then another round of Aodh's treasure chests were brought in, years' worth of plunder and tourney championships, hauled up onto the tables, overflowing with gold and coins. The clerk's scrutiny grew less disapproving. Indeed, it grew downright lustful.

Ré leaned closer, and as the men debated whether or not it was worth sending an emissary to one of the smaller princes, he said quietly, "That clerk can be turned."

Aodh nodded, not taking his gaze off Walter. "He is a windmill of opportunity. Whichever way the wind blows, so follows he."

Cormac tipped his head into their secret council. "I'd as lief trust the lass over him. At least she bears her weapons openly."

"That does not mean he doesn't have his uses," Aodh replied quietly, then raised his voice. "Clerk."

The other conversations in the hall died as if a boot had

stamped on them. Walter's head jerked around, yanking his gaze off the treasure chests. Tancred looked up too, then, glancing at Aodh, he murmured something. Walter got to his feet.

Cormac made a sound of disgust. "Bleedin' snake," was his final mutter before Walter drew up at their table.

"I saw you watching the chests." Aodh touched the one nearest to him and lifted the lid. Walter's eyes flicked to it, then held as he saw the golden coins within.

"One cannot help but notice, my lord." His bald dome had a faint sheen. "The fire last year caused great damage, and a few years past, the sheep fold was decimated. The other estates had to be sold off. Rardove has been without for some time, sir. My lady has been without."

"How highly do you value your loyalty?"

His gaze lifted off the coins. "To whom, my lord?"

Aodh smiled.

Beside him, Cormac muttered again, "Bleedin' snake."

Aodh tapped the chest, and the coins inside rippled like a golden sea. "There's more where this came from, clerk. Make yourself useful, and I may remember it."

His hooded eyes met Aodh's. "What would my lord consider useful?"

"I'm sure you'll think of something."

R⚔W

RÉ WOKE HIM at dawn, informing him a missive had already arrived back from the powerful MacDaniels tribe. Their leader would be here on the morrow to treat with Aodh.

"He's interested," Ré said, grinning. "And he has three hundred men under his command."

ROGUE WARRIORS

CHAPTER 17

THE DAY PASSED as if shards of glass had been embedded in it. Every minute was a slow torture, every hour a slice of impotent fury. She could change nothing, only endure.

As evening fell, Katarina took a break from her restless pacing and sat on the wide stone seat under the tall, curved window in the high tower.

Sunset had already done its brief deed, and was nothing but a thin red scar on the horizon. It would be a short twilight. Already the sky was a brilliant sapphire blue, darkening to ebony. And on the horizon, storm clouds built.

Hearing a step out on the landing, she turned her head, then uncurled her body, heart hammering. Was it fear or hope? Fear that Aodh was coming up.

Hope that he was.

Ridiculous.

An urgent whisper drifted through the keyhole. "My lady," a voice said softly. "My lady, 'tis I, Walter."

Resignation mingled with admiration. How had he got out? She hurried over and crouched before it. "Walter, I am here."

"My lady, are you well?"

She whispered back, "I am fine. How goes it belowstairs? Are you all safe?"

His next whisper was less solicitous. "Have you lost your mind, girl?"

She sighed. Even in whispers through keyholes, Walter was

a force for shame. "No, I simply realized accession was not the route to our greater goals."

"He'll kill the garrison for what you've done."

"No, he won't," she said, realizing the truth as she said it. "But he might kill you," she added solemnly.

That earned an exasperated sigh from outside the thick oak door. "He's locked us all up."

"You seem to have made it out."

A pause. "I had to go over the books."

She touched the door. "Seeing as you are yet at liberty, Walter, you must be the one to get a message out."

"A message!" He sounded shocked. "The castle is locked up tight, my lady. Wind barely gets out, and only Irishmen get in. I could not get a fly out, let alone a person with a message."

"But you must try, Walter." She scooted closer to the door and dropped her voice lower. "The queen must be told that Rardove has been taken. She must be told we stand firm."

A long silence followed. "My lady, I have been thinking..."

Oh no.

"Perhaps your course was wisest after all."

Now *she* was silent. Had that been a compliment? A concession? An admission? Had she struck her head? Had *Walter* struck *his*?

"What do you mean?" she whispered back.

"Perhaps it would be wisest to play along with the savage's desires."

"Whatever happened to the funeral pyre?" she asked angrily.

"He has imprisoned the entire castle, my lady. No one may leave, no one may enter. It is locked down entirely. Because of you."

They had already covered this ground. "It is locked down because they are in the midst of a rebellion. Now, dear Walter, seeing as you are *not* locked up, please *do* find a way to get a message out. Send two, by separate means, perhaps a village child? If they can get so far as — "

"To what end?"

She stared at the door. "Your meaning?"

"To what end would we invite the retribution of a man such as Aodh Mac Con? For what reason risk his fury?"

"Why—"

"Whatever happened to 'serve two masters,' my lady?" His words were sharp, almost a reproach.

She gaped at the door, unable to form a sensible reply, but was saved the trouble when Walter hissed, "Hush."

Low and gritty, boot steps sounded faintly on the stairs. Then, Aodh's voice, low and rumbling, came rolling up.

Another male voice joined in, not Walter's, and then Walter did say something; two of the three voices drifted away, one fussing as it went, and a single set of boots came toward the door.

R/W

SHE BACKED UP QUICKLY as Aodh entered the room, carrying a bundle of something. He kicked the door shut behind him.

"I do not like your steward," he announced.

"Lock him up," she retorted, not inclined to be friendly.

"I just did." He dropped the dark bundle onto the bed. It looked red, a rich wine color. Silken.

He crossed the room, relighting oil lamps on the walls as he went, and setting a burning ember to ignite the wicks of the multitude of rush lights set around the room. In the growing illumination, the hard, muscular power of him was revealed. She drank in the sight of him almost despairingly.

Why must this Irish rebel be so precisely the manifestation of her secret desires?

A moment later, servants appeared, scurrying in with trays and small chests, setting them on the floor, then hurrying out again as Aodh crossed the room and knelt in front of the fire.

Midnight blue shadows stretched across the room as he knelt and struck a flintstone into the kindling, a few times, then leaned forward to blow gently on the tiny sticks.

A few sparks glinted in the blackened maw of the hearth, then, small and orange-bright, flames began spearing up.

"Stop doing this," he said quietly.

"Doing what?"

"Sitting in the cold."

"I am not cold."

He swiveled his head around. "Then why is your nose red again?"

She chose not to reply. It was, in fact, cold. She simply had not noticed.

The fire began to snap and crackle as more flames caught. Soon, a miniature inferno was burning in the stony firebox. The flickering flames lit his face as he stared into it, then said quietly, "I have some questions for you."

And so it began. The breaking down, this time by a direct, frontal assault. Menacing questions, banked fury, steely threats…

"Tell me of the defenses."

"No."

He reached for a few larger pieces of wood and set them carefully atop the flames. "Then I shall tell you. The west wall is in disrepair. The southern tower was undermined some time ago."

She shrugged faintly.

"Until they met rock. Rardove is built on bedrock."

As if she did not know what her castle was set upon.

"So the foundations are firm, but the other parts less so. The gatehouse is weakening, and the portcullis may last through the summer. Or it may not."

It would not. The logs for its repair were in the northern bailey, half-sawed, half-snowed upon.

"Those planks in the northern bailey ought to have been put up months ago, before the winter came," he said.

Yes, indeed. Before the flood-wet autumn came, before the sickness came, sweeping through her men, disabling them in successive waves. Yes, before all that.

"Or at least before you came," she suggested.

Hard-packed muscular thighs bunched as he turned to look up at her, a forearm draped over his knee. "There is a field of mud out there, Katarina. Fronting the castle on every side but the north, and that is where the cliffs are. An entire meadow of mud."

"It is not an *entire* meadow," she demurred modestly. "There is a small pathway safe for passage, far to the east..."

"So that is how you did it," he murmured, a note of respect in his words.

But then, Aodh did not seem reluctant to show respect; she suspected it was one of his greatest traits. He had no trouble giving others their due. "The way you were able to hold Rardove with ten men? You tricked and maneuvered and built fields of mud, and you prevailed."

She shrugged. "It was not so difficult. Firstly, the Irish do not know I only have ten men."

"Neither do the English."

"My marchlands, my defense, my purse," she said firmly. "The queen sends nothing to support the defense of her realm, and—" She stopped short. It would not do to complain of the queen to a rebel. "One does what one can."

"Indeed," he said drily. "Such as build meadows of mud."

"En*cour*age them," she clarified, and was rewarded with one of his half smiles. "And then, of course, I do not go about *antagonizing* people," she added significantly.

"Ah. Fascinating approach."

"I could recommend it to some."

"Who?"

The lazy drawl brought a reluctant smile to her mouth. She hesitated, then added, "Additionally, my men are ever brave."

"And ever loyal."

The compliment surprised her. "I serve them a great deal of meat."

He pushed to his feet. "That is not what their loyalty feeds on." The larger logs caught and flames began licking up all around.

He passed within inches of her, ignoring her completely as he strode to the items stacked against the walls, the crates and sacks and bundles, all sitting atop the huge, oak table. He stared at the collection a moment, then moved everything off with a powerful sweep of his arm and grabbed a corner of the table.

She stepped forward. "Oh, 'tis too heavy, you cannot—"

He hauled the end away from the wall, stepped behind it, and bending at the hips, set his palms against the edge and shoved the table across the room, squealing all the way, until it stood directly in front of the fire that was now crackling merrily.

Well.

"Then you'll not be pleased to know your clerk has told them to stand down?" he said.

Her gaze flew to his. "What? No. That is impossible. You are mistaken."

"You may have a point." He went back for a chair. "I am unfamiliar with your steward. He said, 'I shall stand down the men.'" He peered at her curiously. "What do you think he meant?"

She scowled and began pacing again. "Why would he have done such a thing?"

He picked up the chair and carried it over. "He seems to believe you are in danger."

She stopped so short, her skirts foamed around her ankles. "But I am not, am I?"

"That depends entirely on you, my lady." He shrugged, as if the matter was out of his hands. She felt her face growing hot, and he made a sympathetic sound. "Aye, it doesn't look good for you, does it?"

She ignored the veiled threat, and eyed him thoughtfully as he carried the other chair over and positioned it by the fire. "But they did not do it, did they? My men, they did not stand down."

"Sadly, they did not. Again, they seem to wish to hear directly from you on the matter." She smiled, but he shook his head slowly. "'Tis as unwise now as it was before, lass."

"Oh yes, I know," she agreed happily. Even a minor resistance, when one was hard-pressed for victory, was satisfying. "Somewhat like you taking Rardove."

"Aye, we're quite a pair." He set a tray of food on the table. "You should marry me."

The urge to smile came again. She resisted it.

Arching a brow, he gestured toward the table. Covered with trays of food and pitchers of drink and several chests that had been carried in by the servants, it resembled a stall at a merchant's fair. "Do you want anything?"

"My liberty," she said tartly. "Peace from the incessant raids of the MacDaniels clan, a hot bath, and a great, large salmon."

That earned a quirk of his handsome mouth. "Well, Katarina, some of those things are easier to secure than others, and one is entirely within your keeping."

"Nothing, then," she said staunchly, then hesitated. "Perhaps...some wine?" *Your exquisite wine.*

"The wine, we can manage." He turned to pour.

She watched the silky red folds of liquid splash into a large cup. He set it on the table then waved his hand carelessly at the rest of the items scattered across the tabletop, items which did not bear closer inspection, for what other treasures might this Irish warlord have in his keeping? Certes, the silent message was clear: *Look at all you can have, once you are mine.*

She sniffed at all his mute temptations, but did take the wine. "May my page visit?"

"Little one, about so high?" Aodh held his hand at about waist height. She frowned. Dickon was taller than that. Although admittedly, he was quite small for his age. Malnourishment, most likely. He'd been near starvation when she found him. "Indeed he may visit you. The moment we locate him. He has thus far eluded detection."

"Has he?" *That* was encouraging, wasn't it? "He is quite nimble," she allowed, smiling.

"He will get himself hurt. If my men stumble upon him at the wrong moment, and perceive the wrong thing..."

His words drifted off but the warning was clear and genuine; these were battle-hardened men in the midst of a rebellion. They would not brook much, certes not a young renegade, be he intent on matters of espionage, or simply hungry.

Taking her goblet, she stepped away and circled the room,

entirely ignoring the chests — *of what?* — that sat on the table. The lid of one had been lifted slightly and beckoned like a siren. Which was no doubt the point, the arrogant devil.

Still, the longer she paced, the higher the flames in the fire licked, the louder the rumbles of thunder outside grew, the more difficult it became to ignore the chests, because they did, after all, look a great deal like *treasure* chests. Anything could be inside.

Only slowly did she become aware of what Aodh was doing as she paced the room. He was shuffling...playing cards.

She stopped short and stared. "Are they...playing cards?"

"They are." He glanced up. "Why, can you not play?"

"Well, I— Of course I can *play*. But...you cannot expect me to sit and play cards."

He raked his gaze down the front of her gown. "You may stand." He went back to his cards. "But no peeking."

Her jaw, already at half-mast, fell entirely. "No *peeking*?"

His pale blue gaze came back up. "Is that going to be difficult for you, Katy? You're not the sort who goes about peeking at other people's cards, are you?"

She pursed her lips together to combat the sudden, almost overwhelming urge to smile. "I shall restrain myself."

"Good." He began dealing. "Putt?"

She hesitated, then said, "One of my favorite games," and swung out her skirts to take her seat.

Rogue Warriors

CHAPTER 18

AODH SAT BACK as she picked up her cards. *Carefully now.*

The thought was a caution, a reminder of how quickly she could be gone, in heart and body. And as he'd spent the entire day in a state of constant erection, making even the simple task of bending over a painful chore, he had every intention of slaking the lust that hammered through him, tonight. In Katy.

She *did* feel something for him, something powerful, notwithstanding her fear of the queen. It was simply buried very deep inside. Coals banked beneath ash.

Aodh knew well the suffocating power of ash; it should be considered a fifth element, as powerful as fire or air, if only to extinguish.

So, *carefully now,* he counseled himself again, *or she will be gone.* Into the ash.

"Shall we wager?" he said casually.

Her gaze drifted up from her downturned face. "Is that a taunt? I have nothing."

"Aye, you do. Open the chest." He nodded toward the chest beside her.

She cast a doubtful glance at the wooden box banded in thick iron, then flipped open its lid and drew in a sharp breath.

"Oh, *Aodh.*" It was a whisper, a breathy, feminine exhalation.

He shook his head in grim resignation as his cock swelled hard. Again.

She dipped her fingertips into the chest, sweeping through

122

the piles of coin inside. They glittered dully and clinked. He held his cards up, watching her warily over their tops. Sooth, he'd been unsure how she would respond to a chest of coins. She might be pleased or she might be…furious. It could happen. Women existed in a state of mystery.

Her head came up, her fingertips still dipped beneath the top layer of coin. "You mean to buy me?"

Ah, there it was. She was angry. This coin, purchased with much toil and pain and one dead man—Rudolph, the idiot—had been reduced to a simple insult.

To his surprise, he felt the bite of anger too.

"I'm not buying you, lass. They are gifts. Or, do you prefer, negotiations. Rardove needs coin, aye?" He nodded toward the chest. "There is coin."

She slid the gold between her fingers with a little clinking, then sat back, wrist still over the lip of the chest, watching him. Like a Roman queen. Like the army commander in her tent.

"Very well, Aodh Mac Con. What shall we wager?"

He smiled slowly. "I can think of several things."

"Say, an angel, to start?"

"Fine."

She lifted out a handful of coins and laid them in a pile before him, then, very deliberately, took a single gold coin out of the chest and laid it on the table between them. He did the same from the pile she'd given him. They nodded at each other and sat back.

For a moment, they were silent, looking over their cards and preparing their respective attacks. Outside, another low rumble of thunder sounded. He cast a surreptitious glance across the table. Katarina's head was bent. A few strands of hair lifted away from the confining braid she'd twisted her hair into, which hung down her back in a thick russet plait, under a pale green veil.

"How goes the rebellion?" she asked as she set down a card.

"Apace," he replied absently, looking at it. "We're building alliances."

"With whom?"

"The MacMahon have sent someone, as did the O'Reilly tribe." He set down a card. "Dalton rode in this morning. He is one of ours now."

She waved her hand dismissively. "He was always one of yours. He has no love of Elizabeth."

They each tossed in another coin. "I will be visiting the town soon."

This earned a dark look from under her brows. "*My* town?"

"I'll send your regards."

"Who else?"

"Bermingham sent word." He laid down a knave.

Her gaze, aimed at the card, flung back up. "*Bermingham?* He is more a snake than a man. I would not trust him in a rainstorm if he said I would get wet."

"Sooth?"

"Sooth. If he requested a meeting, do not go." She laid down a card firmly as she spoke. "It is surely trickery, black and foul."

He swept the pile up. "Interesting, for Walter seemed to believe it might be a beneficial alliance."

"Walter? *Walter* said that?" She nibbled on her lower lip. "I would bid you caution you on this matter."

"Well now," he murmured, throwing in another coin. "Your purposes are a mystery to me."

"You think I would lie?"

"Think?"

A reluctant smile touched her mouth. "Well, I might. But I am not. These are things you will learn soon enough, and I would not see Rardove suffer for a few reckless deeds."

"Such as yours?"

She arched a brow. "Mine are stubborn deeds. *Yours* are reckless."

"Och, lass, you've been a bit reckless."

A flush rose up her cheeks. "Yes, well, a hazard of being a marcher lord. It quite goes with the territory."

"And you enjoy it," he accused softly.

Startled, her eyes widened, then another faint smile touched her mouth, lifting her cheeks. "I do."

Outside a bright streak of lightning lit the sky, then a rumble of thunder followed almost at once. The storm was coming nearer. A few splatters of rain fell through the open window.

Aodh strode over and shut the outer shutters, latching them tight. Then he folded in the hinged glass windows too, battening them inside. As he strode back to the table, Katarina reclined in her seat, pulling the cards in toward her chest.

"No peeking," she admonished.

He retook his seat with a smile.

"And what of The O'Fail?" she asked idly, tossing in another coin and setting down a king.

Half-bent to yank in the chair, he levered up his gaze. "Brian O'Fail is loyal to the queen," he said slowly as he retook his seat, "a thousand years old, and hung with leeches most days. He has not ventured out for battle in two decades, and his sons from half a dozen wives have torn the clan limb from limb. The O'Fail has no central power anymore. They do naught but war, allying for minutes at a time to oust a common enemy, then falling upon each other again like a pack of wolves."

She pursed her lips at the assessment. "Ah."

"What do you know?" he asked grimly.

"More than you."

In truth, he knew a good deal about the O'Fail tribe, for they'd once been the closest of friends and allies to the Rardove clan, surrogate families and foster fathers.

They were also disloyal, dishonorable cowards who'd not honored an alliance when it mattered most. Sixteen years ago, neither Brian the Elder nor his sons, nor any of the smaller tribes they claimed suzerainty over, came to the fight in Munster, and as a result, the Irish tribes had been wickedly outnumbered, and viciously defeated.

Aodh's cousins and uncles had died on that battlefield, his father and grandfather captured, condemned to die as traitors.

Aodh would never call upon the O'Fail. Past betrayals aside, they could not be trusted.

But Katarina, it seemed, knew some things too.

"The O'Fail princelings did indeed battle for years," she said, examining her cards, "and the land was torn to bloody pieces, but a year or so ago, one of their number took hold of all the warring pups and assumed command."

"Who?"

"Keegan. He is now *The* O'Fail. Their leader. He keeps to himself, occupied mostly with preventing his brothers and cousins from killing each other off."

Aodh smiled grimly. Keegan. Clever, powerful, dishonorable Keegan. Just coming into his own sixteen years ago, he'd been twenty-five years old and intent on safeguarding whatever he could for himself. He'd been his father's chief councilor, the chief voice urging the O'Fail not to fight, not to send troops, not to honor old alliances.

Aodh had not heard Keegan had taken control of the tribe. The queen surely did not know it either. She believed the old man Brian was still their feeble leader, and dissention among the historically rebellious O'Fail ranks served her well.

"I am surprised you do not know this," Katarina said.

His gaze met hers slowly. "Did Rardove treat with him?"

"Never," she assured him, swift and certain, the swiftest and most certain she'd been thus far except when she was telling him 'no.'

He smiled. "Why do I not believe you?"

A flush spread across her face. "Perhaps because you have me locked in a tower, and feel I cannot be trusted?"

"That would be why." He flipped a card down, which won the game, and swept up the coins, leaving one behind to begin the new trick. "Deal."

She reached at once for the pile and shuffled, then dealt. He immediately set down a nine. "Katarina?"

"Yes?" she murmured in distraction.

"How long are you going to hold out?"

She looked up slowly and their eyes met across the table. She examined her cards, plucked one out, and set it down. A ten. "Aodh, I have seen the queen's wrath."

"When?" he said, moving the cards they'd laid down to the

side, making a little pile. Her win pile.

She laid down a knave with a snap. "When I was a child. Unleashed on my father. And mother."

He countered with a two. "Tell me."

She swept the cards to the side—a pile for him—and he immediately laid down his last card, a king. She stared at it for a second, then laid down her last card, a two, with a smile.

"Take it, Katarina," he murmured. "And tell me what happened."

Aodh watched as she scooped the coins into a pile before her, dipped her hand into the chest and removed one more.

In silence, they laid down their wagers. He dealt.

He was beginning to think she wouldn't answer at all, when she spoke, her head bent, eyes on her cards.

"My mother and father had a great searing passion," she told him, fanning the cards in her hand. "It quite burned through them. The love of a lifetime, which was just as well, for it was the death of them.

"My father been sent to subdue the Irish, and found himself quite subdued. The queen sent for him when she heard he'd had a liaison with my mother, and when she discovered they'd actually wed, her wrath carried us all across the water." She looked up at him. "Your turn."

He set down a nine. "Go on."

She glanced at her cards. "My father was locked up for a multitude of reasons, then executed for them. Treason, conspiring with the Irish, making the queen angry. I suppose congress with an Irish princess constituted all three. As for my mother...When we first arrived in England, and things seemed most hopeful for my father, she was quite happy to be away from Ireland, whereas I felt I could not quite breathe."

Her fingers fluttered over a card, then pulled back. "You and my mother had something in common, Aodh: Irish folk who are not so fond of Ireland."

"'Tisn't Ireland, lass," he said quietly. "'Tis the choice between dying or being subsumed."

Her gaze swung up, dark and penetrating. "Yes. Of course. I

understand."

It was a low murmur, but she might as well have shouted at him; he felt pushed back by her words.

She set down a king. "In any event, when my father died on the block, my mother died of a broken heart. Or perhaps was frightened into death by the queen's wrath. One can hardly blame her. I was eight."

Eight. Aodh had a sudden vision of her, her beloved parents gone, alone in the world, with a vengeful queen hovering like a wasp.

"Your turn."

Her gentle prompt jarred him, and he laid down a card without thinking.

"I'm surprised you do not know this history, Aodh," she said quietly. "It is Rardove's."

"Who says I don't know it?" A flash of lightning could be seen around the edge of the shutters, then a few seconds later, a long roll of thunder rumbled into the room.

"Then if you know it, you must know I cannot turn to you. Don't you see?"

He wiped his hand along his jaw. "The queen killed your father, so you will be loyal to her. I confess to being confused."

She shook her head impatiently. "The queen was *good* to me, Aodh. Kind to me, despite what my parents had done."

He plucked a card out of the fanned assemblage in his hands and laid it on the table. "And what had they done, lass? In truth, what had they done?"

Her jaw dropped at this assessment in the form of a query. She stared at him, her cards on the table, her shields dropped, her defenses gone down like a drawbridge hitting the earth, and he simply strolled into her heart, through the pathway of her eyes.

Hurt. Scared. Betrayed. Abandoned.

All the things one was wont to feel after the careless, selfish choices made by others smashed through your heart like a cannonball.

Upon a time, such feelings had lurked within him too. They

did not now—he'd gone as cold as the emptiness scalding his heart. But dimly, he recalled them. The horror, the fear. The screams. The endless, aching chasm of loneliness and fear, and knowing you were alone in it, forever alone.

Then, quick as a flash, it was gone, and she was Katarina the Bold again, Katarina the Fierce, sitting tall in her chair and regarding him with an expression pinned at the intersection of affection and desire and anger, which was debilitating in and of itself, to know affection lurked there too, tangled with desire.

The anger bothered him not at all. Katarina was fire. Fire burned.

But she could be won. She must be won.

For her sake, as much as his.

"The queen allowed me Rardove," she went on softly, perhaps not realizing he'd just seen into her soul. "When my father had been found guilty of treason, and my mother was dead. Allowed it when I'm quite sure other voices spoke against it."

Oh, aye, they had, he thought grimly. Aodh's father's had been the loudest, demanding the return of his ancestral lands.

The queen had not listened, as was ever her wont when it came to Ireland.

And so the rebellions followed not six months later, turning parts of Ireland—and all of Aodh's heart—into a bloody battlefield.

"The queen took me in wardship, brought me in from the wilds, to England—"

"But you did not want to be brought in, did you?"

"—and finally sent me back, under my step-brother's care. And when he died, she allowed me—*me*, Aodh, a woman alone—to rule her marchlands. She even sent me my father's steward, Walter, to assist."

"For that alone you should turn on her," he said grimly.

She smiled a little. The cards were entirely forgotten now, scattered across the candlelit table, interspersed with gold coins. "You may laugh, Aodh, but when I was younger, Walter was a mighty presence. He wrought precisely what he was intended to. I became a box, he my lock."

"And what was he intended to lock up?"

She hesitated. "I never did a Humphrey again."

He laughed. "And the Humphreys of the world are the worse off for it, lass." But he was pleased. And realized Walter had some purpose in life after all.

"Oh, he brought me alternatives, of course."

"What alternatives?" Aodh said, stiffening.

Delicate and pale, her fingers twisted about themselves on the table. It was a telltale twitching for a woman so self-contained. "Bertrand of Bridge. You may recall him?"

"Vaguely. In what way was Bridge an alternative?"

"An alternative bedmate, Aodh," she said almost sadly, that he had not understood. "Husband. If the passions could not be tamped down, they could be channeled. Bertrand was a perfect choice. He was of a long-standing noble family. We had land, he was impoverished. He very much wanted Rardove, and had the...will...to contain me. It was a perfect match, really. But I was stubborn. I refused." She lifted a faint smile to him. "You see, there it is again, stubbornness. Certes, I am doomed."

"Spirit is not stubbornness," he said grimly. The notion that someone had tried to tame her...as he himself was doing.

Something in his gut twisted, and a weight descended on his chest. He pushed it away. What he was doing here was different. Much different.

Wasn't it?

"On occasion it is," she said, as rain began to lash at the windows. "In any event, I said no. Which mattered not at all; Bertrand is a resourceful man. All the situation required was a little ruination.

"He came to my room one night. It was very dark, and I'd only seen him once, across a crowded courtyard, so at first I did not know who he was. I was terrified. Then when he told me who he was, and what he wanted.... Me, Rardove." She shrugged. "I'd already been disgraced, you see."

Darkness veiled his vision. "Did he hurt you?"

She looked up swiftly at the low, menacing tone. "No, Aodh, no. Just...frightened me."

"I will kill him."

Her eyebrows arched. "I thought that was already your plan."

"I will kill him twice," he vowed.

Katarina smiled faintly, and her fingers trailed over the cards on the table. "And yet again, the queen was good to me. I said I did not want Bertrand, and she allowed me that. Instead of throwing me into the sea, or the Tower, she gave me Rardove. Aodh, she could have done any number of things, none of them good. Time and again, I was the product of misbegotten passions, and looked to recreate them ever and anon. And still, she gave me Rardove to rule."

"Until she gave it to Bertrand after all."

"And then you came," was her tart reply.

"Thank God for small favors," he said with feeling.

She laughed, and a smile lingered after. The secret smile, the one that housed something sweet and hidden, and it was aimed right at him.

Soon. Very soon, she would be his.

Chapter 19

KATARINA DRAGGED her gaze away from the clear intent in Aodh's eyes: he wanted her. She looked at the treasure chests, then the map, then turned slightly to examine the bundle of silk he'd tossed on the shadowy bed. She nodded toward it.

"And what is that? It does not look like something won in a pirate raid."

"I am not a pirate, Katy." The words were quiet, but hard as steel.

"Good. What is it?"

"Silk. Soon to be a gown. For you." He reached out and pushed the bundle closer.

She got to her feet and touched the fabric, then swept it up and held it against her body. It was a gorgeous, luxurious piece of fine-woven silk. She stroked her hand across it, then looked up to see his ice-blue gaze climbing from the fabric to her eyes.

"You said you would accept a gown."

Her fingers curled into the silk. "Aodh, you do not have to bring me gifts."

"Aye, I do." He sounded grim and sat forward. "Does it please you?"

She shrugged dismissively, pulling her mouth into a pout of indifference as she glanced at the fabric that was finer than anything she'd ever owned. "It is pleasing. Is this what they are wearing over the sea?"

"Some."

She lifted a handful of the silk and slid it over her cheek. "I recall in England, the…thing worn…about the neck? A bit of lace…?" Her fingers fluttered against her throat.

His gaze dropped to the movement. "Och, Katy, it's more than a bit."

This little nickname he'd chosen for her, it fairly intoxicated.

"'Tis truly awful." He shook his head sadly.

She lowered her hand. "How awful?"

"Awe-inspiringly awful," he assured her.

"I'm breathless to know more."

"Well then," he drawled, and got to his feet, then flipped open one of the chests and drew out pens and paper and stoppered bottles of ink. My, he was a veritable chancery, this warlord.

He laid the parchment on the table, and, holding it with the edge of one fist, moved the candlesticks closer, swept up one of the pens and began sketching.

She stared in silence. Bent at the hips, sword dangling, muscles of his back evident beneath his shirt, he held the pen with strong, callused fingers and sketched her the likeness of a very pretty dress.

She made a little noise.

He tipped his face up, pen poised in the air, midway through the hemline of what appeared to be becoming a bodice. "Aye? You've something to say?"

Clamping her teeth together, she shook her head. Nothing. She'd said nothing.

The room was silent but for the crackle of the fire and the scratch of his pen. Finally he straightened. "Aye?" He motioned to the paper.

She dragged her gaze from him, down to the page, which depicted a woman in a gorgeous gown, flowing skirts, a golden snood, and…

"Good God," she murmured.

He laughed.

The sketch, it was…ludicrous. The stiff circlet of lace,

confining the neck, opening out like an angry, fluted flower to plume under the chin in the most unappealing of ways. And so wide…it seemed to go on, and out, forever.

"Well," she said softly.

"Well."

She cleared her throat. "After all…"

"After all that."

The tempered amusement in his drawl made her smile. "How would one ever eat?"

"Well now, that is an interesting question. One lady, a very fine baroness, had a two-foot long spoon." He demonstrated how she would lift it far out, away from her body, then bring it back in, the way a hawk might land on a tree limb.

She laughed out loud. "I thought it a jest." She touched the ink. A tiny blot of green came away on her finger.

"I assure you, lass, in a thousand years, I could not have thought of that." They considered the sketch, then he added, "And I've thought of some fine, awful things."

This time, she let her head fall back on a laugh, rustling the drape of whisper-soft silk she still held against her body. He smiled at her, but repressed energy strained beneath the surface of him. Aodh was like the power under the waves, rolling through the world.

And now he'd rolled into *her* world, this warrior who gifted gowns and had known a fine baroness who ate dinner from a two-foot spoon.

How had he come to know such a person? How had he come by his treasures and his pretty playing cards and his very fine wine?

Aodh was not a simple man, and she realized with a shock that she knew nothing of him.

"Aodh?"

"Aye?"

"Where did you go?"

His eyes came up, pale blue and burning. "What?"

"When you left Ireland, where did you go?"

For a moment, surprise shone in his expression, then it was

shuttered. "Many places."

"I was hoping for more particulars," she said gently.

"Aye? And I was hoping to have you laid out on the bed by now, crying my name."

Her cheeks flared with heat. "Yes, well."

"Aye, well," he drawled back.

They smiled at each other.

He sat back down and picked up a cup, with whisky in it, most likely. "What do you really want to know, Katarina?"

Oh, the way he said her name was seduction enough. She would have to tell him to stop, but then he would know how much it affected her, and would say it *endlessly*.

She sat down too, silken fabric in her lap, for she could not quite bear to set it aside yet. "I want to know about the treasure chests. And the Latin…"

"The Latin, is it?"

"Yes, the Latin." Because the Latin had told her something, confirmed something that had been growing in her mind, a cord of thought strummed by the clerk and Aodh's huge, scrawling signature.

She'd known he was intelligent. Now she was sure he'd been educated too. Or else in the company of cultured, expensively educated folk.

An uncommon course of events for dispossessed Irish warlords.

"I've been to Rome," he said, so dismissively, so casually, it took a moment for the words to penetrate.

When they did, she sat forward sharply. "When?"

He shrugged, as if he could not be bothered to recall the dates. "Years ago."

"Where else have you been?"

"Paris. Venice. The Netherlands. Constantinople. Bohemia."

"No," she whispered, enchanted.

"The Canary Islands," he added with a flourish of his hand. "Where your wine is from."

"What did you do in Rome?"

A brief, but very definite, pause. "Met with people."

135

"Catholics?"

He tipped his head to the side. A hedging affirmation, then.

"What was Rome like?" She flung the question like a dagger.

"Dirty."

"Paris?"

"Dangerous."

"Constantinople?"

His nostrils flared slightly. "Exhilarating."

She inhaled a cool breath. How wonderful, the word he'd selected. "Is it true the outer wall has over ninety towers? And the sea wall almost two hundred? Did you see the Hagia Sophia? Is it not the city where Marco Polo launched his journeys from…?"

A slow, knowing smile crossed his face. "I'll make you a deal, Katy. You marry me, and I'll tell you everything."

Disappointment coursed through her. She sat back, affecting disinterest by means of a miniscule shrug.

A low rumble of laughter met this; he knew she'd been practically *speared* by the desire to know more.

"'Twas a mere curiosity," she assured him.

"What I want isn't mere, lass." Low and lazy, it was a confident, masculine drawl, followed up by the immeasurably more confident, and equally masculine, command, "Come here."

Heat swept through her, everywhere. "No."

He gave a faint smile. "Getting tired of that word."

Shivers, hard and pricking, like falling stars, rained across her belly and chest. Traitorous body, to turn into a night sky simply because this warlord had issued a command.

And he knew it. Knew every shiver that ribboned through her body, for he pushed to his feet and came around the table and lifted her out of the chair. He skimmed the fabric she still held to her chest with the back of his hand, then closed it around the silk and tugged it away, tossing it to the side, a slithery pile of silk at her feet.

Nothing lay between them now, nothing at all.

He watched her. Waiting. She should walk away.

She did not walk away.

"Aodh," she said, feeling strangely desperate. On *his* behalf. "You do not know what you have done here, by taking Rardove. Your arrogance will be your doom."

"I am not arrogant. Rardove is. It sits on bedrock. With sea cliffs behind. It can hold off an army for years."

She stared at him. "That is the extent of your plan? To hold them off for years?"

A shrug from the powerful shoulder. His gaze slid off hers, trailed down to her chest. "If all else fails."

"Else?" A tendril of panic uncurled in her belly. "What *else* are you planning?"

"Negotiations. There are worse things than having an Irishman hold a castle in Ireland."

"You cannot mean to try— You cannot think the queen will negotiate with you? Aodh, she will *annihilate* you. You must see—" She stopped short as a new shot of fear went through her. "Does the queen know you are here?"

He nodded. "She ought. I wrote her myself."

She felt flushed and feverish. "You wrote her? Oh no. Did you mention me?" She couldn't keep the panic from her voice. "Aodh, did you mention *me*?"

His gaze came up from where it had been trailing down her body. "Is that what is worrying you, Katy?"

Her hands were shaking. "'Tis treason enough to harbor priests, but to harbor rebels…"

"I told you, Katy, I will protect you." He turned his hand and slid it along her jaw. "I swear it, on my life. I will not abandon you."

She stared into his eyes, dumbfounded, as if she'd never heard the word before: *abandon*. No one had abandoned her. Her father had been executed by the queen, her mother died of a broken heart, too swaddled in pain, perhaps too frightened, to stay alive anymore.

"Abandon me?" she whispered.

"Never," he murmured, and skimmed his hand to the ties of her bodice and tugged on one frayed silk ribbon.

She watched his hard hand being so gentle with her, and

began to tremble. "You are taking your life in your hands, Mac Con." Her voice shook.

He slid his gaze up. "Right now?"

"By taking Rardove."

"Ah." He tugged on the laces harder.

"The queen will be enraged."

"Are you?" he asked, his head bent, watching what he was doing to her bodice.

"You do not understand. The queen will *destroy* you."

He leaned closer, put his mouth by her ear. "The queen will *try*."

And somehow, with his body so close and his confidence firing the room, it actually seemed possible this Irishman might succeed, against the most powerful monarch in Christendom.

Madness. Hopeless, reckless, madness.

She curled her hands into fists. "Aodh, listen to me. It is not too late. We could write her. *I* could write her, on your behalf."

His gaze lifted from her bodice. "You would do that for me?"

Her mind raced. "Yes, of course, I will write the queen—"

"There'll be no messages," he said firmly. "But I thank you." Ever so gently, he kissed her cheek. "For worrying on me." He skimmed his hands to her hips and, in a single move, lifted her and set her down on the table.

Before she could release a shocked gasp, he'd stepped between her knees.

"Aodh, what are you doing?" she whispered.

"What do you think I'm doing?"

An exhale of desire broke from her as she felt the hard heat of his body, so near hers. "But we c-cannot..." Her words drifted off, as she almost forgot what they could not do. "People do not..."

He bent his head so it rested directly beside hers. His hair-roughened cheek brushed hers. "Which people?"

Sane people. Wise people.

Scared people.

"There is nothing I will not do, Katarina." Her blood began

to course in a heated river through her limbs, down low into the juncture between her thighs. "There is nothing we cannot do, you and I."

Nothing we cannot do.

What did that mean? She almost didn't recognize the words, arranged in such an illogical order. There were a thousand things she could not do. Should not do. Must not do.

His head tipped closer, and his dark voice spoke again, a siren for her hidden passion.

"It is but a matter of you, Katarina. What do you want? For right now, I would do anything for you."

Rogue Warriors

Chapter 20

LOW AND COAXING, his words rumbled through her hair, equal parts temptation and threat, for what Katarina wanted right now was unutterable. Thrilling and confusing. She wanted him to take off his clothes, wanted to see the painted lines covering his body. How far did they go? She imagined dark, inked flames licking over his entire body. Did they go across his chest? His hard stomach? Down his thighs?

She wanted him to keep talking. Keep telling her what he wanted. Keep telling her all the impossible things they could do together.

She breathed into the space under their downturned faces. She could taste him, smell him. Leather and steel, musky masculinity. She felt almost weak from wanting.

"I want..." she whispered, shocked at how the words sounded leaving her lips.

"Aye?" Fierce male desire filled the word. Barely patient, wanting her. It urged her on.

"I want to see how far your paint goes."

His body stilled. "'Tisn't paint," he murmured, then his arms bent, his hard muscles flexed, and he dragged his tunic up and over his head.

"God in heaven." The words emerged as breath.

He was magnificent.

Stunning, foreign, and beautiful, he towered before her like carved marble. The entire left side of him was covered in

140

painted lines. Curving, arcing lines, like comet trails across his body. He was a sorcerer. The lines seemed more spell than ink, winding across him like a landscape, across his chest, around his arm, down his flat stomach, until they disappeared under his waistband.

She felt as if butterflies had landed on her skin, thousands of butterflies with red-hot little feet. Shivers broke and ran down her body.

She reached out to touch the inky flame that licked up the side of his neck and felt his body shudder.

She traced the curve with her fingertip, down his neck, across his shoulder, his chest, over his nipple. His breath hissed. She turned her finger to scrape her nail down his flat stomach, following the trail of ink.

His muscles rippled as he let her explore his body. She felt as though she'd entered another land. She was as far from the rules as the sun was from the earth. She was a shooting star, rushing away from everything she'd ever known in a fiery trail of desire.

Her hand drifted to his waistband, then fell away. Their eyes met.

Then, Aodh did the same thing to her as she had done to him. His hand became a mirror of hers.

He ran a calloused fingertip down her neck, over the rise of her breasts and down her belly. As he went, he caught the loosened laces of her bodice between his knuckles and gave another long pull. It tightened the fabric against her already hardened nipples and the corset, once bound like a fist around her ribs, suddenly loosened.

The breath rushed out of her. The ribbons dangled down in front of her gown.

"Now, Katy, there is no one here but you and I." His fingers pushed into her hair. He fisted around the veil and tugged it free. "There is no one to see you, no one to disapprove." He tossed the veil aside, slowly dismantling her, stripping her bare of all the trappings of propriety. "It is only you and I. Let us be."

She felt dizzy at his words, his touch. The want in them. The hope in them. "And where will it stop?"

His gaze swept to hers. "I will stop whenever you say."

She gave a small, hiccupped laugh. "Aodh, you never stop."

"I will stop, for you." He touched the tip of his tongue to the seam of her lips, so gently. Oh, so gently. He bent his head to the side and brushed his mouth over hers, a stroke of lips over lips.

"Let us be, Katy. Let us try."

The bulwark that had held her up all these years, the wall that had held all the passion at bay, was simply washed away under the power of Aodh's intentions for them.

She tipped her face up and opened her mouth for him.

With a last hard pull, he tugged the final ribbon free and swept the bodice from her body, peeling it away from her skin, leaving her bare and flushed, and then he claimed her mouth.

So gentle the pressure of his tongue, pushing in, parting her lips for him, so gentle, but so explosive. It ignited an arc of fire through her body that grew hotter as the kiss became deeper, more demanding, more open-mouthed, more *everything*, until her head was back, cradled in his powerful hand, her spine arched, her body unfurling beneath the wicked, wonderful slow lashing of his tongue.

His hands tested the length of her, skimming over everything he could touch. Detoured momentarily by her braid, he swiftly uncoiled it, loosed the plait and ran his fingers through the banded tresses to let it flow down her back. Then he resumed his exploration of her body, skidding down to her hips.

She did the same to him, utterly lost in him, sliding her hands over the hard bulge of his arms, down his muscled back, her fingertips raking into the valley of his spine until he hissed and nipped at her neck, both punishment and invitation.

With a breathtaking move, he pushed his hands beneath her bottom and dragged her forward, until the thrust of his erection pushed boldly into the fabric of her gown, into the juncture between her thighs.

It was a stroke of pleasure, a perfect push. Heedless now, she pressed forward, until she was right up at the edge of the table, her thighs dangling on either side of his hips. She straightened against his body, pressed her bared breasts to his chest, and leaned up to taste his neck.

The rough scratch of hair abraded her lips, heightening her pleasure. Her mouth moved down the strong column of his throat, unable to stop. Dangerous, this was so dangerous. So irresistible.

"Katy." It was a ragged, male plea. He cupped her bared breasts in both hands. His hands, so hard, so capable of destruction, brushed gently over her nipples.

A firestorm of sparks raked down her body.

Everything about him was hard intent now. He put a hand on her shoulder and tipped her back to the table, onto her elbows, her body laid out like a sacrifice. He stood above her, rock hard with restraint, and raked his gaze down her. "*Leannán.*"

The fierce male approval lit a fire inside her. The rasped endearment meant *lover*. Perfection in the heart.

He planted a palm on the table and bent to her body, ran his tongue up the swell of her breast then slid away, a hot stroke, a cruel tease. She gave a frustrated pant. Teasing soft, he licked around the outer edge of her breast, over skin so sensitive, even his breath was like touch. She arched for him, waiting to receive the touch she so wanted, the brush of his hot tongue over nipples almost painfully hard, peaked by desire.

But his mouth skimmed away again in a taunting dance, swirling around the dark nub, but never touching.

She made a sound of impatience.

He gave a low laugh, sending his breath across everything he'd just licked wet. Then, suddenly, giving her no time to adjust, he closed his mouth over her breast and sucked.

Her head whipped back and banged the table.

He did it again, only slower this time, sucked her into his mouth, and flicked his tongue across her nipple, a hard, swift swipe.

It tore the breath from her lungs. Still holding her in his mouth, he shook his head gently back and forth. The tugging pressure rolled excitement through her body. Then he scraped her nipple with his teeth, dark, dangerous pleasure, and more dangerous yet, his hand slid down her legs, and began tugging up her skirts.

Her entire body trembled as his fingers skimmed between her thighs. When they slicked through wetness, evidence of her desire, his head lifted, and his gaze swept to hers.

"Och, lass, that feels good."

It was a dark, carnal compliment that should have shamed her, but it quite lit her up. She felt as if sparks covered her body, glittering bright. He turned his hand and, without pause, slid a finger up inside her.

Her head jerked back as if yanked on a string.

"Aye, like that," he said with dark approval.

He laid claim with another slippery push, nudging in deeper, forcing her flesh to part for him. The blunt tip of his thumb skimmed through her folds, then stroked across the nub at the apex of her.

Her body bucked in helpless pleasure.

"Again," he commanded, and did it to her again, and again, stroking her harder, for more.

"*Aodh.*"

The broken gasp of his name coming from her lips, ignited Aodh's blood. No more waiting. He straightened slightly and kicked the chair away from the table so he could drop down into it.

"Lie back," he ordered in a low voice.

Her heavy-lidded eyes parted slightly, and she made a little sound of frustration, confusion. She tried to reach for him as he dropped down into the chair and dragged her hips forward.

"Let me show you mad pleasure, Katy," he said, a horse rasp, as he put a hand on her knee.

If she said no now…

Her eyes, passion-dark, stared at him. Then she let her knee fall to the side, letting him in.

Everything became a roar in his head, surging heat in his body, as he ran his open palm along the length of her trembling legs. *His.*

He skimmed his knuckles up the satin-smooth skin of her inner thigh until his fingers were inches from her womanhood. He could feel the dizzying wetness and heat.

He bent his head and touched the tip of his tongue to her.

Sweet, hot woman.

Her body jerked. "Aodh," she sobbed.

He flicked into the dark heat, then moved in deeper, tasting her with long, sweeping strokes, circling through her slick folds as she cried out, then he flattened his tongue and brushed over the nub again.

Her head rolled on the table. He tasted her again, a long, deep sweep, from the bottom to the top of her and when she froze, her spine held, half arched, her body taut and waiting, he nudged his tongue hard into her.

A sob broke from her body and her knees fell apart. He half rose out of the chair, his head bent low to her, and took her relentlessly, with tongue and teeth, quickening the pace. Her body jerked and, dizzy with lust, his body taut with restraint, he pushed two fingers up inside her, deep into the swelling tightness.

"Aodh, oh, *please.*"

He curled his fingers slightly and did it again. And again, attending which strokes made her leap and shudder, then doing them slow and deep, then faster, and harder. When her head began to toss on the table, when her cries became helpless moans, he straightened and stretched his body over hers.

Keeping his fingers deep inside her, he leaned to her mouth and rasped, "This is you, Katarina. This, now, is you. Your fire." He pumped again.

Katarina exploded. Jolting, wicked pleasure, the climax came so hard and fast, her body bucked and she flung her head, crying out as the spasms rocked through her like a storm.

He was there, bent over her, hot and approving, kissing her, whispering half in Irish, half in English, "Och, *mo ghrá thú*, you please me." His arms went around her.

She was heedless, senseless, knew only that he had lifted her. He carried her across the room, his kisses continuing to rain down over her neck, her cheeks, her lips. She turned her head, trying to catch each one.

He laid her down on the bed and knelt above her, propped on one hand while the other reached down to unlace his breeches, and then, oh *then* sense came rushing back. It sliced like a knife through the stupor of her passion, the drugged pleasure of being at the center of Aodh's attention.

He pulled at the laces of his breeches. The long hard curve of his erection bulged against them.

"Oh no!" she cried, dazed and dragged out of the sea of pleasure. "No, Aodh, no."

He went still.

Dark fear mingled with passion as she stared up at him. His gaze burned into hers, fierce and furious, then raked like a brand down the length of her still-shuddering, half naked body.

He was utterly silent, completely motionless, except that his arms were shaking. Rampant desire, thwarted and bent.

"Marry me," he commanded, his voice a low stroke of desire.

"I cannot," she whispered, a caution more to herself than a rejection of him, for Aodh could not be rejected. She saw that now. The most she could hope for was to hold on.

But what he wanted from her — treason — she could not do.

Everything on him was taut with restraint: the muscled arm propped beside her, the painted chest and stomach, only inches away, radiating heat.

She reached up and ran shaky fingertips down his face. A shudder of restraint moved through him. "I am sorry," she whispered. Such a strange, tortured place.

"Just let me take you," he said, his voice rough with desire.

Her body shook, she wanted him so badly. "No."

His head dropped and for a moment, the hard power of him was motionless. His head hung an inch above her body, in the valley between her breasts, his breathing ragged.

Then without a word, he pushed up off her and left the

room, locking her back inside.

She shook all night. With fear. Desire. Desire of the heart as much as the body. She was steeped in want, distilled in Aodh.

R/W

DOWNSTAIRS, he sprawled in front of the raging fire in the lord's chambers.

His hose were loosened, his hand around his cock. He stroked himself, long and hard, picturing Katarina with her eyes half-closed, her knees spread for him, hot pink flesh glistening with her own desire. Hearing her little moans as she let him trail his fingers through the wetness, then the broken gasps when he pushed up inside the tight fist of her.

Then the pleading, when he'd bent his head and stroked her with his tongue, whispering his name...

Katarina, even barely unleashed, was luminous with desire. She had more to give. She was barely tapped.

Abruptly, furious that he was using his hand and not buried inside her, he flung himself up and out of the chair. His cock stood at attention, aching with want.

He'd *known* it. From the moment he first touched her, he knew the truth: she was fire. He had teased it out, set it aflame, then she'd snuffed it out again.

Women were from Lucifer.

Relacing his breeches, he swung open the door and hollered for Ré and Cormac. They appeared, bleary-eyed, and stopped short when they saw his dark, furious face.

Ré closed his eyes and blew out a breath as he took a seat.

"How goes the wooing?" Cormac asked more bluntly. "Can we rely upon her?"

Aodh strode to the fire and began throwing in wood. "We're going to need more allies."

They met until late in the night.

In the morning, another round of emissaries rode out bearing the news: the Hound of Rardove had returned and was seeking allies.

CHAPTER 21

SPRING RECALLED ITSELF with a vengeance, and as the sun rose the following morning, winter was forced to relinquish its hold. The air was almost balmy. Spring breezes frisked up skirt hems and blew through the high tower window.

Katarina stood at it, inhaling the scent of heather. In the distance, at the edge of her vision, she saw the sea, churning and unstoppable.

Closer to hand but sharing the same characteristics, Aodh stood on the battlement walls, amid a group of men engaged in animated conversation. Their armor glinted in the sun, swords hung from their hips, and pistols were strapped across their bodies. They looked like land-borne pirates.

The spritely spring breezes tugged at their hair and brightly colored capes, snatching the occasional deep-throated voice and winging it through the air, high up to her tower window, where Katarina tried, unsuccessfully, to decipher the words.

But eavesdropping on rebels was not the only reason to lean one's elbows on the window ledge and poke one's face out into the sun. The stones were already warm and sea salt was in the air. She knew why the horses being put through their paces were kicking up their heels, tossing their heads with such spirited abandon: spring had sprung, with all its riotous, intoxicating fuel. The day seemed made for rebels.

Katarina leaned out as far as she could and squinted at the small group on the walls. Several of them were unfamiliar

Irishmen…not Aodh's…not….

Her eyes narrowed. Why, was that…MacDaniels?

For a decade now, the clan leader had shunned all of Rardove's overtures of peace and treaty. With a castle of stone and hundreds of far-flung warriors he could bring to hand at a moment's notice, he'd barely responded to some of Katarina's missives over the years, and not at all to the others.

He was not actively hostile, but neither was he docile; he boldly trespassed just inside the borders of Rardove land with his hostings on occasion, when easier routes lay south and east, as if he'd decided the English barony was in need of silent reminders of his might.

He did not balk at more overt reminders either. He was responsible for half the raids on the Rardove cattle herd.

Yet here he was, being entertained by Aodh. Laughing with Aodh. Joining with Aodh.

Just as Aodh had said they would.

Clad in leather and steel and his loosely swinging sword, Aodh was carved from essential things, impenetrable, unbendable, wrought-by-fire things. Iron and steel and stone.

It was very disconcerting, to be standing in old silk and have Aodh be so much a castle in his clothes.

To be so much more of what the Irish marches truly needed. Far more than she and her worn velvet and lying title.

But then, who cared for titles when the winds bore down and the nights grew cold? One wanted heat and might and certainty, and Katarina did not have those things.

So she wove lies.

She acted certain when she was unsure. She exuded calm when she wished to rage. She demanded rents she could not possibly have collected if her tenants refused to pay. She pretended it was not a crushing blow to find half the sheep fold dead, or Spanish soldiers washed up on her shores. She pretended there would be food for all, and somehow, ensured food for all.

She wore the lies like a gown. Donned them by day, discarded them at night, when the darkness opened up like the inside of a cave and she was all alone in her bed, unsure if breaking the lies out again would suffice for one more day.

Or, if instead, someone like Aodh would show up.

Or Bertrand. Or the Queen of England. Or the Irish.

Or all of them.

And yet, she loved Ireland so, loved Rardove with the desperate, fierce love that came from having—and wanting—nothing else.

Rardove was worth pulling out the lies for every morning. It had pierced her, like a dart laid in her heart, the love for this scarred, wild, windswept land, and the notion that Aodh Mac Con belonged to it more than she, was...*infuriating*.

Aodh's blond captain was pointing away into the valley. Everyone looked in the direction of his arm, except Aodh.

His lightly bearded face stared directly at her.

Katarina wished she had a slingshot. A pebble, aimed directly at his head, should do the deed.

His captain lowered his arm, and the group of men moved farther down the walkway. Aodh watched her a moment more, then, with a graceful shove, pushed off the wall and followed after.

R⚔W

"THIS WALL HAS BEEN ablated."

The sun was rising bright, and Aodh was up on the walls with Ré and a few of the men. Cormac had just led MacDaniels and his men off to the hall, and Ré was pointing to a section of the eastern battlement wall.

Aodh dragged his gaze off Katarina's face in the high window. If she'd had a bow, he'd be dead.

"It should hold," Ré was saying, "but it will be weak. Best if we draw their attention elsewhere, and man it heavily. We'll set up listeners, to detect any undermining activity. We'll have to spare a few men from the walls for the task, and we haven't many extra."

Aodh shook his head. "We shall use townsfolk."

Ré smiled a little. "You are assuming they will side with us."

"I intend to be persuasive when I visit them."

The sun hit the walkway as it rose, lighting Ré's blond hair. "How persuasive?"

"A chest of gold persuasive. And my winning charm, of course."

Ré snorted, but smiled.

Under the damp morning air lay a faint softness, as if spring was breaking through. The sky was already pearlescent, pink and orange mists glowing bright and brighter, spreading out as the sun battled its way up over the horizon.

In Ireland, everything was battle, even the dawn. Even Katarina. Especially Katarina.

"I sent out a few men to explore the sea of mud," Ré was saying. Aodh dragged his attention back to their survey of the defenses.

Ré pointed over the wall. "'Tis a veritable swamp. At points, an actual one."

"Quicksand?" Aodh asked swiftly.

Ré shook his head. "The villagers report 'tis more of a sucking mud. Horses won't make it far. Cannons will die where their wheels first roll. The only way across is the way we came, along that narrow stony path. Anyone who spreads out will sink." It was a single track. Very narrow. Fine for wagons and deliveries and friendly visitors. But for an army...

Ré said, "Elizabeth will never get an army across that. God could not get an army across that."

They smiled at each other.

Clever Katarina.

They peered over the battlements, to the wide, sweeping vista of valley and distant hills, aglow now with the rising sun. Mists swirled low to the ground down in the dells. In the distance, green hills rose, thick with forests, deep and verdant. Aodh recalled them well. And under all this fertile, vivid, creeping dawn came the salty scent of the sea.

Something stirred in his chest.

He glanced back at the tower, but they'd walked too far, and he could no longer see the high window.

Ré followed his glance. "What are you going to do with her now?"

Shoving his cape back to let the nascent sun warm his skin, Aodh said simply, "She is no fool. She will come around."

"Why would she do that? And further to the point, if she does not?" Ré's face was tense and dark.

Aodh rested the heel of his boot on a joist jutting out from the wall and crossed his arms over his chest. "Have you something to say?"

"I am saying it. I think it unwise to keep an enemy combatant in our midst."

Aodh smiled a little. "Combatant?"

"Lest it slip your mind, she pulled a blade on you. Twice."

He frowned. "That was but an initial reaction. Fear, confusion, anger." *Great, unbiddable passion.* "Understandable."

"And now? Now, what is fueling her fire?"

He gazed out at the green grasses of spring marching down the valley walls, dew-wet, illuminated by the misty light as if cast in some faerie spell. Ireland was beautiful in spring. He'd forgotten that.

"Aodh, methinks the lady was not confused in the least," Ré pressed quietly. "And I do not think she will come around. Why would she? Nothing is going to change about her circumstances, nor ours. She will still be the queen's bound lady, you will still be the rebel. She will still lose her castle if we prevail—"

"Not if she weds me."

"—or her head if she joins us and we do not."

"'Tis a momentary setback," he said curtly.

"Are you certain?"

"Absolutely." He'd never failed yet in his life. He was not about to start now with the woman who made a fire burn in his loins and his cold, empty heart.

Ré's gaze was pinned on his profile. "How? How, Aodh, do you intend to overcome this setback of the lady of the castle being held, a hostile captive, in the midst of our rebellion?"

"I have plans."

"What do they include?"

Their gazes locked. As the sun rose, it shone on Ré's eyelashes and the hair falling down over his shoulders.

"It would be far wiser to send her away," Ré said quietly. "But you do not seem to want to do that, and for the life of me, I cannot understand why. Women have never held any but the most fleeting allure for you, Aodh."

"I'm not sending her away."

"Why not? What is she to you?" Impatience and confusion hardened Ré's voice. "What matters *she*, to *us*?"

Their gazes locked for a silent moment.

"I suggest you leave off this," Aodh said quietly.

Ré nodded curtly and pulled his own cloak tighter around his shoulders as they drew near the southern tower and guardhouse, where men were assembling to change the morning guard.

"Very well, Aodh. But you had better convince her, swiftly, ere someone gets hurt. Most likely her."

Aodh wanted to smash his head into the wall. What else was he doing *but* trying to convince her? And he was so close... Last night, she'd been so wildly aroused, her body had almost ignited under his touch. It had driven him mad.

Mad, indeed. He'd have done anything for her, anything to keep her under his spell, whispering his name, wanting him more than anything in the world.

He glanced back at the tower, but they'd passed on. Then a call went up from the gate: a rider was cresting the hill at full gallop.

Kicking up dust and pebbles, the rider hurtled down the path they'd just been discussing. He wore an Irish *brat* and a simple hauberk.

They hurried over in time to greet him at the gate.

He brought a message from the O'Mor tribe. Their chief welcomed the Lord of Rardove home again, and mentioned how well he recalled Aodh's father.

He also mentioned they had four hundred warriors ready at a moment's notice.

Ré and Aodh looked at each other and grinned.

A cool rush moved through Aodh, the one that generally preceded the culmination of maneuverings aristocratic or militaristic. It was a familiar feeling, and welcome, and he'd come to rely on it for sustenance, a surrogate for deeper emotions, but he knew the truth: it had no staying power. It was a cool dab on a fevered brow.

But Katarina... What he felt with her reached all the way to his bones. It would last. If only she would turn to him.

R/W

KATARINA HEARD a shuffle at the tower door and spun.

"My lady?" said a small whispered voice. Not Walter, then.

She hurried to the door, touched the seam where door met frame. "Dickon?"

She heard an outbreath of relief from the other side. "Aye, my lady. Are you... Have you...?" His voice faded away. Beyond his station and, depending upon her reply, beyond any remedy within his means, the questions were entirely out of his realm. He let them fade away.

"I am fine, Dickon, fine," she assured him, affection warming her heart. "Do not fear for me. Be strong for me."

"I will, my lady. For you."

"So they did not lock you up?"

She heard a dismissive, snorting sound. "They tried."

Amid all the trials pressing upon her at the moment, a smile lifted her mouth. "Did they?"

"Oh, aye." A pause. "They're so *big*." Yes, they were. "'Twas a simple matter to get away."

"And have you been eating?"

"Oh, I pinch some bread on and off, and I found some eggs sittin' in a bowl by the kitchen door." A pause. "I s'pse I'm a bit hungry."

She pressed her fingertips to the door, as if by this, she could feed him.

"Do you...do you need anything, my lady?"

She laid her cheek against the cool wood. "Yes, Dickon. I need you to be caught."

"What?" Confusion and outrage spiked his voice.

"And then I need you to ingratiate yourself. Be nice."

A disapproving silence flowed through the crack, then on its heels, an equally disapproving "My *lady*."

"Dickon, heed me. You will eventually be caught, and it will not be pleasant. And you need food. And I need to know you're safe, not wandering and starving."

"Not *starv*in'," he muttered.

"Go to him, turn yourself in, apologize, be docile…"

"As you are, my lady?"

She frowned at the door. "If you mean to gainsay me, then do so right off and I shall find myself another champion."

"Champion" seemed to do the deed. She could almost feel him straightening on the other side of the door. "No, my lady, I can do it. Is there anything else?" he asked grudgingly, no doubt worried she might ask for even more outrageous acts, perhaps washing his face, *with soap*, or some other such indignity.

"Yes, Dickon, one small thing." She leaned close to the door. "I need you to bring me my sword."

R⚔W

BRAN RAN INTO WALTER in the darkened stairwell. He almost plowed him over and tumbled down the stairs, but Walter's hand gripped his shoulder and stopped him from falling. Then it dug in and pinched around the fabric.

"Where have you been, boy?" Walter demanded.

"About," Dickon snapped vaguely, tugging to be free, but Walter's fingers pinched harder; he was a good pincher. Dickon cast up a derisive, bitter, but defeated look.

The light of oil lamps in the stairway turned Walter into a towering, monolithic shape.

"Where were you just now?" he demanded, disapproval flowing down from his lofty, clerical heights

Dickon despaired of ever being half as tall as the egg-domed steward, which was half the reason his dislike bloomed so strongly. The other half was the manner in which he treated her ladyship.

Yet right now, Walter was the closest thing to a friend he had.

"Visiting my lady," he muttered.

Walter's hand tightened on his shoulder. "And?"

"She wants me to bring her her sword."

They stared at each other.

"And then to...surrender myself." Shame laid his voice low.

Walter made a sound that, were it anyone else, he'd have interpreted as sympathy. "She counsels us all to surrender, and yet she does not. Fool woman."

Dickon drew himself up. "My lady is not a fool."

"You are," Walter snapped. "I should beat you for your devilry, running around like a rat, putting us all in danger —"

Dickon struggled, but the clerk had superior pinching powers. He gave Dickon a shake and frowned down at him.

"How would you get your lady's sword?"

Dickon rolled his eyes. "I'd break into the master's chambers where he keeps it. O' *course*," he added derisively.

"Fine. Then bring it to my room."

Dickon gaped as Walter released him and started down the stairs. "Then do as she bids, boy, and turn yourself in. Ere they find you themselves, and you learn what a true barbarian is."

Dickon snorted. "They'd never find me."

"They will if you keep stealing eggs from beside the kitchen door."

Dickon's jaw dropped. "How do you know about the eggs?"

"Just get the sword."

R⚔W

WITHIN THE HOUR, another round of emissaries had ridden out.

Aodh was out fast on their heels with his own contingent. Cormac and fifteen others rode at his side as the golden sun sent long rays over the tops of the walls, making the shadows retreat down in the baileys.

As they intended to win the town, and not conquer it, they bore few weapons and several heavy chests.

Ré stood on the wall just above the portcullis gate, in command of the castle in Aodh's absence. As he passed under, Aodh stayed his horse.

"Station a guard at her door the entire time I am gone," he ordered.

Ré nodded.

"Free the rest of her household. Not the garrison, but her servants."

Ré nodded again. Beside him, Cormac gave a grunt of approval, for this meant the maid with the bouncing breasts would be freed too.

As they passed under the gates, Aodh added over his shoulder, "Send her up a bath. And a great, large salmon."

R/W

KATARINA WATCHED him ride off. The horses seemed to wade through the low-lying mists down the valley, then they began climbing the far side. She watched until they were out of sight.

Aodh's small hosting contained more soldiers than these hills had seen since Finn MacCumhail's band of Fianna warriors, and that had been a thousand years ago, and a myth into the bargain. But Aodh Mac Con's rebellion was far too real.

Queen Elizabeth would be enraged.

ChapteR 22

"My Aodh?"

The majority of Queen Elizabeth's councilors stared vapidly up at the rafter beams or whichever whitewashed stone was in their direct line of sight. A few others, absent rafters or stones, peered out the nearest window into a swiftly dying sunset as the queen reread the missive from Aodh Mac Con, who had, apparently, turned rebel.

How like an Irishman.

"*My* Aodh?"

The hollow shock in her voice created a shuffling of slippered feet as the men drew their averted gazes off the walls and windows and looked at each other in silent, furious query: *Where in God's name was Burghley?* Only Cecil could manage the queen when she was bent, now that Dudley was dead.

Finally Sir Walter Mildmay, Chancellor of the Exchequer, cleared his throat. "Your Majesty, 'tis a small enough thing, a trifling. So an Irishman has turned. It is what Irishmen *do*. They are savages, after all. 'Tis in the blood—"

"Trifling?"

Mildmay froze mid-word, his lips wrinkled around the effort of not saying what he'd been thinking of saying, and was now most definitely *not* going to say.

"A trifling that one of my most trusted councilors has forsworn me? That one of my best captains has commandeered a castle on my Irish frontiers and turned it into a rebel stronghold? A trifling that he has aban—"

The queen stopped short. *Abandoned me* almost rang in the air, but she did not say the words, and no one else ever would. They simply watched their steely queen as she set down Aodh's message and picked up the camellia flower he'd sent with it. A token of his affection. A reminder of times past. He'd always known how to touch her heart.

Ireland had been a simmering pot of rebellion for the past twenty years, embroiling everyone from the queen's own cousin, the Earl of Ormond, up to the powerful Desmond earl and *his* brother, down to the man who'd replaced Desmond after he'd been imprisoned, fitzMaurice.

Ireland, quite simply, turned men to rebels.

These rebellions—and the Crown's threats and reprisals afterward—created even more fierce opposition amid the Irishry. It incited uprisings in the south and agitated a few pebbles loose in the unruly north too, mostly defanged Irish potentiates hoping to reignite their own aspirations.

The most noteworthy had been the Rardove clan.

The Rardove barony was named for the region, and the legendary dyes that used to be associated with it. *Ruadgh dubh*— "roo" and "dove," the queen had obediently repeated the lyrical words Aodh had taught her—the Irish words for the colors red and black, the deep shades of the legendary Wishmé dyes that had once come out of that wild region.

The reappearance of such a long-forgotten, warlike tribe had been an unsettling blow.

Fortunately, in the end, the rebellions had been put down, and the overly ambitious Rardove warlord had been beheaded, quite painfully, too—she'd been told it had taken four blows. Cousin Butler had come to heel, the earl of Desmond had been imprisoned (until he was released to rebel again a few years later), and FitzMaurice had sailed to France to seek Catholic allies to begin another rebellion.

But Aodh...Aodh had come to her.

He'd laid his sword at her feet and pledged himself, with a condition: he wanted his ancestral lands back.

Bold bantam chick. But bantam, nonetheless.

Against the will of her Privy Council, Elizabeth agreed to his proposition, in theory.

"Prove yourself to me," she'd commanded, flattered and amused—and impressed—by the boldness of this dark-haired Irish boy about to become a man. Rebel man, or one of hers?

Best to keep him close to hand and find out, for he had a dauntless spirit.

To the astonishment of the Council, he'd proved himself a hundred times over. Charming and capable of standing alone in unpopular opinions—he had none of the untrustworthy prettiness of so many others—Elizabeth found herself desiring to keep him closer and closer to hand. Even at the expense of honoring her vague, theoretical promise.

She hadn't thought it could matter so much. After all, it was only Ireland.

"I cannot lose you to Ireland, Aodh. Francis is weakening, Dudley is gone. Bertrand can go tend Ireland; I need you here. You are my man," she'd said with great affection.

He'd listened respectfully, as always, then leaned near and, taking liberties no man would dare, no man but he and Dudley, ran his finger down her forearm and said in that dangerously male lilt of his, "I am indeed your man, my lady, and have been for the better half of my life. I am not your puppet."

Then he'd kissed her hand and left.

So. Aodh had shown her he was not her puppet.

Now, Elizabeth would show what she was not: a fool.

The Irish could not be allowed to simply *have* Ireland.

She snapped out of her stillness, crumpling the paper in her hand until it resembled the knot in her stomach. The men would never see that, though. They hadn't the sight. They thought her indecisive, waffling, unwilling to commit. They knew nothing of the things she committed to, over and over, in the dark nights of her soul, the wretched ripping apart, dual courses torn asunder, striding the one path, leaving the other behind like a distant shoreline.

They never cared for what was left behind. Men so rarely

did. The opportunity to try again always came to them.

She flung the crumbled paper atop the camellia and swept the room with a cool glance.

"Send for that fool, Bertrand," she said curtly.

"Already done, Your Majesty," Robert Beale, clerk to the Council, assured her. "He is en route."

"To spending some goodly time in the Tower," she snapped. "What was he doing up in Northumbria in the first place, for God's sake?"

"He said he received a missive from you directing him there."

Elizabeth snorted. "He will acquit himself on this excursion or I will see him shackled for a twelvemonth." She cast her steely gaze around the room. "And so, the postern gate of Ireland once again becomes a matter for England. Did I not say it would? Did Leicester not know? Was two decades of war not sufficient to learn us our lesson?"

Silence met this array of questions. It seemed nothing would ever be sufficient for Ireland.

She got to her feet. The room erupted with a squeal of chairs.

"Send an army to acquaint Aodh Mac Con with my displeasure."

A loud chorus of voices resounded off the walls: dissension, cheers, Elizabeth had no idea. She was too deep in a swirl of memories. The faces of the men she'd relied upon, then lost, swam up and receded. She'd lost Dudley, how many times?, but he'd always come back, until, finally, now, he would never come back again.

And now, *Aodh*?

Her chest felt hot and knotted. She turned toward the door she knew was there, but it was difficult to see, shimmering as it was behind unshed tears. But she never stopped moving toward it.

One could never stop. It was the only way.

Rogue Warriors

Chapter 23

AODH RETURNED from a triumphant visit to the town at twilight, four days later.

The castle was bustling. Men were patrolling on the walls, others were hammering and sawing boards to strengthen the gates, others were training in the yard.

He bypassed them all, calling for Ré, striding like a storm to his chambers.

For the past four days, all he'd been able to think of was Katarina. Pushing her out of his mind had proved impossible, in part because she was so well regarded in the town.

Folk were close to exultant that he'd graced the town with a personal visit, and close to crushed that Katarina had not. She was well liked, and more to the point, well respected. She sent the town food when times were lean, medicines when sickness came, and dealt fairly in all matters of court and taxes. So when Aodh showed up bearing gifts from Rardove, they simply assumed Katarina had joined this son of Ireland, and thereby legitimized his rebellion.

As Katarina turned, so did they.

Aodh did not see fit to correct their misperception, although he and Cormac did exchange a silent glance over the heads of the mayor and guild leaders at the feast dinner hosted in his honor.

"Aye, she was sore sorry she couldn't accompany us," Cormac had muttered, looking at Aodh. "Sore sorry, that's for certain."

The other reason Aodh could not set her from his mind was because every time he closed his eyes, he saw her. And every time he saw her, his body readied.

Sporting a partial erection for four days was painful in the extreme.

So when they returned home and the gates fell down behind them, he dispersed his men on tasks of food and sleep, passed by Katarina's newly released servants and maids, one who was particularly flushed with curtseys and color when she saw Cormac looming behind him, then made for his chambers, Ré fast on his heels, reporting developments.

"They are coming, Aodh," he said as they burst into the lord's chambers. "They send messengers and emissaries, but they do not commit. Oh, a few have, but not the major clans."

Ré began lighting candles as Aodh tossed the windows open. Blue-black twilight poured in.

"They are wary," Ré explained, turning to the hearth, which had been set and stoked less than an hour ago. He gave the coals a push with the iron rod and tossed more fuel in, then waited for Aodh to do as he always did, stand directly beside the flames, so close he was practically *in* them. But he did not come.

"Why are they wary?" Aodh asked as he unbuckled his sword belt and tossed it on the table, then tugged off his tunic.

"They want to know where Katarina is."

He reached for a washrag. "Why?"

"They think perhaps this whole thing is some trick, some ruse."

"That doesn't make any sense." Aodh plunged the rag into the stone cistern set in the far wall, where fresh water sped down from the rooftops, then he wrapped a cake of soap inside the rag and swiftly washed his torso.

Ré dropped into a chair and put his boots up on the table. "Indeed it does. Either she has been sent away, or she has joined the rebellion. But she has, apparently, done neither. No one has seen her face, nor heard word of her leaving. I warrant that's making them uncomfortable."

Aodh lifted an arm and laved his armpit. "So she is respected. I knew as much."

"Or disdained for being the queen's paw. But in either event, she is a polarizing force. And a female, which makes a few of them more wary than if she were a viper. But no matter where they come down on the matter of female rulers, Aodh, the fact that she is here, amid us but not *with* us, is making them mightily uncomfortable."

Aodh snorted as he stripped off his breeches and, splashing the soapy rag into the water again, washed between his legs.

"And there are rumors," Ré added significantly.

Aodh paused, eyebrows up.

"That she's been imprisoned."

He flung the rag into a bucket and rinsed with clean water.

"That did not sit well, Aodh, even among those who do not want a woman in command. If she stands amid us but against us...we may as well have a lit fuse in our cellar." Their eyes met. "Or our tower."

Aodh reached for a clean tunic and finished dressing in silence. He shoved his boots on, then, as he slid his sword belt off the table, ready to buckle it back on, he went still.

He stared straight ahead for a moment. "Where is the sword?"

Ré dropped his boots off the table. "Sword?"

"The short sword, that lay here." He pointed to the pile of Katarina's weapons he'd had brought back in and left in a heap on the table, a constant reminder of what he was up against. The danger of her. The fuel. The fire.

Ré shook his head. "I have not touched them, and no one else has been allowed in your chambers whilst you were gone. Only this evening was the door unlocked again." Ré glanced at the pile of weapons, then said, "I did see her little urchin darting around the other morn, but was unable to catch him."

Aodh turned. "Was he abovestairs?"

"That he was."

Aodh was silent a moment, then said in a low murmur, "Oh, Katarina."

CHAPTER 24

KATARINA EYED the bathtub warily.

It was not the first bath Aodh had had sent up. There had been one a day for the last four days. But Walter had never overseen their preparations before. She shifted her wary glance to him.

Her clerk stood in the doorway, arms crossed as he directed the servants. His face was silently reproachful as buckets of water came in, hotter than any before. Even more water was being heated at the fire. Fresh soaps were laid out, and piles of folded towels.

He might be fretful, but Walter was an excellent manager.

Katarina waited until the servants finished pouring the bath, and began filing out, before she said quietly, "I see you are still at liberty, Walter."

"I have work to do," he replied stiffly.

"Such as standing down my men?"

For a moment, his eyes met hers, then he gestured toward the bath. "There are soaps."

"I see."

He moved the direction of his pointing finger. "And towels."

"I see them too."

He frowned. "See that you use them."

"I shall do my best."

"One holds out hope."

They were growing positively sarcastic with one another. She said in a low voice, "One might be forgiven for thinking you forget whom you serve."

The bushy eyebrows on his forehead lifted. "I recall quite well, my lady. I serve two masters now, you and the Hound."

He turned and left the tower.

Tendrils of scented steam wafted up from the surface of the tub, and finally succeeded in drawing her attention off the door. The tub was set beside the hearth, and flickering orange flames burned through the mists, so it looked like a fiery swamp. She eyed the scene with a mixture of longing and deep suspicion. As if the tub itself were up to some mischief.

Aodh had sent it. Mischief enough.

Surely it was unwise to relax even the smallest bit. But Aodh was gone, the sun had set, twilight was evocative, and the evening breezes were so very soft and alluring.

In the end, though, it was the soaps that did her in.

She examined one cake, then reached for it and lifted it to her nose. A wave of weakness went through her. So fragrant. So silky smooth.

Abruptly, she snatched a towel off the top of the pile and turned to the steaming water. Behind her, the pile of towels toppled over.

It was a hardly noticeable event, the towels being so soft, the fall so short. Indeed, she would not have paid attention at all, if there had not been an unexpected thud as it hit the floor.

She stopped and looked over her shoulder.

There, visible at the edge of the towels, poked the tip of a decorated sheath, and the edge of a buckle.

Her sword.

Dickon.

She caught her breath and knelt for it, grabbed the belt and unsheathed her sword with surprising affection; she'd trained with this sword for years. It was as dear a friend as Susanna, and she had not realized how much safer she felt with it close to hand. But as soon as her hand curled around the familiar hilt, she felt better.

Pistols were good, but they were obstinate and fickle and did not always aim well. If you were not careful, or sometimes even if you were, they were as likely to shoot off your hand as the other man's head.

But her sword...oh, she'd trained with it, had its hilt specially made to fit her hand, and her bias for beauty, so that it was inlaid with an image of tiny harps and England's crown, traced with the faintest silver, to bind the two, as they were bound here in Rardove.

A small nub of discomfort knotted in the center of her chest.

She had no plan for the sword, but having it made her feel safer. It was enough.

Laying it along the rim of the tub, she slid her hard boots off and stepped onto the fur pelt Walter had ordered laid. Her toes sank into its plush silky warmth, another luxury of Aodh's. She unlaced her gown and slipped into the warm, enveloping steam.

Softly scented, the hot water closed around her. The fire crackled beside her. She tipped her head back, and let her eyes close with a deep breath. From the bailey below came the muffled snort of horses and the ring of horseshoes on stone.

A relaxed breath slid out of her. She washed herself, the soap fragrant and luxuriant. She worked it through her long hair then, holding her breath and screwing up her eyes, she ducked under the water and rinsed the soap from her hair

She had a great lot of hair, and when she came up for air, she was sputtering.

That's when she felt Aodh in the room.

He spoke, low and dark behind her. "A sword?"

Terror gripped her. She slammed her hand down around the hilt of her sword a second before his came down on top.

Beating him to the hilt made absolutely no difference, for he simply clamped his hand over hers and pressed down, pinning her hand to the hilt of the sword, and to the rim of the tub.

She jerked and tried to rise, but he stretched his other arm out and trapped her other hand to the rim of the tub too.

She was immobilized, arms stretched out, one impotently clutching the hilt of a sword.

His voice came beside her ear. "I underestimated you, Katy." He sounded very, very angry.

She tried to struggle up again, to no avail. Warm water sloshed around her breasts as he held her down.

"I should have known." His mouth brushed her ear, light and terrifying.

"Aodh..." she whispered.

"What were you going to do with it? The sword?"

"Naught, I swear to you. I simply feel safer—"

"Who? Who brought it to you?"

She tightened her jaw, shook her head.

He made a soft sound. "I cannot allow such defiance, Katarina. Surely you can see that."

She shivered. It sounded like a prelude to something. A warning.

"Aodh, I vow..."

Her words, already weak, trailed off as his lips brushed her ear. Her mundane, utilitarian ear, never tended until Aodh and his tongue. "What, Katarina? What do you vow?"

"I am, I am sor-sor—"

"Och, are you going to tell me you're sorry?"

His words were hot mockery, a taunt at best, but her body responded as if he'd touched her somewhere secret and private. Heat rolled through her, and shivers marched like armies across her skin.

"I'll take your apology, for a start. 'Twill not be the end."

Murmuring, whispering, frightening, arousing, his mouth moved down her wet neck, her hands still trapped on the tub. Her breasts bobbed in and out of the water, her nipples breaking the soapy surface, then sliding below. The alternating sensations of warm water and cool air added to the mad pleasure. Her head dipped back to rest on his shoulder, her arms still stretched out on either side.

He shifted to the side and slid his mouth down the front of her, to her slippery breasts now pushed up out of the water. He stroked his tongue over her nipple with a growl of possession. She was already wet, warm from the water, but the nudge of his tongue exploded a firestorm between her thighs.

He let go of one of her hands but kept the other clamped firmly under his.

"Do not move," he commanded as he slid his hand into the water. His tunic sleeve was drenched at once, turning the cobalt-blue fabric so dark it looked black. His hand curled around her inner thigh and pulled it to the side. Without preamble, he pushed up inside her. She watched his painted fingers enter her flesh, and her mind shut down.

Her hips bucked up, pushing him in deeper. She tipped her head back as far as it could go, turning to the side, reaching behind her with her free hand to curl around the back of his head, and pull his mouth to hers. He took her in a savage, demanding kiss.

Wicked to be so trapped, to be so aroused at being so trapped, to be so worked by this man, stripped of everything but her desire.

"I am going to be inside you soon," he growled against her lips. "You're going to beg me." It was a masculine promise, a fierce, beautiful threat.

"Not if we must wed," she whispered, dizzy, ragged and broken, but certain of this one thing: she was not a traitor.

For a moment, he was motionless, except that the arm holding hers down was shaking with...fury. Then, soft and menacing, he whispered by her ear, "You want to fight, Katarina?"

His voice was silky smooth and cold, like wine laid in ice.

Oh *no*.

"*D'accord*." He pushed up and strode away from her, across the room. "Let's fight."

Rogue Warriors

CHAPTER 25

"WHAT...?"

She scrambled out of the tub, water streaming from her body, and grabbed for her chemise, tugging it on. Its linen length clung to her wet curves, her hardened nipples, her trailing, knotted hair.

He grabbed her sword belt off the table, sheathed her blade into it, and tossed it over. "Put it on."

It clattered into her hands, ropes of leather and steel. She fumbled for it. "Aodh—"

He grabbed his own belt, which he'd tossed onto the bed, and slung it around his hips. Her heart both sank and sped up, until it felt as if it was hammering a thousand beats a minute, down in the pit of her belly.

"Aodh," she whispered.

"What?" He was curt, his head bent to buckle the belt. One of his arms was dripping wet, the cobalt sleeve sticking to his roped forearm.

"I do not think—"

"Do you not?" Oh, his Irish accent was thickening; fury was flowing. "What is the problem now, Katarina? Can you not fight openly, in the light of day? Or *will* you not? Only subterfuge and dark shadows for you, is that it?"

Her fingers tightened around the leather. "You know naught of the choices I have had to make."

"I know a few." Striding over, he dropped to his knees and, shocking her into silence, buckled the sword belt around her hips, then got to his feet and retreated a few steps, his hand resting at the hilt of his own sword, waiting for her to draw on him.

"Oh, Aodh," she exhaled, helpless. Her chest felt cold, her brain frozen.

"You've a fire to fight, lass. Let's burn it out."

"Someone might get hurt," she protested

"People are already getting hurt, and there's a world of it to come."

Her throat was dry, making it difficult to form words. "I mean here, in this room."

Something flickered in his gaze. "I'll never hurt you."

She straightened. "I meant you."

He laughed.

Her hand touched the hilt of her sword. "I have been trained, you know."

"Have you?" He tapped his fingers on his belt, then shrugged. "You'll not be as good as I, Katy, but that is not the point, is it?"

She drew her sword from its scabbard.

He smiled and drew his own.

"You might be sorry, you know," she said, an echo of her earlier words as she began to move about the room. He turned with her.

"I doubt it."

They circled each other, parrying, testing each other as they moved. She stepped forward, and he backed up as they took a circuit around the room. He gave the table a hard shove with his hip as they passed by, pushing it out of the way, and as he did, she lunged forward, gave her sword a little flip up, nudging his aside.

With a surge of power, he tightened his hold and let the movement lift his sword up and around, a glinting arc of steel, then brought it back down again to hit her away, but she'd already danced backward.

"You've some talent, lady," he said as he swiped his sword northwest, a flashing move.

"I know, my lord." She swept around in a clockwise arc, out of the way of his blade, and returned her sword to its original position, lethally level, tip pointed at him.

They moved about the room, Aodh setting a rhythm that matched her mood. She took regular swipes at him, left, right, backing him up in predictable motions, then, when she used the natural flow of their parry to make a swift lunge forward, he stepped to the side, out of the way.

"*Contratempo*, Katarina," he murmured as she stumbled forward.

She righted herself at once, blowing hair back from her face with the grace of a cat. His blood fired.

She was made for this.

"What is this word?" she demanded, circling him again.

"I created a rhythm, you fell into it, then I disrupted it. *Contratempo*."

"I shall recall that to mind."

"Do."

"And pray, sir, who taught you such things?"

"The Corporation of the London Masters of Defence."

Her gaze flew to his, then snapped back to the sword. "That is a great many words. I know what none of them mean."

"Aye? Well, you needn't use words, lass. Just look." They parried.

"You are five stone heavier than I." She punched off his parry and backed up. "Most of that between your ears."

"You are paying attention to the wrong thing, Katarina. You keep watching the tip of my sword. Watch me — my posture, the grip of my hand; be *aware* of my sword."

"That sounds like trickery."

He laughed. Katarina frowned. He was laughing a great deal. Under other circumstances, she would welcome such lightheartedness. As it was, he was pointing a sword at her, so it rather unnerved.

"Drop your shoulders," he instructed. She bashed away his

blade. "They're way up here, by your ears. And bring your elbows in."

"Oh, hush up," she muttered as they circled one another. Her face was bright, gleaming with sweat and energy.

They moved around the room, advanced sharply to engage, then retreated. He wasn't toying with her per sé, but he could have ended this thing anytime. The reason he had not was because he was an insufferable, arrogant *mule* and he wished to torment her with this little drama as a metaphor for their larger struggle.

Still, she admitted, brushing back her hair, it *did* invigorate.

"Do you intend to make some point by this display?" she demanded, tucking loose strands of hair behind her ear as she bobbed to the left.

"What point could I possibly be making?" His tone was so dry, it could ignite.

"It escapes me," she assured him.

"Come, lass, disarm me."

She scowled. "You *are* making a point."

"If you detect one, far be it from me to disagree with a lady."

She tossed her head, flinging back her hair, and stepped to the left, moving her sword in a backswing arc.

He stepped to the side and deflected it lightly away rather than engaging, then swept free and slid his feet backward.

"Aye, you *are* good, Katarina."

"I know."

A loud crash broke the silence of the room as he kicked a bench out of the way.

"Who trained you?"

"Just the boys."

"The boys, is it?" He laughed.

She lunged.

DOWN IN THE BAILEY, Cormac and Ré were returning from the barracks, where they'd conducted yet another fruitless session with the Rardove old guard, all of whom were younger than they. Striding across the bailey, they glanced up at the high tower as they passed beneath.

Two of the hinged windows were pushed open, and there were tinkling sounds and faint smashes, coming from within…was that metal? Or glass? And then…a male laugh?

"What do you think is going on?" Ré inquired grimly.

Cormac stopped and listened, then scratched his chin. "Sounds to me like a swordfight."

"That's what I thought, too." Ré started walking again.

"You dinna think he's *fighting* with her, do you?"

"He might be doing anything. He's already done things I've never seen him do before."

"Well, there's a frightening thought, isn't it, seeing as the list of things Aodh'll do is long and impressive."

"I know." Ré was silent a moment. "Son of a bitch."

A shout from the gates disrupted any more detail on this considered opinion. Another rider had just returned.

R⚔W

"YOU LOOK GOOD, lass. Your chemise…" Aodh swiped his free hand down the front of his body. "All wet."

She gasped, but there was nothing to be done. "I hate you."

He laughed.

"Moreover, the queen will hate you."

"Some days, the feeling is mutual."

She eyed him suspiciously. "What does that mean?"

"Some days, I'm not too fond of the queen myself."

"Of course you are not fond of her," she said warily. "What do you mean, 'fond'? You do not know the queen."

"Aye, I do."

"You *know* Elizabeth, Queen of England and Ireland?"

"She's the one."

Her mind, torn between his words and his sword, rebelled. "But…how? In what capacity do you *know* her?"

"Councilor."

"*Councilor?*"

He shrugged. "One of them. Member of her court. Friend."

Slowly, her jaw dropped. "You cannot...that is not possible...what you say...no."

"Aye."

The single word was more compelling than an argument. "In what *manner*? In what way, did you..." She waved her sword ineffectually, so stunned she could hardly speak. "For how *long*?"

His lips pursed. "Nigh on sixteen years."

"*No.*" It was barely a breath. She stopped short, her sword tip dragging across the ground. "You are lying. I do not believe you."

"Well, that's a shame, for I am telling the truth."

"But, I... *Why didn't you tell me?*"

He lowered his sword too. "I thought it would only complicate things."

She gave an incredulous, gasping laugh.

"What difference would it have made?" he asked in a low voice.

"Oh, Aodh, it means *everything*."

"To you?"

"To the queen." Katarina knew very well what happened to the queen's favorites when they did a thing that even *hinted* at betrayal.

When her mother had been accused of being a witch, a maker of the ancient dyes of Rardove, as well as a priest harborer, her husband, Katarina's father, had stood surety for her. Claimed her innocence to the queen's representative in Dublin, and then to the queen herself.

The claims had meant nothing. Indeed, they may have doomed them even more in the queen's eyes, if for no other reason than jealousy.

The way they saw it in England, an Irishwoman had stolen the queen's captain, then bewitched him, then turned him *Catholic*.

Even a hint of disloyalty could doom a man.

Aodh had much more than hinted. He had stolen a castle.

Oh, this was far, far worse than she'd thought. An Irish warlord rebelling was a matter of course. But one of the queen's favorites?

This was treason on a high scale.

Aodh would be dead before Elizabeth finished giving the command. Lashed to a table, his body cut open, disemboweled while still alive, then his arms and legs half-severed and tied to horses…

She actually bent forward, sickened by the thought. She did not think she could survive that.

Oh, curse him, he had *ruined* her.

"Aodh," she said in a cold whisper. "This is terrible. The queen will destroy you."

"You're concerned for me?"

"I'm *horrified* for you."

With a twist of his wrist, he spun his sword and wrenched the blade from her grip. It tore free and clattered to the ground and he moved in, flinging his sword away as he came, driving her back to the wall. He drew up in front of her and put a hand on the wall on either side of her head, his arms stretched out straight.

"Aodh, this is madness." She touched his jaw with trembling fingers. "Are you not even *frightened*?"

He skimmed a hand down her ribs, his hand catching on the damp chemise before he hooked it around her waist.

"I have been through fire, Katy. I have no fear left in me. It all burned away when I saw my father's body torn limb from limb. Whatever happens will happen. I will not shy away." He brushed his beard-roughened cheek across her soft one. "This, right here, now, between you and me, 'tis meant to be."

She leaned her head forward until her forehead touched his. "I do not know what to do with you. You are mad."

"Aye, mad. Join me."

She gave a broken laugh. "I cannot."

His head came up a bare inch. "You keep saying that, but most things are indeed a choice." His voice was a low rasp. "Not a fine one, nor a pleasant one, not the one we wanted to have, but a choice, nevertheless."

"And I am to thank you for offering me this one?"

"I am not offering it. It *is*. What you do with it is the choice. This moment may not be the one you sought, Katy, but it is here, before you. Choosing not to make it, that too is a choice. This moment, here," he tightened the hand on her hip, "this is our life."

"Oh, Aodh, you think I am not choosing you. I am not choosing *treason*."

He must have heard the tremble in her voice, for he moved in, no doubt sensing surrender. His other hand came to rest on her hip, and he dropped his head to press a kiss to her shoulder.

"Choose me," he said, so simply it almost broke her heart.

She spoke softly into his ear. "I hear your words, Aodh. But do you? Does this all not mean you, too, have a choice?"

He stilled.

"You could choose something different. You could change this matter entirely." Her words sped up as excitement grew. She cupped his jaw and made him lift his head. "You could admit you were wrong. Please, let us write the queen. *I* shall write her —"

"No." He slid his hand up from her hip and hooked it over her shoulder, so it hung there, half a caress of affection, half a warning. "My plans are the plans of generations, Katy, an entire people. My father, his grandfather, and his, and his. Rardove is four hundred years of waiting. I cannot lay it aside, nor have it endangered, not even for you, *a stór*."

Her skin heated from the endearment. "What do you mean, *even*?"

"You must know how I esteem you."

She shook her head angrily. "What would tell me so? Being locked in a tower?"

"Not being dead should tell you."

She inhaled sharply. In the dim room, he was a force of nature.

"Not being sent away should tell you." His voice was low,

coaxing her to see this his way. "The gifts should tell you."

"Stop giving me gifts," she pleaded.

"No."

He bent his head and claimed her mouth, kissing her as if they were sinking, the land falling away beneath their feet, her mouth the only thing holding him up. She met him, lash for lash, her arms around his shoulders.

He backed her to the wall and plunged his tongue deep into her mouth. It was a dark, wild, unforgiving, primal, insanely arousing demand of a kiss. She returned it in the same fashion, reckless, willing, her body pressed to his, until he broke the spell and tore his mouth free, looked down at her, his breath heavy, his eyes dark with desire.

"Tell me, Katarina, do I stop?"

She leaned her shoulders against the wall, her hips pushed out to receive him, drowning in want.

"Should I stop?" he said again, in his rough, perfect voice. He rocked his hips forward, the hard power of him fully ready to take what she so clearly wanted to give.

"All you need to do is say stop."

She said nothing.

He bent to her ear. "Do you not see? We are fated. What more proof do you need? You cannot say no, and I cannot stop coming for you."

His vision of their union scorched her heart, because she *did* care, and she could *not* say no, and still, she could not give him what he wanted.

Coldly, he stepped back, his gaze at once burning and distant. Without another word, he turned and strode out, leaving her standing, bereft against the wall, the sword at her feet.

But it mattered not at all, for she'd already been disarmed.

Chapter 26

AODH BARRELED down the stairs into the hall. Soldiers lounged on benches and played games of dice and cards, while servants drifted in and out. The pretty maid Cormac seemed smitten with was sitting with him and Ré and a few others at a table by the fire, talking quietly. All heads lifted as he entered.

No doubt his expression was darker than whatever Bran had seen the other day when he stormed out of the bedchamber, for most of the men got to their feet instinctively, then swiftly retook their seats and averted their eyes. All but Ré, who, once again, just shook his head.

Aodh passed Walter, who stood in conference with Tancred, pointing to something in a book. As he went by, Walter's gaze drifted to the stairwell, then the clerk shook his head.

"She always was defiant, my lord," he murmured in sympathy.

Aodh's hand flashed out and closed around the man's throat, pushed him back to the wall, arm flexed straight.

Walter's eyes flew wide as he began to choke.

Aodh leaned in close. "Do not speak to me of Katarina again, viper."

Ré was there by then, and Cormac. They pulled him off the steward, who stumbled away, hand to his throat.

Aodh stalked to his chambers, leaving the hall in shocked silence.

A moment later, Ré and Cormac appeared at the door. He

179

waved them in and reached for a whisky jug. Splashing drink into three glasses, he pushed them unceremoniously across the table and fell back into the lord's chair and lifted his cup.

"*Sláinte*," he said dourly, then stared into the fire.

Cormac and Ré exchanged uneasy glances. Cormac lifted his bushy eyebrows as high as they would go, then put his hand in a fist and wiggled it back and forth, tipping his head ever so slightly in Aodh's direction.

Ré blew out a noisy breath and turned to Aodh. "Did we hear swords upstairs?"

The flames danced bright red and blue. "Aye."

Cormac sat forward, grinning. Ré made a sound of disgust. "What the hell are you doing up there, Aodh, using swordplay as...prologue?"

"Epilogue," Aodh muttered, then sat forward and lowered his forehead to the table. "Betwixt." He lifted his head an inch and banged it back down, once, twice.

Ré leaned forward on his elbow, staring. "Betwixt? *Betwixt?* You took her *after* the swords?" He smashed his hand over his face and wiped it up and down a few times. "Whatever the hell you're doing up there, Aodh, you need to do it faster. And much, much better."

Aodh lifted his head with a cold look.

"We haven't much time." Ré's voice was grim. "The queen's army is coming, and we need allies."

Aodh threw himself back in his chair. "Sent out more riders."

Ré and Cormac exchanged a glance. "Have you considered the O'Fail?"

"No O'Fail."

AODH SLEPT a few brief hours, in the chair in front of the fire. It was a hot, hazy sleep filled with dreams of Katarina, her knees parting for him, her eyes half-lidded with passion as she reached for him.

A touch on his shoulder ripped him from his slumber with a jutting erection. He sprang to his feet, sword drawn.

Bran leapt backward, hands out. "My lord, I am sorry!"

"Jésu, Bran," he muttered, resheathing his blade with a shove. "How many times have I told you, do not *do* that."

He unbuckled his sword belt and threw it on the bed, then plunged his cupped hands into the stone cistern.

Over the fire, a bucket of water warmed, and he washed with it, dressing as Bran reported on the nighttime developments.

"…fully stocked, so we can do a late slaughtering, and Tancred reports the Coward has gone over the accounts fully now, and while most are in arrears, there is a cellar full of wool fells that will be worth a great deal, and there are other reserves that should be…worth…some…thing…"

Bran's recitation stuttered to a halt.

Bent over the bucket, water dripping off his face and chest, Aodh looked up.

A small figure stood in the doorway, grimy hands clasped in front of an even grimier tunic.

For a moment, he stared, uncomprehending. Then a shot of satisfaction went through him. Katarina's little page.

Bran glanced at Aodh as the penitent scraped his toe across the floor. Voice rough as if it hadn't been used in awhile, he muttered, "I'm to turn myself in, my lord. And…be nice."

Aodh straightened. "Upon whose orders?"

The urchin lifted his head, a derisive twist to his mouth. "My lady's, o'course, milordsir. There ain't no one else's orders I'd listen to."

"Right," he agreed slowly, then reached for a towel. "What is your name, boy?"

"Dickon."

"Richard, is it?"

"Dickon, sir."

"Very well, Dickon." Aodh began toweling off his head, then threw the towel aside and gave his head a shake. "Where have you been for the past week?"

"About," came the vague, defiant mutter.

"Mm. You've run my men a merry chase. That is difficult to do."

A faint smile touched the boy's downturned face. "They're awful big."

"So they are. I've reprimanded them on the matter several times."

The boy's gaze lifted, but not his head.

"Still, 'tis quite a feat, what you did. Commendable."

The boy paused. "Walter said he'd beat me for it, milordsir."

"Well, fortunately for you, we do not adhere to Walter's dictates."

The boy's eyes came up at that, but Aodh had dragged a tunic over his head and was unavailable for scrutiny, so he turned his regard to Bran, half a decade his senior and clearly the next rung on the ladder in Aodh's world. He took Bran's measure for a moment, then turned back to Aodh.

"What *do* you adhere to, milordsir?" he asked impertinently.

"Horses." Aodh reached for his sword belt. "I can think of several ways a man like yourself can be useful, Dickon." The boy's head lifted as if pulled by a thread. "Know you much of horses?"

"Horses, milordsir? I'm not allowed near the horses."

"Are you not?"

"I race about too much," he admitted in a low voice.

Spirit shone in Dickon's eyes, as did defiance and intelligence. He could be trouble, but once won, he would be invaluable. Aodh crouched down. "Come here, lad."

The boy tossed Bran an enigmatic look, then, dragging his feet, he came. He arrived in front of Aodh, head still hung low.

"Look at me."

He did.

"We must have out on one matter."

Guilt flashed across the boy's face. "Sir?"

"Did you bring your lady a sword?"

His head dropped so far, his chin rested on his chest. He said nothing. Aodh waited a moment, then said quietly and firmly,

"You cannot do anything of that sort, ever again."

The boy shook his downturned head. "No, sir."

"Neither bring things, nor take them away, nor put a nail in a post, without my leave. Aye?"

He nodded his chin into his chest. "Aye, sir."

"Very good, then. I'll need your pledge of loyalty. You know your lady's garrison is locked up?"

Suspicion clouded the boy's gaze and made his eyelids rise to half-mast. "Aye."

"And you know why."

"Aye." He hesitated, then added in a low voice, "I know you could do the same to me."

"Then it was brave of you to come. But I do not lock up boys."

This drew a swift, almost bitter grimace. "Thought I was a man."

"In matters of loyalty and honor, we shall proceed with you as a man. In matters of prison, you are a child. *D'accord?*"

He studied the lord suspiciously. What the hell did *dahcour* mean? "Aye, sir."

"Heed me now, Dickon, for I shall expect the same of you."

"The same, sir?"

"The garrison is loyal to her. I expect the same from you. If you are here, now, you are pledging to me. As my man."

Dickon's face paled a bit. He was used to being cuffed on the back of the head when he was noticed at all, except by her ladyship, who, almost worse, or at least more infuriatingly, treated him like a child. Which he was not. He was ten, almost eleven. Nigh on to being a man.

"I have your pledge, then?" The Irishman thrust out his hand, just as if he was nigh onto being a man.

Dickon reached out slowly, and the hard callused hand curled around his and shook so hard it rattled his teeth. He would not forget this pledge anytime soon.

"Aye, sir," he affirmed, his teeth clicking together.

Aodh met Bran's gaze over the boy's head. Bran rolled his eyes. Aodh smiled faintly, then straightened and started for the door. "Good, then, Dickon, we are joined. Come, there's something I want to show you in the stables."

The boy was already trotting at his heels. "What, sir?"

"Horses."

R/W

FROM THE TOWER WINDOW, Katarina watched Aodh walk to the stables, Dickon at his side, and her heart broke a little. Dickon appeared to be chattering happily, and Aodh rested a hand on his shoulder and bent his head to listen. Dickon's face tilted up, then he pointed, and Aodh smiled.

She was so far away, it ought not to have had the impact it did, like a blow to the belly.

Perhaps it wasn't even a smile. At this distance, it was impossible to tell for certain. But she had seen Aodh smile often enough, knew its effect on her, and saw the same now in Dickon; his step became more buoyant, the sway of his shoulders looser.

Water, wine, Aodh.

She swallowed and looked away, not wanting to see how happy Dickon looked, walking beside Aodh.

Not wanting to face how much she wanted to be the one walking at his side.

ROGUE WARRIORS

CHAPTER 27

AODH CROUCHED IN the stables the next afternoon, on his heels in front of his favorite horse, running his cupped hands down the gelding's fetlock, murmuring.

St. George had stumbled on the ride back from town yesterday and had been stabled since, his leg wrapped in linens and cooling ointments. The fiery charger was not happy about it.

Around Aodh's feet were several sacks and pouches, retrieved out of chests temporarily stored in the stables until better housing was found for them. They contained the lesser items: less needed, less valuable, less likely to rot in moisture.

But while what lay inside was not vital to winning a war, it might help win a lady.

The sacks resembled the ones that held George's horse bread, and the gelding was snuffling around Aodh's boots, trying to nose his way inside one.

"Not for you." He gently nudged the horse's muzzle out of the way. George snorted impatiently and tossed his head. "I know, you did nothing wrong, yet you are being punished."

Placated, George blew out a breath and nuzzled down Aodh's back, to the waistband of his hose, which he proceeded to nibble on lightly.

"I have never once stored a treat down there," Aodh murmured, feeling slowly around the knee. No swelling.

"Aodh."

He looked over his shoulder. Ré stood in the doorway.

Bright, slanting afternoon sunlight lit the bailey.

He got to his feet, immediately alert. "What is it?"

"You have a visitor. Bermingham."

"The baron? Is here?"

Ré nodded. "It appears he decided not to wait for your response to his written message."

Aodh scooped up the pouches at his feet and came out of the stall, tossing all the satchels but one back into the chests stacked by the wall. "Katy does not think it is wise to ally with him."

"Does she not?" Ré's voice was tight.

"Think what you will, Ré, she knows the people and lands."

"I think she is trouble."

"Only if we do not win her."

"Bermingham has a hundred men at his command."

Aodh pursed his lips, then gave George a final pat. "Well, then, let us see what he has to say."

"I know what he has to say," Ré said as they turned for the door.

"What?"

"He wants his wife back."

Aodh stopped short. "Wife?" He thought a moment. "Do we have his wife?"

Ré nodded grimly. "Turns out we do. Cormac's girl. The one we thought too fine to be a maidservant? She is too fine. She's a baroness. And Katarina has been hiding her. For two years."

R/W

KATARINA LEANED over the map Aodh had brought up, tracing the outlines of Bohemia in the sunlight pouring through the high window, thinking of how little she knew of Marco Polo's travels, and how she must ask Aodh what he knew, when a key sounded in the lock.

She looked up. Aodh pushed the door wide. Tiny and rose-petal light, the vibration of a stringed instrument drifted in.

Aodh did not come into the room, just leaned his shoulder against the frame of the door and looked in at her.

Uneasiness crept down her spine. "What is it?"

"Iron Piers Bermingham has come for a visit."

She gasped.

"What do you think he wants?"

"*Susanna.*"

She flew to him. Curse the man, Bermingham, coming here, now. No doubt back from whatever campaign he and his awful, criminal brothers had launched on the borders of whatever unfortunate town or tavern had drawn their attention. He'd been gone for six months, and practically leaking beer and incomprehensible—and uninterested in his wife—for the twelvemonth prior to that.

But it seemed dear, sweet, vulnerable Susanna was, in the end, worth something to him. And now he had come for her.

"No, Aodh," she pleaded, her face flushed. "You cannot send her back."

"Why not?"

"He is cruel and brutal. She will not last a week."

"She is his."

She touched his tunic, felt the power of his chest beneath. "Aodh, please, you do not know Baron Athelrye."

"I know him some."

"Then you know what sort of man he is."

"She is his." The repetition was ominous.

"No. Aodh, no." She tightened her fingers on his tunic. "She divorced him, under Brehon law. She was wed to him for a year, then divorced him. Per the law."

His gaze fell to her hand on his tunic, then tracked back up. "That is not English law. Nor Catholic. He claims those rights."

"Aodh." Her voice was so low, even she could hardly hear it.

Laughter from soldiers on the battlement walls drifted in the window, a cheerful backdrop to their deadly serious conversation. "He would make Rardove a good ally. She would be a good peace offering."

"Aodh, please, you cannot. He is changeable... unpredictable. Violent."

"Then you chose a bad man to make an enemy of."

Her face hardened. "It was no choice."

For a moment, she knew her cause was lost, that Susanna would be sent back to the monster, and—

"Give me a reason."

She breathed in a gasp of hope. "What would you have of me?"

He watched her a moment more, then rolled his shoulder off the door frame and strode off without a word.

She stood at the window for an hour, hoping for some sign, some sound of horses or sight of riders, perhaps gunfire, if Aodh was sending Bermingham off and the man did not wish to go.

But why would Aodh risk such a thing, not only for her, but for a woman whom he did not know, a woman Katarina had visited and found bleeding and broken one afternoon two years back? She'd brought Susanna home with her, set her up in the household as a maidservant, to disguise the fact that she'd helped a noblewoman escape from her noble, awful husband.

Not even Walter had known who she was; he assumed she was another wandering waif Katarina had latched on to, like Dickon, like the itinerant priests who had visited Rardove and begun all this madness of "treason," to the half-dozen other waifs and misfits who'd found a home at Rardove.

But eventually, even Bermingham's drink-sodden brain had put it together, and he'd demanded Susanna's return. Twice. But each time, he grew distracted by drink or whoring or whatever else the man did, and had let it go.

The arrangement suited Susanna perfectly well. Her father might have been the Crown's man in the north of Ireland, meting out justice and collecting its proceeds, but her mother had been sweet and entirely unsuited for a life of greatness. Neither was Susanna.

She was more than happy to serve Katarina, to have a friend. To not be beaten daily, or whatever her accursed, violent husband saw fit to do to her when he returned home from the bawdy houses or raids.

But none of this should matter to a marcher lord, because in the end, Bermingham had a large fortune as a result of those raids, and many men to ride with him when he was in the mood for mischief. Many men to bring to a fight against the Queen of England, whom he'd always served with the thinnest thread of loyalty.

So now, Aodh had a choice. A simple one, if he sought an ally. Return to Bermingham what was rightfully his.

She paced and paced, biting her nails to stubs.

Late afternoon sunlight was pouring through the window by the time he returned.

Again, the twist of a lock. Again the low squeal of iron hinges slowly rusting, turning, then the door swung open.

Aodh stood in its opening. Backlit by the warm glow of oil lamps in the landing, he was a dark silhouette.

Beside him stood Susanna.

ROGUE WARRIORS

CHAPTER 28

SHE GAVE A CRY of happiness and rushed forward, wrapping Katarina in a warm, tearful embrace.

Katarina hugged her back, her eyes filling with tears, so that she had to bend her head to hide them.

"Bermingham came, my lady, as we knew he would, one day," Susanna said as they hugged each other. "He came, and his lordship sent him away."

"Did he?" She trusted nothing else to leave her lips, or she might weep.

"That he did. And Cormac. Oh, Cormac was quite wonderful." The warmth in Susanna's voice brought Katarina's head up.

"Cormac, the drinker?" she said, surprised.

"Oh, no more than you, my lady," Susanna assured her happily, her cheeks flushed, her round face aglow in a smile. "He is quite fine."

Katarina smiled. "Sooth?"

Susanna squeezed her hand again. "Very true." Then, tightening her squeeze, she whispered fiercely, "Thank you."

"I did nothing. Do not thank me."

Susanna leaned closer. "I have already thanked your master, and I shall again, and again, and again, until the day I die."

Neither of them looked at the object of their conversation, who sat sprawled back in the chair, watching them with steel-blue eyes under dark brows, like some pagan king overseeing his subjects at revel.

Susanna squeezed Katarina's hand again. "It is *good* to see you, and to see you looking so well."

She smiled in surprise. "Do I look well?"

"Very well, my lady," Susanna said firmly, then, adding in a mischievous whisper, "One would almost think being locked up in a tower suits you."

She left soon after, and when the door shut, Katarina tipped her face up to the ceiling and blew out a breath. Then she turned to him.

"Thank you." There was nothing else to say, but the words were horridly inadequate.

He bent his head in a nod.

"What happened? How did he take it, Bermingham?"

"Does it matter?"

She paused, then shook her head. "No. It does not. So, now, Aodh, what would you have of me?"

"The same thing I have ever wanted. It has not changed."

"Oh, I don't know." She came a step closer. "You have wanted a number of things from me. You want me to marry you, and to commit treason, and to swive you."

A smile broke the dark intent of his face. "*I* swive *you*, lass."

She waved her hand. "I am certain I could swive you too. However it is meant to work."

The smile faded. "I can show you."

She took another step toward him. "I suppose you gave up a great deal, to keep Susanna here with us."

"I gave up nothing. That man is a calamity."

"You gave up something. For me."

"Did it make you happy?"

"Deeply."

"So come and make me happy." He held up his hand. "I have something for you."

She drew up in front of him.

"Give me your hand."

He was still reclined in the chair, but everything about him spoke of vitality and movement. Even the dark inked lines on his neck and arms seemed to move in the sunlight with each subtle shift of his body.

Slowly, she held out her hand. He dropped something into it and folded her fingers around it.

She opened them and stared down at the strange gift. It was a fat three dimensional glass object, crystal clear.

"What is this?"

"A prism."

The stone was heavy in her hand. "And what is that?"

"I will show you." He got to his feet and moved across the room. He shuttered the window, plunging the room into darkness, then arranged coverings until only a single beam of sunlight rayed into the chamber.

She watched, bemused. "What are you doing?"

"Patience, lass."

He dug around in one of the chests and extracted a piece of parchment and held it vertically behind the prism, at a slight angle. Holding the stone up into the light, he let the single ray of sun through it. It emerged on the paper as a prism of color, a rainbow projected onto the parchment.

"Oh," she said, enchanted.

He made a gesture, beckoning her, and she reached out with her thumb and index finger and very carefully took it from him. "Hold it there," he ordered. He backed up with the parchment, and took another, curving glass stone, cut slightly different, and lowered it down, passing it, too, through the beam of sunlight. The rainbow stayed projected on the parchment. Then he slowly pulled the parchment back further.

The rainbow became a single beam of white light again.

"What did you do?" she said at once. "What happened?"

He shook his head. "I don't know." He pulled the paper back further, and the rainbow slowly reappeared, the colors now blurring up the page in the opposite order.

Her eyes widened, and she looked up to smile at him in astonishment, then returned to watching the show he'd given her. "It almost makes one think the colors are...*within* the light."

His gaze flew to hers. "Aye," he said, a low hum of agreement.

"But that cannot be," she said, although not in a rejecting way. In a…hopeful way.

"Anything can be, Katy." He ran his hand through the beams of light, and they fluttered in bands of color across his hard fingers. "Go on, touch it," he urged softly.

She bent and put her face into the rainbow streams of light.

Her nose became streaked with red and orange and yellow. She moved slightly, and it turned violet, blue, the slightest sliver of green. Her eyes came up to his, and the light shafts sprayed across her face, across her eye in red and gold, like a pathway leading in.

He lowered the second prism and came to her, folded her fingers around the stone and brought her fisted hand to his lips. He kissed her knuckles. It was nothing but skin and bone, but it felt as if he'd broken her open.

"Why are you giving me this?"

"Because it makes me think of you."

"Aodh," she whispered. "Please, stop."

"No," he murmured. He knew precisely what he was denying her; as if to prove it, he turned her hand over and kissed her inner wrist.

She shivered. "Why are you trying to win me, Aodh? Why does it matter so much?"

His hand slid to her waist. "My intent is not to win you."

She stared up into eyes so blue it almost hurt to look into them. Blue like the sea, blue like blood under the skin. "Then what?"

"You are a fire that was almost extinguished, Katarina. And I need your flame."

"Oh, Aodh."

He tugged on their entwined fingers, guiding her forward as he backed up, leading her to the bed.

"This thing you want of me, it almost ruined me. It destroyed my parents. I do not care if you need my fire; I do not need it," she said in a desperate whisper, hoping he would save her from herself, because she was swiftly losing the fight.

He showed no mercy, just kept backing up, leading her

forward like a wild creature, coaxing her to the secret truth of them: passion bound them in a fated way.

She shook her head even as she came to him. "I have spent my entire life trying to suppress that which you desire, Aodh."

"I know," he said, and dropped onto the bed, pulling her down with him. "I cannot let you do that."

She lowered herself to straddle him, one hand twined in his, her other still closed around the prism.

He released her hand and began unlacing the crisscrossing ribbons that ran up the sides of her tunic. He swept the gown up over her head, so she was clad only in her chemise.

"This is wrong," she whispered.

"I do not care. I care only if it pleases you." He tipped forward and touched his tongue to her breast, still covered by the soft linen. Her nipples peaked to gemstone hardness. His gaze swept up.

"Tell me, Katy, does that please you?"

A ragged cry broke from her lips.

He moved his mouth to her other breast, graced it with another hard stroke of his tongue through the thin linen shift. She curled her fingers into his hair.

"We are doomed if we do this thing."

"Surrender to it."

"Then I would lose everything. Everything I am, everything I have, would be lost."

"Maybe that is the very thing you need." He lifted the chemise.

"Then I would have nothing."

"You would have me."

She gave a broken sob. "Don't you see, you will *destroy* me?"

His hands stilled. "I vow it, I will not. Your heart knows."

"What does my heart know?"

"Look where it has brought you. To me. Again."

He was right. She was wrecked. "You will ruin me."

"Get up, then, Katy. Get up and walk away." His body was taut with restraint. "I'll not stop you."

Her thighs trembled from holding herself up above his lap. "I am locked in."

"The door is not locked."

"The castle is."

"I'll have you on a ship, to anywhere you wish. Just walk away."

"You would...let me leave?"

"You must leave, Katy. You are mine, or you are gone. There is no other way." His gaze was like a cord, a tether. She felt bonded to him by a single, shivering strand of sight.

"I do not want to leave," she whispered.

"Good. Then let us begin."

Begin. How like him, to word it so. Everything about him felt like the edge of the cliff. Irrevocable, life-changing.

He cupped her face and claimed her with a kiss.

It was an open-mouthed, unforgiving, conquest of a kiss, his hands holding her face, pulling her down to him. She returned it with full ardor, their tongues tangling. They paused only when he leaned her back with a muttered instruction, so he could sweep the chemise up over her head and fling it away. Then she was naked before him.

He made a dark sound of approval. Cool air washed over her breasts and no matter that she'd been bared to him once before, the urge to hide was the strongest thing in her. It came to the fore, and she began to cover herself.

"No, Katy. I want to see you."

He took her wrists and gently lifted them, parting her arms, holding them up in the air, stretched out wide, so he could stare at her body.

The breath burst from her. She closed her eyes, unable to withstand the force of desire she saw in him. For she knew it was in her too.

"I'm going to take you now."

Threat, promise, warning, it was all those things, and her body felt as it he'd strung her up on bolts of lightning.

"Hard and deep."

Her wrists hung in his hands as he leaned forward and flicked his tongue across her breast.

"I'm not going to stop."

He grazed her nipple with his teeth. Her head fell forward with a broken gasp.

"Until you're laid out, tossing your head and crying my name." His gaze swept up. "Then I'm going to take you harder."

Breath, blood, fire: in the end, she was a simple thing. Aodh had reduced her to her most elemental form.

She lifted her head slowly, inch by inch, as if dragging it through honey. "I cannot marry you, Aodh."

"To be honest, Katy, I'm not thinking of marriage just now."

The words poked a hole through the mounting tension, and she laughed. And trembled, now frightened beyond measure, far more than when the castle had been taken. A castle was stone and wood; it was meant to be captured. But Aodh had conquered her.

She'd thought herself insurmountable. A cold mountaintop. Oh, but he'd summited her with hot kisses and cold insights. It was enough that he saw her, truly saw her, even unto what had happened with the swords. Because she had so *clearly* wanted to fight, and he had seen that, and honored it—given her her fight—when no one else would.

He'd given her a map of the world.

He'd given her a prism of light.

Aodh even knew enough to lock her away, for it was her freedom she prized above all else. And he'd unleashed passions she'd never known were inside her.

He knew precisely where to aim, saw every chink in her armor.

Oh, he was a formidable enemy. But he would be an even more dangerous ally. More exciting. More inspiring. More...everything.

"Just give me a chance," he rasped.

"I will give you more than that," she whispered, surrendering to it. To him.

At once, he slid his hand between their bodies, and began to unlace his breeches. Her hands followed after, greedy to feel the hard thrust of him. If she was going to do this thing, she was going to do it with all her heart. All her body. Give everything she could short of treason, and take everything Aodh would allow.

With a muted curse he put his hands on hers, stopping her. He slid off the bed and stood, swiftly freeing himself of garments: kicked off his boots, tore off hose, tunic, breeches in swift sweeps, until he stood naked before her.

She felt blown back by the force of his hard, male beauty.

The entire left side of him was marked, down past his waist, just as she'd wondered. *Hoped.*

The inked lines roped from the back of his skull to the column of his neck, over his powerful shoulder and down his back and chest. They swirled like spells down his flat, ribbed stomach, over his hips, down the hard muscles of his thigh, through the hair of his shin and calf, all the way to his toe.

And rising up from the center of his magnificent, ensorcelled body, jutting out from the dark thatch of hair between his thighs, was a bold, thick erection, curving back almost to his belly.

Unthinking, knowing only that she needed to touch him, she began to drop to her knees, reaching for him.

He swept her back to her feet. "That is not a good idea just now, Katy." His voice was a taut scrape.

He pulled her to the bed, laid her down on it, and knelt between her thighs, his face taut and rigid. "I'll go slow," he said, at odds with the rampant energy she knew was roiling through him.

"Just don't stop."

He propped himself on a palm, leaned to the side, and reached between their bodies. His painted hand grasped his erection. She was breathless at the erotic sight, wanted nothing but to watch his hand curl around himself, but there was no time, for he settled between her legs. The hard, silken head of him bumped into her folds and with a little shove, he breached her, pushed up inside the barest inch.

She froze, her lips rounded around a hard, silent gasp.

He pulled his hips back and brought them forward, sank in a

little further. Her head flung back, jerked by whipcord lashes of arousal. His eyes flew to hers.

"Aye?" Ragged, whispered, it was barely a word.

"Oh, *aye*."

His chest moved in rapid breaths; he was breathing as fast as she. Which meant his head must be spinning as hard as hers, his heart must be thudding with the same frenzied beat.

Never looking away, he repositioned himself, propped up on his palms and stretched out above her. Then he rocked his hips forward. It was an unstoppable thrust, slow mayhap, but very hard, very deep. Very much intending to take her fully.

Her body spread for him, sensitive inner flesh trembling as he stroked into her.

He pulled out and sank in again, a slow, carnal possession. Beautifully slow, painfully slow. The muscles in his arms were tautly defined as he held himself up and rocked again. A shudder took his body. His head tipped back, his eyes shut, the muscles in his neck stretched taut as he plunged into her yet again, harder this time, going in deeper.

It was a viciously gentle breach of her defenses.

Katarina had been prepared for a crushing sensual assault, expected him to storm her gates with fire, after such a long siege. Aodh was vigor and endless movement, a roiling storm cloud; she'd known that to be taken by him, meant to be taken entirely.

But this slow subjugation, this gentle rout of her body, was like being set on fire with a long fuse. It was cruel, vicious, unkind. Perfect.

As if she were the land and he her sky, he stretched out over her, and she laid herself out for him more with each thrust, until her arms curled helplessly above her head. Her hips rose to meet each controlled penetration, her head tipped up to receive every kiss he saw fit to plant on her mouth. Inside her, a hot bank of pressure built. She felt like a storm about to break.

His eyes were so dark, so dilated with desire, she could disappear into them, as if into night, and never be seen again. In this moment, she wanted just that, to disappear from the world, and never be seen by anyone but Aodh.

"Ready, lass?"

Bands of excitement coiled around her. She nodded.

He shoved his hips forward in a deep, fierce thrust, shocking her with the suddenness, and the pleasure to be had from the hard, fierce *taking* of it. She wanted to be taken by this man, hard and long, until she wept from it.

Then he stopped, as if he hadn't meant to do it so forcefully.

But she had *loved* the force of him.

"Please, Aodh." She curled her hands around his hips.

"You like that?"

"Oh yes." She pulled on him, urging him on.

He set a rhythm then, matching himself to the thrust of her hips, the toss of her head, how high her back arched to him.

"Aye, Katy, take more of me," he commanded, shoving her knee wide to the side.

The powerful arms on either side of her head shook as she lifted her hips, opening for him. He dropped to his elbows, laid his mouth on her neck, and took her hard. His hips rolled between her thighs in fierce, hard thrusts. Their bodies grew sweaty, slicked together, then slid apart. He pushed her legs apart farther until she was splayed out for him, sprawled, her head tossing. She could do nothing but whatever Aodh bid.

His mouth plowed her open, tasted her, then left her gasping when he tore away and moved to her ear, then her neck, then her breasts. Everything he touched felt as though it sparkled. She held her breasts up for his suckling, tangled her fingers in his hair to move his head where she wanted to feel his caress next. She nipped his neck, his shoulders, let him do things she had never dreamed of, and reveled in it. He was a wave she was riding, powerful and unstoppable.

It was untended and untamed.

It was magnificent.

She closed her eyes to better focus on the sensations running rampant through her body, the scalding pleasure brought by Aodh's possession of her. Her hips began to thrust up more frantically, her head to toss more unevenly. Her gasps kept breaking off mid-cry, as each new twist of pleasure coiled through her.

Hard and fast now, their union ascended. Pleasure built in dizzying sweeps. She was cold and desperately hot. He slid his hand down under her body, cupped her bottom and lifted, holding her up and shifting their angle. A bolt of pleasure snaked through her.

He surged into her again, then again, and again, until the pleasure was intolerable, so intense it scorched. Her back arched, her breath arrested, poised at the edge of a precipice.

He bent to her ear. "You see, there is nothing we cannot do, Katy, you and I. Whatever you want, we will be."

"*Oh.*"

"You are mine."

Her head whipped back, her body jerked from within, then she exploded. "Yours."

The climax picked her up and tossed her. Helpless in the smashing, churning pleasure, she could do nothing but fling her head, rock her body, and cry Aodh's name, just as he'd promised. He roared his completion then too, and the flood of male heat that surged through her coaxed her body to summit on another wave of pleasure.

They continued to move against each other until the last vestiges of climax were spent. Then he dragged himself off her and drew her to lay beside him.

She sprawled, stunned, her hips still rocking forward, as if a dream of arousal clung to her. He dragged her knee up onto his stomach to let her move against him, curled his hand under the sweaty length of her hair, and lifted it up, so cool air could brush over it.

She whispered her thanks, planted a messy kiss on his jaw, and her head fell back to the bed. Almost before it hit the sheets, they were asleep, sweaty limbs entwined, carnal lusts sated, for the moment, their minds protected from what this all meant. But of course it meant something.

It meant she was his.

Rardove was, in every way now, in the hands of a rebel.

Rogue Warriors

Chapter 29

SHE WAS AWAKENED by the feel of his hand lightly stroking up her naked back, under the covers. The furs were warm, the fire was burning—he must have made it up, because it crackled and popped with fresh fuel. The furs were silky across her body.

His hand slid up between her shoulder blades, and, still half in sleep, she stretched into his touch and pushed her leg out, long under the covers.

Aodh's hand, warm and hard, tugged her knee up over his stomach. She curled into him like a cat.

Then he dragged her entirely onto his body, pushed his knee between hers, parting them, and with a swift, confident lift of his hips, thrust up inside her with a slippery, pressured push.

"*Oh*," she breathed, still half in sleep.

"G'morning," he whispered by her ear.

"Is it morning?" She tried to straighten.

"'Tis after midnight."

"Morning," she agreed dazedly, pushing up on her elbows. She shoved the hair back from her forehead and looked into the eyes so close to hers. The sharp angles of his warrior's face, hardened by the world, were softened now, partly by a morning covering of facial hair on his cheeks, but mostly by the heated passion in his eye.

"I dreamed of you," she whispered.

"And I, you," he said quietly, but the resonate rumble sounded loud in the firelit room. He lifted his hips, pushed in a little deeper.

"Is this a dream?" she whispered.

"Aye."

She bent her head and touched her lips to his. "It feels very real."

"Does it feel very good?"

She tipped her head to the side. "I suppose it will do."

He brushed the sweaty hair back from her cheeks and temples. "What of this?" Another lift of his hips, sinking him in deeper. Bright ripples snaked through her body.

"I think I like that."

"Then rise up, and let me take you."

Addled by pleasure, by this sudden erotic awakening, she pushed to sit up on him. He curled his hands around her hips and as she shifted, he slipped in deeper.

His hands brought her hips forward in a hard pull. "Take more of me," he ordered roughly, and his thighs flexed as he lifted his hips and buried himself inside her.

She loved his rough words, how he demanded things that were so erotic, so dangerous, so perfectly matched to what she wished to give.

She rocked her hips, just a little, by herself. He leaned back, his hands now almost motionless, and let her set the pace. The depth. The rhythm.

At first she moved slowly, leaning over him, hands on his shoulders, her hair swaying beside them. Each measured movement forced him in a little deeper. Her knees slid out, and she began to move faster, their breaths pushed by the rhythm of her rocking.

His hands curled tighter around her hips, and he began moving her too, slowly increasing their tempo, harder, faster.

Bands of pleasure tightened around her: her breasts, her legs, the slippery swollen flesh Aodh was taking possession of. It was splendid torment. She leaned lower, her breasts before his face, and as he suckled them, his hips came up in a long, hard thrust. A shivery pulse of heretofore unknown pleasure snapped up her back like a whip.

Her head jerked back and she cried out, then dropped her

head down, heavy with passion, and locked her gaze on his.

"Oh, *Aodh*." It was a hot exhale of pleasure.

"Aye, *bahn sidhe*, we'll do that one again." And he did, lifted his hips just as he had done before, gripped her hip just as he had done before, and the long, hot cord of pleasure came for her again, lashing her with wicked force.

Her body bucked. Following the sensations, she let her hands fall off his shoulders and sat up straight.

He lay back on the bed and watched her, his gaze raking down her body.

She felt unleashed. To be so bared before him, to move for him so, to have him approve of it all, approve of her, she felt as if she'd been cast in liquid gold. Hot, glowing. Each lift of his hips forced the thick thrust of him in deeper, made her spread a little wider to take him. There was no retreat from this possession. She wanted no retreat. She wanted only to follow the whipcord slashes of pleasure that were slowly deepening to gold-hot undulations down her back and up her legs, and deep, deep inside her.

Aodh kept his hand on her hip, kept moving her, ensured she was dragged under the sea of pleasure. The pulses expanded, until she could do nothing but rock on him like some wanton, her shoulders back, her face up to the ceiling, her hair trailing down her spine, brushing over his thighs, like some mad, magnificent dream.

He pushed up on his elbows. "Aye, rise up, arch your back." His words were like gunpowder, exploding her. "This is what I want from you, Katy. I am not afraid of you."

She had a sudden, blinding flash of insight. She well knew the true danger of woman to a man was passion. She knew men's desire for it, and their disdain for it. Their condescension to it.

But mayhap...mayhap they were *afraid* of it.

All this time, afraid...? Afraid she would do something. *Be* something. Something stronger than they.

The certainty of it stunned her. It was as if a flame had suddenly been lit in a dark room, and she was right up in front of it, staring into its blinding white-hot light.

Men did not disdain her.

They were scared of her.

Aodh was not.

The shocking, earth-shifting nature of the insight drove her over the edge, exploded her body. Wrecked and racked by deep undulations of pleasure, she could not nothing but cry his name, then collapse atop him, her body still shuddering, and he took her mouth, swallowed her cries of pleasure.

He took her then, carelessly lifted her up, and flung her back on the bed, pushed her legs apart with his knee and took her again.

She welcomed him, her body already broken by pleasure, a temple of their desire. He forced her to come again, weakly, almost whimpering. He drove her mad, took her over and over and over, pounded into her until he roared his own completion, and collapsed atop her, barely held up on his elbows as he breathed onto her neck.

He held himself over her until he could not anymore, then rolled away, pulling her with him, but also pulling out of her. She gave a little whimper of distress, but there was nothing either could do about it now; they were too spent.

For long minutes, they lay there and breathed, while the fire cast shadows across the ceiling and walls.

Aodh felt a deep, hot hum inside him, as if he'd been filled with...music? As if a steel bar had been rung, and the reverberations were moving through him.

Katy's slender hand trailed across his chest. He watched the idle movements a moment, then said sleepily, "We'll sign today."

"Sign what." She leaned up to kiss his neck.

"The betrothal papers."

"Oh," she whispered dreamily as she ran her fingertips over his face, then snuggled into his chest. "I told you, I cannot marry you."

Christ on the Cross.

The smoke-blackened rafters were beginning to glow as

dawn light came in. "Why not?" he asked, very calmly.

"Because I cannot. It would be treason." She shifted on the bed, curled closer to him. "I hold Rardove for Elizabeth, Aodh. She is my queen." Her hand slid over his chest, lazily tracing the swirls of ink. "Of course you can see that."

More calmness. "You said you were mine."

Her tracing finger stilled, then she pushed up on an elbow. Her face was soft in the aftermath of passion, her mouth swollen from his kisses. He reached up and brushed the hair back from her face.

"You said you were mine, Katy. When I was in you, as deep as a man can be, you looked in my eyes and said you were mine."

She peered at him. "You are not the sole possessor of me, Aodh."

He forced himself to breathe slowly. "What does that mean?"

"I too possess me."

She was the most infuriating woman alive. "And so you do. But you said you were mine. I thought that meant…"

She straightened a little more. "I am not responsible for your thoughts. I am, indeed *yours* in…in that way." Her face flushed a delicate color. "That does not mean I am not also my own. And I am not marrying you."

She did this to him every time, tore him in half. He wanted more from her than she would give.

"Go to sleep, lass," he said quietly.

She hesitated, watching him a moment, then lay back down. He pulled her into his side, his arm firm behind her. She sighed and kissed his neck and snuggled in. Soon, her breathing was soft and steady. She was asleep.

He slid out of the bed, threw on his clothes and boots, and left the room.

He locked the door behind him.

R⁄W

WHEN SHE AWOKE, Aodh was gone.

She lifted her hand and pushed the hair out of her face, then stretched languidly, her body warm and aching and…wonderful. Belowstairs, she could hear the sounds of the castle stirring. Today, she would join it.

Mayhap it was this, maybe some other conduit to clarity, but in the dawn, after knowing Aodh as deeply as she had, in every way, she knew now exactly what she needed to do: send a message to the queen.

But not the message she'd been intending to send. Not one alerting the queen to a rebel presence, nor a message informing her how best to launch an attack.

A message to inform the Queen of England why Aodh Mac Con was precisely what their marchlands needed.

She would throw herself on the queen's mercy if need be. Surely Elizabeth would understand, could be made to see reason. She always had before, every time Katarina had written on matters of Ireland.

She plied her fingers through her hair, combing it, feeling each muscle stretch itself in a new way. On one particularly languid stretch, through a gap in the canopy that hung on all sides of the great bed, she caught sight of the oak door, and saw it was shut tight.

A small note of discomfort rang.

But why? So a door was shut. Drafts ran rampant. Yet…why was her heart suddenly beating faster?

Pushing back the covers, she got up and padded to the door, and turned the knob.

It wouldn't turn. It was locked.

She was locked in.

Aodh had locked her in.

Fury burst from her like a dam crashing under the pressure of too much force. She hammered on the door, beat on it like an impotent, caged beast, her hands fisted, her feet kicking, shouting as loud as she could, "Aodh, *you bastard!*"

Her shouts bounced around the stone walls of the room. She battered senselessly and uselessly at the door until, finally exhausted, admitting defeat, she slumped against it, leaning on a shoulder, breathing heavily. It had been growing for three hundred years before it had been turned into a door. Banging at it with her fists or her shoulders or even a battering ram was not going to accomplish anything.

Time to be clever, for being stubborn had got her nothing at all.

Just as Aodh had predicted.

R⁄W

DOWN IN THE BAILEY, Ré was escorting a local Irish prince from the stables to the hall, when shrieks broke out and could be heard wafting down from the open window of the tower room.

Startled, the Irish clansman looked around. "What in God's holy name…"

Ré hurried him along a little faster. "Singing," Ré assured him. "English song. We heard a lot of it over in England, as you can imagine. Sounds a bit like caterwauling, doesn't it?

"Sounds like a *bahn sidhe*," the Irishman said with a shiver. "In full regalia."

"You've no idea."

Aodh appeared at the castle door, and they quickened their pace.

Rogue Warriors

Chapter 30

Up in the tower, Katarina copied out two messages. That was the minimum, in case one was captured, the messenger drowned in a river, or some other all too common misfortune.

Hand shaking, she stuffed them under the pelt beside the fire, then went to the door and rapped softly.

The guard outside her room—there'd been one ever since the sword incident—opened the door. It was Bran. She brightened, but his face was sober. She issued an invitation for Aodh to come visit her that night.

"And send up whisky," she added offhandedly. "There are barrels of very good stuff in the cellar, in the farthest chamber, on the northern side. Mind your head; the lintel is low."

Bran seemed clearly torn between a desire to do as she bid, and great, abiding suspicion. "Whisky?" he repeated.

She nodded.

"Barrels of them?"

"Dozens. Pull from the barrel nearest the back. It is an oak barrel with the image of a clamshell burned into it."

"A clamshell," he repeated, stretching it out, the words filled with confusion and growing suspicion. Understandable. After all, she was locked in the tower. There had been sword-fighting. "Do you *drink* whisky, my lady?" he asked hesitantly.

"Upon occasion."

He blinked. "I did not know."

"Now you do."

"Yes, my lady."

She blew out an impatient breath. "Or have Aodh bring his own if he prefers, to ensure I can't put a dropper of henbane in it. It is all the same to me. Honestly," she said, turning back to the tower, "if I'd wanted to kill him, I have had a thousand chances thus far."

R℞
W

"AND I AM TO BRING...whisky?"

Aodh repeated the message slowly, in case something had been misunderstood.

He's spent the day in council with too many lords to count, and it was certainly possible that he was simply suspicious of everything. But something about this seemed...very suspicious.

Bran nodded. "That is what Lady Katarina said, sir. You're to bring it yourself, to make sure she does not poison it."

He sat back. "She said that?"

"Aye, sir."

"That she's thinking of poisoning me?"

Bran looked horrified. "No, sir! She suggested it to allay any concerns, you see, so you would know she *hadn't*."

"And were there concerns?"

Bran shuffled uncomfortably. "I might have asked a few questions about her request. Caused her to think I was suspicious."

"And were you?"

"Well...it is unusual, sir. I mean...whisky. In barrels. In the cellar."

"Why did we not know of them?"

Bran looked shamefaced. "I saw the barrels, sir. I thought they were wine."

Aodh nodded thoughtfully. "But they are whisky."

Bran started to smile.

Oak barrels of whisky, in the cellars of Rardove.

His men would bow down at her feet.

"But," his squire went on, "she said not to worry, that she

could have slayed you a dozen times already before now."

Aodh's head came up swiftly.

"If 'twas truly her goal. I suppose that means it is not her goal?" Bran framed it as a hopeful possibility.

Aodh turned and looked though the open window at the sunset, reddish gold and stretched to the edge of the world. "Do not fear, Bran, her danger is not of that sort, even if we do have to keep her locked in a tower to prevent her from ruining the plans of a lifetime."

"Yes, sir."

Aodh got to his feet. "Send for the whisky. Take it from the barrel with the clamshell mark."

He picked up two glasses and went upstairs.

Rogue Warriors

CHAPTER 31

THE ROOM WAS lit with candles, and a fire burned bright. She'd pulled the windows shut and shuttered them, so the room was warm, rolling in shadow and flickering, amber firelight.

"I thought I was a bastard," Aodh said as he stepped into the room. "As did everyone within three miles of the castle."

She cleared her throat delicately. "I may have overstated the matter." Then she peered pointedly over his shoulder at Bran.

Aodh followed her gaze, tipped his head and sent Bran on his way.

She stepped away from the door and drifted into the room. He followed and set the cups on the table. A moment later, a knock came, and a small pitcher was brought in.

Katarina smiled at her servant, Agatha, who seemed bursting with happiness to see her. She bobbed a curtsey, then brought the whisky over. "It is *excellent*, my lady." Agatha lowered her voice a bit. "I tasted it to be sure."

Katarina smiled her thanks. Agatha set it on the table with a bow, nodded to Aodh, and backed out. The door shut.

Aodh watched Katarina pour the drink into his glasses. She handed him one and said companionably, "I saw a messenger with Cunningham's livery arrive this morning."

He blew out a sigh and sat back with the drink. "Aye. He'll join us if the others do. Same old story."

"They are not so bold as you," was her encouraging reply. "It is a matter of vision." And she took a dainty sip of the whisky.

He took a swallow too, then pushed to the edge of his chair and crooked a finger beneath her chin, pulled her closer until their noses almost touched.

"What are you up to, lass?"

"Nothing," she whispered.

His gaze fell to the drink in her hand, then he curled his fingers around hers, made her lift the cup and drink it down.

She shuddered faintly as the heat moved down her throat, into her belly like fire. "Well," she said softly, "shall I get us another?"

His lips brushed hers, his tongue sliding into her whisky-soaked mouth, then he pulled back. "Aye."

Drugged not from the drink but from Aodh's careless kiss, hot and muddleheaded, she poured them two more.

"Come sit on my lap," he said, reaching for her.

She tumbled down onto his thighs, his arm curved around her back. She leaned close and said, "I'm glad you came up."

His gaze dropped to her mouth. "I've no idea why. Although I see you've developed a strange and sudden affection for whisky."

She shifted on his lap. "This is Rardove whisky. Do you like it?"

"'Tis quite fine."

"Indeed it is. It produced more income than the wool last year," she said proudly, then lifted her glass. "To Rardove whisky." She drank and smiled at him.

He sniffed his cup with an excess of suspicion. "I thought you didn't drink the stuff."

"I do not. Usually. But that does not mean I am unable to." Or that she couldn't hold her own when asked to. Indeed, it was one of her hidden talents: she could drink anything, in great quantities, with almost no effect.

He hesitated, then sipped.

"Oh, don't be scared of it, Aodh," she teased.

"You think I'm scared of whisky?" He sounded indignant.

She shook her head. "No. I think you're scared of me."

He lifted his glass. "To Rardove women. They're a frightening bunch."

She drank too, then splashed more whisky into their cups. "What shall we toast to next?"

"Why are you trying to get me addled on the drink?" He broke gaze and took a slow visual sweep of the room, as if looking for clues.

Her heartbeat sped up. "Maybe I am not trying to get you addled. Maybe I am trying to get myself addled."

He finished his perusal of the room. "To what end?"

She frowned. "Must I have an end?"

"You mustn't...but you *do*." But he seemed to be growing distracted. It was evident in his gaze, the way it kept drifting to her mouth. In the hard thrust of manhood pushing against her hip.

She smiled at him, then her focus drifted to the beautiful inkmarks visible above the collar of his tunic. "Aodh?"

He stretched out a leg, which shifted how she sat on him, and as she lolled on his lap, he said, "What?" very, very warily.

"Did it hurt? When they painted you."

He hesitated. "Aye."

"Are they Rardove dyes?"

"The legend dyes? That they are."

"So it is not a legend."

His eyes met hers. "Do you want to see them again, lass?"

"Oh, yes," she breathed.

Aodh watched her a moment, certain she was up to some mischief, but it hardly mattered; she was sitting in his lap, breathing unevenly with desire. For the time being, at least, she was entirely his.

He leaned forward, bent his elbows, and dragged the tunic over his head.

Her gaze traveled greedily over his arms, his chest, her eyes growing heavy-lidded with desire.

Then she reached out and ran her fingertips down the inked lines. He held his breath, holding himself in check as she trailed down his arm, to the bend of his elbow, then made the small but important leap to his stomach. And then down, to the band of his breeches.

Swiftly, she unlaced him, and he let her, did nothing but say, "Let down your hair."

She did, watching him as the hair spilled over her shoulders, then together they tugged off his hose. But when he put out a hand to draw her back into his lap, instead of taking it, she dropped to her knees between his legs.

He closed his eyes and said a silent prayer of thanks.

He would have to ensure this woman drank whisky every day.

She settled in, her palms resting atop his thighs, and stared at his body, her brow now furrowed, her fingertips trailing lightly over his chest. "Why did they do this to you?" she asked softly.

"To mark me."

"As what?"

"A savior."

She looked up. "Of what?"

"Rardove."

"Oh, Aodh." The words caught in her throat.

"I do not want to talk of Rardove," he said harshly.

"No. No, we must not."

His body almost vibrated with lust. His hair felt as if it stood on end; his blood churned. He debated, briefly, leading her to the bed, but even that much movement might blow a breath of reality on the moment and she might spark away again. In any event, he was perfectly happy to have whisky in his blood and Katy on her knees, so he sat back and let her be.

Head tipped back slightly, chin in the air, she skimmed her fingers down the length of his erection. It quivered. He hissed in a breath, and she released a little pant of desire, then tipped forward, bringing her hot mouth closer to him.

"You best be certain, Katy," he rasped.

"I am," she assured him, her words breathy, and curled her hand softly around the length of him and gave a little stroke. His hips jerked up.

She did it again, a light stroke. Her eyes, bright with excitement, lifted to his. "Like that?"

"Not quite," he said tautly. "Harder."

Her body trembled. "Show me."

He curled his hand overtop hers and made her squeeze tighter, much tighter, then moved their hands in a stroke up the length of him, a long, hard pull.

"Oh." She was all hot breath and pink cheeks. She was excited.

Katy would try *anything*. And love it, he thought with fierce, grateful affection. Her adventurous spirit was entirely unappreciated by any man but him, thank God.

He drew their entwined hands up the length of him again, faster this time, and his bollocks tightened.

"So hard," she whispered.

"Aye. Hard. That's how I like it."

A little pant broke from her as she tried it herself, moved her fist up him, a fine, hard stroke, then looked up at him.

"Is that proper?" she whispered, trembling.

He smiled. "Not a'tall, lass. 'Tis quite wicked." He moved their hands again.

"Wicked," she echoed, her lips parted in a pretty, wet pant.

"You like wicked, Katy girl?"

Passion-heavy eyes lifted to his. "I like *your* wicked."

"Then take me in your mouth. You look good. I want to feel you."

Her head tipped back helplessly. Words alone could take her to a climax, he realized now. One day, he'd set himself to the task.

She leaned over him, and took his cock into the hot, wet cave of her mouth.

Every day, the whisky.

Leaning her forearms on his thighs, she took him in, her head bobbing, her hand gripped beneath Aodh's, circling the root of his shaft. Together they pumped him in long, rhythmic strokes, up to her mouth, then down again. Then he loosed his hand and sat back, lifting his hips ever so slightly, not wanting to frighten her, but wanting very much to have deeper carnal relations with her mouth.

She let him in.

He made an inarticulate sound, something between a growl and a curse and a plea. He would marry this woman, if only she would let him.

"Can you take more, *leannán sidhe*?" he murmured, coaxing. He rested his hand lightly on the side of her head and tipped his hips up. She shifted on her knees and moved down on him, taking him in deeper, to her throat.

He descended into a vortex of lust. There was nothing but Katy's hot, wet mouth. He closed his eyes and let her manage everything, just fisted his hand gently in her hair and held on.

The end came swiftly. It crested over him in a hot, thick wave. He tightened his hand in her hair and gently pulled her up just before it burst from him. He pulled her onto his lap and took her mouth as he came, and they stroked him together through the climax.

He used a linen towel to wipe himself clean, then drew her back down onto his lap. Dazedly, she sat, and he kissed her throat, intent on the next step.

"I know what we toast to next," he said.

"I'll get the whisky," she gasped, fumbling for the cups.

Rogue Warriors

Chapter 32

IT TOOK TWO HOURS, but finally, Aodh Mac Con, son of a hard-drinking Irishman, bred on peat, passed out cold from drink.

The moment his breathing was steady and low, Katarina wrapped herself in his heavy cape and hurried out the door, her body still pulsing from all their 'toasts.'

She hurried down the stairs to Walter's chambers and scratched at the door. Cold drafts drifted along the floor like fog. The door slowly creaked open.

Walter's single strand of hair floated eerily in the drafts atop his otherwise bald head as he stared at her in amazement. "My lady!"

She hurried him backward into the room.

"Curse you, Walter, why did you tell Aodh to go see Bermingham?" was, inexplicably, the first thing she said.

Walter seemed equally surprised, but perhaps that was from being awakened out of a slumber in the dead of night. "Why, my lady," he said, all innocence, "I did but offer my opinion. But what are you doing here?" He peered at the door, then back at her. "Are you freed?"

She frowned and held out the letter. "Not at present. I need you to see this delivered. It must go to the queen, or her representative, if one is already en route to Rardove."

His bony fingers pinched the missive. "And what does it say?"

She scowled at him. "It provides directions for the army."

She left Walter and swept to the lord's chamber and peeked into the antechamber. As hoped, little Dickon was curled up on a cot. No Bran in sight.

She crouched beside him and shook him gently. He popped up, bleary-eyed and confused.

"'Tis I, Dickon."

"Oh, my lady." He scratched his head and shifted on the pallet. "What is it?"

"Dickon, I need you to get this message to the town."

He stared at the folded parchment between her fingers.

"Can you do that?"

He nodded miserably. "My lady, are you certain—"

"I swear to you, it is to help Lord Aodh." She patted his shoulder. "Be careful," she whispered.

He swallowed. "I will."

She hurried away, making her way to the barracks through the dark night. Through a barred window at the back of the building, she was able to speak to Wicker. Even touch his hand.

"Are you well?"

"They're growing tired of watching us."

"Yes, I suppose they are."

"Something will have to give soon."

"Yes, something must." Or someone.

"I guess an army's coming?" he said. It was difficult to determine from his tone how he felt about this.

"I don't know," she whispered.

"He doesn't seem a bad sort. Spent some time in here with us."

She tipped her head back, surprised. "He has?"

"Aye."

"Doing what?"

There was a small pause. "Eating."

"He has supped with you?"

"He has."

She hadn't expected that. "Well then, what do you think of our conqueror?

Another pause, a bit longer. "If he is your enemy, my lady,

then he is ours."

Oh, this was awful. Even her soldiers were turning to him. And she could not.

She reached her fingertips through, touched his, and gave a little squeeze. "Be safe, Wicker," she whispered.

"And you, too, my lady."

"Do not worry, I shall not be reckless."

"Oh, we've no problem with reckless," he said easily, his hand slipping away. "Just be *right*."

The heart of the matter, then, in that simple reply.

"I must go. Eat, keep up your strength, and Wicker? I trust Mac Con with my life. I urge you to do the same."

His wary eyes peered back at her. He was not confused by her words. He knew as well as she that Aodh was what Rardove needed. She just could not give it to him yet.

"Now, I must away."

Her nighttime travels had taken longer than she'd intended. A gray opalescence was beading up the mists, rising out of the dells as if the coating of a pearl were floating through the air.

She hurried back to the castle and slipped inside. Even under the hood, her hair was damp with mist. Shaking it as she hurried up the stairs, she swung off the cape as she reached the landing and slipped back inside the darkened room.

The fire was almost out; it had not been stirred. The room was still warm.

Ducked over, barely breathing, she shut the door, twisted the lock, and set Aodh's cloak on the table. Shaking out her hair one last time, she turned to the room.

Aodh was sitting in the chair, watching her.

Cold rivulets of fear rolled down her chest. "Aodh," she said on an exhale.

He said nothing.

"You are awake. Is your head hurting? We overindulged, did we not?" She started toward him. "I can get you something for it—"

"Where were you?"

"Oh. I was..." She swallowed. "I..." Why could she not lie to this man?

Her voice trailed off as he rested his bent elbow on the table and lifted his forearm. Pinched between two fingers was a folded letter, sealed with cobalt-blue wax.

Her wax. Her letter.

Fear slid down her back. "How…?"

"That does not matter."

Walter.

"Oh, St. Jude," she whispered.

"Even he cannot help you now." Aodh pushed to his feet.

She bolted. Fumbled for what seemed like forever to unlatch the door, then flung it open, Aodh a step behind. She hurtled for the stairs, but he caught her before she made it two steps, wrapped a steely arm around her waist, and hauled her back inside.

The moment he released her, she raced to the far side of the room, around the edge of the bed. She gripped the bedstead as he locked the door and turned to her. His eyes were darker than she'd ever seen, reflecting little glints of firelight. He looked cold and calm and…furious.

"Aodh, please…"

"Please what? What could you possibly plead for right now that I should give you?" He started toward her.

She circled the bed. "Aodh, do you not see? I cannot betray her."

"I see. Only me."

She blew out a breath. "I took a vow. An oath. And she has given me so much—"

"Aye, a father imprisoned for loving a woman who must have made starshine seem dull, until he had his head cut off for not renouncing her. Your mam ripped from her home, her heart broken in two on account of the queen's petty jealousies, so terrified, she chose to die over protecting you. Then she gave you a castle at the end of the world, understaffed and unprotected, which you were somehow to make a go of, and Jesus God, always send the money back to England. Oh, aye, she's given you much."

Katarina stared, dumbfounded, at this rendering of her relationship with the queen. Worded that way, it sounded pitiful. But that was *not* the way of it. And even if it was... Her father had been *executed*.

As would she, if she turned traitor.

As would Aodh, too, if that missive she had just sent out was not delivered to the queen. That, and that alone, might save him. But only if Katarina remained loyal.

Traitors did not make good advocates for other traitors.

"I know you are angry, Aodh—"

A short gust of laughter met this. He began circling the bed.

She scooted up on the mattress, over to the far side. "—but did you read my letter?"

"Why would I do that?"

Oh, coldness emanated from him like steam. He had no patience for the reasons why, nor the good that might have been done. He cared only for the deed.

"But, Aodh, you must *read* it," she insisted, skirting the table as he stalked her. "I told her everything."

"Excellent."

"No, my meaning is...I told her everything about you. And me. Us."

He mirrored her every move, as she dodged the table and hopped back behind the huge bed.

"Do you know what I said?"

"No, Katy, what?" Slow, calm, tautly controlled, he was beginning to terrify her.

"I praised you," she breathed, circling onto the other side of the bed.

"Did you?" He sounded absent, as if he were barely listening. His gaze drifted between her eyes and her hips, as if deciding which to pay attention to. She tried to move neither.

"I did indeed. I said you were a good man." He stepped forward, and she swung around the corner of the bed, her hand gripping the post for support. "A good master for Rardove. I told her I had come to care for you. That I had fallen for your charms." All the truths were falling out of her now. "Aodh, regard: I told her she was *wrong*."

His gaze caught on hers. "You could have done nothing worse."

A tremor of unease, deeper than her fear of Aodh's wrath, moved through her. "Why?"

"Elizabeth is jealous. She does not want to be shown up, she does not want to be told she was wrong, and she surely does not want to be told a rebel is right. Such things do not matter. Nor does she want to be told you care for me. She loves me. She did not want to let me go."

Katarina's heart tightened at the words. She knew precisely how the queen felt.

"More to the point, telling her you cared for me would have been the worst thing you could have done, for it would have revealed to her that I, too, care for you. That is why you are fortunate this letter was brought to me."

Her heart skipped a beat. "There is a second."

He stilled. "A second what?"

"Missive." Her voice dropped lower. "I gave one to Walter, and one...to Dickon."

"Oh, Katy."

Her heart sank. It was a cold progression down her chest and belly, a musical scale of coldness.

"You made a mistake, lass."

Cold straight down to her toes.

"You went behind my back."

Cold, into her bones.

"You were seen. People know you snuck out, without my leave."

"Aodh." It was a pleading exhale.

His demeanor was level, almost detached. Inscrutable. He held out his hand. "Come here."

"No. Why?"

His gaze, unflinching and impassive, told her everything she needed to know, so in truth, she did not need any words. "I'm going to punish you."

"No," she whispered.

Tall and resolute, he watched her. "You can leave, I'll see you to that ship, or I can punish you, but it'll be one or the other. I cannot have you going behind my back, countermanding me. You are mine, or you leave. This is your last chance to choose."

"I do not want to leave." *Leave Ireland. Leave you.*

"Then come here."

"No!" Fear flushed through her. Her hands closed around the post at the corner of the bed. "What if…what if I marry you?"

The words, flung in desperation, finally stopped his advance. His eyebrows lifted. "Now? You'll marry me *now*?"

"Yes!" It was all an outbreath. "Yes. Yes. Yes." She tried to say yes as many times as she'd said no, which was a great many times. They all hung in the air.

"*D'accord*," he murmured slowly.

"Oh, good," she breathed, relief washing through her. She let go of the bedpost, her muscles relaxing.

His hand stayed out.

She went to him, and when she was close enough, he tugged her the rest of the way over and kissed her. It was a slow, lingering kiss. A kiss of consummation, a kiss of devoted union, and she felt the adoration coursing through it. Her hands twined around his shoulders, pulling him down to her mouth, until she was breathless from want.

He began tugging up her chemise. His mouth drifted to her ear. "Let's get this over with, Katy."

She froze. "What?"

"I'm going to punish you."

"No…but I thought…"

His pale blue eyes held hers. "Thought what?"

She backed up. "I said…said I'd marry you."

"So you did. And I'm very pleased. I'll make you happy, I swear it. And that is all for later. Right now, you need to lie down over my knee."

She backed up another step.

His eyes were dark with intent. He meant to do this thing, whether or not she wished it. Her breath staggered out in unsteady gasps, unable to believe this was happening.

"You don't want me to have to come and get you, lass."

Head bent, face flaming, she took an extremely small step his direction and peeked out from under lowered lashes. He'd sat down on the edge of the bed.

Bolts of cold fire lanced across her breasts. Her breath came faster and faster as she laid her hand in his.

He tugged her to stand before him.

Her breasts heaved. They felt full, trapped. He cupped one, his hand hot through the fabric, then he slid his palm down to her waist. His fingertips pinched her chemise.

"Pull it up."

She pulled it as far as her knees, trembling.

"Come closer."

She did, at once stunned and stupefied. Her body felt as if it would float right up out of the window. He took her fingers, kissed her knuckles. "Lie down."

She started to lie on the bed, but he stopped her. He patted his thighs. "On me. On your belly, lass. Right here."

Fire flared across her cheeks. "Oh, *Aodh*."

He took her hand and made her bend her knees, drop to the floor, then tugged her forward to lay her body over his thighs.

Thundering heart, whirling head, blood firing in hot pulses. The room all but spun. Hard-muscled thighs pushed against her breasts. She stared ahead at the wall, the tiny decorations of swirling patterns, hearts and clubs. He rested one palm gently on her bottom. Through the thin linen shift, it was an imprint of heat. She made a tiny sound.

"Pull it up."

Her body jolted. She reached down for the thin fabric and tugged the chemise the rest of the way up, baring herself to the hips. "Don't hurt me," she whispered.

"Och, I'm going to hurt you, lass." He skidded his palm gently over the cool curve of her bottom. "But I think I'll make you like it."

He lifted his hand and brought it down hard.

Her body jerked as if lightning had surged through it, a shocking, hard shudder of...*pleasure*. Her head flung up, her mouth rounded around a silent cry.

He bent by her ear. "Did you like that?"

Oh, the devil he was. He *knew.*

He did it again, a hard slap, first one side of her bottom, then, swift and red-hot, the other. She jerked with a panted cry, her hands still fisted around the hem of her chemise, holding it up for him to do as he would with her.

"You look fine, laying there for me, Katy."

Her face flamed, but her legs parted when his hand slid between them. For a moment, he didn't move, and she knew he was staring down at her, spread wide for him. The backs of her legs were cool from the air, the front of her hot from Aodh. Her bottom *flamed*. And ached for more.

He brought his flattened palm down on her again, hard and swift.

Her body shuddered and her head dropped, so her hair spilled across the floor. Her hips rose up to take the next one.

"Tell me you're sorry."

A sob broke from her. "I am sorry."

"Good." His hand came down again. "Say it again."

"I am sorry."

He spanked her again, then again, and again, first one cheek, then the other. Hot, hard, stinging pleasure. Occasionally, his hand would drop lower, smack against her upper thighs. Each time she rose to meet him, shocked breathless by the sword thrusts of pleasure it sent slicing through her body. Each time, she gasped, each time her head dropped farther.

"Now, lass," he said, and this time, when he struck, it was oh so softly. "I don't want to have to worry about you every time I turn my back."

"No," she agreed in a ragged whisper.

"Nor every time I take a drink." He brought his hand down again, soft, on the other cheek, then his fingers skimmed into the wetness coating her inner thighs.

She could barely gasp, her body was so lightning saturated, so ready to fall.

"We understand one another?" His hand gently circled her

bottom. Again, his fingers detoured to press into her swollen folds.

"Oh yes," she whispered.

His fingers pushed up inside her. "I think you like this, Katy." He slid out again and traced her swollen entryway. "Do you like it?"

"Yes."

The tip of his finger pushed back in, skimmed up to her bottom. "Should I stop?"

"Please...don't stop."

Immediately, he lifted her off his legs and slid her to the cool sheets of the bed, then laid her on her belly, where she collapsed. He tore his clothes off and dragged her back up to her hands and knees. She swayed as if drunk.

He knelt behind her, his thighs hard, the hair scratching the soft skin of the back of her thighs. He rested a hand on her hip, and then, for a moment, simply held them like this, unmoving.

She dragged her head around and peered over her shoulder. His body, ranging behind hers, rose up like a mountain. His dark eyes pinned her.

"Aodh," she whispered raggedly, reaching back. "Please don't stop."

"Katy," he said in a hoarse whisper. "There'll be no stopping, ever again."

He gripped her sweaty hips and breached her with no prelude and no gentleness, all push, no stopping, just as he'd said, a single, long, thrusting penetration, until he was buried in her to the hilt.

She screamed from the pleasure.

He pulled back and entered her again, slowly and unstoppably, a long stroke. Her arms began to shake. His pace grew more intent, more driven, as he kneeled up high, one hand light on her hip. She sprawled, bottom in the air, elbows out, gasping from the mad, unspeakable pleasure.

Her knees weakened, slid out, and she dropped to the bed.

"Good, lass?" The dark query came beside her ear, his body burning and slick with sweat above hers.

Pleasure flattened her. He dragged her back up to her knees, and she cried from the pleasure of that too. Then, hands on her hips, forcing her to stay up, he pulled her back to him as he surged forward, and she climaxed, a bright, hot, explosion that rocked her in shaking shudders, and rent her heart open.

His voice came by her ear, a fierce whisper. "Now, you are mine."

Weak and dizzy, she nodded. "I am yours."

He kissed her, and thrust inside her again and climaxed in a surge of male heat and seed and driven intention, and she was, truly, his.

Now the trouble would begin.

R⚔W

"MY," THE QUEEN SAID, as she stood in the rain-soaked courtyard, hood pulled far forward over her face. "What a lot of letters from Ireland these days. How lively it has become."

She turned to the man who towered beside her, Sir Charles Ludthorpe, captain of the force she was sending to acquaint Aodh Mac Con with her displeasure. "A bit too lively, wouldn't you say?"

"Indeed, Your Majesty."

"This most recent message is from Bermingham, Baron Athelrye. He reports Aodh Mac Con is well ensconced in the castle, and the lady of Rardove has acquiesced to him."

"So he says," was the noncommittal reply.

"You will find out for certain."

"I will."

"No negotiations."

He nodded.

"We shall call Aodh's bluff, if bluff it be. If he wishes for a fight, then a fight he shall have. And when he is captured... If it is as we think...bring him back to me. If it is worse..." She averted her gaze. "See to it there."

He nodded.

She was quiet a moment, then said briskly, "The message to

227

Katarina has gone off, telling her of my displeasure. Aodh Mac Con will see it as well, they will all see it, but that is quite the point. She will do what she must, or I will destroy her. This is her last chance."

"Perhaps she does not have a choice," Ludthorpe suggested gently. "Her castle has been overtaken, Your Majesty."

"Yes, and *how*?" the queen retorted. "After all these years, *now* it falls? One would almost think she opened the gates to the man."

She tapped her chin with the note, then gave a brisk nod. "Very well, Ludthorpe, see to this matter however you will. Give her a chance to prove her loyalty. If indeed she has turned on us, then turn on her. If she has not…" The queen waved her hand in a vague fluttering. "Perhaps you can use her as bait, for if Bermingham speaks true, a *tendresse* has developed between her and Aodh." Her jaw tightened, then smoothed again. "But if there is the least question of her loyalty…"

And of course there had to be the *least* question, didn't there? If only because there been no word from Katarina. No news of inhabitants fleeing, of dispossessed ladies seeking refuge at loyalist castles.

If only because Aodh, reckless, charismatic Aodh, was at the center of this thing.

Ludthorpe nodded his inscrutable nod. "Very good, Your Grace. I shall manage the matter of Mistress Katarina and Aodh Mac Con."

It was an unfortunate pairing of names, and she spun sharply to the servant who stood behind her. "And where is Bertrand?" she snapped.

"Lord Bertrand is en route, my lady. Another day at most. The rains, you know…"

She whirled back and stood in silence for a long time, then addressed her captain. "You used to know Mac Con, did you not?"

Ludthorpe's armor was a perfect reflection of the cloudy skies and the gray rain starting to spit down on them. Still, Elizabeth did not retreat indoors. Ludthorpe, being a seasoned soldier, had no compunction about standing in the rain until the sun came out again, and merely nodded as water ran in rivulets down his helm.

"He served under me, Your Majesty, years ago."

She nodded, tapping the most recent message from Ireland on her bottom lip. "What did you think of him?"

"A rogue," he said at once. "Charming, dangerous, and looking for trouble." Ludthorpe paused. "But not a rebel."

She lowered the paper. "And yet he is precisely that, is he not?"

He nodded, his gaze sliding away.

"Is he not?" she said again, sharply. "He has taken a castle of mine and holds it even now, against my wishes. What else could he be *but* a rebel?"

Ludthorpe's gaze came back. "He is whatever you say he is, Your Majesty."

She stared blankly ahead, then a moment later, shook her head, as if replying to some inner conversation.

"No. I cannot have Ireland come at me from behind. Not even for Aodh."

ROGUE WARRIORS

CHAPTER 33

KATARINA WAS UP the next morning as soon as the first ray of sun hit her eyelids.

The first thing she noticed was that the door stood ajar.

She flung herself out of the bed, grabbing for her gown as she went, then her boot, far too excited, considering she'd just wedged herself deeper into a bond with a rebel. But for now, all she felt was…buoyant. The sun was shining and Aodh was out there, waiting for her.

She tugged on her boot as she hopped across the room to where the other lay, on the floor beneath the table. She bent for it, putting her nose a bare inch from the table, so for a moment, she didn't realize what she was seeing, lying there on its surface.

A half-curled roll of parchment, covered in ink. At the bottom was Aodh's signature, large, scrawling, and red.

It was the betrothal agreement.

It had been torn in half.

She stared, her heartbeat speeding up, then she straightened with a snap and flew out of the room, snatching up her veil and pinning it on as she went.

She found him in the training yard, clad in armor and sweat. Engaged with one of his men in swordplay, puffs of dirt rose from under the men's feet as they circled each other. Their tunics were unlaced, hems hanging down to muscular thighs clad in hose and boots. At the far end of the bailey, another set

230

of men worked on the target field, shooting arrows. The stables bustled with men leading horses in and out, and from over the wall came the faint ring of gunshot; men were training beyond the walls, too.

She leaned her shoulder against the wall, content to wait to be seen. He caught sight of her when their circling brought him around, and he smiled even as he slashed his sword.

She smiled back.

His opponent knocked the blade out of Aodh's hands, then danced backward, astonishment on his face, but laughing in triumph.

The rest of the soldiers who'd been leaning against the walls roared in laughter too, to see their commander beaten. Aodh swept up his blade, and the group enjoyed a few moments of enthusiastic revilement of Aodh's abilities — or lack thereof — until he dipped his head Katarina's direction.

They all snapped to attention, then flushed and apologized and nodded and bowed and very quickly drifted off. Aodh came to her side.

"Did I do that?" she asked apologetically. "Make you lose your sword?"

"Aye." He wiped sweat off his brow with his forearm, then hooked his arm behind her back and hauled her to him. "Entirely your fault. Mayhap I should punish you."

He kissed her, a swift, possessive kiss, showing her he recalled all the things she'd taught him about what she liked, then he released her, setting her down on wobbly feet, her face flaming. "Good morning."

"And good morning to you, sir," she said breathlessly, straightening the veil he'd pushed askew.

He snatched a skin of water off the ground and drank deeply before he poured a good portion over his sweaty face and neck, and wiped it off with his tunic.

"Did you like my gift?" he asked, without looking at her.

So, he was unsure of himself. Or perhaps of her.

She was very, very sure. "You mean the betrothal papers?"

"Aye." He slammed the cork back into the skin opening.

"The one torn into pieces?"

He dropped the skin on the ground. "Aye."

"Oh yes, Aodh," she assured him softly. "Very, very much."

His gaze swept to hers, then he kissed her again. She took the kiss until, her eyes opened dazedly and she saw the crowded bailey had ground to an almost complete halt. People stopped and stared as Katarina, who'd been trapped in a tower, stood with their new lord, getting properly kissed.

She pushed him away and tried to catch her breath. "But *why?*" she asked, ducking her head, keeping her voice low. "Why did you tear it up?"

He shrugged. "I was wrong. I'll have you willing or not at all. Nothing else will do."

This was the sort of thing that could make a woman not care who was watching. She pushed up on her toes and touched her lips to his. "That, sir, is almost enough to make a lady consider being reckless."

His hands closed around her before she could step away. "This pleases you? This tearing up of things?"

She nodded. "Greatly."

"Then I shall begin tearing up things immediately. Papers, trenchers of bread." His hands interlaced at the small of her back, not letting her retreat. Which was quite his way. "I'll rip the tapestries to shreds."

Katarina laughed and rested her head on his chest for a moment, not caring who was watching or what they thought. Her skin was awash in chills comprised of laughter and passion and...yes, happiness. When had she last been happy?

She could not count the years. Life was not made for such things. Happiness was nonessential, but oh, how it pleased.

Again—and again, and again—how Aodh pleased.

"And I believe, sir," she said, looking up at him, "that as you going to tear things up on my behalf, I will...stand down my men on yours."

"Ah," he said slowly, then bent his head and kissed her.

They walked to the keep together after they'd released the garrison. He slung his arm over her shoulder and they strode through the bailey. She walked close at his side, discussing what she wanted to speak to Cook about for the evening meal.

He barely listened. It was enough she was here, chattering happily, her slim body curving up to his. The hum was back, the emptiness filled, the coldness gone.

Miniature reunions erupted all across the bailey as her household drew close to speak to Katarina, hug her, to ask questions or advice on various small matters.

Surely they did not need her opinion on whether to boil the chicken or purchase additional lye for the laundry. They just wanted to be near her, touch her hand, bring her sprigs of spring wildflowers—Dickon shoved them into her hands and rushed off before she could catch him—so in the end, it was almost an hour before they were back inside the keep.

He took her directly to their chambers. He had no specific plans, but a great many general ones.

They spent the rest of the day there. They left only for the evening meal, when the household finally pounded on the door for Aodh. And for Katarina.

R/W

"WEAR THIS."

Katarina was in their chambers, rummaging through the wardrobe, casting aside all the gowns that would not do for such a night as this. But they would *all* not do.

Her muscles were gloriously sore and well worked. Muscles she had not known she possessed were still sensitive and trembling. She felt aglow.

And she had *nothing* to wear.

She turned at the sound of Aodh's voice, and almost caught her breath.

He stood in the doorway, his hair damp from a bath, fresh and windblown and smelling of vitality and spring and maleness. And wearing...velvet.

His broad shoulders filled out a black tunic, studded with rivets across the front. His dark hair fell down over it, melding with the darkness of the fabric. Black hose completed the ensemble, down to polished knee-high boots. He looked like danger incarnate. In fact, the only hint of color was his ice-blue eyes.

Magnificent indeed, a beast in his prime. And he knew it.

Over his arm hung...the red fabric from the tower. "The servants made it into a gown for you," he said.

"Tandy," Katarina said fondly. "She is a master seamstress."

"She had helpers. You've a talented staff."

Katarina touched the rich reds and pale yellows of the fabric. "They have had to be, for I am not."

On his arms, in addition to the gown, lay a pale shift, with lace along the edges, and silk stockings, with silky threads falling from them, and a long girdle with hammered silver links, not hers. A gift, then.

"Wait outside," she said softly. "I will change."

He handed everything over and backed out.

She could have called for Susanna, or one of the others, but she did not want to share this moment. Aodh could help her finish. The silken gown fell in skirts of pale yellow and red, with wide, flowing sleeves edged in lace. It became a tumble of yellow and dark red, one color overfalling the other, a frothy concoction of bright sun and red shadow. It had an open, darted bodice, the tight yellow tunic showing through the red silk ribbons like a sun. The tops of her breasts rose up above.

The long, linked girdle banded her slim waist, double-looped in orbits of gold, and falling below her belly. She braided her hair and wrapped the long plait around the crest of her head, and pinned it. Over it she wore a simple, unadorned veil that flowed to her hips, banded by a circlet of gold around her head.

She bent and peeked a moment at her reflection, intending to pinch her cheeks, but they were already flushed with color.

Taking a breath, feeling oddly shaky, she opened the door and stepped onto the landing.

Aodh spun as if he'd been pacing and stopped short. His gaze trailed down the front of her, a long, lingering, and utterly *male* regard. Her body responded: washes of heat in her belly, prickles across her breasts, hardening her nipples.

Their eyes met.

"You are beautiful, Katarina." The simple, unadorned compliment made her feel as if she'd been laced with gold.

"As are you," she said despairingly.

The hard lines of his face relaxed, and a smile touched a corner of his mouth, and oh, it had the same impact as when he'd first smiled at her, in the bailey, when she did not yet know he was taking over her life, and they'd shared a smile over the stubbornness that made her hold a castle beyond the Pale with only ten men.

She felt quite battered by his smile, just as she had back then.

"Men are not beautiful, lass," he informed her.

"You are."

"Just don't let Cormac hear you say it." He reached up to her face and slid his hands under her veil, to the nape of her neck. His fingers were cool against her skin, as he clasped a necklace around her throat.

"A gift," he murmured.

Her fingers flew to it, touched the hard, smooth, knitted metal.

"Come see." He led her back inside.

She bent before the small mirror again and caught her breath. It was a carcanet, a jeweled choker, studded with garnets and pearls. From the center hung a pendant, on a long chain, dipping into the hollow between her breasts, depicting a soaring bird.

Behind her, also half bent over, peering into the mirror just above her shoulder. was Aodh.

She smiled at him in wordless pleasure.

He tugged a little pouch from his pocket and dumped it into his palm, then turned her around and began tucking little bodkins into her hair. They were tipped with gems, garnets and emeralds, so they sparkled as she turned her head.

"You make a fine maidservant, sir," she laughed.

"You should see me with stockings," he said, intent on

tucking one above her ear, and even as she laughed, a quiver of excitement went through her at the image of Aodh's hands on her stockings. Untying the bows behind her knees, his hard fingers scraping her soft skin, then rolling them down...

Quickly she returned her attention to the mirror, her fingertips skimming the little sparkling studs across her hair and veil. Their eyes met in the mirror.

"You look like the night sky," he murmured.

She thought he would try to kiss her, if not take her outright, their afternoon exertions notwithstanding; their current position certainly invited a taking, him bent over her back. Indeed, it made her face flame. But he only straightened, and extended his arm.

"Shall we?"

She laid her fingers on his forearm. "We shall."

Rogue Warriors

CHAPTER 34

HE LED HER to the stairwell, bright with torchlight and the hum of excitement. Of revelry. There had not been revelries here for years. Not enough money. Too much danger. Now, Aodh had brought it all back. Feasting and music and laughter and...rebellion.

No, she told herself firmly. Not tonight. She would not think of it tonight.

Ré stood at the archway to the great hall. He, too, was dressed for feasting, and smiling, which quite transformed his grim warrior's face.

My, Aodh did surround himself with great lusty men.

Ré swept her a low bow. "My lady." She returned a curtsey, feeling quite charmed, then Ré slid his gaze to Aodh. "A word?"

Aodh stepped to the side while Katarina waited impatiently. When their conference went on an additional minute, then another, she stepped forward and poked her nose into the hall, to see the festivities.

A face appeared at her side. "My lady!"

She jumped back, then smiled at the mayor whose round face and big bulging eyes were peering at her earnestly. Mayor MacDougal. A very earnest man.

"Master MacDougal," she said warmly, holding out her hand. "It is *good* to see you. It has been some long time."

"Indeed it has, my lady."

"I greatly miss your wife's cheeses."

"I will have some sent up immediately," he assured her. "And we greatly miss your whisky." He grasped her hand and pumped it with enthusiasm, then bent into a clumsy bow from which he peeked up hopefully. "Will you have a new batch anytime soon?"

She smiled. "I will have some sent down at once."

Aodh came up behind her, and she half turned toward him, saying, "Master, I would like to introduce you to..." Her words drifted off.

She would have stumbled over "the lord of Rardove," or indeed any other such term, had she time to stumble. Instead, she only had time to be amazed.

The moment Aodh appeared in the doorway, the entire hall turned toward him. Then, almost as one, they fell into deep bows and curtsies, a show of deference, nay adoration.

The mayor practically bent himself in half, swept off his hat, and doffed it to the ground. "My *lord*," he breathed.

She stared in amazement.

The son of Rardove had come home, and they were pleased.

Among the soldiers and various warriors, a huge roar broke out. Cups were raised and some great, happy Irish shout went up—it was too loud to actually understand the words—then the stringed instruments that had been playing prettily beforehand were drowned out by the sound of a...bagpipe.

The sound lifted up in a beautiful, wailing cry, like something rising up from the earth. It swelled through the hall. Eerie, stirring, evocative, as elemental as blood pumping, it washed over her, made the hair stand up on the back of her neck.

The hall stilled, as if caught in an enchantment, but when it faded away, another huge roar of approval rocked the room, calls and whoops and stamping feet. They were not enchanted; they were ecstatic, and they wanted more.

The stringed instruments joined in the celebration this time, and as the music pulsed over the heat and bodies, the revelries seemed to actually speed up as Aodh moved into the gathering.

Katarina stood back, watching him clasp hands and clap backs, entirely at his ease. She felt stunned, confused...fascinated. The faces around her, the smiles, the rustling silks that her mother had dreamed of, became a blur.

She'd never had such crowds here, had never been *able* to have such crowds, with only ten men to guard the place and a questionable countryside to rule.

Katarina's largesse, indeed all her alliance work, had radiated outward. She'd traveled and visited, gifted large and small, but she never entertained. She could not. She could not invite others here, for the truth of Rardove would be turned against her.

But Aodh had opened the gates and welcomed them all in, and they reveled in it. In him.

Such an irony: Katarina had opened the gates to him, and he'd opened the gates to all this...magnificence.

Aodh reached back for her and pulled her to his side, into the light and the heat. Into the magnificent.

Person after person was brought forward. They would grasp Aodh's wrist or, if they were Irish-looking, might yank him into a bear hug, then they would turn to her with a bow.

Many she knew already. Irish princelings or warlords she'd known by visit or by letter, or, as the case may be, had been *shunned* by visit or letter. So it was rather satisfying to be in the position to afford a gracious nod when MacDaniels was brought forward, affecting a clumsy bow.

There were a shocking number of Englishmen here too—or at least Aodh said they were English; one could hardly tell.

She began taking hands, returning nods and greeting and smiles and curtsies.

"Katarina!" called a voice from amid the deepest part of the horde. The crowds parted to reveal the barreling approach of the florid-faced, burly chested, exceptionally English lord, Geoffrey Bellingbloke, Lord of Wingotten.

Katarina stared in amazement. Wingotten was a loyal English marcher lord—or so she had *thought*—with three castles, one only a half day's ride away.

That fact had put her in close contact with him over the

years. They'd shared troubles, contributed to the common defense financially, and he'd always been steadfast in the queen's cause. So Katarina felt shocked to see him here, now.

Aodh had been drawn into conversation a few steps back so she had nothing to distract her from Wingotten's surprising conversation.

"Lady Katarina," he exclaimed, beaming at her. "How fine to see you! God grant you health."

"And you, my lord. It is most good…" Her words faded. "I admit to being *surprised* to see you here, my lord."

"Ahh." He winked and waved his arm about. Wine splashed out of his cup. "As I am, to see *you*."

"Well, after all, I do live here," she began, but his next words cut her off.

"The Straight Lady of Rardove turns," he announced cheerfully.

She was startled into silence. "I beg your pardon?"

He bowed slightly. "My lady, forgive my impertinence. It is this wine; quite fine, is it not?"

"No, please, my lord, tell me. This is all so…new and surprising." She waved her hand at the gathering. "It is sometimes necessary to gain the insights of an outsider, one who sees things from a different perspective. You have found me…straight in the past?"

"Like an arrow, my lady, if you will. Surely a grand trait, but out here…" He made a sound. "You have always been so loyal to the queen. Unalterably. Unable to hear even a single complaint."

"I did not know—" she said weakly, but he drank more wine and went on.

"Unable to even consider any differing views. Always following the straight and narrow," he said, and stood his hand on its side in the air and pushed it forward, as if it were sliding along a track. "Whatever the queen says is right and proper." He made a sound of disgust. "Which is why it is so surprising, and refreshing," he added warmly, and drunkenly, "to see you've become a rebel."

Heat flooded her cheeks. "A rebel?"

The baron waved his hand. "Well, of course, one hopes it will not come to that."

"In*deed.*"

"But then again, I'm all in favor of a good shaking up. Quite in the mood for it."

"Yes, of course, a good shaking up." Katarina felt entirely upended. Wingotten was in the mood for a shaking up? She'd never known.

What else did she not know?

"Aye," confirmed Wingotten, the Englishman turned Irish. But he was also a good lord, one of the few permanent English landlords—most stayed absent, raped the land, and left their chaff behind for others to manage—so maybe this was the only way. You lived in a land long enough, and the next thing you knew, you were *of* that land.

Have I become Irish, she wondered suddenly.

"In any event," Wingotten went on, "it would be difficult to do a worse job than the English Crown."

"Would it?"

He lifted his cup as if to drink, then held it in the air and gazed across the room with an expression she could only describe as satisfied. "We've been wanting this for some long time."

"Have we?" Her replies had taken on the note of echo.

"In any event, your Aodh will do a better job than ever Elizabeth did out here on the marchlands."

Her Aodh.

"What have Elizabeth or her agents ever done for Ireland but reap what Ireland sows?" Wingotten drank some more, seemingly unconcerned that this speech alone was enough to lose him his head.

As if reading her thoughts, he dropped his gaze to her. It was rather fierce. As were all the other gazes in the room. Pleased, celebratory, but...fierce. Prepared. These men were ready for whatever came next. Wanted it. And it was Aodh who had stirred their blood.

"The English crown takes our harvests to fill her belly, takes our money to pay her bills, takes our men to fight her wars. What does she return? Laws and strictures and religions we do not want."

"Indeed," she echoed weakly. That was an entirely novel way of looking at it.

"And who better to lead a rebellion than one of the queen's own?"

"Indeed," she said, quite taken aback.

"Your Hound." He nodded his chin toward Aodh, who stood in conversation a long pace off, "used to be the Queen's man. Councilor, sea dog, all that. A second Dudley, they say, only better, for Aodh was ready to the fight."

She opened her mouth—to say what, she did not know—when a small, darting figure, ducking under a tray being set on the table, smashed into Wingotten. It was a glancing blow, but the baron stumbled backward, as one does when one is drunk, and banged into a trestle table.

Katarina reached for him, as did a few others, and she had a chance to see the shooting star who'd caused the damage.

Dickon.

Excusing herself, she made her way after him, dodging people as she went. She caught up with him just as he was trotting up the stairs at the front of the hall.

"Dickon."

She bent and put her arms out and caught him up, his skinny, bony, strong little body that had almost starved to death before she found him.

For a second, he clung to her, and she to him. Then, as if suddenly recalling he was almost eleven years old, not a hugging age, he disentangled himself. Wiping his hair, he stepped back and tugged on his grimy tunic, but he was grinning as he looked at her.

She straightened and said brightly, "You look well, Dickon."

He gave a clumsy bow. "Milady."

"Are you all fed up now?"

"Quite," he assured her, and rubbed his belly. "I'm getting

fat."

She laughed.

"And I'm to help with the horses." He whispered the last word, as if saying it too loud would remind someone he ran too much around them, and take the privilege away.

She wanted to hug him again. She put her hands behind her back to resist the urge.

"Dickon, I wished to thank you for all that you did for me." His face flamed red. "And to tell you you shall never be asked such things again."

Her solemn words made him look directly into her eyes. "Milady, you saved my life. You know I'd do anything for you."

She smiled warmly. "I know, Dickon."

"And so, I'm awful sorry I could not…"

Her eyebrows lifted.

"…deliver your message."

She blinked. "You did not deliver my message?"

"Well, I delivered it to the *master*."

"Well, yes," she agreed weakly. "Of course you did."

"I pledged an oath to him, you see, milady." His little face was tipped up earnestly. "He told me I must be as loyal as the garrison was to you. That is exactly what you always told me too, milady, about loyalty, so it seemed right."

She stretched out a hand and squeezed his shoulder. "And so it is. One must honor one's vows, or what is the point of making them?"

Relief lightened his features, and as he darted off with a jaunty salute, she straightened and turned to the hall.

So, Dickon had been the one who'd delivered her message to Aodh. She'd assumed it had been Walter.

She saw the steward now, across the hall, sitting at a low table and tapping his foot to the music. She made her way over and stood behind him for a moment. People were slowly making their way to their seats, now that Aodh had arrived. She could see Aodh, looking around for her.

"Good evening, Walter," she said.

The clerk looked decided grumpy as he rose. "My lady."

"Please, sit."

He did.

"A fine night, is it not?"

Walter harrumphed and began drumming his fingers. "If you're partial to barbaric music."

"Some are."

His fingers stopped drumming.

"Walter, did you deliver my message to the queen?"

"Did I not say I would, lady?"

"And did you bring me my sword wrapped in bath towels?"

Silence, then he huffed, "The boy said you wanted it."

Neither looked at the other. Their gazes were pointed at the hall. "I thank you," Katarina said. "It was bravely done."

"Loath as I am to see a woman handling weaponry, it seemed a small enough thing to give you, after all that has been taken away. In any event, someone must fight the Irish beasts." He sniffed. "I thought you were going to *use* it."

Katarina looked over the gathering. Aodh stood at the center of a group of men by the fire. Wicker seemed to be acting out a story. The group broke into laughter, and Aodh clapped him on the shoulder. He grinned up at his new lord.

"I did not choose the sword," she said quietly.

"Then the sword will choose you."

She looked down quickly. "Do you not think, having seen him now... Do you think he might be *good* for Rardove?"

"The Irish Hound? Never, my lady. You see what is happening already." Walter waved a disdainful hand at the gathering. "Irishmen everywhere."

"After all, we are in Ireland," she reminded him.

He made a contemptuous sound.

"I have had great success talking to the queen over the years. Aodh believes if he can but speak to the queen, we may avoid the sword entirely."

Walter turned in his chair. "The Hound had years to speak to the queen. And in the end, he chose the sword. This will end in bloodshed. Theirs." His eyes met hers. "The sword always chooses Ireland."

Chilled, she looked away.

"I suppose I am the only one with English sense left in this whole keep," he muttered and in a fit of self-pity, crossed his arms over his chest.

Their conversation was cut short as Aodh arrived at their side. Walter looked away and settled back in his seat. Aodh slid a hand around her hip and nodded toward the dais.

"They await us, lady."

Walter's eyes slid to the touch of his painted hand on her body.

Katarina let him guide her away from Walter's chilling assessments. What did Walter know of it? His mind was a lockbox of prejudged verdicts. He had no vision. Moreover, he had no power to effect any of the awful things he saw in Rardove's future.

Thank God, she sent the silent prayer up as Aodh led her to the dais, his hand steady on her back.

"They are glad to see you, lass," he murmured, pulling out her chair.

"They are gladder to see the roasted pig." She nodded at the huge platter being carried out to great cheers as it passed between the tables.

"It is a fine pig," he agreed, taking his seat beside her. "Shall I send Walter away?"

Startled, she looked over. "Oh. I... Why?"

"He makes you unhappy."

Aodh really did see a great deal with his ice-blue eyes. She rested her hand lightly over his. "He means no harm."

"He means all harm," Aodh retorted, turning his hand over to fold over hers. "I can send him away tonight. Give him a mule and a bagpipe, see how he does."

She burst into laughter and dropped back in her seat, Aodh still holding her hand. She, still holding his.

"Let's let him at least practice a bit first," she suggested.

"Mm," was all he said, then the pig arrived, and the feast began.

"I am famished," she announced, reaching for a napkin.

"Aye." The word was all sensual intent. "Let's not linger."

The night was filled with food and music and laughter. Throughout, Aodh's leg occasionally and intentionally brushed up against hers under the white linen tablecloth. Every bit of food he laid before her became a transmission of male intent, every passing of the shared goblet an excuse to touch.

Aodh lifted her to her feet before the sweet cakes were brought out.

They went to the bedroom and reveled in each other all night, talking and touching, whispering mostly of nothings, although Katarina felt compelled to offer a few somethings.

"MacDaniels is a cheat in all things," she informed him after he'd taken off her gown and knelt at her feet.

"Inform Cormac, not me," he said, unlacing the little ribbons at the back of her knees. "I ne'er gamble with men who display the food they eat as they are eating it."

She nodded in sympathy. "Thank you for setting him far away from me."

The stockings came sliding off, and as he tossed them aside, she rested her hand on the side of his head. "And Aodh, heed me, you cannot deal with Wingotten directly on matters of state. It is a lost cause."

"Fine." He laid her back on the bed.

"He is ever in the drink."

"I noticed."

"You must deal with his wife. She is wise and reliable, and far more steadfast. At the least, she remembers things."

He knelt on the bed. "And what do you know of Dunn?"

"Garrett Dunn? In my experience, he wavers until the final..." Her words drifted off as he pushed her knees apart. "Aodh?"

Propped up on an elbow, a hand fisted around his erection, he paused and looked at her. "Aye?"

"Are we going to...talk? While we...?" She angled her head to the side.

He grinned at her slowly. "You like when I talk," he said in a sly tone that quite made her heart speed up. "I've watched what happens to you when I talk."

"Well, I'm quite sure it won't happen if we talk about Garrett Dunn."

He laughed and settled in between her thighs, his arm above her head. "Very well. We'll talk about how deeply I enjoy being inside you."

Shivers spread across her body as he entered her with a slow thrust.

"And then we'll have you talk to me of how much you like it too, and maybe what else you might like me to do."

Excitement snapped through her. "*Else?*"

"You see. It's happening already."

"Well," she allowed, moving into his rhythm, which he kept slow, "this is certainly better than talking about Garrett Dunn."

"Later we can talk about Dunn."

"I'll tell you everything I know."

He rewarded her for her intelligence in ways that proved being a rebel was not entirely a thing of sacrifice after all.

Chapter 35

THE NEXT AFTERNOON, Katarina was in the kitchens with Cook, discussing whether the beets they'd overwintered would be suitable for the next day's meal, when Susanna came in wearing an uncertain smile.

"Katarina."

She paused, two leeks in her hands, held up to examine them.

Susanna came a step closer. "Cormac asked me to find you. The master wants you."

Katarina lowered the leeks. "Wants me? Where is he?"

"In council."

They stared at each other. Susanna looked apprehensive.

There was only one reason Aodh would be calling her to a council meeting with his rebel forces today: to prove herself. Not to him, but to them. He had taken a risk and set her free, but that did not come without a cost. Yesterday had been a reprieve. Today, the payment came due.

She could not be here, at Rardove, in their midst, standing against them. Standing against Aodh. She might not have to marry him, but she did have to join him. In a manner the others could see and recognize.

The men pushed back their chairs and rose as she entered the council room. She tread lightly into the room, the way you might if passing through the meadow bog all around the castle, which would be a foolish and fatal thing to do, unless you knew

248

precisely where to lay down your boot.

She walked to Aodh through the silence. He nodded to the seat beside him, and when she sat, so did everyone else.

"We were speaking of Wingotten," Aodh said without preamble. "Did you not say his wife is the one we ought to deal with?" His gaze was direct and firm. He expected a reply.

The room was silent as the men waited to see precisely who, and what, she was.

She nodded. "When he is drinking, yes. And he is always drinking."

"Tell them what you told me."

She turned to the tableful of men and told them everything she knew. There was no other way.

When she was done, she pulled her chair back slightly, putting herself just outside their circle. Aodh did not touch her, but he did hold her in a long gaze, then gave a single, approving nod.

She breathed the first easy breath she'd had in some long time, a breath of relief. Such things did not come easily out here on the marches. She'd done well in his eyes, and just now, nothing else mattered.

Furthermore, she felt safe. Ensconced in a castle with rebels all around and an army marching for them. Safe because Aodh *approved* of her. She'd made her choice, met his expectations, and now she was…his.

It was a very definite thing.

He had vowed to protect her, and made her think he might actually prevail. *Hope* he might.

Quite simply, he made her hope.

And that, she saw now, was the deepest layer of Aodh's danger. When there was clearly no hope at all, still, one believed.

The council resumed its talk, slowly at first, then, perhaps forgetting she was present, more openly. She listened in surprise to how much they knew. They had gathered intelligence, and a lot of it. What they needed were allies.

Which she should not care about at all.

What an odd sort of holding place her home had become.

She became aware they were talking of sending a messenger — Bran — to the Rathbourne clan, deep in the mountains. They planned to send him by the coastal path, the Glencoe, a twisting, treacherous way. A faster way to reach the hidden trail that led into the mountains, indeed. If one survived.

She tipped forward into their conversation. "The Glencoe path will have washed away by now. Or if it has not, it shall very soon, likely as Bran is riding upon it."

They all turned to her.

She shrugged. "It happens every spring. It is impassible after winter. Bran will need to take the high road. 'Tis longer, but he will get through with his life."

A shuffling moved through the room, then more silence. More suspicion.

"Well, after all, I do not want him to die, do I?" She sat back and folded her hands over her belly. "Additionally, he should take a gift. Something sweet. MacErrogh has a fearsome sweet tooth. Let me see, we have honey in the cellars…"

Every eyebrow had lifted, every finger which had been drumming with repressed emotion, stilled, and more than a few gazes narrowed suspiciously at her.

One of Aodh's men laid a hairy forearm across the table. "The high road will add a day to his travels, lady."

"The straight path will add a lifetime, for he will never return."

The men exchanged wary glances.

"I tell you, the road appears solid, but horses and ponies and men have been sliding off into the surf since Yule." More silence met this. "As for the sweets… MacErrogh has cut off the heads of emissaries and messengers before if they did not come with proper respect as well as good news. Since I do not know whether he will consider your news *good* — that the Queen of England is about to send an army marching through his lands en route to Rardove — you should ensure your messenger has something he *does* consider good: honey. Trust in me, I have exploited MacErrogh's sweet tooth before. And there is a great deal of honey in the cellars."

Ré looked at Aodh. Katarina looked at Aodh.

Aodh slowly took his gaze off her and moved it to Bran, who stood, booted and caped, ready to be sent on any mission the council deemed worthy.

"Take the high road," Aodh said. "And stop at the cellars on your way, for honey."

Bran gave a swift nod, smiled at Katarina, and turned for the door.

R⚹W

THE NEXT WEEK passed in a blur. Bright sunny days were filled with a flurry of garden planting and a deep spring cleaning for the hall and bedrooms. Evenings were filled with music and laughter, their newly joined households mingling happily with the Irish who'd come in from tribes both great and small.

The nights, long and hot, were filled with Aodh.

In such idyll, one could almost forget war was coming. Especially if one was trying to.

One morning, the men were changing guard duty on the walls. The hall always bustled at such hours, and Aodh stood with a few men, leaning over a table together with a swiftly sketched rendering of the hills to the west, while Katarina hurried the servants to bring in more bread and cheese.

Into this flurry of activity, Dickon stumbled in and almost tumbled down the stairs, shouting as he came. "My lord, a messenger has come!"

Fast on his heels came one of the gate porters. "From the queen, my lord. 'Tis from the queen!"

The hall went still. Cold rivulets of fear trickled down Katarina's chest. She swung her gaze to Aodh, but he was already striding toward his gateman, hand out.

The porter handed it over, saying, "It is for my lady, my lord."

Everyone turned to her.

Aodh looked at her, then handed it over.

With trembling fingers, she cracked the seal and opened the

missive.

Elizabeth, by Grace of God Queen of England, Ireland, Scotland, and Wales, to the lady of Rardove, Katarina. Know our deep displeasure in your accession to the Irish rebel Aodh Mac Con. Our castle of Rardove, held by you in Our name, in trust, is now forfeit to the Crown. Be prepared to surrender it to our man.

Drafts eddied through the air and made the page tremble.

"Without evidence?" Katarina sat down hard and lifted the paper into the air, in front of her eyes, as if staring at it harder or longer would somehow make it seem right. Or fair.

Inside her chest, there was a falling-away sensation, not so much a tumbling as a slippage. The ice shearing off again, this time into a much deeper, more turbulent sea.

"So, the queen did condemn me, without evidence." She looked up at Aodh with a bitter smile. "Without a trial. Without a conversation. Somewhat in the manner you suggested she would." She looked at the message again. "She did this all in her mind, turned me traitor and finished the deed."

Aodh sat on the bench beside her. "I am sorry."

She looked over into his beautiful, complicated eyes. The oddest thing. He who'd all but forced her into this rebellion, now apologized.

"You should leave," he said and nodded to his men. "Ready an escort. Deliver her ladyship to the ship, thence, to wherever she wishes to go."

The men went into motion immediately, but Aodh stayed them with a sharp addition. "Take three of the chests with you." He looked at her. "I have friends in many places, Katy. We can find you harbor, you can stay there, safe, until…"

"Until what?"

"This is over."

She got to her feet. "What do you mean?"

He got up too. "I have a ship, in a hidden cove, at anchor. It will take you wherever you want to go. Although if you choose the queen… I would recommend against it. But if that is your wish, my men will see it done."

She felt shocked that he would think such a thing. The falling-away sadness of a moment ago, the empty, foundationless slippery feeling of loss, was gone entirely, replaced by a spark of anger.

"I am not going anywhere, Aodh. You did what you did, and had your reasons. I did what I did, for my reasons. But the queen, she had no reason. She assumed the worst of me. A lifetime of giving over, and giving up, and pressing on, all as the queen willed it, and she simply…turned on me. As she did on my father. As she did on you."

She straightened her back and let the message flutter from her fingers.

"The queen gave me no choice, Aodh. You did." She snapped her attention to Ré. "Is there still no word yet from The O'Fail?"

Ré went a careful sort of quiet. Everyone turned to Aodh.

"What?" she said, turning to him too.

Cormac examined the room and the ensuing silence, then threw up his hands. "We've not sent anyone to the O'Fail tribe, ma'am."

"Not sent anyone… Saints preserve us, why not?"

The men exchanged another silent look.

Aodh felt Katarina looking at him, felt everyone looking at him. "He cannot be trusted," he said in a cold, clipped voice.

She glanced around the room, then came forward and stood very near him. "How do you know that?"

"I know him."

"Oh. What happened?" she asked quietly.

He shook his head. "I know Keegan O'Fail. He will not aid us."

"How do you know?"

"He did not come to battle when called, sixteen years ago. The entire O'Fail clan betrayed us, left us to die on those fields alone." He kept his words simple; no need to describe the carnage. But when she didn't argue, just let the silence linger, he added, "All my uncles died on the field that day. My cousins, my friends. My father and grandfather were taken and tortured, then were killed. In one swoop, we were all taken. The O'Fail destroyed my family that day, betrayed us all."

"Betrayed you."

Aye, himself. He'd been fostered at the O'Fail's, had trained with his warriors. Indeed, Keegan himself had taught Aodh to whittle, made him a little horse Aodh had kept on the mantel of his home until the English burned it to the ground with Aodh's mother inside. Keegan had been more than a decade older than Aodh, but they'd been foster brothers, closer than blood. And Keegan had not come to the battle that day. And Aodh's family had died.

Katarina bent nearer. "Aodh, I am sorry."

"We are all sorry," he said coldly, not in the spirit to be comforted.

"But you do not know what forces were at work."

"I know he did not come. I know he took an oath, and I know he turned."

"As you have asked me to do?"

He looked up sharply.

"Aodh, it was a long time ago. If Keegan O'Fail promised, then he should have come. Maybe now, he knows that." She gave a little shrug. "Maybe now he is sorry. Maybe we could at least...see?"

He heard his men waiting, boots shuffling.

"He has many men at his command, Aodh," she urged. "Perhaps near to a thousand. It was his summons that raised five hundred for a hosting several years ago, and by it almost decimated the English forces. He has droves of supporters. Is it not worth at least inquiring?"

He was not inclined to grant this request. Beg for an alliance with a worm?

In the background, Ré shifted and said quietly, "We do not know where The O'Fail is at present, my lady."

Katarina's head lifted. "He itinerates constantly. Like as not he is at his keep of TorRising, for Easter is nearing, and that is but a long day's ride from here. Still"—she nibbled on a fingernail as she stared across the room at one of Aodh's tapestries—"we ought to send messengers to Pike's Deep and the glen at Dark Lough. He often visits there."

The room was silent under her musings. Aodh looked at Ré, who shrugged, then said, "That's a great many men traipsing about the countryside on questionable missions."

"You must risk large to gain large," she countered.

Aodh thought a moment, then shook his head. "Ré is correct. We haven't men enough to send a few to the main castle, a few to the Pike, and yet more to that godforsaken lough. Not with an army marching for us."

She nodded briskly. "Then go only to TorRising. I am certain that is where he will be."

"No."

She frowned. "Why ever not? I swear to you, he is worth the risk. The time, the men." She paused a moment, then added in a more musing tone, "You may have a point, though."

A sigh of relief moved down the line of men. Aodh just watched her through faintly narrowed eyes.

"The O'Fail can be notoriously unwelcoming," she said, her tone thoughtful. "Sometimes violently so. It would not do to send low-level emissaries." She got to her feet. "I will go."

In startled unison, the men pushed to their feet.

She reached for her cape. Spotting one of her servants in the distance, she gestured. "Emmitt, please instruct Wicker to saddle my horse and gather an escort. I shall require...seven," she decided, affixing the large Rardove pin to her cape before stepping out from behind the table. "I will not be gone more than four days—"

She walked directly into Aodh.

He put a hand on her arm, gently, but most decidedly stopping her. The others stared in a silence that could be shock, or perhaps horror. It was difficult to tell, among one's so recent enemies.

Aodh's expression was the most unreadable of all.

"Leave us," he ordered quietly.

"You are always clearing the room," she complained as everyone scattered.

"You are always saying and doing such room-clearing things," he replied, drawing her toward the fire. "Katarina, you cannot simply march off with my men."

"I was going to take my men."

"They are all my men."

She stilled. Of course. What was she doing? The castle was Aodh's. Her will, her orders, her desires, were secondary now. And if Aodh did not heed her, her will meant as much as a bag full of feathers.

He must be convinced.

She curled her fingers around his arm and said earnestly, "Aodh, I vow to you, The O'Fail is a necessary addition. He is greatly like…" She paused a moment, searching for the right words. "A beating heart. Through him flows a network of clans and loyalties. He is like the center through which the blood flows. If you gain him, you gain them all."

He considered her a long moment in silence.

"Aodh, I thought it suited you for me not to be a thing to be done with," she said.

"It does," he replied gruffly.

"What makes Ireland so good to me is the freedom to be out from under anyone's thumb. I must be able to do things. To think things, to be heeded."

A dark scowl touched his features. "Have I not sat you in my council?"

"Indeed, you have. And then said we could not do what I suggested."

"We do not always do as a man suggests."

She leaned in closer. "I know Ireland, Aodh. I know these men. You asked how I survived out here? I did it through union. Relationship. Trade. That wood out there? Sent by The O'Fail, in exchange for a barrel of Rardove whisky. And the iron we melt for arrowheads and bullets came from a trade with O'Reilly that served us both. I know these men, their families, their petty wars, and their fierce loyalties. I believe I *am* them now, to Elizabeth's chagrin."

He looked her over. "An Irish princess."

Her cheeks flushed faintly. "Not precisely, but it will do. You would be wise to heed me in those things of which I know more of than you. And that is Ireland."

His hand fell away and he walked to the window. Sunlight poured through and illuminated him in colors: the vibrantly colored *léine* hanging just below his knee, red and green and cobalt blue for Rardove; tall black boots. From his hips hung a belt strapped with sword and daggers. His face was lightly bearded and the inked lines swirled down his neck. The sun lit one side of his face, leaving the other in shadow.

He rested his forearm on the wall beside the window and looked back at her. "You may know more of Ireland, Katy, but you do not know more of war."

"I know more of The O'Fail."

He sighed. "You are not letting this go, are you?"

She sighed back. "I will try to be docile, but I fear it will fail."

"I'm familiar with the feeling," he said grimly.

She crossed to him and held his cheeks between her hands as he had so often done to her, and smiled into his worried eyes, as he had so oft done to hers. "You are worrying too much," she teased.

"You're not going to The O'Fail," he replied.

"Oh, Aodh—"

The resumption of their argument was cut short by another messenger who came flying into the keep, shouting at the top of his lungs.

"My lord! My lord, they are coming! The English army is marching, burning as they come!"

ROGUE WARRIORS

CHAPTER 36

THE MESSENGER stumbled to a halt and dropped to his knees in front of the dais, chest heaving. Aodh bent to eye level as the man dragged his sweating, red face back up.

"The English, my lord. I was sent to tell you...they've dropped anchor, and they are marching... *They are burning everything.*"

Silence rent like a bolt through the fabric of low conversations filling the hall. Katarina got to her feet. "Burning? Burning...Ireland? Oh no, they cannot do that." She turned, dumbfounded, to Aodh. "They cannot *do* this. Those are my people, my lands."

She fell silent, then, as if the thought had just occurred, she said softly, "They must be stopped."

She hiked up her skirts and flew to the stairs, calling for people as she went.

"Ready a messenger," she shouted, hurrying across the bailey, up to the walls, into the wind, her cape flying out behind her. "I will need three riders to survey the damage," she called to one man as she rushed by. His gaze trailed past her, over her shoulder. "Emmitt, bring me a pen and parchment. And for God's sake, someone bring me Wicker! I must send word, at once. They cannot be allowed to burn my lands."

She pushed the hair behind her ear and whirled, flinging out her hand. "A pen!" she shouted impatiently. "I require a—"

Her hand connected with Aodh's chest. "Oh, Aodh," she

gasped in relief, as if she'd forgotten him. She gripped his arm. "We must send a message to the commander of that army, to stop them."

"So you said. That would be unwise."

"And then we must send food to the villagers, and— Unwise?" She blinked. "No, it is *necessary*. Essential. They must be stopped."

"You will not be the one to stop them."

She was already peering down into the bailey, at a handful of soldiers hurrying by. "Saddle my mare," she called to them.

Wicker looked up, lifted a hand that fell to his side when his gaze shifted to Aodh. She turned too, and for a few beats, she and Aodh stared at each other.

"Katarina," he said carefully.

She knew that tone. It was the "no" tone, the one that said his will, not hers, would be done. Again.

"No." She claimed the word first. "You cannot gainsay me on this. We must send help."

"At best, 'tis a ruse, lass."

"A ruse?"

"Intended to do precisely what you are about to do: open the gates. Make us ride for them. We must do the opposite—"

"But—"

"Hush."

She trembled with fury. "Did you tell me to…hush?"

"I am telling you to cease. Right now." His voice was level and hard. "Our people are watching."

Indeed, all along the walls, and down in the bailey, soldiers and villagers and castle folk were watching the argument between the lord and lady of the castle. She swallowed.

"So, aye," he confirmed quietly. "Becalm yourself. And if you cannot, then return to the castle, and I will manage this matter."

She stared, not seeing him anymore, but every person who'd moved through her life, telling her what she should not, could not, must not do.

It was the story of her life.

And now Aodh? Instructing her to silence her voice? She felt it as a betrayal, sensible or not.

"Do not tell me to *calm myself*," she replied in a furious whisper.

He shook his head almost sadly. "Katy, I will toss you over my shoulder if I must."

She gasped. He held out a hand, directing her to the stairs, back to the keep.

She didn't move.

"Do not make me do it," he warned.

"Stop telling me not to make you do things, Aodh," she snapped. "You will do as you will. Did you not plant your flag on that claim? So, then, do what you will." Her eyes were fierce, pinned on his. "As will I."

He watched her a second longer. Something about the silent regard introduced the barest hint of, well…fear. Perhaps terror. Certes a grave and great discomfort in the pit of her belly.

She swallowed. "Aodh, if you would but listen to me—"

He bent and swept her up in a single move and tossed her over his shoulder.

"Good *God*!"

Shock wrenched the words from her mouth, then fury moved in, fast and hot. She began kicking with her knees and pounding her fists on his back. "Set me down this *instant*."

He said nothing as she raged, just clamped his arm around her legs, pinning them to his chest, and walked her down the stairs.

Her face was scarlet with embarrassment, which mattered not at all, for her nose was bumping his back, and her hair was a thick dark curtain swaying back and forth over her head and down the backs of his legs, the ends trailing on the ground as he carried her inside to their bedchambers.

Once inside, he set her on her feet. She stumbled back, taking a moment for the blood to return to her limbs.

"How *dare* you?" she gasped.

"I dare much," he said coldly. "You think this castle can survive, riven in two? Some who heed you, some who heed me?"

"No, I..." Her words fell away.

"It would not last the night," he said harshly.

She felt strung up on the strands of a dozen conflicting emotions, some of which were due entirely to the fact that, for the first time in their many complicated, high-passion encounters, Aodh had never looked at her as he was right now.

As if she could not be trusted.

"Never again," he said, and turned to walk out.

"Are you going to lock me in again?" She flung the words at his back.

He kept walking.

"Anytime things do not go as you will them, you stamp on whatever stands in your way? I swear to you, Aodh, we shall have a troubled time if that is how it is to go. Arrogant, mule headed *amadán*."

"I see you learned a few foul Irish words," he commented, swinging the door open.

"Mayhap I was wrong, but you are too. *Loscadh is dó ort!*"

He slammed the door shut and came back around.

She met him this time, her boots planted. "You think it is all yours to take. You think of nothing but taking, of winning. I think of our *people*. I think to save their homes, and our crops—yes, *our* crops, for how else do you think we will winter next year? I am thinking to save them a few of the horrors that you and I"—she pushed her fingertips to his chest—"have had to go through. Have you ever had your home burned to the ground? Have you ever watched loved ones die in flames? I did, last winter, when the fire raged. It was awful." She pushed at him again.

He caught up her hands, bent them to her chest, and pulled her to him. "I well know the horrors, Katy. I have had my home burned thrice. I watched my mother die when I was nine in a fire set a'purpose by Englishmen."

"I did not know," she whispered.

"No, you would not." His eyes were hard blue ice. "I do not want you to know. *I* do not want to know. What I am telling you, Katy, is your path is laid, and it is *my* path. Our path. And battle is coming, whether you wish it or no. So knowing that, you stand fast. And Jesus God"—his voice broke—"you do not let them *lure* you."

His hands gripped her elbows so hard his knuckles were almost white. His face was taut, his voice rasping, the eyes staring into hers so filled with emotion, it almost broke her heart.

He was afraid *for* her.

They stared at each other, then, as one, their mouths met in a violent kiss.

They staggered back to the bed, grappling at clothes as they went. Her skirts were hiked up before she hit the mattress. He knelt between her thighs and tore at her bodice as she fumbled with his hose. His erection sprang out, full and hard. He pushed her knees apart and entered her in a single thrust.

She flung her head but did not look away. This union was about a different thing from all their others, and it did not require kisses, which was just as well, for there were none. It required intense, unceasing contact of body and gaze.

Fierce and relentless, he took her, holding himself up on one palm, the other hand gripping her knee to his side, spreading her, allowing him to sink in with urgent, rolling thrusts. She lifted her hips with each surge, put her elbows on the bed and pushed to meet him, battling to take every hard plunge.

Then suddenly, he gave a curse.

"Jesus, Katy," he muttered, and rolled them so she was on top. Her hair fell down around them. His body, still fully armed, lay beneath her.

"Go on," he said hoarsely. "Take me. Say whatever you mean to say."

It was an amen. Her eyes filled with…were those tears? Her voice, when she replied, was thick.

"I mean to say…"

She looked down at this man who'd defied every rule, ascended every summit, overcame every obstacle, and accomplished every outrageous goal ever set for him. Councilor to a queen. Pirate and lace-sketcher. Courtier and conqueror. Captured a castle, locked her in a tower, and never touched her without her permission.

He'd had a vow imposed upon him, to come claim his ancestral lands, his skin pierced by the promise they'd demanded of him.

And he had done it. Against all odds, against all the world's desires, he had done this mad thing.

And he was *hers*. He wanted her, this man of power and mastery. He sought her out, moved toward her like waves move toward the shore.

And in the midst of it all, at the vortex of his mad, bold, perilous self, perhaps the most unforeseen magnificence of Aodh Mac Con was this: he'd brought hope. To them all.

Surely 'rebel' could not weigh so heavily as 'hope' on the scales of honor.

"I mean to say," she whispered brokenly, "I love you."

His eyes widened, then his head dropped back to the bed and he murmured something—it sounded to be an Irish prayer—then he lifted his head and kissed her, gently, so gently. "And I, you, Katy."

Her tears fell onto their kiss. "I am sorry," she whispered.

He said nothing, just lifted his hips, rocking into her.

"But I…" she moved on him. "Aodh, the world may hush me, but not you. When you did, I quite lost my mind."

"Aye, you did." He curled his hands around both her hips.

"We will find a way," she promised.

"This is our way." He pulled her slowly forward, spreading her open as he sank in farther. Her head fell back as a sluggish undulation of pleasure moved through her.

"I was dying without you," she said, a whispered confession.

"I died a long time ago, Katy."

She leaned over his mouth. "You are not dead." She kissed his lips. "You saved my life. You are flame and fire."

"No. You are the fire. I will tend you." She closed her eyes, focused on the sensations rippling through her, the scalding pleasure brought by Aodh's slow possession of her. His acceptance of her, his need for her. Her hair swung, her breasts swayed.

He held her hips, took over the rhythm. "I will listen to you, Katy, when you have something to say. And I will consider it well."

"I know."

"But you cannot do that again."

"I will not."

"And I will not hush you."

"Good."

"That said…," His words drifted off in an ominous way.

Her body, splayed by him, stilled.

Shifting so that he reclined on only one elbow, he slid his hand between their joined bodies, abrading her slippery-sensitive skin with his thumb, pushing into her wetness, a hard pulse over the nub at the crest of her. "When we are in our bed, Katy, this is mine," he said, and did it again.

Heedless, she flung her head, trying to breathe, trying to nod.

He sat up and cupped the back of her head. "And when we are in our bed, your mouth is mine." He slid two painted fingers into her open mouth.

She turned to him, closed her lips around his hard fingers. He stroked them in and out, at the same rhythm she was rocking her hips. As the hard thrust of him pushed up inside her, so his fingers took her mouth. Golden pleasure, hard pleasure, hot shudders of pleasure, filled her.

"When we are in our bed, your body is mine, whatever I want, however I want it," he instructed, and his mouth closed over her breast, both tongue and teeth.

She arched her back as he took her hard, his mouth alternating between her breasts, their hips meeting in a hard, striking, relentless rhythm. Her body shuddered under the storm of pleasure.

It was over almost before it began. She climaxed with huge, shattering undulations that moved through her body in successive waves. Aodh came deep inside her, a hot, cascading eruption, urging her to come again, and again, as he held her and whispered in her ear of how much he loved her.

Less than half an hour after they left the walls, Aodh was back on them, making plans with his men.

R̸W

"YOU SNORE," said a voice, yanking her out of sleep the next morning.

She rolled over. Pale sunlight illuminated the bedroom. Aodh stood beside the bed, fully clothed, in armor and cloak.

She struggled to a sitting position. "Snore? I most certainly do not." She clutched the sheets to her breasts.

"Aye you do." He tossed her her cloak. It settled over her face. "Come."

She wrestled it off, her hair sparking as it lifted in wild arcs. "Come where?

"We ride for The O'Fail."

ROGUE WARRIORS

CHAPTER 37

THEY RODE ACROSS a landscape exploding with spring life for two days, twenty-five Irish warriors, Aodh, Katarina, and four barrels of Rardove's finest whisky.

Finally, late on the third day, atop a far hill, the fortress of The O'Fail appeared. A stone castle thrust up from within a perimeter of high battlement walls. No simple pele tower this; this was a fortress of strength.

"Are we certain he's no' a Saxon?" Cormac muttered warily as they started down the hill and crossed the meadow toward the towering stone ramparts. Small pinpricks on the walls solidified into men wearing armor, patrolling the battlements.

They rode in silence up a dirt pathway and clopped over the wooden draw.

They were admitted into the outer bailey, and the portcullis gate winched shut behind them with a squeal of iron. It banged as it hit the earth.

The outer bailey was large and hosted a huge contingent of stables and shops, smithy and kitchens. Cormac had been right; it was more like a bustling English town than an outpost on a marchland. As they passed, everyone stopped and stared.

They rode into the inner bailey, and drew to a halt in front of the high, narrow stairs that led to the keep.

Ré and Cormac dismounted. Twenty other soldiers did the same, almost in unison, a sort of dance of men who'd long worked together.

Aodh stayed on his horse, looking at the keep. Katarina cleared her throat.

"By the way, did I mention…?" A significant pause ensued.

His gaze slid off the tower. "What?"

She smiled. "'Tis nothing. Nothing at all. The O'Fail and I once…shared a kiss."

Stillness radiated out from him like a stone that had set in the sun all day. Ré and Cormac exchanged a wary glance.

"Why?" he asked, very slowly.

It was only a word, but it made Ré reach out and put a hand on his arm. Katarina touched his other arm.

"It was years ago, Aodh. *Years.* It was so trifling, and so long ago, I'd entirely forgotten about it. Until just now." She smiled brightly.

"Just now, is it?"

"Yes, just this very moment." Another bright smile.

"And what was the occasion of your trifling kiss with the Irish prince?"

"He was one of several princes, you must understand, years ago. A potentiate. Nothing of regard. But…" Her voice drifted off. "In any event, a union had been proposed. Bandied about, as such things are —"

"You were going to *wed* him?"

" —but in the end, it came to naught. So, there you have it." She smiled again.

"I've something," he agreed, the Irish lilt a little stronger, implying strong emotion, but his words were level and seemingly devoid of emotion.

She patted the hard length of Aodh's arm. "It is not even worth a mention."

"And yet you are mentioning it."

"I simply did not want it to arise in discussion without you knowing."

His gaze was fixed on her. "You think it will 'arise'?"

"No, of course not. Come, he has likely forgotten about it, in much the way I did. One does, you know. Let us forget it ever happened. We shall present our case, and see what he has to say."

Ré and Cormac had a fairly good idea of the case Aodh was currently preparing in his mind. They watched him close his eyes, take a deep breath, and get off his horse.

"Fine." He strode to Katarina's horse, put his hands on her hips, and swung her to the ground. "What is he, twenty years older than you?"

"Closer to fifteen. He is quite virile," she added absently, tugging at her gown.

Aodh's finger crooked under her chin and tipped it up. "Quite, is it?"

She shook her head. "Not very. Not at all."

"We'll talk about this later."

She smiled and let him adjust her hood. "There is nothing to talk about."

A figure appeared on the highest step of the castle, in front of an arched, carved oak door.

"That is he," she murmured. "The O'Fail."

Tall, long-haired, neatly bearded, and expensively booted, wearing a deeply dyed cape that was tossed off to the side to reveal a sword and two pistols, he was the epitome of a marcher lord. Precisely the sort of man you wanted to lure into an alliance. Assuming he could be lured.

They began the trek up the stairs. Aodh lifted Katarina's hand and guided her up, then passed her on ahead of him when the stairway narrowed. Tension emanated out of him like sound.

"Katarina," The O'Fail welcomed her as she joined him on the top step, his Irish accent so thick it always took a moment to acclimate.

She took the hand he held out and began to curtsey, but he lifted her up and, leaning forward, kissed her cheek.

She could almost feel Aodh starting to ignite behind her.

The O'Fail must have felt it too, for he moved his gaze to Aodh as he stepped onto the landing. For a moment, the two Irish warlords looked each other over. The O'Fail was more than a decade older, still robust, but Aodh was a beast in his prime. And behind him trailed a long row of armed retainers, clad in armor and the colors of Rardove.

"Aodh Mac Con," The O'Fail said quietly. "Some laid wagers you'd never return to Ireland. That you were content to be cosseted by a queen instead of settling for an Irish kingdom."

Aodh smiled, but it was cold. "'Tis true, I do not settle. Unlike some."

The O'Fail's hooded eyes narrowed. "Your meaning?"

"You well know my meaning. An oath is hard work. Some are content to settle for scraps, for whatever they are given by others."

Katarina felt the beginnings of true fear.

But she could do little other than step between them and wave a pistol about, and as it had not yet come to blows, that seemed a bit excessive. Barring blows, or perhaps including them, these two would simply have to work the matter out.

Up on the walls, the O'Fail soldiers stood, bows aimed at the armed band perched on their castle steps.

The O'Fail considered Aodh. "What you speak of, Con, was a long time ago. Your father and grandfather joined a rebellion that was not theirs, when they were not ready. Rash and reckless, as ever they were."

"Brave," said Aodh, his voice granite hard.

"Aye, very. Enough to put the rest of us to shame," he said willingly enough, and reached for Aodh's wrist.

Aodh held a moment, motionless, then he clasped The O'Fail's arm back.

"As were you, Con," the older prince said, gripping Aodh's forearm tightly. "I saw you on the field that day. Fourteen-year-old berserker, you were. We were sore sad when you went to England, and the Red Queen took you for her own."

"I am back now."

He clapped Aodh on the back twice, then released him. "Your father and grandfather had high hopes for you, which you seem to have realized." His gaze grazed the tattoos visible on Aodh's neck before it swung back to Katarina. "Although I admit to being surprised the lady acceded so swiftly."

She sniffed. "Firstly, I was tricked."

"And secondly?"

She sniffed again. "I was convinced by various…persuasions."

Amusement glinted in The O'Fail's eye as he took her hand and lifted it to his mouth. "As I once tried?"

"Not precisely," she murmured as he bent to kiss her hand. Over the top of his head, Katarina met Aodh's glare with a silent, warning command: *Stay*. "As I recall, my lord, in the end, 'twas you who declined the union."

"I declined a union with the Queen of England," he said, straightening. "Only a madman would decline a union with you."

She smiled. "You received my thanks for the wood?"

The O'Fail's smile grew broader. His face was starkly handsome, and the gray strands in his beard and braid dangling by his temples only added to the sense you were in the presence of a mighty presence, like an oak tree, or a storm. "A single barrel of Rardove whisky far exceeds the value of a few planks of wood, my lady."

"Those planks have trebled in value of late, as they will help rebuild the drawbridge. Aodh has brought you more." She waved toward the barrels of whisky sitting on their fat sides in the bailey.

The O'Fail glanced at them briefly, then looked back. "You want something."

Katarina shrugged. "A trifling."

"A war," Aodh said, a bit more bluntly.

She frowned at him, but The O'Fail just nodded. "I thought as much. Well, come inside. There is freshly brewed ale, and we've just slaughtered a hog. It will go well with Rardove whisky." He leaned to the side and murmured to Aodh as they stepped inside, "If you do not know it yet, your lady is quite fond of bacon."

R⚔W

INSIDE, THE FEAST was laid and the fires roared, and the Rardove contingent was entertained in rich fashion by musicians and dancers.

When the meal was over, as the revelries pressed on, Aodh and Katarina sat at the high table with The O'Fail drinking—Katarina, wine; the men, Rardove whisky—and Katarina spoke of the coming troubles.

Aodh said little. If he spoke, too much would come out, all of it anger, none of it useful right now. So he let Katarina do the talking.

When she finished, she took a last dainty sip of her wine and said, "I must say, my lord, you do not seem overly distressed by these troubles."

"Why should I be distressed? They are your troubles, not mine," he said, lifting a jug and dumping whisky into her now-empty cup.

Aodh met her eye over the chief's shoulder, a brow lifted. She gave a faint shrug. His brow went down. She sighed and slid the cup away.

The O'Fail settled back in his seat. "In any event, troubles with England are the way of it in Ireland. Akin to holding your breath under water; a necessary thing if you wish to go swimming. Politics are a tricky thing. A man can hardly complain. He's just got to know when he's in too deep." His gaze slid to Aodh.

Aodh stared out across the tumblers and dancers, the laughing couples and roaring fires. This is what *he* wanted to create, this home, this warmth, this refuge. Reclaim what had been stolen from his family, over and over and over again.

He was so close now. So close, sitting beside the man who had all but ensured the failure of his father's dreams, and his traitor's death.

He felt Katy's hand on his arm and jerked his gaze up, realizing his jaw had clenched. He unfastened it with a low outbreath.

"Perhaps one is not always given a choice, my lord," Katy said softly, still touching his arm but looking at The O'Fail. "Sometimes one is simply thrown in, and must swim as best one can."

The O'Fail shrugged. "True enough. And yet some try to

drag others down as they go."

Aodh looked over slowly. "Do you mean me?"

The O'Fail met his eye. "I mean your grandfather. And your uncles. And your godforsaken, beloved, reckless, *stupid* father."

"Oh dear," Katarina murmured.

A fist of fury punched low in Aodh's stomach. Every muscle in his body tightened. He pushed to his feet. The heavy chair squealed as it slid over the floor.

"My father died because of you."

The O'Fail looked up at him, his face tight but his gaze clear and calm. "Let's have this out, then, Aodh, why don't we? Your father died because he moved too fast, too soon, without waiting to gain enough strength, or sense, or allies. As was ever his wont. He was fire, Aodh, like in a forest, not a trough. He burned himself out, and scorched a thousand other men as he went. So perhaps swimming and drowning are not the right words at all. He burned, Aodh. He was all wick. And a lot of good men died in the flames of his glorious, pointless rebellion."

Aodh's body tensed from head to boot, tightening around the flashes of memories scorching through him: his father and grandfather being captured on the battlefield, marched to their deaths, their heads rolling off…

"What would you know of it?" Aodh said, his jaw barely unhinging to speak the cold words. "You did not come to battle. You stayed safe. As is ever a coward's wont."

The O'Fail rolled to his feet.

Katarina got up too. The three of them stood in a little group while the hall reveled on.

The O'Fail spoke again, his voice no longer calm, but still quiet, so that it cut through the music and laughter.

"I know because I loved your father, Aodh. I watched him burn in reckless deed after reckless deed for twenty years before he finally went up in flames. He was my friend, my brother, and he chose to leave us all behind in a blaze of stupid, irresponsible actions. I begged him not to go to that fight. We all begged him. Before your mother died, *she* begged him, to show restraint, to be wise, to stop burning the world. But did he? No." The O'Fail's voice broke. "He left us. He was to be our shining star, the best of us all, and he left us. He chose that."

Aodh could barely hear him, his head was pounding so hard. Because...The O'Fail was right.

And Aodh knew it.

His father had been stubborn and headstrong and driven, and had chosen to die on the pyre of his ambitions, rather than save them all.

The O'Fail laid a hand on Aodh's shoulder. He wanted to throw it off, but could not. He couldn't move; his body was knotted.

"He left you too, my boy, and that was the worst. I swear to all the gods, we tried to get you back. But you were gone."

"I went to England to get Rardove back," Aodh said, his voice hoarse, as if he hadn't spoken for a long time.

"I know. We thought we'd lost you." The O'Fail's hand fell away. "And now, you've returned. Jésu," he muttered, wiping his hand across his face. "After all these years, you're back. We thought...."

"You thought what?"

"We thought you'd left us too. You chose a different path than your father, but still...England, taking you both from us?" The Irish prince gave a bitter laugh. "Hard to not hate it."

"You thought I'd left forever?"

"You were furious Aodh. To this day, you see me as the cause of your father's death. Jesus God, what *would* you come back for? The rain? You had the queen's favor, ships—oh, aye, we heard the tales of your adventures. You'd a rich life with England. Everyone said you were gone for good."

"And what did you say?" Aodh asked harshly, because somehow, it mattered what this man thought. This man who had once been his mentor, his father's friend, his family's boon ally, this man who had not come when called.

But perhaps the call should never have gone out.

The O'Fail's gaze was unwavering. "I said that one day, you would be even greater than your father. The greatest of us all."

His breath felt hot, balled up.

"I always knew you'd come back, Aodh. Laid money on it. And now here you are, and you've brought an army to our doorstep." The O'Fail smiled bitterly. "Just like your father."

"Not precisely like."

"What is different?"

"This time, you are going to help him," Katarina's soft voice broke in.

The O'Fail barked in laughter and Aodh dragged his gaze over. She'd retaken her seat and was sitting back, eyeing The O'Fail appraisingly. The battle commander in her tent. Aodh wanted to rush the man, crush him, hit him, bury him deep in the ground, unfair or no. But Katy was cool and reserved as she considered the chief.

"You owe Aodh a debt." She picked up the cup of whisky and met The O'Fail's eye. "Fortunately, my lord, honor is not so tricky a thing as politics." She threw the drink back in her throat, downing it in a single swallow.

The O'Fail's eyebrows flew up as she poured again, burbling whisky into the cup, then pushed it across the table toward him and Aodh.

"Will you join me, my lord?"

She did not specify which lord, the rightful one or the rebel. She did not clarify what, precisely, 'join' meant, the whisky or the rebellion.

The O'Fail looked at the cup, then muttered a curse and reached for it, tossing it back as Katarina had done.

Swift as a hawk, her gaze sped to Aodh's, and her eyelid dropped in a miniature wink.

Then she was the battle commander again, sitting back and nodding regally at The O'Fail as he slammed the cup on the table, poured more whisky into it, and turned to Aodh.

"Well?" the king said impatiently. "Are you drinking with us or what?"

Aodh would take her against a wall tonight and suck the whisky off her bottom lip.

Headstrong, willful, glorious woman.

He swept the cup into his hand as heat moved through his limbs. The heat of relief, of triumph, he didn't know; it didn't matter anymore. The heat was inside him now, in Katy's eyes as she smiled ever so faintly at him.

"Well now," The O'Fail said, retaking his seat, "let's have it. Where do things stand? How long do you have before the queen's army arrives?"

Aodh said simply, "Not long."

"How many men do you have?"

"Not enough."

The O'Fail wiped his hand down his beard. His gaze met Aodh's. "What would you have of me?"

"What can you give?" Katy asked.

The king's gaze slid away, across the hall. "Rardove is an anomaly. It has been great under great masters, and under poor ones. It has been great under English rule and Irish. Somehow, through all the years, Rardove has never faltered nor fallen into the mists. It is charmed.

"There are rumors of dyes. Legendary ones. Magical ones." His gaze fell on Aodh and his tattoos. "But whatever the reason, Rardove has stood the test of time. But then, no royal army has ever marched directly for it. In such an event, it might fall. Be broken. Something might be destroyed."

"It might at that, my lord."

"I do not think Ireland can stand the strain of any more of her magic being broken. For that, I can give much."

He looked at Aodh. "For the son of the Hound, I can give even more."

CHAPTER 38

THE RUMOR OF WAR WAS everywhere as they rode back to Rardove. Towns were locked up tight. Entire villages had fled. The land had a waiting, watchful feel.

All around, they detected the presence of riders, just inside the line of woods flanking them. Up and down the line, Aodh's men cast suspicious, wary glances at the wood.

"They are The O'Fail's," Katarina explained quietly. "We are under his protection now, while we are on his lands."

"It's unnervin', that's what it is," Cormac muttered.

But Katarina felt safe. So odd, after all the years she'd lived here, closeted inside the thick stone walls, always faintly afraid, now, in the company of a rebel, riding on the open hills, she felt safe.

They entered Rardove's bailey as evening fell. Abuzz with villagers and town folk and castle folk and even more Irish than when they had left, it was a fairly joyous mob scene as they rode through the gates. Wagons and cartloads and bushels of foodstuffs were being brought in from the surrounding countryside, and riders were constantly coming and going, bearing messages and burdens. Rardove had the air of celebration, of fête or fair, not preparation for a battle. Their hopes were high.

Because Aodh's were.

They had barely removed their hoods and were standing in front of the hearth, shaking mist off their cloaks, when a messenger arrived, pushing through the bustle with a missive for Katarina.

"From whom?" she asked, surprised.

"The mistress of Carrickdon," the messenger said with a bow. "Inquiring as to your health and the coming spring fair. She has sent a gift for you too, my lady." He handed over a small package.

Aodh and she exchanged a silent glance. The soldiers' gazes flitted from her to the package to Aodh. Then to her.

They did not yet, not quite, trust her.

She extended the package to Aodh. He gave a curt nod and waved one of his men forward, who took it and tore it open.

It was a little bundle of lace, wrapped in linen, with a note from one Lady Carrickdon, which spoke of the coming spring fair, and suggesting that if Rardove had any wool fells, they would fetch a fair price.

Katarina had had a friendly correspondence for many years with Carrickdon's mistress. She was older, widowed, and resided within the Pale, but she was of old English stock, very loyal, very dependable, and Katarina felt a small knot of discomfort in her throat, thinking of how the news of this rebellion would be perceived by the venerable old lady.

Aodh read the letter in its entirety twice, and one of his men examined the fat little bundle of lace skeptically, but it was difficult to hide weapons in lace, and everything was finally handed over to her.

Katarina sat at the dais table while the others settled down to drink and tell stories before the evening meal was served. She unfolded the lace and laid it on the table to examine it more closely, and went cold when she felt a thicker section of the lining along one edge.

She slid out a small, tightly folded scrap of parchment with a message written on it.

In mercy, Her Grace the Queen gives you one chance to regain her goodwill: turn over the Irish traitor. Impressing upon you the importance of this deed, we leave the means and methods to your discretion. Should none should appear, on the second night after our army arrives, leave the back postern gate open. We will send in a man.

Say nothing to anyone. Burn this missive, and you will not suffer the same fate.

Katarina laid a hand over her forehead. Oh dear God, it was a terrible cycle, everything a mirror of the past, winding its way down to this moment.

She felt so cold she began trembling. She was now, truly, her father's daughter. Her mother's daughter. Branded a traitor in her sovereign's eye, she was being given one last chance to avoid a traitor's death.

Turn her back on her Irish consort. Turn her back on Aodh.

In her secret heart, Katarina had long ago turned her back on her parents. Repudiated everything about her father and his overweening passion, his treason. Rejected utterly her mother's rejection of her. Katarina had no parents, only a queen.

She had promised the queen, and herself, that she would be different. She would be the loyal subject her parents had not been.

Now was her chance to prove it.

She'd thought all she would have to do to prove her loyalty was marry the wrong man. Not see to the death of the right one.

Merriment abounded in the great hall. Strings of lute, masculine laughter, and the soft murmur of female voices drifted throughout. She looked up. No one seemed to notice her. How long had she been staring at the paper?

A fire burned in the hearth, a foot to her right.

Aodh stood with a group of men—his, hers, their Irish allies—in front of the long fire trough in the center of the hall. They formed a loose, relaxed circle, rumps on tables, boots on benches, as they tried out each other's swords, but Aodh was clearly at the group's center. A natural-born commander.

The choice was here, then. Now. The fire of the flames, or the fire of Aodh.

She got to her feet. The movement drew his eye, and he smiled. Then it froze as he looked at her hand, which she was holding out, the missive from the queen extended between her fingers.

He took it and read it without a word. Her breath grew shallow as the seconds passed. He said nothing.

"Aodh."

He thrust out his hand and dropped the message into the hearth. It contracted into thick, black curls, then combusted, subsumed into the larger fire. He watched it burn.

Still, he said nothing.

"Aodh, you must know —"

His cold blue gaze swung up from the burning fire and landed on hers.

"Aodh," she whispered, shaking her head. "You must know, I would never —"

He reached for her.

" — could never —"

He pulled her into his chest, his arms tight around the small of her back, which was for the best, as her body almost crumpled with relief. "I would never have —"

"Katy, I would tell you to hush if I did not think you would bite me," he murmured against her hair.

She pressed her cheek to his chest. "Please, tell me to hush."

"Hush," he whispered, kissing the top of her head.

Someone cleared his throat. They turned to see Ré watching them warily.

"Lady Carrickdon's messenger is leaving," he said, looking at Aodh. "He has requested a reply."

"I have a reply," Katarina said loudly enough to be heard by all in the hall, including the Carrickdon messenger, who stood near the stairway to the front doors. "I suggest 'Lady Carrickdon' never again call the lord of Rardove a traitor in my presence.

"Furthermore, there are unimaginable benefits to having this Irishman rule in Ireland, and while I am willing to open the front gates to anyone who wishes to be educated on the matter, the back gate will remain closed. Tell him to pass that along."

Aodh swept her out of the hall even as the buzz erupted. The hum grew, comprised of *'What did she say?'* and *'She did not!'*

and loud stringed instruments beginning to play and laughter and iron bars being thrust through bands of steel as the doors were locked. Exhilaration hummed though the castle as Aodh pushed her into their bedroom, already kissing her.

But when the moon rose that night, after Aodh built up the fire again and returned to the bed, as he pulled the furs back over their bodies, she whispered, "We are doomed."

"You cannot give up, lass," he said, pulling the covers up to her nose, and fluffing her pillow.

"I am not giving up." She kissed him. "I am marrying you."

He stilled, mid-fluff. "No you are not."

"Yes, I am."

His expression flattened. "No, you're not."

"We are getting married, Aodh."

"Och, you're beautiful to me. And I'll not have you do treason on my behalf."

She laughed. "You were willing enough for it earlier."

"Aye, well, I was a fool. I only *wanted* you then. I did not love you."

Her heart felt both full and horribly squeezed. "We are getting married, Aodh."

"No, we are not, Katy."

R⁄W

THEY WERE MARRIED the next day in the great hall as the sun went down.

As they said their vows, they could hear the sounds of the army coming down the hills outside.

ROGUE WARRIORS

CHAPTER 39

NIGHT FELL. The revelries continued unabated. Indeed, they may have been whipped to a greater frenzy by the approaching army. A defiant wedding, then. It fit.

Music played endlessly. Song and dance erupted in every corner, as did much kissing. There was juggling and mock sword fights, winners and losers toasted with equal fervor. All they wanted tonight was celebration, and anything that resembled it would do the deed.

Aodh and she partook in every moment. Aodh even took to the floor, Katarina on his arm, and showed the hall a dance from England. It was a delicate, precious thing, and much as Katarina liked it, the Irish roared in laughter, and then a few worked their own booted magic on the hard plank floors, bashing away. Then afterward, they fell to playing ancient, evocative music that quite broke the heart, on *bodhrán* and flute.

And instead of escaping to their bedchamber, Aodh and Katarina stayed for it all.

Wedding night or no, with an army amassing outside the walls, they were needed here in the hall. The people needed to see them, to watch them be calm, to play cards together at the dais table, while around them music played. They had all night—neither would sleep. They would go to their bed later. Tonight was for Rardove.

They stayed on the dais after the music stopped, after soldiers and the overflow of guests were bedded down on the hall floors and bedchambers above. They stayed as long as any voices could be heard, murmuring about the wedding or the army outside the gates. Bran curled up at Aodh's feet, and Katarina stuffed a pillow under his head. They played a card game, just the two of them, talking about the map she'd laid on the table beside them, asking him to show her all the places he'd gone.

"We will mark each place you have visited," she said, laying down a five of the trump suit, spades. "And when you were there."

He glanced at the map. "That would take a great many marks." She watched his gaze slide to the New World, then return to the cards in his hand.

"Do you ever regret not going?" she asked quietly.

"Where?"

"To the New World."

He glanced at her, then tossed a card onto the table and sat back. "Regret is a very specific thing. The adventure of it, aye, that lures, but in the end, there are adventures everywhere. I had the opportunity to go, and I did not choose it. I chose Ireland."

"And I am glad," she said lightly, as lightly as one could say she was glad her heart had come to find her body.

His gaze traveled leisurely down her gown. "After all this, and the army outside your castle, you are glad I'm here?"

"After it all, I am glad."

His slow smile was like an ember lit inside her.

"And you, sir, are you glad you did not send me away when you had the chance?" She examined her cards. "My presence may make things more difficult for you with the queen."

"I would die for you, Katy."

Her head jerked up, the blood draining from her face. "Do not say such things."

His smile stilled.

"Never, *ever* say such things."

He looked shocked. "Why, Katy —"

"You will not *die*. 'Die for me.' What is the meaning of that? No, you must *live* for me." She closed her hand into a fist and held it over her chest. "You must live. For me."

She was babbling now. She hit her chest a few times with her fisted hand. Her eyes grew hot and wet and oh *curse* the tears, one spilled over. Aodh could not *die*. On account of her?

They would not become her parents all over again. God save her from that everlasting fate.

Aodh was on his feet, reaching for her. He brought her around the table, down into his lap, soothing her.

"Do not say such things," she whispered, as he kissed her mouth, then her cheeks, then her ear. "Do you hear me?"

"I hear you."

He seemed more intent on kissing than listening, though, so she held his face between her palms, as he had so often held hers, and forced him to look at her. "What does your dying serve, Aodh? Promise you will live for me."

"I promise," he said with an easy smile.

She tightened her hands around his face. "Vow it."

"I vow it." He lifted her to her feet and took her to their room.

Only later did she realize she had not asked the far more pressing question: *Given a choice between Rardove and me, which would you choose?*

Rogue Warriors

Chapter 40

Aodh was up on the walls before dawn. The weather was gloomy, befitting the start of a siege.

Large, smoky-black clouds patrolled the horizon like sullen sentinels. Down on the ground, the English army assembled in the valley. A somber mood prevailed throughout the castle, a far cry from the festivities and enthusiasm of the past few days.

"I think they will try a feint to the west side," Ré was saying, pointing.

Aodh nodded. As they talked, he counted. He had almost a hundred men in-castle, with another a hundred or so Irish allies inhabiting the woods around. The O'Fail were coming, but it would take time to muster them. For now, Rardove was on its own.

The English army had at least five hundred.

It was both satisfying and unsettling that Liz had sent so many. And Ludthorpe... Aodh knew the man, had served under him. He was both competent and decisive. It was highly unlikely that Elizabeth had sent such an experienced commander to parley, rather than engage.

So be it.

The matter was hardly yet decided. Even from this distance, the invaders were clearly uneasy: the camp never settled, sentries walked the perimeter constantly, and a low hum of nervousness hovered over the land.

"I've set up villagers to listen for attempts to undermine the castle…"

Ré's voice drifted off as he stared over Aodh's shoulder. Aodh turned to see what had rendered his captain speechless.

Katarina was striding toward them…in full battle armor. She clutched a handful of arrows in her hand, and had a bow slung over her shoulder. Guns were strapped to her hips.

"Feeling barbaric?" he inquired as she drew up, nodding toward the weapons. And the armor. And the guns.

She smiled and tucked a few loose sprays of hair behind her ear. "Rebellious, I should say."

"Katy, you should not be up here."

"Certes I should," she exclaimed.

He blew out a breath. "I should send you back down."

She smiled at him and Ré, then turned to include Cormac in her mad happiness. "But you will not, because you do not always do as you should."

He eyed her grimly. "I might."

She gave her sword belt a little tug, settling it around her hips. "What if I ask very nicely?"

Ré looked to Aodh, his eyebrows high on his forehead. Cormac grinned.

"Please?" she said.

Silence extended, then Ré said quietly, "If she wants to fight…"

He blew out a breath. "Truthfully, Katy, for all that you've called me 'mad' a thousand times, 'tis you who's the mad one," he muttered, but inside, his heart was beating hot.

This woman had been made for him.

"It is in the water," she agreed, her eyes bright. "Or perhaps the soil. They were correct after all: Rardove does breed rebels."

He smiled, fully intending to plant a kiss on her mouth then turn her and send her somewhere safe—perhaps the cellars, chained to a wall—when he was distracted by the sight of an unfamiliar armored figure arriving on the high tower battlements. Then he saw another. And another.

More were coming, climbing up the stairwells that ascended the interior of the battlement walls, lines of armored figures, belted with weaponry, stepping out on the walls, from north to south, east to west, taking up places beside his men.

"*Dia ár sábháil*," he muttered, and looked down at Katarina. "What have you done?"

A smile lifted her cheeks and pride brightened her eyes. "You did not think I could hold Rardove with only ten men, Aodh, did you?" she said, half teasing, half scolding

"Who are they?"

"Do you not know?"

He squinted and saw long, feminine hair flowing from under many of the helms.

"The women," he said in amazement.

Behind him, Cormac said something in a hushed Scottish brogue that sounded both impressed and impious.

"That is how no one knew you had only ten men," he understood slowly. Aodh's men stared in mute astonishment as the women drew up beside them, but Katarina's garrison simply stepped to the side and made room. "Because you had *women*."

"Dozens of them." She leaned close and said in an almost gleeful whisper, "We quite line the walls, don't we?"

He looked down at her, her shining eyes, her swords and pistols, her endless, boundless vibrancy, and knew he would not be sending her anywhere. Oh, he could carry her off again, lock her up somewhere, but that was not what Katy was meant for. Not what she was made for.

She was made of fire and meant for passion and, at need, for fighting. God knows she'd fought him enough. And yet, for all that, she was not stubborn like his father, nor ambitious, like him. She was simply passion enshrouded in the form of a woman, a warrior in her own right. This was her fight, now, as much as his. She'd chosen it. He would not take it away.

It made his heart full to bursting.

He unfolded his gauntleted hand and curled it gently under her chin, tilting her face up. "You are quite something."

"I am, am I not?" Her eyes were shining.

His gaze slid back to the walls. "They may get hurt."

"They may indeed. As may you. I hope not. I hope none of

us do." She curled her slim fingers around his gauntleted hand. "Aodh, I swear to you, I have no point to make here. If my women were not trained, they would not be up here. But we prevail, or we fall, together. What good are they down below? And can you not make use of a few dozen more well-trained hands?"

"That I can," he said, looking over the new members of his regiment. "You are certain they can use weapons?"

Pity touched her features. "Aodh, my love, what use would a soldier be if she could not use a weapon?"

He dropped a kiss on her nose. "If you are here for battle, Katy, this is the first thing that must go." He tugged the coif off her head. Her hair billowed out like streamers of silk.

"Do I look more barbaric this way?" she asked brightly.

"Much," he said grimly, and gestured to Bran, who came up and handed over his helm. "Go get an extra for yourself, lad."

Bran threw a grin at Katarina and bounded off to do as bidden, while Aodh tugged the linked hood of her hauberk up over her head, smashing her hair down as well as he could. He dropped the helm atop with a gentle pat.

"Your head. Let's keep it safe."

She leaned up and kissed his chin. "And yours."

There was a small commotion just then, near the front of the English army camp, and a mounted contingent rode out from its depths, flying the flag of Elizabeth above a flag of truce.

"Parley," Ré declared quietly as the rider cantered up the pebbled path. "They want to talk."

R⚔W

THEY MET on the field between castle and army.

"Aodh, good God man, what are you about here?" called Sir Charles Ludthorpe, the queen's lieutenant commander and once Aodh's captain, from across the field.

"You're the one who called this meeting," Aodh called back, and Ludthorpe laughed in reply.

They dismounted as they drew to the center of the field.

Behind Aodh, Ré did the same; he and Ludthorpe had brought one man each to this midfield conference, within bowshot of the Rardove soldiers who lined the castle walls, and the English army encamped behind the meadow. The two commanders were open targets for everyone, which was entirely the point.

Ludthorpe vaulted from his horse before it fully stopped and strode over. "I'd never have predicted our reunion would take place here," he announced boisterously, then reached for Aodh's hand and pumped it. "As I recall, Con, you never much cared for Ireland."

Aodh said nothing. What was there to say? That now that he stood again on its green earth, he felt his blood flowing as it never had before? That he knew now he could thrive nowhere but Ireland?

None of that mattered to Ludthorpe. Only surrender mattered. And that could never be.

The buckles on Ludthorpe's vest winked in the sun as he put his hands on his hips and examined the castle defenses. Then he looked back at Aodh. "Well, what are you doing here?"

"I should think that would be obvious."

"Very well. Then *why* are you doing it?"

"I should think that would be equally obvious."

Ludthorpe blew out a gust of air. "The queen is not pleased. Not pleased at all."

"Nor am I. She made me a vow she did not keep."

"That is her privilege, Aodh. She is the queen." Ludthorpe appraised him for a long moment. "Will you surrender, before this descends into further madness?"

"Will the queen honor her promise?"

"It was never a promise. You think we have not all had vague vows snatched away, at inopportune times, given to less worthy men, for reasons of politics or passion or whim? What if we all went about taking castles that did not belong to us?"

Aodh nodded thoughtfully. "But Rardove does belong to me."

Ludthorpe gave a short bark of laughter. "No talking to you, is there?"

"I will talk. Moreover, I will listen, if the queen has something new to say. But if she says what she has ever said, '*Yes, no, never,*' then there is no need. I've heard it a hundred times. She was in error. I am rectifying it. Furthermore, I have offered to hold Rardove for her. Rardove can be loyal. Or it can be rebel. 'Tis up to her."

A begrudging smile touched the captain's face. "I was not sent with the authority to discuss terms other than complete and unconditional surrender."

Aodh shook his head.

Ludthorpe nodded slowly. "And what does the lady say? Lady Katarina?"

Aodh regarded him coldly. "Why?"

The commander shrugged. "Ever has she been loyal to the Crown. Now you arrive, and I receive a letter praising you to the heavens and begging for mercy on your behalf."

"She should not have sent that."

"But she did. Which makes her neatly into a traitor too."

They stared at each other.

"Why do you not at least send her out to me?" Ludthorpe proposed. "Let her step aside, away from this madness, while we handle the matter. She need not be implicated, nor have any blood on her hands. In fact..." He eyed Aodh. "If you send her to me, I will protect her, destroy her note. The queen need never know she turned, not even a quarter turn. She will be blameless. And in that wise, however this matter turns out, whosoever prevails, she will be protected."

His chest felt tight. It was an unexpected offer of kindness, one that would, indeed, protect Katarina no matter what transpired. Aodh had no vision for the future but success, and yet...and yet, Katarina should be protected at all costs, by whatever means.

And yet....

He took a slow breath, then turned and pointed at the castle walls.

"Do you see the soldier in the front of the northwest tower?" he said quietly.

Ludthorpe nodded.

"See the hair?"

Ludthorpe stared, then made a sound of surprise. "That's a woman."

Aodh said nothing

"Methinks I see such hair on a goodly number of them."

"You do. They are hers. And that is she. In the northwest tower. The lady of Rardove."

"Armed?"

He nodded.

"Good God." Ludthorpe whistled in a low breath. "On your behalf?"

Pride and fear moved through him in equal measure. "Aye."

Ludthorpe turned, squinting against the rising sun, his teeth bared in a grin. "You are not to be believed, Mac Con," he said in admiration. "Send her to me and I swear, she will not be harmed."

"It is not my choice to make."

Ludthorpe looked confused.

Aodh turned for St. George. Ré followed, a silent shadow.

"It will not be pretty," the commander called as they swung up on their horses.

"No, it will not." Aodh gathered his reins and nodded toward the tree-lined hills that surrounded them. "There are a great lot of Irishmen out there."

"My scouts estimated a hundred," Ludthorpe revealed. "Not so many."

"More are coming."

Ludthorpe's face tightened. "That is good to know. I do not intend to be here long." The commander pointed to the bright green meadow that stretched in front the castle. "That thing ate one of my cannons." The top half of the long gray barrel of a cannon could be seen, pointing up at an odd angle out of the vibrant green. Its back end and lower portion had been sucked under.

Aodh smiled faintly. "It'll eat everything: armament, horses, men...'tis a hungry meadow."

Ludthorpe laid his hand flat over his brow and peered at the keep. "So the path is the only way," he muttered. "The cliffs behind are far too treacherous."

"The path back to England remains open to you."

Ludthorpe lowered his hand and clapped it against his thigh. "Well, that's that, then. I am sorry it has to end this way, Aodh."

"As am I. Would your men want some whisky?"

The commander's eyes lit up. "Jesus God, man, yes."

Aodh smiled. "I'll have some sent out."

"Anything to lift their spirits. These winds, this wet..."

"God-awful."

"How does one *do* it?" Ludthorpe asked with a burst of impatience. "Live out here, in all this...this wild green?"

"Ireland isn't for everyone."

Ludthorpe met his eye. "But it is for you, eh? At all costs?"

"All of them." Aodh and Ré reined about.

"Elizabeth always favored you, Aodh," Ludthorpe called out. "She would be lenient."

"The queen was always lenient if I did her bidding. Under all other conditions, she is perilous. If you think otherwise, Charles, you do not know her."

R⁄W

BERTRAND, LORD OF BRIDGE, stared at Ludthorpe as he rode back into camp. "You mean to say you simply let him go?"

"I did," Ludthorpe replied curtly, sliding off his horse and striding purposefully into his tent.

Bertrand followed, scowling. "Why?"

"I was within arrowshot of a hundred bowmen."

Ludthorpe bent over his small camp desk and scribbled out a few words on a piece of paper, then handed it to a young soldier who stood waiting.

Outside the tent, the campfires were burning. Soldiers stood around them, eating cold food and drinking warm ale and glancing up into the hillsides and forests that surrounded the valley. Unease flowed through the camp like a fog. All around, the trees seemed to move and whisper as evening winds kicked up. But it wasn't the winds rustling amid the trees; it was the Irish.

No one had expected him to amass allies so swiftly. And if Aodh spoke true, more were coming. Ludthorpe saw no reason to doubt it. Indeed, he'd just received intelligence reporting the O'Fail tribe was mustering, and that was trouble. They would be here in a few days. All the more reason to get the hell out of Ireland.

Aodh had always been exceptionally persuasive, Ludthorpe thought with grim admiration. In only this one matter, of Rardove, had the man failed to get his way.

And it was upon this one that his life would hang.

A pity, such arrogance, such foolish *commitment* to a cause that did not translate directly into money or comfort. For Ludthorpe, causes were a waste of time and manpower. Food and featherbeds mattered more, particularly as he got older. If he handled this matter of Aodh Mac Con to the queen's satisfaction, he would get precisely that, via a grant of the monopoly on the pepper. A rich retirement awaited.

Still, Ludthorpe had to admit, he admired Aodh. And he certes *liked* him far better than the noble idiot now crowing in his ear, Bertrand of Bridge.

"You should have lured him closer to our side of things, and we'd have had a clear shot at his head," Bertrand complained.

"Even if I had I lured him into my tent, Bridge, we were still in parley. Those are the rules of parley: you do not kill one another." He stared out of the tent. Through the flap, which was tied open, pale sunlight lightened the sky, but campfires still shone as bright red dots across the valley floor.

Bertrand came up behind him. *"Rules?"* At the high-pitched angry word, soldiers turned to stare. "Against the Irish, the only rule is burn them out. Stomp them flat. You are a fool, Ludthorpe, if you think—"

"Have a care, Bridge. Rules are the only thing keeping me from taking a broadsword to you right now."

The commander started out of the tent, then swung back

suddenly and spoke in a low voice.

"I know not what the queen sees in you, Bridge, but heed me: do not gainsay me in front of my men again. If you do, I will push you outside the perimeter myself, and let the Irish have their way with you."

ROGUE WARRIORS

CHAPTER 41

WALTER APPROACHED KATARINA in the gardens the next afternoon, while she was laying down a new row of onions.

She could stare at the queen's army only so long. Nothing seemed to be happening—Aodh was correct, no army could lay an effective assault on Rardove. So it seemed they were in for a long siege. Rationing had begun, but again, even there, Rardove provided: men had tromped down to the seas by the treacherous cliff pathway just this morning and netted a large catch of fish.

Being in the garden not only gave her something to do, it was soothing to be kneeling in soft piles of dirt, concerned with nothing but how to make something small grow. Beside her, Susanna crouched, her happy, undemanding chatter as soothing as the sun and earth.

A shadow fell over her, and an urgent voice said, "My lady, come swiftly."

Startled, she yanked her hands out of the dirt. Walter's face was sooty, and he smelled of smoke, as if he'd been standing over a fire. "What happened?"

"There was a small fire—"

She shot to her feet. "Where?"

He waved his hand. "All is contained now, my lady. But you must come. Hurry." He glanced around nervously as he said it.

She wiped the dirt from her hands and swiped her arm across her forehead. "Walter, I—"

"Come my lady, 'tis most urgent."

She let him hurry her to the northern side of the bailey, which backed up to the cliffs below. This portion of the castle was generally deserted, used mostly for storage: old barrels were stacked by the wall; several half broken-down carts stood ready to have someone finish the job; lumber lay ready for use. The old bakehouse listed sideways and now housed small scurrying creatures instead of cook fires.

Up on the walls, soldiers were moving off in the direction of the smoke, leaving the northern side unmanned.

"What is it?" she asked in a faintly complaining tone.

"Someone to see you," Walter said, drawing up at the little postern gate that opened just over the cliffs.

"See me?" she said in surprise.

"From the village."

Originally built to allow small parties of occupants to leave without being detected during sieges, the postern gate led to an extremely narrow pathway, rocky and slick with sea spray, that scaled down the hillside toward the village. Occasionally, at great need, villagers still used it, when they wished to reach the castle quickly, since it was a much more direct route.

It was also much more treacherous. Villagers used it only at times of great need.

With a chill of fear, she hurried toward it. Walter swung the door open and ushered her through. He shut the gate and two English soldiers stepped in from either side.

Katarina stopped short and stared for an uncomprehending second. Then she took a step backward but before she could scream or get inside, they grabbed her, gagged her, wrapped her up, and carried her off to the army camp.

Walter hurried behind.

R⚔W

"I AM SORRY to have been so underhanded in my methods of inviting you up to visit me, my lady," said Captain Ludthorpe as Katarina was escorted into his tent. "But it was imperative that I speak with you."

Still reeling from the capture and Walter's duplicity, Katarina took the cushioned seat he offered. "Some men simply send messages," she told him weakly.

He laughed.

The soldiers had taken her almost all the way to the village to avoid being spotted by the Rardove garrison lining the walls. They were met by a few Irish spies who, it turned out, Walter had enlisted, men who had either no interest in joining a rebellion, or great interest in the coin the soldiers poured into their hands. In any event, the deed was done, and under the disguising cover they provided, Katarina was taken to the army camp.

"The captain merely wishes to *speak* with you, my lady," Walter had kept assuring her as he'd hurried along behind. "I am concerned your mind has been turned by the Irish barbarian and his...attentions."

She'd aimed a lethal glare at him, but Walter kept on.

"Women are, you know. It is not your fault. So I wished to bring you hither, so the captain could hear your petition, and put his to you directly, out from under the influence of the Hound." He cast her a glance. "After all, you said you wished to talk."

That, and the gag in her mouth, kept her from calling him a host of terrible, unchristian names. For if this was true, and the captain was indeed intent on negotiation, perhaps she *could* speak to him. Persuade him.

In any event, she was utterly unable to resist.

Captain Ludthorpe stepped toward a small table. "Yes, well, your clerk indicated it might be difficult to ascertain your true feelings on the matter while inside the castle. He offered to assist me."

"When did he make this offer?"

"He oversaw the whisky delivery," Ludthorpe said with appallingly large smile, and lifted a glass her direction. "Aodh had it sent out. May I offer you some?"

"No. But I would very much like a moment alone with

Walter. And a pistol."

Ludthorpe smiled but shook his head. "He says he only has your best interests at heart."

"I very much doubt that. Where is he?"

"We...have him now." There was something vaguely satisfying about the pause before he said that. Perhaps Ludthorpe did not like Walter much either. "In any event, your clerk felt your head has been turned. And I could not be sure Aodh spoke true, when he said you were fully his, of your own volition."

She held her tongue as the commander sat opposite her in another of his little camp chairs, cup in hand. For a moment, they regarded each other, then he dropped his elbows to his knees, leaning forward, and stared hard at her.

"It would be a most odd development, my lady, for you to have turned. You've always been exceptionally loyal to the Crown. Her Highness was quite taken aback. I counseled that we speak to you directly. That perhaps the news we'd been receiving was not true."

"News?"

"From Bermingham, for one."

"That snake," she snapped. "He bears only ill news."

"Yes, well, if that is all the news there is to bear, one is rather at a loss, is one not?" He peered at her, perhaps waiting for her to indicate she was bearing good news.

She folded her arms over her chest. "What do you want me to say, Captain?"

"The truth."

"Aodh Mac Con is precisely what the queen needs out here on the Irish marches. That is the truth."

Ludthorpe straightened off his elbows. "Aodh has a way of making people think those sorts of things."

"You know him?" she said in surprise.

"We have fought together."

"Then you know he is stalwart, a natural leader of men."

"I know he is in open rebellion."

"And already forming alliances that have eluded me for

years, sir. With both the Irish and the English. And he…"

The commander was shaking his head slowly. "Open. Rebellion."

She cleared her throat. "I do think he can be persuaded to come to terms."

He laughed and set down his cup. "I do not know if Aodh told you, but I offered sanctuary, my lady. To you."

"Sanctuary?"

"Let us say pardon, then. The queen is willing to be forgiving to you."

"How forgiving?"

He shrugged. "Your decision here was not so surprising, in the end. Your castle was overrun, you were under duress, trapped, perhaps forced to…do things." Their eyes met. "Mayhap even to send messages with your name affixed to them. Perhaps to ride with the rebels, and broker alliances with other rebels."

So, they knew of The O'Fail. Curse Walter.

Ludthorpe's voice became more persuasive. "In such circumstances, the queen would be strongly inclined to be forgiving, lady. I give you my deepest assurances." He lifted his eyebrows, giving her the chance to simply confirm his guesses, and settle the matter, once and for all.

She leaned down as the captain had done, elbows on her knees, and lowered her voice as he had done.

"I am under no duress, Captain, and Aodh Mac Con is England's last, best chance out here beyond the Pale."

He snapped back in his chair and his gaze traveled down her gown. "I saw you on the walls. You, one of the most loyal nobles of the realm, in open rebellion. *With an Irishman.*"

She extended a hand. "Then I offer that as my proof, Captain: if he can convince even the Crown's most loyal supporters that he is the best man for Rardove, and furthermore, if he does not *wish* to rebel, but wishes to serve, then perhaps he is precisely what the Crown needs. As you point out, he has fomented a rebellion that stretches across the entire northern portion of Ireland in a fortnight. From whence do such powers come?"

"The devil?" suggested the commander drily.

"From within." She tapped her chest. "If a single man turned, so be it, such things can be dismissed as little more than self-interest, or foolishness, a man too easily overawed, some such."

"And if one woman does...?"

She pressed on. "But that is not the case. Aodh has persuaded all manner of men to turn to his cause. Both the small and the powerful, English and Irish."

"Yes, the English concern me greatly."

"As well they should. It is a testament to the need for a change, do you not think, that even the English are willing to join this rebellion? He has roused them, but only because they wished to be roused. Matters cannot go on as they are, sir. Aodh has indeed fomented open rebellion. He can just as easily dispel it. I tell you, sir, these men did not join a revolution. They joined *him*. If Aodh is here, in command, and loyal to the Crown, they too will be loyal."

"I do not think it is so simple a matter, my lady."

"But it can be. If you wish it to be, sir, you could avoid much bloodshed here. You could carry my entreaty, present it to the queen, explain the matter."

He drank slowly, watching her, and faint hope rose in her chest. "I was not sent to avoid bloodshed, my lady."

Coldness stabbed through the bubble of hope that had started rising. "No, indeed," she agreed coldly, sitting back. "For if you were, you would not have burned my lands."

"I would not have had to burn your lands if you had not rebelled against your queen."

"They did not rebel." She pointed out the tent at the rest of Ireland. "You have made enemies here, Commander, which I am fairly certain is *also* something you were not sent here to do."

She forced her breath to calm, for it had accelerated as the certainty grew that Ludthorpe was not here to listen at all but to command.

His eyes narrowed at her scathing assessment of his tactics

and her veiled warning.

"It is your actions that have brought them to this state, lady. Nevertheless, remedies exist for one who has been so loyal for so many years. If you were willing to show sense, we could find a compromise."

"How would I show sense?"

"I have instructions that you may stay in residence, should you prove yourself to me, and re-pledge any…honor that may have been lost to the rebel." Innuendo curled his words into something dark.

"Prove myself how?"

"Turn over the Irishman. The queen wishes only for Aodh Mac Con."

"Only him, is it? And then?"

"Then, you will be…left here."

"I meant what then for Aodh Mac Con?"

His battle-gnarled hands lifted the glass. "Do not concern yourself with rebels, my lady. That is what I am here to manage."

"You cannot manage Aodh, sir. In any event, I am already intimately concerned. I have wed him. Did Walter not mention that?"

A ripple of impatience tightened his square jaw. "He did not."

"Do you not wonder what else he may not have told you?"

He hesitated, suddenly wary. "Wedding the outlaw was a reckless thing to do, lady."

"Yes, yes, I am well aware of that," she said impatiently. "A lifetime on the Irish marches has seen that deed done."

"You were reckless long before the marches, Katarina," drawled a voice from the shadows.

She turned sharply and saw Bertrand of Bridge step into the light.

Even now, years later, the sight of him was powerful. Throat-tightening, hand-clenching powerful. He drew closer and she suddenly recalled the way he'd smelled that night all those years ago, of sour ale and garlic, exhaled wetly across her face.

"Slicing your face open with a blade was not reckless, my Lord Bridge," she said coldly. "It was self-protection."

The commander looked between them, his eyebrows high in surprise. Then he surveyed the faint ladderlike row of stitched scars that bumped down Bertrand's left cheek. "You know each other," he intuited.

Bertrand held out a hand. "Come, my lady, I have made a case for you to the commander." Ludthorpe's eyebrows went higher yet. "The Crown will be merciful to you."

She laughed. "As it was to the peasants en route here?" He seemed startled by the mention of peasants. "As it will be to Aodh?"

"Aodh?" Bertrand's face twisted. "You call the Irish rebel Aodh? Oh, you have gone to the devil out here on the marches, lady. In England, we call him traitor. He has gainsaid the queen, fomented rebellion, stolen a castle, and countermanded orders. That is your 'Aodh.'"

She folded her hands over her belly. "I see you have heard of him."

The commander's mouth twitched. Bertrand fabricated a stiff smile and stretched it across his mouth, so level it did not even bend the thin, trimmed moustaches that topped his upper lip. "His Irish wit has infected you."

"It comes down in the rain, my lord. Perhaps if you spent some time here, it would infect you as well. But you have never spent any time in Ireland, have you? And nevertheless think you can rule it."

He stared in amazement, glanced at the commander, then back at Katarina. "You...you cannot expect the *Irish* to rule Ireland?" He laughed in astonishment. "Why, even a woman would be better than one of them."

She cast him a derisive glance. "The marches would gnash you in their teeth before a week was out. I have ruled here for seven years. How long have you ruled anything at all?"

A flush of anger and embarrassment scalded red across Bertrand's face. "I am a nobleman, lady, born to lead."

"Aodh Mac Con is twice the leader you shall ever be." Now the flush of red was bright, like a stain. "Know you how many English souls have cleaved to him out here, amid peril and uncertainty?"

"Fools."

"They do it for love."

"Is that why you do it, cunt?" He grabbed her elbow and yanked her to her feet. "Share your charms with a dirty Irishman and not me?"

She jerked on her arm, but he shook her so hard, her teeth rattled.

On the other side of the table, the commander got to his feet. "That's enough, Bridge," he said coldly.

"It is not enough. These marches need an iron grip. Your rebellious spirit is proof of it, Katarina. The way you rule these people is you grab hold," he shook her arm, "and squeeze." He tightened his fingers into a painful circlet of anger. "And you never let up. That is how you rule a lawless land and a barbarous people. The Irish understand nothing less. Apparently, neither do you."

He backhanded her across the cheek.

"Stand down, Bridge," shouted the commander.

She reeled away from the blow, her mouth bleeding. Bertrand yanked her back, but the commander hauled him away and spun him as he released, so Bertrand ended up on the far side of the tent.

"I said stand down," Ludthorpe said coldly.

Katarina, cheeks burning, lifted her chin. "You are wrong, Bertrand. Neither I nor the Irish will ever submit to one such as you, no matter how hard you squeeze or how much blood you draw."

He lunged for her, but the commander pulled her out of the way and put a hand out, stopping Bertrand. Then Ludthorpe looked down at her.

"I am sorry, my lady, but we are wasting time here. You are not what we want. Open the gates for us, and you will be spared."

Blood pooled hotly in the corner of her mouth from her split lip. Shaking, her breath coming fast and shallow, she realized now there was no hope. None at all. Nothing but open defiance.

She had become her father.

"No, my lord, I will not. Even if I wished it, I have not that power. Aodh commands the castle now, and he will not open the gates for anything."

The commander eyed her a moment. "I doubt that," he murmured and turned for the tent flap.

She took an instinctive step after him. "What do you mean?"

"Bind her and bring her to the front," Ludthorpe ordered the guard outside.

A knife blade of fear slicked through her belly. "What are you doing?"

Ludthorpe glanced back. "I'm going to stand you up on a cannon and offer Aodh Mac Con a choice: he surrenders, or you die."

ROGUE WARRIORS

CHAPTER 42

AODH STOOD on the southern wall, chewing a piece of bread and talking with Ré as they surveyed the army below, when a small group broke free from the main English camp and came forward.

"Does the end of the day bring any further clarity to your stubbornness, Aodh?" Ludthorpe's voice carried thinly through the speaking trumpet up to the battlement wall.

Aodh shook his head and turned to Ré. "Reckless. We are being *reckless*. Why do they keep calling it stubborn?"

Ré lifted an armored shoulder and let it drop. "Translations."

Aodh cupped his hands around his mouth and called down, "I remain as clear as ever. Rardove or death." He paused. "Your westward cannon is sinking." He pointed.

"Let me add an additional consideration."

There was a shifting of the men who flanked the commander, then a lithe figure with blowing skirts was pushed to the front and thrust up to stand on the cannon beside Ludthorpe.

Katarina.

"Jesus God," someone muttered.

"My lady!" someone else gasped. Rippled exclamations of horror and outrage moved along the walls, a wave of curses and shrieks.

Aodh stared down at the sight of Katarina, her hands bound behind her back, her chin up, her small, pale face pointed right at him.

He gripped the stony walls tighter and tighter, until hard bits of rubble broke off in his hands. They bit into his skin like fangs. Blood dripped down his hands, but he didn't notice. His head pounded.

"We have your stubborn lady, Aodh," the commander called.

"Reckless," Cormac muttered.

"I will see she has a traitor's death, unless you surrender yourself."

Sickness soured his belly, and he dropped his head as the images held at bay for so many years were finally, finally unleashed on him.

His father, bleeding on the battlefield, clutching Aodh's shoulder with a mangled hand, making him vow to get Rardove back by whatever means necessary. His father, dragged away by his heels through the mud, black earth mixing with red blood. His father, hanged and taken down while still alive, tied up and cut open, disemboweled, his traitorous parts flung to the far corners of the kingdom.

Katarina, facing the same.

Slowly, his hand fisted around the rubble, he started to go down to his knees.

He heard someone curse and there was a jerk on his arm, then Ré was there, holding him, pushing him up against the high crenel with a forearm, his hip against Aodh's, holding him up. "Aodh. Aodh!"

He shook his head, clearing it.

He jerked free, then wiped his hand over his mouth and swung back to Katarina. Her gown flowed around her. The small figure of Ludthorpe moved, then lifted something to her face. The trumpet. She was to say something to him. No doubt a call to surrender.

"Do not!" Thin and tiny, her voice came up. One of the soldiers holding her gave her a hair a shake. Aodh almost lunged over the forty-foot wall. "You promised," she called again through the trumpet, wrenching free from the

constraining arm. "*You promised me.*"

He whirled back around and stared into the horrified faces of his men. Ré, Cormac, Bran, all staring at him in stupefied silence.

Aodh stared back at them for a heartbeat. Here, then, was the true danger of Katarina. She could do what armies and mercenaries and kings and queens had not been able to: make him give up Rardove.

He spun and hurried down the rampart wall, making for the stairs. "Open the gate."

Ré cursed and hurried after. "Wait, Aodh, speak to me."

"Walk with me." Aodh leapt down the last two steps and hit the bailey ground in a puff of dirt. Ré jumped down after.

As they passed through the bailey, people turned and stared, as the news began moving through the castle.

They strode past staring eyes and dropped jaws, the inhabitants and allies of the lord of Rardove struck dumb by this disastrous turn of events.

There were more people within the walls of Rardove at this moment than had ever been there in its history, yet silence reigned as he and Ré strode through its center of it.

The only sound was the squawking of chickens and the jingle of horse tack and knightly gear: bridles, buckles, sword hilts. Somewhere, far back, a dog barked, and drifting in from over the walls, the low murmur of smoke and death an army always carries on its back.

"You cannot go out there," Ré insisted, his face sweaty.

"I am to leave her out there?" Aodh replied, grabbing hold of a rope that hung by the gatehouse and swinging himself up five or six steps, then taking the rest three at a time, climbing to the top of the gatehouse, en route to the inner stairwell that would lead to the door outside.

Ré followed after. "I shall go in your stead."

Aodh stopped short and spun, clapping Ré on his shoulder. "Never, my friend."

"*Please*, my friend," was all Ré said, his voice tight and low. It echoed off the stone of the gatehouse they'd just entered.

"They need you here."

"They need her."

"They need you *both*."

"Very well. But if there can only be one, 'tis better she than I. You know this is true. She has been here longer than I. She loves it more than I. I brought brief glory and war, but for nigh on a decade, she ensured peace and safety."

Ré said in a furious, low voice, "We shall have you both. We will work something out...come up with some plan..."

"There is no time." He turned into the gatehouse. It was cool and dark. His boots echoed as he clattered down the stairs.

Ré grabbed his shoulder and spun him back around. "Aodh, it cannot end like this."

Aodh's gaze searched his, then he smiled faintly. "God's truth, Ré, who said this is an end?"

Ré's angry eyes met his. "If not an end, then what? What are you doing?"

"I'm going to get Rardove back."

"You're going to get killed." *Hanged, disemboweled, beheaded.*

"Katarina is Rardove, Ré. I'm going to get her back."

His soldiers stared as he passed them by, clattering down the inner stairway, patting them on the shoulder as he passed. He reached the bottom and pushed the door open.

Golden sunlight poured inside. In the distance, like little poking sticks, the army waited.

Aodh glanced back at Ré's ashen face. "Do not let Cormac have St. George."

"Goddammit," Ré muttered, his voice cracking.

He stepped out into the sunshine.

CHAPTER 43

"YOU COULD HAVE BEEN spared all that is to come, my lady," Ludthorpe said to Katarina as he pulled her down off the cannon.

She felt the cold, in her chest, down her belly, great folds of it, like a frozen *léine* was being wrapped around her.

"How?" she whispered, staring at the castle. Aodh's figure was no longer on the walls. He must be coming. Coming for her. Coming for his death.

"You are English. It did not need to be this way."

She looked over. Her neck seemed to have stiffened, her arms and shoulders too, so it took some time for her to turn. "I am Irish, my lord, to the marrow of my bones. And you cannot take it from me, nor me from it, without tearing out my very bones."

"Then tear them out we shall."

"You cannot grind them so small that it will disappear."

He looked at her a moment, his nostrils quivering. "Then I am sorry for you."

"No, sir," she said coldly. "You are afraid of me." Then she saw the gatehouse door open, and her heart stopped beating.

Aodh's tall, unmistakable figure appeared, coming down the hill. From a thousand yards away, she would have known it was him.

"No!" she screamed, jerking against the ropes and Bertrand's constraining hand. "Go back!"

308

Bertrand grappled to catch hold of her again, but she ran forward, out of his grip, shouting in Irish, "You vowed you would live for me. You vowed it!"

Behind her, a chorus of startled English shouts rose up.

"What did she say? Is that a spell?"

"Is she a witch?"

"Accursed Irish garble."

Then, louder than the rest, "Grab her, for God's sake."

She made it perhaps twenty yards before she was grabbed from behind and wrenched backward into a soldier's chest. She hung there in his armored grip, hands tied behind her back, panting, watching Aodh come up as if nothing were amiss, as if he was meeting her for a picnic out on the green grass. The wind blew his hair, his eyes locked on hers, and the archers trained their arrows on his chest.

Even when they shouted at him to stop, he did not stop looking at her. He stopped walking, but he did not stop looking at her.

And when they ordered him to remove his sword and blades and pistols, he did not stop looking.

And when they ordered him to kneel down, and put his hands behind his head, he never looked away from her.

Tears, fat and hot, birthed themselves from her eyes, a nursery of tears. She wrestled uselessly against her captor's hands as they bound him and lifted him to his feet.

"Aodh, *dúirt tú go mhairfeadh tú domsa,*" she called when he was brought near enough. *You said you would live for me.*

"*Shíl mé go raibh muid ag labhairt teoiriciúil,*" he replied.

"Theoretical?" she repeated, incredulous he could jest at such a perilous time. "*Níl, Aodh, tháinig na focail ó cheartlár mo chroí.*"

"As did I," he said, being dragged nearer, his eyes intent. "Every word." He glanced up, then hollered loudly enough to turn heads. "Ludthorpe!"

The commander was deep in discussion with his captains, and already, tents were being broken down, men hurriedly grabbing bundles and tossing them onto wagons, hitching up horses.

At Aodh's call, Ludthorpe turned. "Welcome to my army, Con!" he called. "I am pleased you decided to visit."

"It was the least I could do, since you had my wife."

The commander smiled. "We're going to take a little trip, back to England, you and I. The Irish press upon one so in Ireland."

Aodh turned toward Katarina and saw her face now, closer up. He went still. "What happened to her?"

Ludthorpe sighed. "It was a misfortune. Of Bridge's."

A ripple moved through Aodh. "Release her. Now."

It was almost obscene for Aodh to be giving commands, bound and manhandled as he was. But nevertheless, Ludthorpe turned to the soldier who held Katarina, but Bertrand stepped up, his face furious.

"No! She comes with us. I decide what to do with the spoils and the hostages," he added hastily when Ludthorpe turned toward him, no doubt recalling the threat about being thrust outside the English lines for the native Irishry to feast upon. But in this, he was correct—being noble gave him certain precedence, for all that he was not in command, and Ludthorpe paused, then shrugged.

Bertrand looked triumphantly at Aodh. "You are fortunate I do not have you beheaded right here, Mac Con," he snarled.

Aodh stared at him. The seconds ticked away and he never broke gaze. Bertrand's face flushed a hot red, then he turned and snapped at a subordinate, cuffing him on the back of the head when the man did not hurry fast enough. Aodh turned back to Ludthorpe.

"May I have a moment with my wife?" he asked quietly.

Bertrand started to protest, but Ludthorpe cut him off. "Concern yourself with matters that matter, my lord," the commander said tersely, and nodded to the soldier who held Katarina. "Let her speak to him. And for God's sake, cut her cords."

Bertrand seemed about to complain, but subsided when Ludthorpe turned a glare on him. "We bound the lady to bring in the Hound, Bridge," he said coldly. "The Hound is here, so we cut her cords. Have you a reasonable argument, speak."

Bertrand scowled mutinously but subsided, stalking a few paces away to glower at them.

Katarina watched as Aodh was led up in front of her. The sky stretched out behind him in glorious, unending blue, Aodh was a dark stroke of masculinity in the foreground, clouding her vision. She could see nothing but him. The soldiers shoved him roughly to within a foot of her, and Aodh, mad thing, bent his head and kissed her.

Arms bound behind his back, hers just cut free, the rope ends still dangling, they kissed, a hot, passionate, diving kiss, more lunging than loving. Aodh gave his powerful torso a mighty shake and, for a moment, freed himself from his captors. At this much liberty, he took another step nearer and leaned over her, opened her mouth beneath his with hard, furious, delving strokes, the last kiss of a dying man.

She wrapped her arms around his shoulders and hung on, kissing him back.

People tried to drag them apart, but Katarina's grip tightened. Bertrand cried out, "I warned you he was mischief!"

Shouts ran rampant, the commander hollered for people to drag Bertrand out of there, soldiers grappled, knocking into each other, and in the midst of the mayhem, Aodh ripped his mouth from hers and whispered into her ear, "*Cruthaigh mé mearbhall, Katy.*"

She looked up into the blue eyes so close to hers. "A distraction?"

"Aye. Slip away. *Ní tusa ata ag iarraidh orthu. Mise amháin atá á lorg acu.*"

"Oh, you are wrong. Bertrand most certainly wants me," she whispered back in Irish. "He wants both of us."

"That is why you must slip away. Nothing is served if we are both taken. Rardove needs you."

"I—"

"Katy," he said in a furious Irish whisper, "if I am not here, and you are not here, Bertrand will be."

They peeled her arms from around his shoulders, forced her

away, dragging her backward. *"Is cuma liom,"* she cried. *"Níl sé ag teastáil uaim. Níl uaim ach tusa. Tusa amháin."*

"It is too late for that, Katy. It does not matter if you want it. You *are* Rardove." They hauled him roughly away. "Be Rardove. I need you to be that, for me. For our people."

With a wicked jerk, they turned him away. The soldiers holding Bertrand released him, and he flew at Aodh in a fury. Aodh watched him come, then drew his head back and snapped it forward just as Bridge reached him, smashing his forehead into Bertrand's face.

Bertrand's legs kicked out from beneath him as he flew backward with a hollered cry, then he hit the dirt, flat on his back, nose gushing blood. He rolled to the side, howling, clutching his face.

The soldiers exploded into laughter. "Bring the Hound here," the commander said, holding out a hand for Aodh.

They propelled him up the hill. Blood trickled from Aodh's forehead down his nose as he looked back at her. "I could not be more serious, Katy," he said in Irish. "Do as I say. Go now. Stay near Ludthorpe. You will see your chance. Take it."

Staying near the man who'd held her hostage for Aodh's surrender seemed like a particularly bad idea. The commander held her gaze a moment, then, very levelly, shifted it away. "Here we go," he shouted. "Everyone, move out!" He snapped back at the soldier holding Katarina, "For God's sake, release her and make yourself useful."

With a jerk, the soldier did, then glanced at Bertrand, who was still sprawled, clutching his bleeding nose, in the mud. "Ought I get him up, sir?"

Ludthorpe shook his head. "Not yet." His gaze came up and brushed over Katarina's. "Let's be off," he said to the soldier, and, very nonchalantly, very definitely, left her standing there, unbound and unguarded.

The soldiers tossed her a confused glance, but having no desire to gainsay their master, and having a great desire to get the hell out of Ireland, they followed him.

The camp turned to noisy chaos as tents were broken down,

wagons loaded, horses saddled. Only Katarina stood, twenty paces out from the main army camp, alone in the field, with Bertrand nearby, sitting in the mud, starting to groan and shake his head from side to side.

She backed up a few steps, then turned and ran.

ROGUE WARRIORS

CHAPTER 44

THE SOLDIERS UP ON the walls gave a shout when they saw her coming. Seven of them braved the open pathway to run to her, surrounding her like dark caped wraiths in the coming twilight. They hurried her back inside the walls.

She rushed straight for the keep, and straight into Dickon, almost toppling him over.

"My lady," was all he said. His voice was broken, his face pale and haggard, his eyes red-rimmed; he'd been crying. "Oh, my lady," he cried, then stilled when he noticed her face, where Bertrand had struck her. "What happened?"

She pulled him to her, then, holding his arms, set him away a little and peered into his eyes. "I am fine, but Dickon, heed me, we have things to do."

"Aye, my lady," he said miserably. "What things?"

She squeezed his shoulder. "We must bring Lord Aodh home again."

His eyes rounded and he straightened his scrawny spine. "Aye! My lady, aye!"

Holding him by the shoulder, as much to comfort him as support herself, she hurried them though the baileys. They were in an uproar. Shouts and yells rang from one end to the other. People ran here and there, shadows cast huge against walls as they passed to and fro. Both baileys were lit with bonfires and soldiers stood at the ready.

"Run and get Ré and Cormac," she said in a low murmur

314

that cut through the chaos. "And then bring my cloak. And sword. And pistols. To the front door, now, Dickon, swift as swift can be."

The boy darted off and she hurried through the mayhem toward the keep, throwing off her hood, speaking to the castle folk she passed, who plied her with questions and fears.

On the walls and in every corner of both baileys, Aodh's men and hers had joined together as one. They hauled buckets laden with wood up the walls and kept the huge kettles of oil boiling, which could be poured on the heads of enemy combatants who might try to breach the gates. Men and women perched together in the gloom, their bows aimed down in the valley below.

Even as she flew through the bailey, cries of alarm turned to cries of confusion, as the English army began moving out, leaving a smaller contingent behind.

Wicker ran past her, directing men with a stretch of his armored arm and loud, firm commands. When he saw her, he flung back his head and closed his eyes, then made the sign of the cross over his chest and hurried to her side.

"My lady," he said, gripping her arm. "Praise God you are returned to us."

"We are going to get him back," she said grimly.

His hand tightened on her forearm and his eyes lit. He went so far as to grin at her, because Wicker's blood fired as hers did, and he had always been her biggest supporter. "How?" was all he said.

"In the way we have done all the rest, Wicker, by hook or by crook."

His grin grew. "I'll ready myself—"

"You'll stay here."

His face fell.

Now it was her turn to tighten her hold on his arm. "Wicker, I need you here. As captain of the guard. You *must* lead the men. You *must* hold the keep. There is no one else I can trust so well as you." She squeezed his arm. "I am depending on you."

Taut lines rippled along his jaw, then he gave a clipped nod.

She hurried to the keep. The shadows of hurrying people were tossed, long and haggard, up across the walls. She charged up the stairs to the keep and reached for the door just as it was flung open by Ré.

He and Cormac stopped short. They stared at her bruised face, their own faces devoid of emotion, but their eyes... Their leader and friend had been stripped from them. On account of her.

It all shone in their eyes: they were not exceptionally fond of her right now.

Most especially Ré. From everything she'd been able to ascertain, Ré had been suspicious of her and her value from the start. Suspicious of how deeply Aodh cleaved to her.

All those suspicions had just been proven well-founded, had they not?

"We are going to get Aodh," she announced.

Astonishment lit their hardened faces. "How?" Cormac said.

She frowned. "How should I know? We ride, we catch up, we...do some deeds that recover him."

A faint smile crossed Ré grim face. Cormac's jaw dropped. "I'd never have believed it of you, lady," he said, wiping his hand over his face as if to clear it of a cobweb.

"And why not?" she demanded, as Dickon came bounding down the stairs, bundled under so many cloaks and weapons he looked like a pack pony. Behind him hurried Susanna, carrying several satchels and strapped with pistols.

Cormac scratched his head. "Well, my lady, meaning no offense, but you're English, and—"

"I am half Irish," she retorted, reaching for the sword belt first.

Ré looked at Cormac. "And I am full English," he said in faint rebuke, then took the cloak hanging over half of Dickon's head and began fastening it around Katarina's shoulders.

"Aw, you're a testy bunch," Cormac muttered, taking a satchel from Susanna.

"Food," Susanna murmured, heaving another pack into his

arms. "Drink." She hoisted another one into Ré's hands. "Powder and shot. And salves." She looked at Katarina. "Be safe," then glanced at Cormac and tipped up on her toes and kissed his cheek. "You too," she whispered.

Cormac's face, what could be seen above the beard, flooded red. He fisted his hands around the baggage once, twice, then, with a curse, dropped everything and flung his arms around her. He planted a long, hard kiss on her mouth. Then he gathered all the bags back up.

"I'll watch out for your lady," he promised gruffly.

"And I shall watch out for him," Katarina said as they turned for the door.

Bran appeared on the stairs. They stopped.

"My lady, may I... I must..." His voice broke for a second. "I am coming with you."

Cormac, after a glance toward Katarina, spoke first. "Lad, you'll be needed here."

"I am coming with you."

Ré spoke almost gently, "Aodh specifically ordered you to stay here, Bran. He wanted you safe—"

"He raised me. He saved me. I am coming."

Katarina saw in his eyes exactly what she felt in her heart. Such things could not be denied.

"Of course you are coming," she said firmly, and flung the door open. Cormac shook his head, and Ré all but glared at her. "He doesn't want to be safe," she told them. "He wants Aodh. Surely we can all understand that. Come, we must be off. The army will move directly for England, and the queen will not be kind to Aodh."

She had no further plan than this. *The queen will not be kind* was not, in actuality, a plan, but these were Aodh's men, built for reckless adventures, and they required no convincing.

R⚬W

NIGHTTIME WAS EVERYWHERE by the time they squeaked open the small back gate and stepped onto the path that traversed the precipice that overlooked the sheer cliff and the drop-off to the rocky, turbulent waters below.

Carefully, they led their horses along the slippery, cliffside. The hard rock trail underfoot was damp, reflecting moonlight off stone like wet obsidian.

"Jesus save us," Cormac muttered, his rumbling murmur bouncing off the stones, "If I didn't know better, lady, I'd swear you were trying to kill us."

"I did not realize you were afraid of heights," she said, leading the way, her hood pulled forward so she was little more than a dark shadow.

Cormac stiffened but didn't look up from the ground beneath his boots, "No' frightened, simply...cautious."

"Since when?" Ré inquired from behind.

"I'm a cautious fellow, at times," came the indignant, if faint, reply.

"Aodh did not mention 'cautious' in his descriptions of you," Katarina said, supporting Ré in this line of questioning.

"Talkin' about me, was he?" Cormac muttered.

"He spoke of all of you." She stepped over a portion of the path that was washed away. Rocks dribbled into the little gorge that had been left behind. A little earth slide cascaded into the miniature crevasse, and bounced noisily down the vee.

"What'd he say?" Cormac asked.

A few more pebbles skidded down and fell blackly into the chasm below. She tightened her hands on the wet leather reins of her horse and walked on a little faster. "He told me Ré was most bold, Bran fiercely loyal, and you were middling with a bow, and lethal with everything else. He also mentioned you were a most valiant drinker of ale. Mind the washout," she added, as if it were an afterthought.

"Valiant, is it?" he railed indignantly. "An' he said nothin' of Ré's drinkin', did he?" He snorted and stepped over the washed-out portion indignantly.

"He said you could drink Ré under the table," she informed him.

"Hardly," the amiable retort drifted up from the back of the line, where Ré brought up the rear. And in this way, they distracted Cormac from the plunging depths to their left until they reached the end of the rocky cliff trail and stepped out onto the grassy earth.

Then smoothly and in single file, caped and hooded, like moving shadows, they rode down the only path of safety through the bog and followed after the queen's army.

R⚔W

THEY TAILED THE ARMY for two days, but it moved swiftly, never stopping for more than an hour or so. There was no chance to intercept it, or sneak inside its perimeter, nor to make any sort of more complicated plan. The army reached their ships and loaded up immediately, eager to return with their prize. No delay, no pause.

Above the town, Katarina, Ré, Cormac, and Bran watched the launch. After two days' riding, they were a motley-looking crew and would never get through the gates.

"I suppose we must hire ourselves a smuggler," Katarina announced, realizing she had utterly turned a corner. Lover of rebels, employer of smugglers.

"We don't need smugglers," Ré replied, reining about.

"Why not?"

"We *are* smugglers." He cantered off down the hill.

Katarina started after him. "Where is he going?"

"To our boat," Cormac said, gathering his reins. Bran followed suit, and Katarina reined around too, their hooves a low thunder as they raced back down the hill.

She'd forgotten they had a boat. How like Aodh, to have provided the very thing that would assist in his own rescue.

ROGUE WARRIORS

CHAPTER 45

"HOW ARE WE EVER going to get in there?"

They stood outside the English army encampment as night fell. Campfires burned inside the perimeter, bright punches of dancing flames amid the dark bodies of tents and soldiers, who were in a celebratory mood.

And for good reason. The English battalion had had an easy sailing across a notoriously shifty sea, after having accomplished their mission for the queen with surprising speed and no bloodshed. Even now, their commander had ridden on ahead to inform the queen of their successful accomplishment, leaving the army encamped outside this small town, as night fell and revelry erupted.

On the morrow, they would bring the queen her prize, the Irish rebel. Which is why they were understandably and intensely celebratory.

The nearby townsfolk seemed of a like mind. Merchants and vendors and whores streamed into the army camp as it lit up under the night sky, and a festive atmosphere reigned. An army marching *into* your town was bad news, but passing *by* it en route to other, non-military business was an entirely different matter. The aspiring merchant or whore could make a lucrative showing.

But exultant and celebratory, the army had not entirely relaxed its guard: everyone entering was being searched.

"We shall get in as merchants," said Ré firmly.

They all looked at the merchants walking by. Every one had a barrel or basket or wagon of goods. The only ones who did not were the tricksters and the whores.

"Can any of you do tricks?" Katarina asked, watching a trained bear go by.

"I can juggle a bit, ma lady."

Everyone turned to the great hulking mass of Scotsman.

"You *juggle*?" Incredulity stretched Ré's voice as if it was on a rack.

A huge shoulder lifted in a nonchalant shrug. "Upon a time. Learned when I was a lad. Earned a penny by it here and there."

"Cormac, every day, you become more of a revelation to me," Ré said in an admiring tone.

"That's just what ma mam said," Cormac replied comfortably.

And finally, finally, Bran smiled. Bran who had not smiled, nor barely spoken, since leaving Rardove. In response, she patted Cormac's arm fondly. "Then juggle you shall, sir. With Ré and Bran as your assistants. And I... I think I shall make a credible whore." She pulled up her hood and tugged on the collar of her bodice. "Do you think I look like a whore?"

They stared. She'd bathed briefly in the cove they'd sailed from last night, where the water came down over the rocks in a pool lit by reflected moonlight, so it seemed to be a home for nymphs more than men. She'd washed her tunic and hair, and tucked it all back under the veil, but perhaps... Well, one could not be sure how one looked after several days of riding a horse, chasing an army.

"You're the best-looking whore I've ever seen," Cormac assured her in reverent tones. He sounded slightly choked up.

Ré smacked him on the back of the head and turned to her. "My lady, you should wait here. We will get Aodh."

"Yes, with a great deal of bloodshed and attention, which will never do. In any event, you cannot stop me. I am going to be a whore."

Ré wiped his hand over his face. "Aodh will have my head," he muttered into his palm.

"I shall stand for you," she assured him. Then Cormac, ever helpful, reached out with huge, beefy hands, and puffed up her hair a little. "They like it a bit more tousled," he informed her soberly.

She thanked him for the insight.

"At least, I should be the one slipping into the tent," Ré said, and Cormac, hands still in her hair, nodded. "Or myself, ma lady."

She sighed. "We have already been over this. There will almost certainly be guardsmen inside the tent, and they will not be distracted by *a man* stepping into their tent, at least not in the way we want. Only a woman can do that. Whereas the guards *outside* the tent will be very distracted by an argument occurring in front of their faces. With a juggler."

Ré watched in dismay, and Bran watched, impassive, as Cormac dropped his hands, her hair apparently sufficiently tousled. She smiled at him and tugged at the laces of her gown, loosening them a little more.

Ré closed his eyes. Cormac examined her with a soldier's eye, then nodded. "You'll do," he said. Ré groaned.

"The green tent is Ludthorpe's," Bran informed her.

She nodded and tugged her hood forward.

"You get Aodh, and you go," Ré said grimly as they started walking. "Do not wait for us. We meet back at the cave."

They all nodded silently, and glided toward the camp.

R/W

THEY MADE IT IN easily, and moved straight toward the green tent. Katarina hung back, head averted, hood up, waiting until Ré and Cormac started a full-on argument that was clearly tending toward violence, then skirted behind the two guardsmen who, as predicted, stepped forward to watch, and slipped inside the tent.

She straightened immediately, prepared to offer explanations and anything else that might be required, momentarily, in order to distract the men and free Aodh. She would just have to hope Aodh could, at some point, offer his own invaluable assistance.

But there were no soldiers. There was only darkness, the pale ambient light of moon and fire that filtered in from outside, and a single figure, slumped sideways on the ground, propped against the tent pole, arms wrenched behind his back, lashed with rope to the pole.

"Aodh," she whispered. "Oh dear God."

His face had been beaten. Dried blood formed a crusted river down his cheek and jaw and neck, stuck to his half-grown beard and clothes. His booted legs were stretched out, half-bent, boot heels dug into the earth. His head hung to the side, as if he were unconscious.

Or dead.

Her body, which had been flushed hot from tension and excitement and endless movement for days now, went cold, full cold, from her fingertips to her toes, and all the way to her heart.

Her heart managed to thud out two sodden beats, then, choking slightly, she dropped to her knees at his side, her knife out. What sort of beast would do this to a helpless man...

His body suddenly twisted up and over in a shocking move, knocking her off-balance. His boot came up and kicked the blade out of her hand. It tumbled away, flashing, and before she could open her mouth, he had kicked her onto her side and wrapped his legs around her, her arms and torso trapped in the grip of his powerful thighs. His hands were still tied behind his back, her blade three feet away.

So much for *helpless*.

"Aodh," she breathed against the hard press of his legs.

His eyes, one of which was almost swollen shut, opened. "Katy?" his voice scraped hoarsely.

"Dear God," she whispered. "What happened?"

"Bertrand," he said, releasing her.

"I will kill him," she vowed, shaking with fury and fear. She knelt beside him as he shifted to his side, presenting his bound hands.

"How...get here?" he croaked. Outside the tent, the

argument raged, the shadows of people pressed onto the walls of the tent.

"Ré and Cormac," she whispered, and swiftly sliced through the ropes that bound him.

In a flash, he grabbed the knife and cut the away bindings trapping his ankles, and staggered to his feet.

He swayed at once, stumbling sideways. She caught him, her arms tight around his ribs as they stumbled together a few steps. His breathing was harsh. She leaned them gently against the center pole and, fumbling with a hand, tugged a flask off her belt.

He downed half of it, trickles of it wetting his beard. She looked over her shoulder. The shouts were ever-present, and by the shadows, it appeared a few punches had been thrown, so the fight was escalating apace, but the shadows of bodies were all clustered around the tent flap. Slipping out undetected would be impossible.

Aodh handed the flask back, wiping his chin with his forearm. "Whisky," he said thickly. "Gave me...whisky."

"Oh, for God's sake, why did you drink it?" she whispered, fumbling for another flask. "I thought it was water."

"Perfect." He pulled her to him, kissed her with his swollen, torn-open mouth, then spun her to the back of the tent. "Under," he ordered in a rasp.

Aodh crouched and slit the bottom edge of the tent with the knife, then tugged it up enough for her to roll under. He came after, then they were off, his arm slung around her shoulder for support, hurrying behind the row of tents, out into the darkness, into the night.

Rogue Warriors

CHAPTER 46

THEY MADE IT to the cave hidden on the western edge of the coast, and crept inside.

Katarina propped Aodh against the wall and swiftly removed her gown then laid it on the hard ground. Aodh fell onto it as if he were already dead. He went down first to his knees, then toppled over. He grabbed her hand as he went, pulling her down beside him.

"Give a lady a moment," she whispered as she pulled her cloak over him.

"Never needed moment…before…to remove gown…for me." His voice was a hoarse, barely guttural rasp, but that he had made a jest at all filled her heart with hope.

"On account of such arrogance," she whispered as she tucked the cape up to his neck, then pulled the satchel with salves and unguents toward her, "I shall make you wait a full hour before my gown is removed next time we are in the bedchamber."

"Who waits…bed…?" A slow, harsh breath. "Ré? 'Mac?"

"Will be here soon," she whispered. She decided not to mention Bran just yet.

"Fools, all." His words, already misshapen due to the bruises covering his battered mouth, were getting softer, more mumbled.

"Reckless." She brushed blood-sticky hair away from his temple.

"Owe you...life."

"Nothing, Aodh," she whispered. "You owe us nothing. We do but return the favors you have done for us."

The hard hand clasping her tightened momentarily, but his words had disappeared into breath before they were fully out, for he had fallen asleep.

She stared at his beaten and bloody body, and since no one was there, and it was dark, she allowed herself the indulgence of one good cry, done quietly and quite wetly, as she knelt beside him and tended his wounds.

They looked worse than they were, mostly cuts, and one that needed stitches, but Aodh barely stirred as she put them in.

Then she washed what needed washing, bandaged what needed bandaging, shifted him gently, and resting his head on her legs, she stroked his hair, watching him sleep and breathe, giving thanks her rebel was still alive.

R⚔W

AODH AWOKE as the linen-white light of dawn flowed in from the cave's mouth and around the corner, illuminating the far wall.

The moment he saw the wall, he knew where he was.

Renegade's Cove.

The huge wall of rock glowed wetly in the pale pearly light, revealing delicate veins of color within. All across its towering face, like some granite tapestry, flowed etchings made by stone edge and blade tip. Silent, visual diaries left by marauders and outlaws and lost souls who'd been driven here throughout the ages.

Renegade's Cove was a lair for, well, renegades. Long before the Romans had ever marched north, men had been stumbling into its hard sanctuary by dint of rumor and hearsay whispered at the fringes of polite society.

It was the refuge of men and women pressed to their last resort, beleaguered, beset by friend and foe, with no place to call home.

Renegade's Cove was a preserve of the homeless, the landless, the outlawed. Broken men dragged themselves here and found a refuge for body and heart, before flinging themselves back into the world again. And almost all of them had left a little piece of themselves behind, in the etchings that covered the rock walls.

The cave was bursting with pictures and scrawled words, little ciphers scratched into the hard rock, unbreakable secrets telling the stories of what had driven the Cove's men and women in here, and what had lured them back out again.

One of the oldest was also one of the most prominent. It appeared to be a dagger, held between two fanged and clawed creatures, rampant, facing each other. Legend said it depicted the arms of King Richard the Lionheart, but what the dagger meant, none knew.

One scratched drawing was of an open book, its locked covers flung open, with leaves being torn out, or falling out.

There was another with what appeared to be piles of coin on a long table, men standing around it, and in a high tower above them, a heart-shaped face at a window, long hair falling down the stony wall.

There was a boar hunt, with arrows flying at one of the horsemen.

There was a huge tree and under it, a court of men in a large circle. An argument was breaking out, swords were being drawn.

There was a tourney with pennants flying and two battered champions facing off in the ring.

One showed a ragged-edged pirate flag, torn in half.

There were several pictures that looked to be maps, sprawling, unknown landscapes with Xs marked inside their tortured lines, but where they led to, Aodh did not know.

It was as if the stories had a life of their own, and were desperate to be told, even if they would never be understood.

There were a great many castle towers. And a great many women. Indeed, in almost all the storied runes, there were women. Long-haired, skirts flowing, the unknown women fairly danced across the hard stone walls.

Women, perhaps the ones who'd driven the broken men in. Women who had certainly lured them back out again.

Indeed, across the ages, the most enduring tale of the Cove was that men had been fighting for their women.

It made a kinship across the centuries, all these lost souls, tracing their lives and loves and yearnings into rock, hoping to leave some trace of themselves behind.

Aodh got to his feet and limped beside the wall, dragging his fingertips over the etchings and the unreadable stories they told.

About halfway down the wall, in a ray of sunrise light, he crouched low.

Here it was, his own unreadable story, made sixteen years earlier, on that hellish, stormy night when he'd landed in England and Ré had dragged him out of the sea.

The years had not dimmed the memories much.

Even now he could hear the vicious crack of breaking wood as the ship wrecked, feel the dark, wet weight of the sea pulling him down with heavy fists. Could still taste the foaming salty harshness of the sea in his throat. Bone-cold fury was the wave that had pushed him, finally, toward land.

He'd crawled up on shore, gritty sand under his hands and knees, spitting up seawater, intent on a single deed: making the Queen of England restore Rardove to him.

Which had led directly to this moment, crawling *away* from the queen, beaten and battered, to Renegade's Cove.

One had to admire the symmetry of it, Aodh thought grimly. The patterns repeating, ever and anon, like the angles of a shoreline or the peaks of a mountain range. He and his father. Katy and hers.

Sacrifice bore its costs. As did love.

He looked over at her sleeping form, curled up under her cloak. The cycles, ever repeating. Until broken.

He'd spent his entire life fighting battles chosen by others. Until Katarina. He'd lied—he had every intention of winning her, it had been his single goal—but she was the only thing, in all his life, that had been of his own choosing and with his full heart. Now he'd won her.

And she'd sacrificed herself for him.

If that did not fire a man's blood, nothing could. This woman, so hard to win, had transferred her loyalties to him completely. He didn't know if he was worthy, but it hardly mattered, for the deed was done. She was his. Under his protection, at his command—*occasionally*, he amended in a spasm of honesty—his in every way, from here on.

As for that here on... They had some decisions to make.

Katy was not going to be happy about his.

But that was for later. He unsheathed his knife and beside the etched lines of Rardove's towering walls that he'd scratched into the cave wall sixteen years ago, he now drew the real magic of home, and the rekindled fire in his heart: Katy.

Then he went to her, dropped down beside her and slid his hand along the warm curve of her hip. Because if there was one thing Aodh had learned in all his years of hard living, it was to seize what you wanted, the moment you saw it, ere it was snatched away forever.

He slid his hand lower.

$$R\!\!\!\times\!\!\!W$$

AT FIRST, KATARINA THOUGHT it was a dream.

A dream that Aodh was uninjured, hardy and virile. Slowly, she roused out of the heady, clouding state of slumber and found him most definitely injured, but also quite hardy and *exceptionally* virile, propped up on an elbow, his head bent to her neck, the other hand working its way masterfully down her body.

"Aodh," she whispered. He lifted his head.

She stifled a gasp. In the dawning light, the evidence of his ravages was clear.

His mouth was entirely swollen on one side, as was one eye. Four days' growth of facial hair lessened the evidence of his battering, but even through the dark hair, green and blue bruises could be seen. One side of his brow stuck out farther than the other.

"Oh, Aodh." She touched his face with her fingertips.

He dipped his head and brushed his cheek against hers. "Kissing will have to wait." His voice was hoarse.

"Kissing? Of course it must wait. All this," she tried to struggle up from the hand he was continuing to slide down her body, "must wait. You need *rest*. You cannot be ready for these kinds of...exertions."

He held her down with a gentle pressure on her belly. "I am quite ready for exertions, Katy. Have you not yet learned, it is a mistake to wait? If a thing matters, and it is there, you take it." His words grew more intent as their eyes met, and his hand flattened on her belly. "That is how we shall do it, you and I. Aye?"

His one good eye held hers, and even that one was a little bloodshot.

"Aye," she said doubtfully, and let herself be drawn back down. "I hope you know what you're doing."

"I know exactly what I'm doing. I'm making love to you in a renegade's cave."

In a thousand years, she could not have predicted this trajectory for her life, nor imagined the joy it would bring.

Hope and fear and desire warred inside her as she lay back, her gaze sliding up the walls. She thought she saw pictures on them. But there was no time for cave drawings now, for Aodh was between her thighs.

"Och, maybe a little kissing is in order," he murmured, and touched his broken mouth to hers.

It was a kiss made of breath and sunrise. Her eyes hot and wet, she kissed the breath of him, just their tongues touching, no lips.

"I thought I'd lost you," she whispered, the words catching in her throat as she threaded her fingers though his hair.

He rocked into her, slow and steady. "You will find I am exceptionally hard to lose."

"Stubborn man."

"Reckless." His smile was lopsided and lumpy.

"Oh, Aodh, I hope you know what you're doing," she said again, softer this time.

"Aye, Katy, hope's the thing."

She managed a smile back, and put her hand on his chest, stopping him. "If we are going to be so mad as to make love in a cave with you looking like bruised mutton, then at least lay back, and let me do the work."

He did, for once obedient, and after setting a pack beneath his head, she straddled him gently, careful not to knock or bump anything that couldn't bear the strain. He closed his hands around her hips. The dawn light made him almost glow, his painted body like some undulation of the earth, rising up out of the cave floor, so he was half of earth, cast in stone, fully male. Her battered King of the Wood.

"What are we going to do now?" she whispered as she moved gently on him.

"I am already doing it." His face tightened with pleasure, and his eyes closed for a second as he lifted his hips, pushing up into her.

Her breathing stopped, then flooded out in a gasp.

His eyes were seared almost silver in the growing sunlight. "There was one moment...when I thought I might never feel you again," he admitted hoarsely.

She pressed her hands to the ground beside his shoulders and hung her head near his, and rocked for him, however made him close his eyes, however brought him pleasure. "Feel me now, Aodh," she whispered. "I am yours, forever."

"Och, I love you so, Katy," he murmured, lifting his hips again, entering her as ever Aodh had come to her: hard, unstoppable, utterly certain.

She loosed a long, shaky breath, tipped her head back and let Aodh's hope rule the day.

HE WAS AWAKENED by the sound of boots at the cave entrance.

Aodh swung to his feet, sword in hand, grimacing in silent pain, his muscles taut and screaming. He swayed slightly as two caped figures rounded the corner of the cave and loomed blackly amid the sunlight pouring into the tunnel entrance. They were all height and width, no depth.

Behind him, he heard Katy get to her feet, then the low hiss of her sword being drawn from its sheath.

Och, he did love this woman.

"Jesus God, you look like hell," Ré's voice came floating into the dimness.

Aodh exhaled a hot breath of relief. He lowered his sword and limped toward them. "Took you long enoug—"

He stopped short when he saw Bran standing behind them.

Bran glanced at him, then bent his head low. "Sir."

"What are you doing here?" Aodh asked hoarsely. "I told you to stay in the keep," he said, not liking the way his chest suddenly constricted. He'd saved Bran's life when the boy was ten, barely a tadpole, bullied and utterly cast adrift in the world. Now he was en route to being a good man, and Aodh did not like how he was *here*, when Aodh had ordered him to stay *there*. Safe.

Bran's head stayed down as he said again, "Sir."

Aodh said a muffled curse then reached out and gripped the back of Bran's neck, pulling him forward.

"I made him come," Katarina said quietly. "He fought me tooth and nail, but I insisted. You must blame me entirely."

Aodh squeezed the back of Bran's head and for a few seconds, Bran hugged him so tight Aodh almost grunted in pain.

"Well, then," he managed to say without grimacing as they separated, "perhaps you've learned an important lesson nevertheless: always listen to your lady."

"Unless it's the queen," Bran quipped, his eyes red and a bit wet, but with a smile breaking through, now that his champion was returned to him.

Aodh's hand fell away. "Ah. Well, there you bring us to the matter at hand," he said as he and Ré embraced swiftly. One could have been forgiven for thinking it was a perfunctory thing, if one had not seen how tightly it was done, or how tautly Ré's jaw was clenched, nor how he blinked repeatedly as he stepped away.

Cormac gave Aodh a far more hearty embrace that finally did make him groan in pain. The Scotsman made a surprised sound, then stepped back with a grin.

"Well now, Aodh, where are we off to this time?"

Aodh smiled back. "I'm going to Windsor, to see the queen."

ROGUE WARRIORS

CHAPTER 47

THE OCCUPANTS OF THE CAVE erupted in various emotions: outrage from Cormac; confusion from Bran; a muttered, "I knew it," from Ré; and outright horror from Katy.

Her jaw fell and her face grew paler than it had been the first day he'd seen her, when he'd retaken the castle of his ancestral homeland and realized that inside, he still felt colder than a winter waterfall. Until Katarina had touched him—in actuality, punched him—and thereby relit the fire in his heart that had been extinguished half a lifetime earlier.

So, her concern here was worth something.

But he would not be swayed.

Not that she didn't try. Cormac too.

"Well, for the love of Christ," the Scotsman said, throwing his hands up in the air. "What the hell did we go get you for, if you're just going to throw yourself at her feet again?"

"Because you are a brave and hearty crew." Aodh included Katarina in the compliment by way of a smile and a nod, but she was entirely underwhelmed; her jaw was still dropped. He swept her cloak up off the gritty cave floor and, giving it a hearty, chivalrous shake, handed it back to her.

"See that Katarina has new clothes," he told Ré as he reached down to grab his own cape.

That launched her out of her stupor. "New clothes... *Clothes?* What are you saying?" She reached for his arm, stayed him when he would have picked up one of the water skins. "Aodh, what are you planning?"

"You four are sailing off, for a port we agree upon, where I can send word. I am going to see the queen about Rardove."

"That is madness."

"Aye, well, no reason to stop now," he said brightly and planted a jaunty, rather painful, kiss on her mouth. He tried not to show that it was painful, for she already looked so worried. Then he leaned over and picked up the skin and held it under one of the rivulets of clear, clean water coursing down the walls of the cave.

"Cormac is right," she said. "Why did you come away with us, if you intended to go to the queen anyhow? Why not just let them take you?"

"I had to get you safely away."

She made an inarticulate sound. "You let me rescue you, in order to rescue me?"

"Aye."

And finally, Ré grinned. Cormac laughed, and Bran smiled. Katarina held her hands to her head and stared at them, then flung her hands down. "I do not know what to say," she announced, and it seemed true. For the next few moments, the only sound was water trickling down the walls. A bright bank of sunlight washed up the main cave entrance.

"He has a point, lady," Ré said quietly. "All this was done in pursuit of Rardove. To leave it now…"

"Just as things get the least bit difficult," Aodh agreed, stuffing the skin into one of the packs and grabbing another.

"The least bit…" Her incredulous echo faded off.

He planted his hand against the wall and began refilling the next skin. Bran came silently forward and took the other two. "Your rescue of me was indeed a rescue," he said, "for it was imperative that I got away, so I could return on my own terms."

She stared.

He shrugged. "'Tis far better to go to Elizabeth standing up, of my own volition, than bound and dragged behind Bertrand of Bridge."

Cormac made a concurring sound, his brow furrowed in

seriousness. "You've a point, Aodh. She likes a strong man, the queen does. You walk in, spread out your arms, and say 'I'm here, as you commanded,' well, she might just be charmed. You did it once before." Cormac's brow smoothed under the power of the new insight, and he began to grin. "Aye, you're a madman, Aodh, and it just might work."

Katarina's jaw fell for the third time. "Why, you are as mad as he."

Ré glanced at Aodh, who was stuffing the now-filled skin into another pack. Their eyes met, then Ré said casually, "I do not wish to be morbid, my lady, but...."

Katy spun to him, clearly frightened by what could be more morbid than what had already been discussed.

"If we leave, now, lady, we're all but giving Rardove to Bertrand."

A soft gasp reverberated against the walls of the cave. Clearly, Katarina had not considered this outcome.

Crouched over the pack, Aodh gave Ré the smallest of smiles. Ré nodded back, just as infinitesimally.

Cormac's nod was more noticeable. "You speak true. And God knows but that that Bertrand arse will bring Walter back into the fold, too. Bleedin' snake."

Katy paced in a little circle, clearly at her wits end. "I did not act like a whore simply to see you turn around and march straight back to—"

The water overflowed the skin as Aodh snapped his gaze over his shoulder. "You did what?"

She stopped pacing. "'Twas a ruse."

"A right fine one," Cormac assured him.

"And entirely unnecessary," she added sourly. "For you appear determined to get yourself killed or otherwise maimed—"

He snapped his hand out, handing the dripping wet skin to Cormac. "A word?" he said to Katy, and led her further into the shadows of the cave, where their voices made sibilant whispery echoes. They stopped a dozen paces in, and Aodh turned her to face him.

"Katy, did you not tell me Ireland is your air? That it fills your lungs and heart?

Her eyes, wide and dark, stared up at him.

"Then why are you so eager to leave it behind?"

"I—" She seemed frozen by the question.

"For that is the choice now before us. Leave, and go...where? Make no mistake, lass, fugitives we shall be, and that limits our choices considerably. Mark that well." He held her arms, setting out the future in cold, bare lines. "Sailing from port to port, never knowing which will be open to us. Always on the lookout for an English ship, or an English man. Knowing that at any moment, you might be spotted, and taken. Have you any notion how extensive is the queen's network of spies?"

"No—"

"I do."

"But all your friends...all over the lands..."

"I have many friends, over many lands. None of them are in Ireland. And that is where we are meant to be. Ireland. Together, you and I."

For a moment, hunger filled the gaze pinned on his, then she turned to the front of the cave, where Cormac stood, stick in hand, drawing pictures in the sand, while Ré crouched beside him and Bran lounged against the wall.

Aodh stepped up behind her, put his arms around her and folded his hands low across her belly. "And them, Katy? It will be their fate too, if we flee now. After all they've done for me, to give them that?"

She inhaled and shook her head. "I don't want to make this choice."

"But you must."

"Why must I choose my worst fear?" Her words were so soft they almost disappeared under the tiny streams of water rushing down the cave walls.

"Then do not view it in such a manner."

"What other manner is there?"

He put his mouth beside her ear. "Choosing your greatest hope."

She turned to him, her face shadowed in the dim light, but

backlit by the bright sun. "So, I must choose. We flee, as fugitives, or stay and try for Rardove. The chances of which are so small as to be almost non-existent."

He smiled. "I'm feeling persuasive today, lass."

She skimmed his jaw with her palm. "You look as if hell sat on your face."

He gathered her closer. "I must do this thing."

She closed her eyes. "I know."

He examined her face a moment then said, with ruthless aim, "What would you have me do, Katy, in such a situation, if our roles were reversed?"

Her lids lifted and her dark eyes locked on his for a long, silent moment. Then she touched his jaw, smiled faintly, and said, "What can I do to help?"

Aodh skimmed his knuckles down the side of her face. "I do love you," he whispered, and bent his head. Their kiss was the gentlest brush of lips.

Then he took her by the hand and led her to the front of the cave.

"I'm for the queen," he announced, a bit triumphantly. Cormac turned and the others got to their feet.

"You mean *we* are for the queen," Katarina corrected.

He stopped short. "We're not starting this again, now, are we?"

Rogue Warriors

CHAPTER 48

AODH CREPT up the secret back staircase at Windsor, an entryway known only to a select few, which he'd gained entry to by contacting the stable master's assistant, who used to be a bit of a gambling partner, and who was engaged, quite amorously and secretively, with the laundress, who snuck him in and up the stairs.

Voices from the downstairs rooms rose up a twist of stairs and coursed down the long corridor that led to the queen's chambers. The throng below was, as usual, celebrating their wealth, or fighting not to lose it, and determinedly riotous in the effort. The queen would be among them. He would wait, hiding in the shadows.

The only threat lay in being seen by one of her ladies- or maids-in-waiting. This was a distinct possibility, but a negligible threat.

Aodh had known the queen's entourage well, and been well liked, for he brought gifts and knew how to compliment without flattering, how to arouse without touching, or at least not much, and they would say nothing if they saw him. Or at least, nothing that would get his head cut off.

The queen, on the other hand, would be very much inclined to cut his head off.

Perils of the adventurer.

He encountered one of the younger maids the moment he stepped out of the back passageway. Sitting outside the queen's chambers, head bent over embroidery, she gave a start when he appeared, then got to her feet in shock.

"'Tis I, Liz," he said softly.

She gave a little gasp, and her eyes flew wide.

"Not a word, now."

She shook her head. "Oh, sir," she whispered, staring at his face. "What happened? We heard you were taken, then escaped. And now here you are."

"Here I am," he agreed cheerfully.

She smiled, but it was troubled. She glanced over her shoulder. "They are at feast. You should leave."

"I mean the queen no harm."

"I know," she assured him swiftly. "You have ever been the queen's good friend, and I do not believe a word they've said about you."

He wasn't sure which part she didn't believe, but seeing as all of it was true, decided this wasn't the time to inquire.

"But if they find you here, Sir Irish," the little maid went on, using their name for him, "you will be the one harmed."

"I need to see her."

His calm earnestness seemed to do the trick. Her brow furrowed, her eyes darted to and fro, then, with a swift glance, she glided to the door. "Come."

She let him into the queen's antechamber and swiftly shut the door behind him. He made his way across the room, a room he'd been in hundreds of times, for quiet games of chess and cards, and turned the handle to the inner chamber, intending to wait.

But there would be no waiting. The queen was already inside.

She sat on a small bench at her writing table, her head bent as she scribbled away. Back in the corner sat one of her ladies, working on embroidery.

When the door swung open, the queen looked up, startled, and got to her feet, pen in hand.

Her jaw dropped and the pen fell, clattering on the floor.

"God have mercy," she whispered, and her lean, unpainted face flushed with color.

Her gaze swept over his bruised face and her hand reached

out, as if to touch him, then retreated again, like a butterfly folding its wings. She rested her open hand over her heart and gave a soft laugh.

"But why am I surprised? Ever have you been my charming rogue."

"Your Grace," he bowed.

"Oh no," she said, warning in her voice. "No. I cannot be charmed this time, Irish. Not anymore."

He sat down in the nearest chair to present as little threat as possible, and also, to a smaller degree, to ensure he did not topple over; perhaps he was the smallest bit weak.

The queen's gaze drifted to the door. "How did you come...where..."

"I vow I pose you no danger, Bess," he assured her. "I wish only to talk."

"Talk?" She laughed. "Oh, yes, the Irish are very good at talking. At lying. We had years to talk, and you never, ever told me you planned treachery."

"I did not plan it. It sprang itself on me quite suddenly, when you refused what you had long promised."

Her gaze hardened. "You were informed, quite clearly, of the reason for my decision on Rardove."

"Oh, aye, I was. Bertrand is an able master; the proceeds from the ironmongers are quite lucrative; you needed me close to hand." His casual recitation of the reasons made her hand tighten. "I heard them all most clearly."

"And none were good enough for you."

"None were."

Her gaze slid to his head as he pushed back his hood and she gave a little gasp. "Your hair. What have you done?"

He said nothing. It was clear what he'd done by shaving it; he'd claimed Ireland.

She made a sound of impatience, then glanced at the lady-in-waiting who stood, shocked, in the background. "Leave us, Catherine."

Catherine bent her head and hurried to the door. She cast Aodh a glance under lowered lids as she passed. Either in support, or because she was going to get the guards, he had no idea which.

Nothing for it now; it was all in Bess's hands.

"And not a word," the queen ordered sharply as Catherine opened the door. She nodded, and as she passed out, she smiled at Aodh.

For a moment, the queen and he sat in silence. "How did you get away?" she finally asked.

"Friends."

"Your Englishman?" said the queen. "And your Scotsman?"

He nodded mutely. No need to mention Katarina.

Bess looked down at the pen still clutched in her hand. She turned it over in her fingers. "And the lady?" she said, her voice pitched to an idle tone.

"Katarina? What of her?"

"You are cleaved to her?"

"Entirely."

"So swiftly."

"From the moment I saw her. As it was the moment I saw you, Your Grace."

"Do not flatter me," she said shortly. "I well recall our first meeting. You were dripping in seaweed and laid your sword at my feet, silencing a crowd of nattering courtiers and self-important nobleman not to mention the Spanish ambassador."

"Oh, he was always worth mentioning, was he not?" he said, smiling faintly. Smiling hurt, so he stopped.

"Hm." She made a little sound. "Well then, your meeting with Katarina must have been quite a thing."

"Quite." He paused. "She punched me. Right here." He ran his fingers along his jaw, then hissed in pain and pulled his hand away. "Then she told me she held Rardove for you, and stole my dagger and laid it against my throat."

The queen stared a moment, then drew up her chair, turned it to face him, and sat down.

"Tell me everything."

She leaned forward, her hands on her knees, and Aodh saw the child she must have been, the young woman, made illegitimate, her mother executed, her father raging mad at times, flailing and powerful. Imprisoned in the Tower when her maniacal sister took the throne, then against all odds, she took it herself, an unwanted pawn who'd somehow outstripped all their ambitions and become, quite simply, magnificent.

He admired her deeply.

And she did love a good story.

Gesturing a silent query toward a flagon on a table, and being graced with a miniature, regal nod of assent, he poured the queen a drink, handed it to her, then retook his seat and told her all about how Katarina would have made her proud.

When he was done, the queen was smiling, sitting back in her chair. "I *did* pick well for Rardove," she said warmly.

"That you did. You could do so again, my lady."

Ah, and there they came to it.

The queen eyed him closely, but her body was reclined in the chair more easily now, as it had been in years past, when it was just they two, and he had stories to tell, and treasure to deliver. "I have not seen Mistress Katarina for many a year," the queen said, and he detected fondness in her words.

"She is a fierce and loyal mistress, Bess, out beyond the Pale. Not many could have done what she has done all. Do you know she held Rardove with ten men? Ten men and…" He looked at the ceiling and reflected a moment. "Approximately twenty-five women."

Surprise brought the queen tipping forward in her chair.

"Householders, serving maids, even the hen girl. Katarina enlisted and trained them all."

"Did she?" Elizabeth sat back and peered at the ceiling too, in much the same spot as Aodh had, a smile on her face. "Did she indeed?" For a moment, the room was quiet. The moon, bleached white and scratchy looking, bobbed into the corner of the tall window. Set against blue-black sky, it looked bright and cold.

"You must have made quite an impression on her, then." The queen's voice made him look back. "For her to have turned to you so utterly."

She was no longer looking at the ceiling; she was staring directly at him, and the smile of a moment ago was gone.

"She remains yours yet, Bess, I swear it."

"Does she? Ludthorpe tells me she seemed quite enamored of you. Enough to wed you against my will. Enough to stand on the wall with weapons trained on my men."

"She is loyal to you, my lady." The message would be repeated however long it took to save Katarina's life.

The queen's gaze drifted over his shoulder, and her voice took on a contemplative tone. "Methinks she is loyal to *you*, Aodh. For her to have come back to save you…twice."

He shot to his feet and turned to see the door being opened by a soldier who was…pushing Katarina in front of him.

"I found her lurking, Your Majesty. She said she had a meeting with you. Want I should show her the cellars?"

Aodh surged forward, but when Bess held up her hand, he stopped.

"I was not *lurking*," Katy said, composed and indignant, and how she did both, he did not know. "I was coming to see my queen, and you were simply the fastest route to getting here."

The queen motioned to the guard. "Leave her to me."

The soldier shifted a gimlet eye off Aodh, released Katarina's arm, and backed out. He shut the door, and the three of them stood in silence.

"You should search her," Aodh said lazily. "She is fond of weapons. All over." He waved his hand at his own body, sweeping it up and down, chest to knees.

"Aodh!" Katarina whirled to him, shocked. "This is my *queen*!" She whirled back, dropped to a knee, and bent her head. "Your Majesty, I have served you faithfully for all my life, until very, very recently, and for that, I would explain. Explain my actions, and my wherefores, and set it all before you, to decide as you see fit. And"—she bent her head farther—"if needed, beg for my husband's life."

"Not your own?" the queen said drily.

Katarina shook her head at the ground. "No. And I do not beg for my own sake, Your Majesty. I beg it for your sake, and

Ireland's."

"Do you indeed?" The queen leaned down and with a slim finger, tipped Katarina's face up. She looked her over a moment, then said briskly, "And what happened to *your* face? Do not tell me Bertrand again."

"If I may not say Bertrand, my lady, I have naught to say."

A hardening along the queen's jaw. She made an impatient gesture. "Get up, get up, and tell me your story."

Katy unfolded herself and despite the urge to put himself between her and whatever threatened her, he forced himself to remain where he was, propping up the wall. She had her own things to settle with the queen, and neither of them would thank him for interfering.

It was al up to the women now.

KATARINA LOOKED over her shoulder at Aodh.

He stood lazily, a shoulder pressed against the wall, looking perfectly content to let her and the queen have their moment. But she noticed his hand hung near the hilt of his sword.

A pose of ease, but as always, Aodh was as relaxed as a panther.

"I don't know what Aodh has been telling you…" she said warily, turning to the queen.

"Much," said Elizabeth.

"But I have always been loyal, Your Grace."

"That appears to be precisely what is under debate."

"I could not let it happen again," she said bluntly. "As it did to my father."

The queen's gaze narrowed, then turned away. Indeed, she turned entirely away and picked up a wine cup that sat atop a decorated wardrobe. The scene was a fresh and lively rendering of sheep and other creatures—nymphs?—cavorting in a green meadow. The queen's hand rested atop the wardrobe, but her fingers curled tightly over the top, into the hair of the nymphs.

"I have long regretted your father's choices, Katarina. He was a good man."

"Yes, he was, Your Grace."

The queen's face came a quarter turn in her direction. "His loss was deeply felt."

"Yes it was."

Elizabeth continued to stare out the window. "Perhaps *his* are not the only choices I regret." She looked over, then turned. "But never my choices about you, Katarina. I never regretted those for an instant."

Katarina smiled. "Perhaps until recently."

"Perhaps," the queen said drily, then blew out a breath through her thin nostrils. "I did not want you to be alone, out there in Ireland, but to keep you here, at Court...?" Elizabeth shook her head.

"You sent me home, Your Grace. It is the only place I ever wanted to be."

"Good girl," she said, and patted Katarina's cheek, as if she'd given her a gift.

"You should see the wool."

The queen, ever alert to ways to enhance her treasury, straightened. "Tell me."

"The flock has been rebuilt such that we can send wool to market. And next year...it will be even better."

"Even better?"

Katarina nodded. "It is beyond compare, I swear to you. And there is whisky." The queen's brows lifted. "We shall have many barrels aged properly by the summer. They will bring in more than the wool."

"Impossible."

"Indeed. We will send you a barrel, Your Grace. As a gift." Giving gifts was something she had learned from Aodh.

Elizabeth considered this. "I've never tasted the stuff."

Aodh pushed off the wall and held out the skin Katarina had given him in the tent. The queen looked at the dirty thing.

Katarina was horrified. "Oh, Your Grace, I don't know…"

Elizabeth took it and raised it daintily to her lips.

"Don't be too careful with it," Aodh cautioned. "Sip, but don't linger."

Over the spout, she met his eye, then tilted back her head and drank.

She coughed only once as she swallowed, then lowered the skin. Katarina glanced at Aodh, holding her breath.

Elizabeth regarded the skin thoughtfully. "Send me three."

Katarina blew out her breath around a smile and shook her head at Aodh, who smiled back.

"And you made this?" the queen asked.

"Rardove made that. Ireland did. And the sheep. And the bedrock under the castle. And the moors, and the winds, and the sea at our backs...."

The queen lowered the skin. "I truly did send you home, didn't I?"

"You did."

"And yet it came to this."

Katarina bent her head. "This has not gone at all how I planned, Your Majesty. I never meant to be chatelaine of a rebel stronghold; nothing could be further from who I was."

"Until Aodh came," Elizabeth said tartly.

Katarina lifted her eyes. "Until Aodh came, we were a small English cork bobbing amid a large, hostile Irish sea. We could not have held it much longer."

Elizabeth paused. "Surely not."

"Surely. No one knows better than I, Your Grace, how dire our circumstances were, nor how thin the thread we held. I built many alliances, yet I was only ever able to hold the line. Never extend it."

The queen nodded. "Beyond the Pale, it is difficult to do much."

"Not for Aodh."

Silence.

"It took him three weeks, and he had an army raised."

"Against me."

"It need not be. Your Grace, I know Ireland. I know what is needed. And in my most humble opinion, Ireland needs..."

The queen raised her eyebrows. "Yes?"

"Aodh." She looked at the queen, pale and penitent. "You

have no idea how well it will go for you if he is there."

The queen shook her head, and Katarina's heart dropped. "Ireland has ever been a dangerous postern gate into England."

"Then it must be guarded," Katarina replied firmly.

"By rebels?"

"By those who have been received back into the fold and know the power of forgiveness." She transmitted a fierce, quelling look in Aodh's direction.

The queen looked at him too. "I do not think Aodh believes he has done anything to be forgiven for, mistress, making it exceptionally difficult to see how such a state would exert any power at all. What say you, sir? Think you 'a forgiven man' describes you well?"

Aodh moved his gaze to Elizabeth and slowly shook his head. "Nay. Fortunately for you, my lady, you do not need men who know the value of forgiveness. You need a storm on your Irish horizons. Your very own storm."

And then, *then* the queen smiled.

Katarina revised the plan that had swiftly developed in her mind, to launch herself over the table and knock Aodh into a state of senselessness so he could not push ever harder at things already precariously balanced in the first place.

But she was learning sometimes the balance must be upset, to proceed to the next thing. Perhaps the balance was of sickness held at bay, or a lethargy that paralyzed. Or fear. Like a wall too precarious to stand, it must be kicked aside.

"And you, Katarina?" The queen's penetrating eye fell on her. "What say you to his assessment?"

"I say he is right."

"You would have Aodh, then, and all these doubtful boons of Ireland?"

"I would have him above all else."

"Above Rardove?

The queen looked between them, and saw the love in their silent, shared glance. This one thing she could not have, but could keep them from having.

"We are at your mercy," Katarina said quietly.

"And if my mercy sends you back to Ireland?"

Against the wall, Aodh straightened. Katarina caught her breath. "We will hold it for you, Your Majesty, I swear it."

"And those who joined your rebellion?" the queen demanded.

"Some joined a rebellion, Your Majesty, but most joined Aodh. He might have suggested holding a fête and that is what they would be doing."

"A fête," Aodh mused from the wall. "Why did I not think of that?"

The women ignored him.

"And what do I make of you, Katarina?" the queen asked almost gently, coming forward to cup Katarina's chin in her hand. "After all your promises and oaths, to see you suchly?"

"Do not ever think it was done lightly, my queen. But if one truly has her sovereign's interests at heart, then must she not speak the truth, and change her mind, no matter the consequences, however inconvenient or perilous they may be to her personally?"

"That is what you are doing now?" the queen said archly. "Safeguarding me, by claiming Aodh Mac Con?"

"Indeed I am. For nothing, and no one, can serve you better out on the marches than the son of Rardove."

"Not even you?" the queen asked softly.

Katarina shook her head. "Not even I."

"Aye, she can," Aodh said loudly.

"Hush," the queen murmured. "We are not speaking to you, Irish."

In the back of the room, Aodh stood, hand on his sword hilt, watching the scene between his queen and his love.

"And if I send you back, and not Aodh?"

"I will die."

The room was silent. From downstairs came the distant sounds of courtiers at their merrymaking. Low and soft, through the room, came Aodh's rough whisper: "Katy."

"You will not die," the queen scoffed, but there was a quaver in her voice.

349

"I will wish to, Your Majesty. That is something you cannot understand, being so great. But in my heart, I will wish to die."

The queen stared at the tapestry on the wall, a moment, then said irritably, "Well we cannot have the chatelaines of our baronies dying off."

Katarina held her breath.

The queen waved her hand. "Fine, take him. There had better be no problems," she warned with a sharp look.

Katarina shook her head, too stunned to be glad. "No, Your Majesty."

Elizabeth touched her shoulder, then moved away, toward Aodh. He knelt before her, then rose and took her hands, kissed their backs, turned them over and kissed the palms, then, devil that he was, leaned in and kissed her cheek, all the familiarities Bess so craved.

"I will miss you, Irish," she whispered.

"I am your man, Bess, as ever I was."

Her throat worked as she touched his face.

"Rardove will wait for you," he murmured. "You must come visit."

"Maybe I will one day. Be prepared," she said in warning.

He smiled, then said, even more softly, "The only reason you did not have this"—he gestured toward Katy—"was because you chose not to. You chose not to have it all, because England needed all of you."

"There have been compensations," she admitted, and leaned forward to kiss his cheek. Then she straightened and became regal and magnificent again. "Now, go, both of you. I have papers to sign and people to see." She swung the door open.

Servants flew up out of their chairs. Ludthorpe, who'd appeared in the waiting chamber, lurched to his feet.

"Where is Bertrand, that fool?" the queen snapped.

The captain bowed swiftly. "He is coming, Your Majesty. He…" He froze when he saw Aodh towering behind her.

She waved to one of her men. "Escort them out the back, and call for Cecil. I have a matter to discuss with him."

The servant flew off. Ludthorpe continued to stare in shock.

Aodh gave a small, friendly wave. Ludthorpe began to smile.

"Come now, Captain," the queen ordered briskly, gliding past him. "We have plans to make." She swept off down the corridor, dragging everyone after her. At the end of the hallway, guards scrambled to aligned themselves along the walls, ready to announce her presence.

"Plans, Your Grace?" Ludthorpe said, hurrying to keep pace with the swiftly-moving queen.

"Yes. What do you think of Scotland?"

"It is even darker, wetter, and more savage than Ireland."

Aodh bent his head to Katy and murmured, "Darker, aye, but no more savage. And certes not wetter." He sounded offended.

"Hush," she whispered back. His hand slid around her back and she leaned into it, feeling weightless.

"Precisely," the queen said to Ludthorpe. "That is why I am sending Bertrand of Bridge there."

Aodh laughed. Katy smacked his chest. The queen continued her majestic promenade down the corridor. "There is a castle in the borderlands that wants Our attention. The Scots are currently holding it. Think you Bertrand is up to the task?"

Ludthorpe snorted. "I do not think he is equipped to manage the ale of Scotland, let alone her warriors."

"Well then, we shall see what he is made of."

"I already know what he is made of," Ludthorpe replied.

"Never fear, I will not send him alone. What was the name of that English clerk you took from Rardove?" the queen asked. "The untrustworthy one you wished to toss over a cliff?"

"Walter," Ludthorpe replied with alacrity.

"That's the one. Rardove no longer requires his services. He shall go with Bertrand. He might come in useful. Or they both might die. It is difficult to say."

Ludthorpe gave a startled laugh. The queen stopped and looked at him haughtily, but the hint of a smile edged up a corner of her mouth. She peered down the hallway to Aodh, his hand curved around Katarina's back. She met his eyes, then turned her gaze to Katarina.

"Go," she said softly. "Take care of Rardove for me."

Katarina, eyes hot now with tears, nodded.

The queen turned and swept by serving maids and guards, calling out irritably, "By all that's holy, where is Cecil? He's not praying again, is he?"

The entourage turned the corner. The queen lifted her hand and held it in the air a moment, a silent farewell, then swept around the corner and was gone.

Silence descended. Katarina looked at Aodh, breathless and almost lightheaded.

"And now…"

"Now we go home," he said firmly, and turned them to the back stairway, where two Yeomen of the Guard stood, waiting.

"This way, sir," said one of them, preceding them down the stairway. The other brought up the rear. Katarina's head was spinning, so she barely noticed the circuitous route they were being taken on, only barely aware of the murmured conversation between Aodh and the guard behind her.

"…Court not be the same without you, sir…"

"…richer for you…"

"…temporary break in my luck…"

"…my arse…owe me half a crown…"

"…double or naught next time, sir," the guard urged, and Aodh laughed quietly.

They came out in a garden courtyard. A fat white moon shone through the graceful latticework of bare tree limbs, which were only just beginning to bud in the nascent spring.

One of the guards nodded into the darkness of the garden. "You'll know the way from here, sir."

"That I do," Aodh replied, taking Katarina's hand and leading her away.

ROGUE WARRIORS

CHAPTER 49

"CAN YOU SMELL IT?" Katarina said as they stood at Renegade's Cove, ready to board their boat. The sun was rising, and the water was smooth and clear, a perfect day for sailing.

"Smell what?" Aodh asked, waiting for Katarina to climb on board their boat.

Cormac was already on, tugging on lines. Ré and Bran would be here soon. They'd detoured to a nearby town to gather foodstuffs.

"Ireland," she replied, excitement in her words. "Can you smell it?" She took a deep, illustrative breath, gesturing for Aodh and Cormac to do the same.

Cormac sniffed obediently. "I think that's fish, my lady."

Aodh laughed.

She threw her leg over the boat, then paused, skirt hem trailing in the water, and looked back up the high hill above the cove.

Aodh turned too. Even now he could see Ré's head coming around the high trail that led down the jutting headlands, Bran at his side. They were riding horses swiftly purchased. They cantered through the high, blowing green grasses and down the hidden trail, and drew up beside him.

Bran began throwing satchels onto the boat. Cormac grabbed them and began stuffing them into various storage compartments, grumbling, "What were you doin', braidin' the rope? We were supposed to be off an hour ago."

"Well we're off now," Aodh said, turning.

"I'm not coming."

Aodh stopped short. Beside him, Katarina froze. On the boat, Cormac spun, making the boat rock. Only Bran continued his tasks of loading bags onboard, his face partially averted, his eyes... Were they red again?

Aodh looked away from his small crew and turned to Ré. Bare-headed in the spring sun, Aodh could see everything about his friend clearly, most especially the resolve in his eye.

"What do you mean?" Aodh asked quietly, but he already knew.

Ré took a deep breath. "You found what you went looking for, Aodh. And then some. Home, and..." He glanced at Katarina, who looked stricken as she came back on land. "Cormac too. Everyone found what they needed in Ireland. Except me."

Aodh nodded slowly. He should be used to this by now, the endings of things that mattered.

But this one, losing Ré, his sea star, his boon companion, his captain and friend, cut to the quick. And yet, it was perfectly right. And perfectly necessary. Ré had hitched his wagon to Aodh's ambitions many years ago, and now they were all met. It was time for Ré to go seek—and claim—his own.

And it was fitting that it should happen here, where it had all begun.

"You saved my life, right here," Aodh said, looking around.

Ré smiled. "And a furious ride it has been." They both smiled. "I could never have dreamed you would take me the places I've been, my friend. I would never have done them without you. I was fated to be a farmer, and a poor one at that, until you came along. In truth, you saved my life."

"Then we are even." Aodh kept his voice pitched low. "But I will miss you with a hurt I cannot express."

"Aw, Jesus," muttered Cormac. His voice sounded thick.

Ré looked away, then swiftly, head still down, he stepped forward and embraced Aodh in a silent, hard hug. He stepped back as abruptly as he'd gone in, his head still down.

"A fitting end," Aodh said gruffly, "for the last time you threw your arms around me was when you dragged me out of the sea."

"Aye," Cormac chimed in, a little hoarsely, from the boat. "And we've been cursing him for it ever since."

Ré reached for Cormac's wrist, took hold and pumped it, but Cormac made a disbelieving sound and lurched to his feet. He came over the side and pulled Ré into a huge hug, then released him almost violently and climbed back on board. He settled onto a seat, looking out to sea, his back to the group.

Ré turned to Bran. "Take care of him," he said with a nod toward Aodh.

Bran lifted his head and yes, indeed, his eyes were red. "Always, sir," he said gruffly.

"And you, lady." Ré turned to Katarina. "You showed me what a woman might be. I will have some ways to go to find someone who can approach the bar you have set."

"Stop." She put her arms around his shoulders and as she hugged him, murmured in his ear. "You were right to mistrust me, and you have always been Aodh's closest, dearest friend. I am sorry you must leave him, and while I understand, you must know, you are ripping his heart out."

"Then you shall have to mend it," he murmured, and backed away.

She took the step with him, unable to let go. Aodh put a gentle hand on her arm. "But where will you go?" she asked.

Ré shrugged. "I have not seen my mother for many years. I will visit. They live not far from here."

"And then?"

"The queen, she remains enamored of adventurers, does she not?" A smile lifted the corners of his mouth. "Mayhap I will be the one to make it to the New World after all, Aodh, aye?"

Aodh began to grin. "You will be."

Katarina squeezed his arm. "We shall invest."

Ré smiled. "Then how can I lose?"

"If you're going, go already," Cormac muttered, still looking out to sea. Ré smiled, then turned away.

"You will come visit?" she called.

He swung up on his horse. "If you will have me."

"Come tomorrow."

He reined around, leading Bran's horse behind. Lifting his hand into the air, without looking back, much as the queen had done, he cantered up the curving path, away through the high, salty green grasses.

Aodh watched until he was out of sight. The grasses were once again disturbed only by sea breezes, as if no one had ever been there at all.

He heard a little sound beside him and looked down to find Katarina staring after Ré, a hand at her mouth. He wrapped an arm around her shoulder and pulled her close.

"Do you think he will be happy?" she asked uncertainly. "Find a home? A wife?"

"He will find whatever he seeks, and he will be happy."

She tipped her face up. "And you? Will you be happy? After all you have done and seen, to leave everything behind and settle down to a remote Irish castle?"

He pulled her to stand in front of him.

"You still don't understand. Everything I ever did was for Rardove, and you. You fear I am leaving things behind. I say I am going to the things that matter most. Home. And you. Stop being afraid. Our life is just beginning."

She went up on her toes. Wisps of her russet brown hair blew around them as she kissed him. "I fear only that I cannot love you enough."

He kissed her back, a slightly deeper kiss, that made her body curve a little more. "Seeing as that's a fear of yours, we'll have to allay it. You can prove it to me every night. And some afternoons. And mornings," he said as he released her. "Mornings are an exceptionally good time to prove your love."

Her cheeks were pink as he tossed her into the boat. Bran handed her an extra cloak and Aodh climbed onboard.

"Are we ready then?" Cormac said, heaving to his feet.

Aodh nodded, already looking across the sea to Ireland.

"Let's go home."

Rogue Warriors

Epilogue

Rardove
Six years later

SHE SAW HIM coming from almost a mile away.

Aodh's grey horse crested the rise of the valley at a comfortable pace. Around him rode twenty men and squires, the contingent that had gone to Dublin and Waterford on matters of government.

Katarina would have gone as well, but the baby had been ill, and Katarina had not wanted to leave her.

Her heart stirred as it always did when she saw her husband, even, apparently, from a distance of a mile. Cries went up all along the walls, "*The Lord of Rardove is returned!*"

Katarina shifted the baby in her arms—little Lizzie made a tiny sound of irritation, then curled back to sleep. Katarina swung her arm back and forth, waving.

From across the valley, Aodh's arm lifted in reply.

"He is home, Lizzie," she whispered to the baby, tucking the blanket around the tiny chin.

Lizzie opened her eyes at the sound of her mother's voice. Piercing blue, they stared up at her. Whether they would remain blue, no one yet knew—Lizzie was barely half a year old—but her brother's had.

Five years old and wrestling with the older boys in the training yards while the men took their afternoon break, Finn had eyes that seemed determined to remain as blue as his father's.

He also had Aodh's temperament: easygoing with everyone—save his sister; self-assured; intent on getting his way. In everything.

Their middle child, Aine, had Katarina's eyes. Dark brown, they would peer up at you from great, soulful depths, as the four year old explained the motivations for her most recent exploits, such as why she'd *had* to punch her older brother in the nose after he'd stolen her princess doll.

Princesses, she'd informed them earnestly, could not be stolen. They must be wooed.

Katarina and Aodh had exchanged a silent glance over the tops of the children's heads.

Young Finn had rushed at his sister, and a brief but energetic tussle had ensued, until Aodh had dragged the children apart, dangling them from his powerful hands like kittens.

Yes, indeed, these were the children of Rardove.

Katarina was so abidingly happy, some days it almost took her breath away.

Not that every moment was blissful. Far from it. Crops sometimes failed, the sheep sometimes took ill, and cattle raids still occurred. She and Aodh still stood toe to toe at times, opposed on matters of rule or home. Sometimes she backed down, occasionally he did, but they always settled their differences in bed afterward. Or against a wall. Once, on a table in the hall when everyone was at a picnic, and more than a few times, up against the battlement walls on the western side of the castle as the sun was going down, all the guardsmen ordered away, as few military dangers pressed upon Rardove anymore, not since Aodh had come home.

Lizzie began kicking her legs irritably. Cormac showed up on the wall beside her and looked down at the fretful bundle swaddled in soft wool in Katarina's arms.

"I could take her for you, my lady," he offered, longing in

his voice.

"Oh, I…" She glanced over the wall at the men riding across the valley. "Aodh will want to see her. It has been a month."

"Susanna would dearly love to have her awhile." Cormac and she had yet to bear a child.

Katarina promptly handed Lizzie over. The baby was a charmer—another of Aodh's gifts—for her face expanded into a smile when she saw Cormac's red-bearded face. She gurgled happily at him.

He was already speaking in low, nonsense words as he took her in his burly arms, cooing to the clearly delighted Lizzie. Her charge so well tended, Katarina went to meet Aodh.

He rode in as he had done all those years ago, on his grey horse, at the head of a small army, and she felt precisely as she had then. As if he was the only man present.

The troop entered the inner bailey to warm cries of welcome. Aodh swung off his horse and tossed his reins to Dickon, now sixteen years old and still utterly devoted to his master. Aodh clapped him on the back with a brief word, then strode to Katarina.

Just as he had done, all those years ago.

She felt as if she were floating, just as she had then. Surely the feeling would pass soon.

She'd been telling herself that for six years.

He stripped off his gloves as he drew up in front of her and, without a pause, bent his head to drop a swift kiss on her lips.

It was a properly decorous kiss, no tongue or teeth or all the other things Aodh so liked to put into a kiss, which was as it should be, considering they were in a crowded bailey filled with dismounting men and women and servants hurrying to greet them.

No one could see his hands under the cloak, sliding boldly up her ribs, his thumbs skimming over her breasts.

"I missed you," she whispered, returning his decorous kiss, while her body arched to his touch.

"I can see." He brushed his thumbs over her hardened nipples.

"I am glad you are back."

"As am I." He gathered her to him, hands circling her at the small of her spine.

"Yes, I can see," she teased back, feeling the hard thrust of manhood push against her.

Aodh smiled then glanced away, looking around the bailey. "Where are the children?"

"Where are they not? Finn is in the yard; I cannot believe he has not yet accosted you yet. Aine is in the hall, doubtless dismantling tables or dumping out kettles or some such, and Lizzie is in Cormac's arms—"

"Da!"

Their son came hurtling around the corner of the castle, full tilt for his father. Aodh crouched and took the hit, then scooped the boy into his arms.

Finn began hugging and talking all at once, his chubby little boy arms around Aodh's neck, regaling him with tales of recent triumphs with a pony, and woes with his sister, all in a single sentence, without needing a reply. "...and I fell right off him, and he was *trotting*, but Mamma picked me up before he stepped on my head, so that was good."

Aodh looked at Katarina. She shrugged. He turned back to his son, wiping away a streak of dirt from under Finn's eye.

"...and Aine stole my horse, the one you whittled me, so I pinched her slippers, and she—"

"You didn't pinch her slippers," Katarina said.

The boy turned to her with wide eyes. "Why, aye, I did, Mamma. You know it, for you told me if I ever—"

"You *stole* her slippers."

"Oh." He reflected a moment. "You're right, that sounds better. I *stole* her slippers. And then she—"

The object of his discourse emerged from the castle, trailed by a servant. She was wearing tunic and hose, because she could *not* be kept in gowns. Tangled hair spilled over her shoulders, and there was some sort of white powder all over her face.

"Flour," Katarina and Aodh said at the same moment.

They smiled at each other.

Her mouth rounded in excitement when she saw her father, then she came careening towards him. He scooped her up, and after a brief tussle for supremacy between the children, Aodh settled them, one in the crook of each arm, and looked down at Katarina.

"I got word from Ré."

She clapped her hands together in excitement. "When? Where? How is he? What did his message say?" The children, detecting their parents' happiness, cried out equally, if ignorantly, excited. "When? Who is he? What is it?"

"He is an old friend, Aine. I told you of him, Finn, the one who dragged me out of the sea. He should be here within a fortnight, love," Aodh finished with a smile down at Katarina.

She beamed at him. "I am happy."

"As am I. He'll stay the winter."

She sighed with a smile. "Good. He will be here for Christmas."

"And through the spring, at least. He says he has news."

She reached for his elbow, the only thing she could touch through the children. "What news?"

"I do not know. All the missive said was news." They looked at each other, then smiled.

"He made it to the New World," Katarina announced. "I know it."

He bent and placed a kiss on her mouth. "The men are hungry. Let's eat."

The meal was festive and merry, and extremely long, as the kitchens hadn't yet prepared food. So it began with cold things—bread and beer and cheeses, and moved to the warmer courses.

Aodh and Katarina did not make it to the fully prepared courses. They tried, of course. They sat on the dais with Aodh's captains as the meal slowly unraveled, relaying the news they'd learned in the south.

"Things are going to become bad for awhile," Aodh explained, sounding grim.

Little Finn sat on his lap, leaning forward to play with his wooden horses and knights on the dais table. Aine stood on the chair on the other side of Aodh, her little feet digging into Cormac's lap as she mounted a spirited counterattack comprised of dragons and princesses that Aodh and Wicker had whittled for her.

Wicker had become quite the whittler, after having married the red-haired lass from the village below, and had three children with another on the way. Susanna sat beside Cormac, holding baby Lizzie.

"How bad?" Katarina asked quietly.

Aodh reclined in his seat, a hand on Finn's back. "Perhaps very. There are more rebellions happening." He stroked Finn's head. "The O'Neill is in open revolt."

She drew in a sharp breath. "Oh no."

"Aye."

She looked out across the hall for a moment, then asked flatly, "And are we expected to help put him down?"

Why did the English Crown insist on pushing at every ache with such vigor? Digging in, intending to root out pus, but instead, introducing more infection. Did they not know it was better to let some things lie?

Aodh shook his head. "Do not worry. I impressed upon the Lord Deputy how unwise it would be to ask Rardove to join a hosting against the O'Neill clan. It would only spur more rebellion."

She swung her gaze to him. "So we are to…?"

"Hold the line. Our strength lies in being England's wall, not its fist. Fitzwilliam seemed to agree."

Relief and wonder made her laugh softly. "Only you, Aodh Mac Con, could convince the English to allow us to sit out a war."

He shrugged. "I've no intention of fighting The O'Neill. I think Sir William saw that." His reply spoke directly to her words, but his gaze was intent on an entirely different matter as it slid down the front of her gown with clear male purpose.

She sat back in her chair. "You told the Lord Deputy of Ireland you have no intention of fighting The O'Neill?"

"I did not have to tell him. I simply explained more rebellions would follow if Rardove were ordered to join a hosting against The O'Neill."

She let the words sink in. "You meant *we* would rebel."

"Perish the thought," he said softly. "Lass, we tend the fires, we do not put them out." He threw back the rest of his drink, lifted Finn off his lap, slid out, and set the boy back on the chair.

"Fight well," he said to both his children, kissed their heads, kissed the baby, then turned to Katarina. "Come with me."

Her body lit as if he'd lit a wick inside her.

They went to their rooms. Aodh was stripping off his clothes even as he kicked the door shut. "Take that off," he ordered, tugging at her gown.

"Yes, well, I was going to," she said breathlessly, pulling faster at the laces. He walked her back to the bed while he was still yanking off his tunic, and kicked her legs apart as she dropped onto the bed.

He was inside her in seconds, hot and fast, dragging cords of pleasure across her body. She was ready for him, pulsing with heat, slippery with desire, so he sank in deep, with a single thrust.

"Ah, Katy," he murmured, leaning down to kiss her neck. "I missed you. Come with me next time I go."

"I will," she whispered.

"You could have helped, with the Lord Deputy."

"You do not appear to have needed help."

He nudged her thigh up and to the side a little more, and thrust in again. "A beautiful woman always helps, especially when she is clever too. They never expect that."

She lifted her hips to him. "You did not expect it."

He stilled a moment, peering down at her. "What I did not expect was to get punched in the jaw."

"Oh, yes, *that* was it. And to have your dagger stolen."

He rolled his hips again. "I admit, that was a surprise. Particularly when you did it a second time."

"I was angry."

"I noticed." He set a hand on her hip and held her firmly as he sank in with harder, more urgent thrusts.

Her breath came faster. She tipped her head back, pressing it into the mattress, and looked up into his eyes. "What will Elizabeth say?"

"Who?" His gaze was fixed between their legs, on their union.

She tipped his face up. "The Queen of England?"

His ice-blue eyes burned into hers. "Katy, there is always a way," he said, ignoring her stated question, and answering the deeper one. The truer one. It was his way. "I swear to you." He surged into her again, strumming her like an instrument.

"I believe in you," she whispered.

"I burn in you."

Their mouths met, in a long, deep kiss of adoration.

This, this with Aodh, this was her home. Their lives, their union, their children. It was home.

She was finally home. In Aodh.

Never The End...

Dear Reader,
I hope you loved Aodh & Katy's story! Don't you love a hard alpha warrior who goes rogue and finds love? Me too!

That's why there are more stories in the *Rogue Warriors* collection. Standalone historical romance adventures set in different medieval eras, each book features a warrior gone rogue.

In *Defiant*, Jamie Lost is King John's most renowned commander, an audacious knight ordered to bring in an enemy troublemaker before rebel forces close in. It's a simple mission. There's only one thing standing in his way.

Eva.

Armed with nothing a small knife and secrets that can bring down a throne, Eva has a single goal: Stop Jamie at all costs. She thwarts him, charms him, distracts him…then makes off with his quarry.

Hunting her down is just the start.

This is one seriously epic road romance!

If you like big adventure with alpha heroes who fall head over heels for whip-smart waifs who infuriate them, charm them, and save them from themselves, you're going to love *Defiant*, next in the *Rogue Warriors* collection.

Links at website & or find the books at online booksellers.

WEBSITE
kriskennedy.net
- Newsletter Sign-up
- Excerpts
- Links to all books
- Author's Notes (including behind-the-scenes peeks at medieval Ireland!)

About the Author

Upon a time, Kris ran a solo business where she loved her clients very much. She also loved the middle ages and writing romances. When life events conspired to make typical office life impossible for a time, she moved into writing fiction with a vengeance.

Kris is a multi-award-winning, USA Today® bestselling author. She's published with Simon & Schuster and Kensington, and also indie publishes. She writes super sexy, big adventure romance set during the ages when hard-willed knights and questionable chivalry reigned supreme.

FIND OUT MORE
kriskennedy.net

Check out Kris's sweet & dirty contemporary romances written as Bella Love.

FIND OUT MORE
bellalovebooks.com

The newsletter is the very best way to be sure you're getting all the latest news, including new covers, release dates, and special deals.

Here's to a long journey ahead, filled with hard heroes, strong heroines, rollicking adventure, and scorching hot passion!

34533852R00227

Made in the USA
San Bernardino, CA
03 May 2019